PACK UP THE MOON

I thought about writing to you for such a long time. I never actually dreamed I'd get around to it, but when I did, it seemed so easy. Memories are absurd things. Some are vague, some crystalline, some too painful to recollect and some so painful it's impossible to forget. Happy times are remembered with warmth and laughter, recalled as an anecdote in the pub, exaggerated for the crowd. The really good ones keep you company on an otherwise lonely evening. The clearest memories are of those occasions when you experience great highs or lows. It's the emotion the situation inspires that you remember. That feeling of incredible exultation or terrible despair enables your brain to note the details that normally pass you by, like the color of someone's shirt, a hand gesture or how warm or cold it was.

You can recall the creases caused by the smile on a loved one's lips or the way tears crept from their eyes. But pain is hard to put into words and in life there is always pain. It's as natural as birth or death. Pain makes us who we are, it teaches us and tames us, it can destroy and it can save. We all have regrets—even Frank Sinatra had a few.

"Fascinating and hugely readable."
—*The Kingdom*

"Crisply written, insightful and moving."
—*Irish Independent*

Pack Up the Moon

Anna McPartlin

DOWNTOWN PRESS
New York   London   Toronto   Sydney

Downtown Press
A Division of Simon & Schuster, Inc.
1230 Avenue of the Americas
New York, NY 10020

First Downtown Press trade paperback edition April 2008

DOWNTOWN PRESS and colophon are registered trademarks
of Simon & Schuster, Inc.

For information about special discounts for bulk purchases,
please contact Simon & Schuster Special Sales at
1-800-456-6798 or business@simonandschuster.com

Manufactured in the United States of America

10 9 8 7 6 5 4 3 2

Library of Congress Cataloging-in-Publication Data
McPartlin, Anna
    Pack up the moon / Anna McPartlin.
        p.   cm.
    "First published by Poolbeg Press Ltd (Dublin, Ireland)."
1. Young women—Fiction. 2. Ireland—Fiction. 3. Death—Psychological
aspects—Fiction. 4. Bereavement—Fiction. 5. Domestic fiction. I. Title
    PR6113.C585P33 2008
    823'.92—dc22
                                               2007036537

ISBN-13: 978-1-4165-5309-0
ISBN-10:   1-4165-5309-6

To my mom
who taught me how to find the smallest glint of light
even in the darkest of places.

To Mary and Tony O'Shea
For being my parents.

To Hallie
just 'cos . . .

Acknowledgments

My love and thanks to Mary and Kevin Flood for always being there. To my friends: Fergus (Jergilious) Egan for the best times I've ever had in a kitchen and teaching me how to write; Enda Barron for being the Darth to my Vader; Tracy (feel the weight of tha') Kennedy for your infectious laugh; Joanne Costello and John Goodman without whom no holiday would be complete; Lucy Walsh for always knowing what to do; Darren Walsh for being the funniest man in Ireland. To Edel Simpson for recognizing when I'm talking through my ass, Noel Simpson for his kindness, Valerie (Hallie) Kerins because she has to be mentioned at least twice, Graham & Bernice Darcy for your support and ideas, Angela (Dorian Grey) Delaney for your divine taste and one-liners, Martin Clancy for all the answers and Trish Clancy for making Martin happy. To those who've stuck it out since our teens: Leonie Kerins for perfecting the waddle walk to the dance floor; Dermot Kerins for New Year's Eve 1996; Clifton Moore for always seeing the best in me; Gareth Tierney for sharing my taste in the nerdy stuff. Stephane Duclot for being French. The McPartlins, especially Don and Terry, for their support. To my family, the O'Sheas: Maime and T, who define the term "role model," Denis for your enthusiasm and warmth, Lisa for your goodness and dirty grin, Siobhan for your splendid and filthy mind, Paul for finding Siobhan, Brenda for being the giddiest person I know, Mark for putting up with the giddiest person I know, Caroline and Ger for being adventurers, Aisling (Bing-a-ling) otherwise know as Xena (Buffy loves you), Dave for taking care of me in NZ. To the kids, Daniel, Nicole, David and my godson Conor—I love you all. To Claire McSwiney, Paudie McSwiney and all the McSwiney clan. Aisling Cronin, I miss you. To David Constantine for your humor. To my workmates David Jenkins, Kevin O'Connor, Suzanne Daly, Sophie Morley and all at Chubb Insurance. Everyone at Poolbeg, including Kieran, all the girls and especially Gaye Shortland for her patience and insight and Paula Campbell for being my champion. Finally my husband Donal for everything.

The stars are not wanted now; put out every one;
Pack up the moon and dismantle the sun;
Pour away the ocean and sweep up the wood;
For nothing now can ever come to any good.

from *Funeral Blues* by W. H. Auden

Chapter 1

The Thin Blue Line

It was early March and raining. The clouds were relieving themselves with a ferocity akin to a drunk urinating after fourteen pints. I looked through the frosted glass, imagining the impact the downpour would have on my whites blowing wildly in the accompanying gale. Then back to the floor, immediately noticing the slight yellowing in the grouting around the toilet.

Men, I thought. *How hard is it to aim for the loo?* I briefly contemplated how it was that my boyfriend could manage to clear a pool table with pinpoint accuracy, park a car in a space the size of a stamp and yet when it came to pointing his mickey in the direction of a large bowl, he had the judgment of a drunken schoolboy. The edge of the bath felt cold under my skirt.

Three minutes.

Three minutes can be a long time. I wondered would it feel so long if I were defusing a bomb. I started to count

1

the seconds but quickly lost interest. The mirror needed cleaning. I'd do it tomorrow. I absentmindedly played with the stick in my hand until I remembered that I'd just peed on it. I put it down. I brushed invisible fluff from my skirt, this being a habit I had picked up from my father although obviously he was not a skirt wearer. It was our response to nerves. Some people wring their hands; my dad and I clean our clothes.

The first time I really noticed our shared trait was when my brother, age seventeen, announced that, instead of becoming the doctor my parents had dreamed of, he was going to become a priest. My mother, mortified by the thought that she would lose her son to an absent God, spent an entire evening screaming shrilly before breaking down and taking to her bed for four days. My dad sat silently cleaning his suit. He didn't say anything but his disappointment was profound. I remember that I wasn't too pushed at the time. As a self-obsessed teenage girl, I didn't share the same concerns about Noel's sacrifice as my parents, although I admit that the thought of having a priest in the family was slightly embarrassing to me.

We weren't very close then. He was your typical nerd, bookish, intense and politically aware. He studied hard, brought out the bins without being asked and was an ardent *Doctor Who* fan. He never smoked, never indulged in underage drinking or for that matter in girls. For a while I thought he was gay, but that theory passed when I realized that to be gay you had to be interesting. Still, we were adults now and, although I could never understand his utter devotion to The Almighty, times had changed and all the traits that made for a nerdish teenager

2

guaranteed a fascinating adult. I now counted Father Noel as one of my best friends.

Two minutes.

I was twenty-six years old. I was in love and living with John, my childhood sweetheart. I had the pleasure of watching my lover grow from a fair-haired, blue-eyed, idealistic boy to a fair-haired, blue-eyed, self-assured man. We'd been together nearly twelve years and for me he was definitely The One. We'd been living together happily since college. We were renting a nice place—two bedrooms, two bathrooms, a kitchen and a cute sitting room—just off Stephen's Green and although it was small and sometimes smelled of sweet old lady, it wasn't that expensive, which was amazing considering the location. I had a good job. Teaching was never my life's dream, but then I considered myself lucky to have been unburdened by ambition. Teaching seemed as good a job as any. Some days I liked the kids and some days I didn't, but it was steady. I was home most days by four thirty and I had three months off in the summer. John was still in college doing a PhD in psychology, but he also managed to hold down four shifts a week as a bartender. Some weeks he'd bring home more money than I would and he maintained that he learned more from drunks than he would in college.

We were happy. We were a well-adjusted happy couple. We had a good life, good prospects and good friends. There are a lot of people who would like to have the kind of security we had with one another.

One minute.

My mother had often pondered aloud as to when John and I would think about marriage. I'd tell her to mind her own business. She'd note that I was her business. We'd fight about the issue of privacy versus a mother's love. At twenty-six I felt too young to marry and this feeling remained, despite my mother constantly reminding me that she had two young children by the age of twenty-four.

"It was a different time," I used to say and that was true. Most of my mother's friends were married with kids by the time they reached their mid-twenties. I was from a completely different generation. The Show Band versus the MTV generation. While she grew up on Dickie Rock, I gyrated to Madonna. Before meeting my dad, her idea of a fun night out was lining up against the wall at the local dance hoping one of the lads would pick her for a waltz. I, on the other hand, was from the disco generation. Besides, none of my friends were married.

Thirty seconds.

OK, that's a lie. Anne and Richard met in college. She was the middle child of a middle-class family from Swords. He was the son of one of the richest landowners in Kildare. They met in a queue to sign up for an amateur drama group during orientation week. They got talking, abandoned the queue to get coffee. After that, they were inseparable. They married a year after college. Big deal, they were the only ones.

Clodagh, my best friend since age four, hadn't managed to hold down a relationship over four months. She had emerged from college a tenacious, intelligent, hardworking career woman, managing to work her way up to senior account manager of a large advertising firm within three years. She succeeded in all she did, with the small exception of her romantic life, and that perceived failure hurt her.

Then there was John's best friend, Seán, dark, brooding, dry and beautiful. Clo called him "the living David." He had not only made his way through eighty percent of the girls in the Trinity Arts block, he'd also managed to nail a few lecturers along the way. His longest relationship to date had been with an American girl called Candyapple (her real name, I kid you not) during a summer we all spent working in New Jersey. She was your typical coffee-skinned, brown-eyed, big-breasted, small-waisted nightmare. She had long curly brown hair that somehow reminded Anne of the Queen guitarist Brian May. Seán called her "Delicious"; the rest of us called her "Brian." They lasted six weeks. He left college and after a few false starts he fell on his feet, landing a job as editor of a men's magazine. His quick wit, sincere worship of football and encyclopedic female carnal knowledge ensured his continuing success. Relationships didn't matter and marriage and family certainly was not a priority.

Ten seconds.

John loved our life. You know those smug couples you meet and instantly hate? He could be smug like that. He never seemed to care that Seán had his pick of women through college. He didn't even mind that he had only ever had sex with one person. He was content, loved up, happy. He was rare. We were rare.

The first time we had sex we were both sixteen. We were in a tent on the side of a hill in Wicklow. It was a warm summer night, not a cloud in sight. The moon was full, round and bright, the sky was navy and thick like velvet, the trees were towering, leafy and smelled of sun. No wind, no breeze, the world seemed still. We had our little campfire, a picnic basket, a packet of condoms and a bottle of wine, which we both merely sipped, our underdeveloped taste buds mistaking its fruity freshness for the taste of rancid crap. Kissing turned to cuddling, which turned to snuggling, which led to nuzzling, graduating to feverish genital rubbing and one hymen later we were lying in one another's arms looking up at the cigarette stains on the blue nylon tent, wondering what all the fuss was about.

Clo had warned me that practice made perfect. We managed it four times before we returned to our respective parents, proud and full of secrets.

Five seconds.

I wasn't ready. I felt sick, praying it was stress-related and not morning sickness.

Oh fuck. What will I do? I don't want to be a mother. I don't want to be a wife. I don't want to feel like I'm my mother before I've lived. I want to do things, I'm not sure what. I want to experience different places, I don't know where. I'm not ready.

I hadn't mentioned to John that my period was over two weeks late nor had I mentioned that I had bought a pregnancy test. I wasn't used to keeping secrets from him but I was sure that I was right not to involve him in this.

Why worry him?

The problem was I wasn't sure if he would be worried. He smiled when my mother teased us about marriage and babies. He'd take time in a supermarket to stop and smile at a dribbling child, while I would push through the throng, impatient with everything bar getting what we'd come for and leaving.

Two seconds.

He would be excited, I could feel it in my bones. Worse than that, he would want the baby. There would be no furrowed brows or tearful decisions to be made. There would be excitement and planning and books and baby clothes. My stomach started to hurt.

I'm not ready.

My hands were shaking as I turned the stick.

Please don't be blue, please God, don't be blue!

My eyes were closed although I don't remember voluntarily closing them. I sighed deeply and this reminded me that I was a smoker so I lay the stick down and ran to my bedroom to grab a packet of cigarettes. I returned and lit up. I inhaled deeply, determined to enjoy what could be my last cigarette for a long time. My intention was to finish the entire cigarette before unveiling my future. However, this plan was obliterated by the sound of John's key in the front door. I hastily put the cigarette out by dousing it in cold water with one hand while waving madly with the other in an attempt to dissipate the smoke, which seemed to billow around the confined space. I could hear his footsteps make their way upstairs and toward my hideout. I was out of time.

"Emma!"

"I'm in here!" I called, a little too shrilly.

He attempted to open the door. I watched helplessly, hiding the stick up the arm of my jumper. It was locked. I sighed with relief.

"Why's the door locked?" he asked suspiciously.

"I always lock the door," I lied, hoping he'd momentarily lose his memory.

He didn't.

"No, you don't," he said, still pushing down the door handle.

"John," I said sternly, "can you just give me a bloody second?" I could hear him walk toward the bedroom. He was mumbling something about me being a bitch when I had my period.

I wish.

I sat back down and turned over the stick. I looked at it for the longest time. I closed my hand over it and then I looked again. I bit my lip, hurting myself in the process. I opened my fingers again, revealing a gloriously white window. Not a hint of blue. I moved to the window to ensure maximum light. Nothing. It was clear. No blue line. I had my life back. I wasn't pregnant. I wasn't even a little bit pregnant. I was just late and I had a party to go to.

Thank you, God!

★ ★ ★

When Richard's grandfather died at the age of ninety-one, he left a very large portion of his estate to Richard, making him extremely wealthy. To this end it was decided that there would be a party to celebrate, an "inheritance party." Anne was initially concerned that it would be in bad taste.

"He was a very old man, who died after living a great life full of love and achievement. Why would having a party to celebrate your good fortune be disrespectful?" I had asked her.

"It's been so long since we've had a party," was John's contribution to the cause.

"Besides, my granddad had a great sense of humor. He'd love the idea," Richard intoned, desperate to enjoy their new fortune.

"It's a fantastic idea! We can celebrate his life and the fact that our good friends are loaded," Seán insisted.

Eventually Anne succumbed and so it came to pass that the day I discovered I would not bring a new life into the world was the day that my world changed forever.

★ ★ ★

I thought about writing to you for such a long time. I never actually dreamed I'd get around to it, but when I did, it seemed so easy. Memories are absurd things. Some are vague, some crystalline, some too painful to recollect and some so painful it's impossible to forget. Happy times are remembered with warmth and laughter, recalled as an anecdote in the pub, exaggerated for the crowd. The really good ones keep you company on an otherwise lonely evening. The clearest memories are of those occasions when you experience great highs or lows. It's the emotion the situation inspires that you remember. That feeling of incredible exultation or terrible despair enables your brain to note the details that normally pass you by, like the color of someone's shirt, a hand gesture or how warm or cold it was.

You can recall the creases caused by the smile on a loved one's lips or the way tears crept from their eyes. But pain is hard to put into words and in life there is always pain. It's as natural as birth or death. Pain makes us who we are, it teaches us and tames us, it can destroy and it can save. We all have regrets—even Frank Sinatra had a few.

Some tragedies are of our own doing and then sometimes things happen that are out of this world's control and when it happens, it can take our breath away.

Happiness is a gift. It washes its warmth over us and reminds us of beauty. It should never be taken for granted. I should never have taken it for granted. That thin blue line represented happiness. I didn't know that it would later represent something that I would never get back. But then I wasn't ready.

Chapter 2

Hoppity-hops, Cigarettes and Lipstick

My little drama concluded, I was now in the bath trying to wash St. Fintan's secondary school away. Despite my good fortune I was in a bad mood and not looking forward to the party that I had partly instigated. The door unlocked, John entered and his grin suggested that my earlier outburst had been forgiven.

"Can I wash your back?"

I told him to piss off.

"Will you wash my back?"

I gave him the fingers.

"Ah, the little bastards gave you a hard time," he laughed.

"Don't call my students little bastards!" I admonished.

"Why not? You do. Besides, when they piss you off, I have to live with the consequences, so I feel I have a right."

He was right.

"All right, I'll allow you to cheer me up," I grinned.

11

"That's good of you," he said, kneeling on the floor and playing with my bathwater, his eyes glinting.

I melted. "Okay then. Get in but don't push me into the taps," I warned.

His clothes were off almost before I got to the word "taps." He sat in behind me and we lay in the warm water, his arms around my gloriously empty stomach and the water sloshing over the side. I let some out, leaned back and asked him how his day went. He responded by telling me about a fantastic psychological test that he had pulled off the 'Net and I was instantly sorry that I'd asked.

"It's great—I've got to do it on you," he threatened.

I looked around at him. "That's sexy," I said.

"It's great—it's a laugh. But you'll need some paper."

"I'm in the bath," I pointed out while trying to get comfortable.

He started to wash my back. "It's very telling," he said ominously.

I told him that, after six years, I was under the impression he knew everything there was to know about me. He smiled smugly.

"There's always more, Em. Sometimes we don't even know ourselves. Like for instance, until yesterday I didn't know that I could eat two Big Macs, a large fries, six chicken McNuggets and a chocolate milk shake in one sitting without feeling sick."

"Christ," I said, "that's disgusting."

He nodded his head in agreement. "That's me, baby," he laughed with his arms in the air.

★ ★ ★

12

Later, he arrived into the bedroom with a piece of paper and a pen.

"John, I'm trying to get dressed here."

He put the pen and paper on the dressing table. "Come on, it's just a few tests. Ten minutes tops. I want to try it out before the party."

I couldn't believe it. "You're not planning on doing this at the party?" I asked incredulously.

"Em, it's a laugh," he said unconvincingly.

So I picked up the pen anyway, knowing I had no choice. "Make this quick. I have to blow-dry my hair," I warned.

He pulled out the instructions from his briefcase and started reading. "Okay, pick a color and write it down."

I thought for a second and wrote.

"Okay, name three things that you associate with that color."

I thought for another few seconds and then wrote down three words.

"Have you got it?"

I nodded yes.

"What color did you pick?"

"Red."

"Good, now what are the three words?" He was grinning smugly.

I read my words aloud: "Hoppity-hops, cigarettes and lipstick."

"What?" he asked, obviously perturbed. His grin faded and he was looking at me funnily.

"Hoppity-hops, cigarettes and lipstick," I reiterated.

"I heard you the first time. It doesn't make any sense— you're doing it wrong."

I couldn't believe it and frankly had had enough of his poxy game. "What the fuck do you mean, I'm doing it wrong?" I screamed over my hair dryer. "It's a psychological test. You asked me to pick three words that I associate with red and I picked them. How can that be wrong?"

Bewildered, his hand reached for his forehead and it became obvious that he was fighting the urge to scratch his head. "How do you get hoppity-hops, cigarettes and lipstick from the color red?" he yelled.

I was struggling with a newfound cowlick and not having the laugh that had been promised, but, as I had anticipated that laughter would not be the outcome of John's little game, I just answered him in the hope that he'd leave me be.

"When I was a kid my hoppity-hop was red. I smoke Marlboro, the packet is red, and my favourite color lipstick is red. It's that simple." I turned up the hair dryer.

"Well, that just doesn't make any sense," he mumbled, rereading the page.

Then he shouted something about the three words and how they were supposed to describe how I saw myself. He was clearly disturbed with my answer, so in an effort to relieve his pain I turned off the dryer and thought for a minute.

"Maybe it's revealing that deep down I'm a chain-smoking hoppity-hopper who likes red lipstick. That's amazing. You're right. I've really learned something about myself." I was laughing now, but he remained perplexed.

"When we did it in the lecture hall it worked really well. You must be mentally challenged, Em. I swear it works with everyone else." He crumpled the page and threw it in the bin.

As he left the room I heard him mutter, "Fucking hoppity-hops!"

★ ★ ★

By the time John and I reached the party it was in full swing. The hall door was open and there was a couple sitting on the stairs kissing. As we passed them, John made a huge wet kissing sound. Fortunately they didn't seem to hear it. We headed straight for the kitchen, where Seán was already sitting at the table skinning up a joint. John plonked down beside him, while I went looking for Anne and Richard and found them in the sitting room. Anne was busy making sure the assembled crowd was having a good time while Richard was throwing alcohol down his throat like it was a gaping hole that required filling.

There was a big homemade sign hanging over the fireplace with the words "WE'RE IN THE MONEY" printed on it. I smiled when I saw it and told Anne I liked her style. She, disgusted at her husband's sense of humor, asked me not to remind her while attempting to keep her back to it.

The music was loud, people were standing about chatting, some were dancing and all were drinking. I didn't really know most of them, they were the workmates of the two hosts, so I returned to the kitchen to find the two lads bleary-eyed and John choking.

Seán looked at me and smiled stupidly. "Have a drag," he said.

So I did and I felt the back of my head blow off. "Sweet Jesus! I need a hat."

They both laughed and Seán told us how a friend of his had posted a sample selection of differing strains of cannabis from Amsterdam. The little plastic bags were name-tagged and accompanied by a menu. We were busy being sincerely impressed when Anne burst into the room with an empty tray. She took one look at us.

"Oh lovely, what a pack of wasters! You're only here five minutes and look at the state of you!"

I smiled at her. Anne was Den Mother. John used to say that she was born an adult. She was the one we all relied on to be sensible and she never failed to deliver.

"Got any glasses?" I asked, unable to move.

She handed me two large pint glasses before leaving the room, with her tray now stacked with sandwiches. I filled my glass with wine and John's with beer. I looked at the wine for a few minutes before taking a sip and made a mental note never to put wine into a pint glass again. Having said that, it tasted fine. Seán had started to skin up again and I was really beginning to relax after my stressful day.

"Where's Clo?"

"She's here," said Seán, while dispersing tobacco with expert hands.

"Where?"

"Upstairs with some guy," he answered, grinning.

I felt suddenly alert.

"I tried to get into the bedroom to leave my coat," he continued. "The door was locked and Clo's voice told me to fuck off."

John started to laugh. I wanted to check it out, but my legs wouldn't work. Anne kept entering and restacking her tray, only staying long enough to warn us about overdoing it. Richard, who was pissed, was holding court in the sitting room. We remained in the kitchen drinking, smoking and laughing at rubbish.

After a while Anne arrived back into the room.

"How's it going?" I asked.

"Richard is on his fourth we're-filthy-rich speech. I really don't know what's got into him," she said and suddenly I was reminded of my mother.

Seán was laughing. "Half a bottle of vodka, four Slippery Nipples and at least two joints," he noted as though reading a shopping list.

Anne remained unimpressed. "Yes, very funny, Seán. You're a fucking comedian."

Seán was so inebriated he was fully sure that her jibe was a compliment. "Cheers!" he said, lifting his glass and John and I followed suit.

"You're a bunch of wasters," Anne said and we fell about the place laughing, delighted with our title. She smiled and threw her eyes up to heaven like an amused parent admonishing bold children.

She was piling more food onto trays when Clo walked into the room with a guy trailing behind her.

"Hey, folks," she said, relieving Seán of his fresh produce. The guy just stood there, not sure where to put himself. She parked herself on a chair and patted the one beside her. "Sit here," she said, smiling at her new friend again.

But he didn't see her, as he was too busy looking at us,

who in turn were staring at him as only stoned people can. He sat, appearing perturbed. We were waiting for an introduction. Clo smiled at us, as if forgetting about the sexual object beside her. Eventually John asked her to introduce us.

"Oh," she said, "this is Philip."

Anne, now finished piling the tray, welcomed him to her home and headed off into the sitting room. We all just smiled at him until he excused himself to go to the loo. The second the door closed behind him, I asked the question on everyone's mind.

"Did you just have sex with him upstairs?"

"No!" she stated categorically while nodding her head yes.

"So where did you meet this poor bastard?" Seán asked tactfully.

"The taxi rank."

We laughed again.

"There really is an awful lot to be said for public transport," she noted and Seán nodded in agreement.

Anne arrived back in. Seán asked her to sit with us, but she was on a mission to find more ice. John called her Doris Day and, as she left, he was given two fingers for the second time that day.

Philip returned and sat down. We all stared at him again. After a few seconds he spoke. "So this is an inheritance party?"

We nodded again.

"What exactly is that?" he asked, appearing unimpressed.

It seemed pretty obvious to the rest of us, but Seán decided to answer him. "It's when a very, very rich grandparent dies at a very old age and leaves you pots of cash."

We all smiled at him, stupidly delighted with the simplicity and honesty of his answer. Philip wasn't convinced. "So, somebody died?" was his question.

John looked at him as though he was retarded.

Seán said, "He was very old." He took a drag of the joint directly after he said it, blew it out slowly and smiled at Philip. He reminded me of Steve McQueen in *The Magnificent Seven* and we stoners laughed again. Philip was a grown-up and therefore not impressed. He excused himself from our presence by saying he was going into the sitting room, but we all knew that he had every intention of leaving the building. We waited till we heard the front door slam.

Seán looked at Clo and stated the obvious. "You do realize he's gone, don't you?"

She smiled at him. "'Gone But Not Forgotten!'" She laughed at her own joke.

I turned to John and with surprising ability grabbed his chin and turned it toward me, looked into his eyes and said in an American hillbilly accent, "I hope you give me somethin' I won't forgit tonight."

Without missing a beat he answered in the same stupid accent: "You and your sister, honey!"

Seán, who was taking a swig from his can, nearly choked at his friend's comic genius and everybody laughed again. Eventually Anne and Richard joined us. Clo passed the joint to Anne, who took her first long and sustained drag, and Doris Day left the building. It was a few minutes before she realized that Philip was missing.

When she inquired as to his whereabouts, Clo responded monosyllabically with: "Gone."

John added, "But not forgotten."

We all fell about laughing and Anne said, "Christ!"

The night pretty much continued in that inane vein. At one point John and I were dancing—well, in fact, merely holding one another up and swaying. Anne put on Prince's "Purple Rain," which was our song. We swayed some more and remembered the night we had listened to the song while christening our brand-new ten-year-old Ford Escort. We smiled at the memory and recalled how amazed we were when the windows actually did steam up. John spun me around at the end of the song and dropped me. Despite this little mishap I felt like Ginger Rogers—again, the power of mind-altering drugs. After helping me back on my feet, he kissed me and I felt sixteen. John could always make me feel sixteen, which was one of the reasons that I loved him.

People started to leave and Clo disappeared to sleep under the stairs, a habit she picked up in college. Unconcerned, we forgot to look for her when leaving. It was three in the morning and Richard and John were in deep conversation about some stupid football game. We were standing at the door and I was tired and cold.

Eventually Anne called time and we headed out onto the street. We hadn't reached the edge of the footpath when I remembered that I had left my lighter behind. I wanted to go back in and get it but John insisted we'd get it in the morning. I wouldn't listen. The lighter was a silver-plated Zippo that Noel had given me for my twenty-first birthday. He had it engraved and I loved it, not just because it was a cool lighter but also because, to me, it represented his acceptance of my hedonistic lifestyle. So despite John's protest I went back inside. He said he'd wait on the street.

Anne and Richard were in the sitting room, picking up cans; Seán was still in the kitchen, smoking yet another joint. I smiled at him and made some stupid remark while looking for the lighter. He offered me a drag for the road. I accepted. He smiled at me.

"You're beautiful," he said.

I smiled, waiting for the punch line that didn't come. The words hung in the air.

"Cheers," I said, a moment too late.

"I'm sorry, I didn't meant to embarrass you," he slurred.

"It's fine," I said, going red. I saw my lighter on the table and grabbed it. Instinctively I bent down to peck his cheek to signify my exit. He turned as I reached his face and I felt a shock run through me when his lips made contact with mine. We both pulled back and he began to apologize profusely. I didn't want him to fuss, as it had been an accident. We were friends and it was no big deal.

Chapter 3

The End Is Near

I was moving toward the door when we heard a screech of brakes closely followed by a sickening thud. I hadn't even properly registered this background noise when Seán was up and running out the door. I heard Anne and Richard shouting. They were calling John's name. Suddenly I was stuck to the floor, still staring at the spot where Seán had been sitting.

Anne was now screaming, *"Oh Christ, oh sweet Jesus!"*

My heart started to beat wildly. My chest started to hurt. I heard Richard screaming at Seán, *"Don't touch him, don't move him!"*

Suddenly my legs started to work. I was moving, running out of the house onto the street. Once outside, I saw my friends. Richard ran past me into the house.

Anne was standing in the middle of the road, staring down at Seán, who was bent over someone who was bleeding very heavily from the head. I looked around for

John. I must have been shouting his name because Seán looked up at me with panic in his eyes. I walked toward him and realized that the bleeding head was John's. I started to shake and it seemed to take forever to get to where he was lying. I slumped down on the ground.

"John, John, John." I kept saying his name over and over again but he wouldn't move. The driver was sitting on the curb, holding his knees to his chest, mumbling something about not seeing him and that he'd just appeared in front of the car. I looked at this stranger biting his lip and crying.

Richard came out of the house saying the ambulance would be here in five minutes. Anne ran back into the house. Seán was talking to John. He was telling him that everything would be okay and that the ambulance was on the way. I told him I loved him and that he was to hold on. It was very cold; John looked very cold. I started to try to lift him up to take him into my arms, but Seán stopped me.

"We can't move him, Em. He'll be okay. The ambulance is on its way."

"Please wake up!" I begged. I just wanted to see his eyes. "Please wake up!"

Anne ran out of the house with towels in her hands as the ambulance came up the street. The medics got out and moved us out of the way. Seán pulled me away and held his arms around me tight, as though he was afraid that I would run away. Richard was staring at the driver who was sitting on the curb, his lip beginning to bleed. Anne was standing in the middle of the street still holding the towels.

I was allowed to go in the ambulance with John; the

others followed in a taxi. I held his hand while they worked around me. They stuck tubes into him and used paddles on his heart. He was still asleep but I talked to him anyway. I told him that we could go on holiday as soon as he was better and not to worry, because everything was going to be fine. I mentioned how much I needed him on a number of occasions and even spoke about some stupid football match he was looking forward to.

We got to the hospital and I was left standing in a corridor while they wheeled him into a room that only staff were allowed into. A nurse took me into a waiting area and asked me if I wanted a cup of tea with sugar.

"Sugar is good for shock," I said.

She agreed and smiled at me sadly. "I'll get you that tea," she said and left.

The others arrived minutes later and waited. Nobody spoke. I was terrified. I knew it was bad.

Please stay alive. Please be okay, I kept saying over and over again in my head.

Holy Mary Mother of God, please save him. Our Father who art in heaven, please save him. Please God, please sweet Jesus, please save him. Glory be to the Father, please, I prayed, then I prayed again.

Seán suddenly remembered Clo. She was still in the house, passed out somewhere, blissfully unaware of this nightmare. Anne went to phone her.

The doctor was walking toward us. I looked up at him and it seemed like hours before my eyes reached his. He asked if any family were present. John's parents hadn't arrived yet. I stood up. I said I was family and walked toward him.

"I'm sorry," he said. "John's head injuries were just too serious. We did everything we could. He wouldn't have felt any pain."

He was telling us that John was dead. My head hurt and my eyes were burning. I wanted to stop my heart from beating because each beat was becoming more painful. The others were staring at me. Anne was crying. I tried to listen to the doctor over the loud buzzing in my ears. He took me into the room where I had been previously denied entry. He stood for a minute, watching me stare at John's body. Then he left. John was in the room but I was alone.

No. This isn't happening. We're at home in bed. I'm having a nightmare.

"Wake up! Wake up!" I called out, pinching myself hard. "Wake up!"

I knew deep down I wasn't dreaming but I pinched myself harder. Then I held him in my arms. He was heavy and still warm.

I whispered into his ear, "Just open your eyes. That's all you have to do. The doctors will take care of the rest."

He wouldn't though. Death was thick in the air, making it difficult for me to breathe with ease. There was a white sheet tucked under his chin. The blood had now stopped flowing from his head and he was clean. I could see his face again. He looked younger, like the teenage boy who had always picked me to play on his basketball team despite my inability to play. I took his hand again and I could feel my heart breaking.

I briefly wondered if I was about to have a heart attack and I welcomed it. He was dead. He was dancing with me a few hours ago, but now he was dead. It was becoming even more difficult to breathe.

"I love you," I said, my voice breaking. "I really wish that you would fucking wake up." I pleaded with him but he couldn't hear me, but I couldn't accept that. I kissed him on his blue lips and rubbed my wet face against his cheek. I whispered into his ear and begged, "Please come back!"

Then I said "fuck" a lot, tears burning red tracks into my face, hands shaking and numb holding on to his growing colder and colder.

"Please come back! I'll do anything!"

I waited—but nothing. I looked up toward the ceiling. I knew it was stupid but I didn't care.

"God, if you give him back to me, I will do whatever you want. I'll be good. Please God, please God, please God, just give him back to me. He's twenty-six—he's only twenty-fucking-six. Please God, please God, give him back!"

It didn't work. I wanted to lie down with him, but I couldn't bring myself to because for the first time lying with John seemed wrong, so I just held his hand and brushed his blond bloodied hair from his face, the face that I had grown up with, the face that I relied on, the face that was as familiar as my own but was different now. The light was out, the spark had faded away, and all that we were and had and all that he was and would be was gone. My boy, my man, my friend, my challenger, my lover, my identity lay growing cold like stone. Tears flowed from the ocean that had once been my heart. I removed invisible dirt from the sheet that covered him. I found his hand and held it tight.

"I love you."

Time stood still and I succumbed to the agony. I've no idea how long I was kneeling on the cold tiles clinging desperately to his hand. At some point Clo entered the room. She was crying. When she saw our boy she screamed. She didn't mean to—it was primal, it just came out, and she couldn't help it. She stood looking down at the body that used to be John and put her arms around me. I heard myself saying: "Bye, baby." Clo was sobbing as I held John's hand. The pain weighed us down, making sudden movement almost impossible. We just stayed still, still like John.

Someone had called my mother. She arrived with my father to pick me up, he silent and four steps behind her, not quite knowing what to do or say. She took control of me and, for the first time since I was a young child, I was grateful for her strength. As they led me out of the hospital I saw Richard comforting his distraught wife and Seán alone in a corner, staring and broken. We went home. I remember sitting in the backseat of the car, watching the night lights blur as we passed them, the reds and yellows of the streetlamps, the shining white of the passing cars. My father's Dean Martin tape was playing. He was singing about love. I looked up at the sky. It was black. Not a star to be seen. The skin on my face still burned. My mother kept turning to gaze at me, almost as though she was afraid that at any moment I would defy her and join John in death as I had done in life.

The house was cold. My mother put on the kettle to make tea, but I just wanted to sleep. She tucked me in and rubbed the hair away from my forehead. I couldn't feel her touch. My father stood in the doorway watching his wife and child. She turned off the light and she lay beside me in the dark and I felt her warmth and an overwhelming sense of exhaustion. I remembered Clodagh's mother and how as a child I thought it odd that her reaction to her husband's death had been sleep. I now realized why. Sleep was the only escape.

Chapter 4

No Good-byes

The funeral took place a couple of days later. John's mother requested that Noel hold the service. It's odd that I don't remember much about it, but everyone said he did a beautiful job. The church was packed. People were there from our old school and college and of course people from work, all there to shake hands and share in the grief. They uttered words of sympathy; some were crying. I was numb. At the graveside people held one another circling the open ground. Noel's choir sang "The Alleluia" while they lowered John into the ground. I could feel my father's strength holding me up, his presence unobtrusive and omnipresent. His heart beat on my back as the coffin was lowered. He held my hand when I threw dirt on the glistening brass plaque inscribed with John's name. I heard his mother's anguish and felt her agony as people passed and blessed themselves. I remember being led away by the firm hands of my parents, passing the gravediggers standing by, itching to cover the hole so that they could go home, like vultures sitting on a tree waiting for a calf to breathe its last.

I remember sitting in his parents' front lounge surrounded by my friends and watching his mother crying while she handed out sandwiches. My mother and Doreen were handing out drinks and whispering to each other, concerned about who had a food plate and who didn't. Doreen was our fifty-year-old neighbor—she had arrived with a sponge cake the first day we moved in and after that she became part of the furniture. John used to say that she came with the house. Doreen was kind, considerate, funny, sharp, strong, passionate and above all a deadly adversary. She was old Dublin and made no apologies. She was a second mother to me and Noel. We often went to her when any problem arose, but this was one that even the mighty Doreen couldn't solve and she knew it, so instead she served food.

John's father sat in the garden on a plastic deck chair alone and drinking whiskey. My father joined him and they sat in silence, both with tears resting in their eyes. There was nothing to say. Anne held on to Richard for dear life, afraid to let go, and I knew how she felt. Seán just sat by the front window, chain-smoking and blindly watching the passing cars. The loneliness and guilt in his eyes was unavoidable and for me it was like looking at a reflection. He caught my gaze and I turned away.

It's my fault.

I stayed at my parents' house for two weeks after the funeral, but it no longer felt like home. I was a visitor. Noel stayed too and it was nice, but we were all adults now and every day felt like an extended Sunday lunch. Everyone tried to say the right things but nobody knew what they were, even Noel. I wanted to go home, but they were worried about too many memories. Nobody seemed to understand that there was no escape from them and that I held them close. I wanted to roam around and pick up his jumpers and tidy them up. I wanted to smell his aftershave and lie on his side of the bed. I wanted to listen to our music and hold his shirts close to my face. I needed to be as close to John as I possibly could be, so that I could say sorry.

It's my fault.

Eventually it was Noel who pleaded with my parents to let their vise grip go. It was he who explained the feelings that I had difficulty sharing. He just knew it was right for me to leave, so that I could start to pick up the pieces. So I did. I went home. My mother cried openly when I left and my father held her and smiled at me bravely. When they hugged me, it was difficult to let go.

My dad held me tight and bent down, whispering in my ear, "He was like my son. We've lost our boy but we will survive."

The tears that had dried up days ago fell once more and I was grateful for the release. My mother nodded her head, agreeing with someone invisible. I sat in the car and looked forward. When we moved off I turned to see my father holding my shaking mother.

It's my fault.

The house was empty and cold. Noel put on the heating. The kitchen was still the mess we had left it. He started to clean up but I stopped him. Nick Cave was in the CD player. John had been listening to his new album that day. I wanted to be alone but instead Noel made tea. I waited for him to talk about God's ways and how it was a plan and that John was much better off but he didn't and I was grateful. He stayed for one coffee and when he was confident that I needed to be alone, he left. I waved him good-bye and told him I would be okay.

Liar.

I sat on the sitting room floor listening to Nick Cave sing sad songs for hours, crying, laughing, talking to John, talking to myself but mostly crying. I played the answering-machine message he had left over and over again.

"Hi, you've reached six four zero five two six one. We're somewhere exotic so leave a message and, if we like you, we'll call you back."

Our home had become a museum and my present was now the past. I sat in the kitchen and gazed at his personalized coffee mug, the Post-it he had left on the fridge reminding me to get the brake light fixed on the car, the piece of paper he had brought from college about his stupid hoppity-hop test. I stared at everything that had been his and cried for hours because he was gone and it was my fault.

Chapter 5

The Five Stages

Grief is all-consuming. Grief is isolating. Grief is selfish. Grief counselors will tell you that there are five stages in the grief process: denial, anger, bargaining, depression and finally acceptance. I think that there are six: denial, anger, bargaining, depression, guilt and then finally acceptance.

Denial
I didn't think about anyone else. I didn't think. I lived in my own past. Locked in my own head, rerunning my life thus far. I had been given four weeks' compassionate leave. Four weeks to mourn a lifetime. I stayed mostly in my room, hiding under my duvet, listening to my grandmother's antique clock tick through time. I slept and slept and slept and when my eyes would force me to wake I would hug my pillow and talk to John.

"Remember when we told my parents we were moving in together? Remember how insane they went?

Even Noel got it in the neck. Remember? My mother used the word 'Christ.' Noel chastised her and she ate him. You calmed her down though. Even Dad was against it and he's usually easygoing. You were brilliant. I was screaming like a fourteen-year-old but you sorted it all out. You were always good at arguing. You could have been a barrister if you'd wanted. You could have been anything."

I could hear the hailstorm outside. The hailstones battering against the window didn't move me. It was a cat screaming on the windowsill that eventually pushed me to get up. I dragged myself to the curtain and pulled it back roughly, disgusted that reality was interrupting a pleasant conversation. I looked out at the hailstones battering down on the concrete backyard. The shed door was swinging wildly, its hinges screaming for relief. The plant pots were rolling, spilling their contents with every spin. It was a few seconds before I remembered the sound that had drawn me to the window. The cat cried out in desperation at the lunatic staring into the middle distance. If cats could talk, I think the words "Let me in, you fucking thick!" would have been uttered. I opened the window, shocked at the sight of the tiniest little kitten clinging on to the windowsill with its underdeveloped claws. I picked up this little sopping creature, who really was just a little pair of petrified eyes surrounded by fur, and lifted him carefully inside. I could feel his little heart beating wildly in my hands. I ran to the bathroom and wrapped him in a towel. I sat on the side of the bath carefully patting him dry.

"You're only a baby. Look at this, John! A little kitten."

I looked into his little face. You could tell he was a boy instantly. He had a boy's face, oval black eyes, black fur that stood straight up despite being soaking wet and a little white smig under his chin. In fact, the longer I looked at him the more he reminded me of John's third-year science partner, Leonard Foley. Leonard had the black oval eyes and a black shock of gravity-defying hair. He didn't have the white smig or the fur, but everything else was pretty much eerily the same. Leonard had made many attempts to sedate his mane—however, in the end the only option other than a skinhead was to gel it to the shape of a mohawk. He looked like an alien, but then he was a big fan of *Star Trek* and thought looking like an alien was cool and, because he was lead guitarist of the only band in the whole school, we had all agreed that indeed it was cool. I played with the kitten's head fur, shaping it into a mohawk. He looked up at me cautiously while rubbing his ass against the towel. He was looking more like Leonard.

"Hi, Leonard? How's the music business? Got a deal yet?"

The kitten wasn't much interested in my rambling. Now dry, his cries suggested that he was intent on being fed. I took him downstairs and into the kitchen, sitting him on the counter while I looked for an appropriate bowl. Once out of my grasp he instantly began to move, although he stopped short at the edge of the sink. He looked down at the floor far below and backed up against the window. It was only then that it dawned on me.

"How the hell did a little dude like you manage to find your way onto a second-floor windowsill?"

He didn't answer.

"That's impossible."

Leonard wasn't much interested in giving away any

secrets—he was too busy walking around in circles. I watched him feeding on two-day-old tuna.

"Where did you come from? Did you send him, John? Did you send him to get me out of bed? You never did like it when I overslept. A waste of a day, you'd say."

Leonard was finished feeding. He wanted to sleep after his ordeal. I couldn't blame him. After all, his encounter with nature's wrath on my windowsill was akin to any one of us surviving an earthquake. I found a shoe box and filled it with a fresh hand towel. When I placed him inside he snuggled up instantly and closed his eyes. I put him on the bed beside me. I got back under the duvet and watched him sleep his troubles away.

"Hey, John, remember the moving statue? Thousands of people made a pilgrimage to pray at the foot of a statue of Mary in some barn in North Kerry. Remember Leonard removed the statue of the Virgin and Child from outside the principal's office? He hid it in the girls' toilets and left a note on the podium saying *'Gone to lunch'*!" I was laughing. "The principal went nuts and called him a blasphemer. Moving statues! What a joke!"

Leonard opened one eye to see what the joke was. I wasn't laughing anymore.

We both fell back to sleep shortly after that.

Anger

Clo would call me once a day.

"Are you okay?"

"Yes."

"Do you need anything?"

"No."

"Do you want me to come over?"

"No."

The call would end and we would both be relieved.

She didn't get four weeks' compassionate leave. She only lost a friend, he wasn't family to her. Her pain wasn't valued as highly. She returned to her stressful job the day after the funeral. She walked into the office to be greeted by seventy pieces of post requiring urgent attention, three press releases, a magazine shoot for Fruit and Veg Awareness Week and a very disgruntled client. She dealt with her post methodically. Her client was placated within minutes. She managed to write three press releases within an hour, meeting the deadline with time to spare.

The shoot, on the other hand, was a nightmare. Two underfed models, one dressed as a cabbage, the other as an apple, cold and cranky waiting for the fruit man to deliver the display. He was caught in traffic on the M50. The girls were fending off teenagers' abuse of their fruit-like appearance while the photographer bitched about the time. Clo remained professional throughout.

She didn't get home until after seven. She entered her empty apartment, deflated. She pulled the coffee from the shelf. It slipped from her grasp and she could hear the thick glass jar hitting her head before she felt it. The coffee jar continued toward the floor. She nearly caught it but her grip let her down once more. It smashed onto her white tiles, the coffee grains bursting out of their glass prison in their bid for freedom.

"Enough!"

Heat blazed inside her. The erupting tears burned her eyes.

"All I wanted was a cup of effing coffee! Is that too much to ask? Fuck, I'm not cleaning up! I'm not dealing with this!"

She was screaming and moving toward the press. She started to pull out glasses, throwing them across the room, watching them hit, smash, then trickle down her kitchen wall. She aimed a cup at a picture of a boat sailing on blue sea. She threw it with the concentration and professionalism of a star baseball player. The glass shattered on impact, leaving the picture torn and hanging from the chipped frame. She screamed and cried and danced on the coffee and glass broken under her feet. Then she stopped cold, her heart beating wildly, attempting to break out through her rib cage, her hands shaking and her thoughts blurry.

Enough.

She was sitting on her kitchen floor, moaning and halfheartedly attempting to sweep the fruits of her destruction into a dustpan when the doorbell rang.

"Fuck off!" she roared, knowing that it was impossible for any prospective visitor to actually hear her four floors down on a busy street. She answered on the fifth ring. It was her mother.

"Clodagh, let me in!"

"I want to be alone."

"Let me in, for Christ's sake!"

"Just fuck off!"

She buzzed her mother inside. She surveyed the kitchen while her mother ascended in the lift.

"Just leave me alone!" she roared at the counter before smashing the plate that lay inoffensively in the kitchen sink. She answered the door a minute later.

"Oh love! Come here to me, you've snots halfway down your face." Her mother took a tissue from her pocket and wiped her nose. "Blow!"

She blew hard and her mother held her while she cried and swore. Her mother cried too.

Later, exhausted, Clodagh asked her mother to speak about the father she had been too young to know.

"He loved the Boomtown Rats. He loved their restlessness, their anger. He was political. He wanted change. Old Ireland is dead and gone, he'd say. He was passionately opinionated."

She was smiling. Clo watched her softening with each memory.

"When he laughed the room laughed with him," she said, still smiling. "He was stubborn just like you."

Clo smiled, not offended.

"He was always right even when he wasn't. He loved the beach and he loved boats."

Clo made a mental note to replace the boat picture.

"He was an overachiever—he always had a moneymaking scheme under his sleeve. He could drive me insane."

"Like me," Clo said, attempting a smile.

"Like you," her mother admitted, stroking her hair.

The Hallmark moment passed quickly and Clo felt the heat rising inside.

"It's not fair. I'm so angry!" she spat.

"I know you are," her mother agreed. "The state of the kitchen is a testament to that."

Clo couldn't help but laugh. She was under the impression that her mother hadn't noticed the contents of the other room.

"You know, when your dad died you were only five, but on the day of the funeral you broke every single cup and saucer in your play set and they were plastic. I knew then that you understood that your dad wasn't coming back. That was your way. Times haven't changed."

Clodagh dissolved. "How?" she asked.

"Well, you're still smashing things," her mother responded.

Clo cried, for her mother, her friend, for me, for herself. All the while her mother held her, safe in the knowledge that she would survive.

Bargaining

Noel called in every few days. He'd stay long enough to know that I was okay. Then he'd leave. He spent most of his time praying. He and John had been friends . . . no, they were closer than that. They grew up together. Noel was two years older than John, but they clicked. John admired all the traits that I had initially found so offensive. He liked that Noel didn't follow the crowd—he liked talking with him about something other than the usual football/cars/girls conversations that ruled his universe. John made Noel laugh out loud and until he was sore in places. He would miss that. He would miss their religious debates; God versus science was an old favorite that they would return to over and over again.

God, please, don't let me forget! If you had to take him, please allow me to hear his laugh!

He wished he could tell us that John was at peace and that his death meant his resurrection in heaven and that we should be happy for him, that we should celebrate his homecoming. He couldn't. His heart wasn't in it. He missed his friend too much.

Please, God, make me understand.

He was working through his pain the only way he knew how. He said Mass; he visited the old folks' home, the hospital; he gave a scheduled talk in the school. At the end of each day he went to the home he shared with Father Rafferty, a Corkman in his sixties. Father Rafferty would watch the news while Noel cooked them dinner. Noel would eat in silence, nodding intermittently at Father Rafferty, who was dedicated to worrying himself sick about the state the world was in. When Noel would at last escape to his room, he'd put Nina Simone on his CD player and listen to her sing about sadness while he knelt at the foot of his bed with his hands clenched in prayer.

Please God, I've devoted my life to you, take this pain away. I bow down before you. Take this loneliness away.

★ ★ ★

As I learned much later, Noel had met Laura at a cake sale. She had baked over four hundred queen cakes in support of breast cancer. She'd lost her mother to it, and she felt fund-raising was the least she could do. She was warm and chatty. A lot of people don't chat to priests, not in an everyday kind of way. Noel was disarmed. He enjoyed her easygoing ways and her openness. She wasn't afraid of speaking her mind, but she wasn't afraid to listen either. They went for coffee and she talked about her mother while smiling and laughing at old anecdotes. She told her sad tale with humor, free from guilt, and he found it refreshing. He had found that he too talked about himself. This was new to him and an unexpected pleasure. They had met again a number of times, sometimes accidentally, sometimes it only appeared that way. They had never been intimate nor would he even consider it, but he had been feeling guilty about his new friendship. That was before John had died and now the loneliness that he had felt so long was becoming unbearable.

Lord, I'm on my knees. Please, I beg you, make this loneliness go away.

★ ★ ★

He grabbed his coat and without a word passed Father Rafferty, who was ironing his jacket. He closed the door behind him and walked onto the street, preparing to hail the first taxi he saw.

He arrived unannounced. Laura opened the door and smiled happily. She led him inside to her warm sitting room. He sank into her sofa. Candles were burning on the mantelpiece. It was dark except for a lamp by a reading chair where her book lay opened. He had interrupted her; he had no reason to be there. His embarrassment caught him off guard.

"Would you be more comfortable if I turned on the main light?" she asked, aware of his discomfort.

"No," he apologized, "I'm sorry, I shouldn't have come." He bowed his head to avoid her gaze.

"I think that's exactly what you needed." She smiled. "Let me make tea and we'll talk about it."

He nodded his head.

Later she sat on her reading chair and Noel told her

about his friend who had been killed in an accident. He told her about his anger and his shame. He talked about his pain, his regrets and he even mentioned a few fears.

Then she was hugging him. Holding him close to her and he cried on her shoulder while she rubbed his back and told him that he would be okay. He felt her breath on his neck and her cheek pressed against his. He inhaled her perfume and felt her breasts pressing on his tunic. He pulled away, startled by the tightness in his pants. "I should go."

She nodded. "If you ever need anything."

He nodded.

She walked him to the door and he hugged her despite himself.

"Thank you," he said.

"Any time," she said sadly.

She watched him walk down the pathway and close the gate. He didn't look back. She closed the door.

Noel walked home. It took him over an hour, but it felt like minutes. His head hurt.

I wanted her. Oh God, help me, I'm so confused! Please, God, I am yours, give me strength!

Depression

Seán left the funeral and went straight to the pub. He sat alone at the corner of the bar, emptied his pocket of all his money, placed it on the counter in front of him and ordered a whiskey, then another one and another one. He kept going as long as he had the money to pay for it. He didn't interact; he wasn't there to be social or to get laid, which probably surprised a few of the regulars. When he fell off the stool, the barman stopped serving him. He didn't argue or throw shapes—he just took his money, pushed it into his pocket and meandered out of the establishment, his exit as silent as his entrance. He'd bought a few bottles in the off-license next door, his Visa taking the hit, when he discovered that his remaining change couldn't stretch to a kebab. He needed help leaving; the mixture of twelve whiskeys and fresh air had hit him hard and his legs were becoming unstable. He didn't recall how he got home. He didn't remember the mode of transport nor how he managed to fit the key into the lock. He found himself sitting on his favorite chair, a tatty, ragged thing that, once you sat in it, swallowed you whole. Clo used to call it "the Lotus."

He didn't leave it that night. Instead he sat in the dark drinking from the bottle, not caring about any possible damage he could be inflicting on his tired body.

What's the point?

He took a long-overdue week off from work and there he remained in his tatty chair, in his small apartment sitting room, surrounded by the books that lined his walls. He wouldn't be reading for a while—his eyes hurt too much. The CD machine in the corner remained silent. Sound hurt his ears. The TV lay permanently idle. Food was a foreign concept; he'd forgotten how to swallow solids without choking. He couldn't sleep. He just drank until there was nothing.

He ignored the telephone and the door. He was in no fit state and after a while he didn't hear them. He'd fall asleep but his troubled mind woke him quickly. His head would loll, and then fall slightly; he'd pick it up, eyes closed. This would occur a number of times before he would finally succumb to a deep sleep.

John would be there and for a moment everything would be fine. He would be sitting in the Lotus beside John's hospital bed. John would turn to him and say: "Jesus, man, you look like shit!"

Seán would nod his head, smiling. "You gave us a scare," he'd say, and John would sit up grinning.

"I do love the spotlight."

"It's not funny. We thought you were dead."

Seán would move to the window, mesmerized by the glowing sun that seemed to dance in the air like a bright orange balloon. He could hear John laughing behind him.

"Nobody dies—we go somewhere else, that's all."

Seán would try to turn away from the window, but his eyes would remain focused on the sun.

"Yeah. Well, I'm glad you stayed," he'd say, battling to turn his face to John.

"I didn't."

Somehow released, he'd turn but it would be too late: he'd be facing an empty bed and then he'd wake, startled by his own cries. The dream was always pretty much the same. The odd detail would change; instead of a dancing sun it would be a yellow moon or a white cloud. Once it was a chocolate M&M.

He'd been drinking for five days when the key turned in his door. Jackie, a girl he had been shagging, entered, still knocking.

"Hello? Anybody here?"

Unable to respond he remained seated, drunk, exhausted, haunted and suffering from a touch of alcohol poisoning. She stood over him, surveying the damage he had done over the previous five days: the empty bottles

45

that lined the floor, the cigarette butts towering over the ashtray, the smell of booze, which almost took her breath away. His eyes were red raw. He was filthy, not having changed his clothes in days. His fingers were yellow and shaking. He was sweating profusely.

"Oh my God! What have you done to yourself?"

He sat staring into the middle distance, drawing deeply from a cigarette, and she wasn't sure if he was merely ignoring her or if he was even aware that she had entered. She walked to the bathroom in search of a face cloth. She slipped on vomit and then gagged.

"You've turned into Shane McGowan!"

She cleaned her shoe as best she could and closed the door as she left the bathroom. She approached him slowly, afraid to make any sudden moves. When she eventually reached him he didn't stir. She knelt a safe distance in front of him, afraid to reach out, and slowly she attempted to make contact.

"Seán . . . Seán . . . Seán . . ."

Nothing.

"It's me, Jackie," she said, nodding and pointing to her own face.

"I know who you are. I'm not blind," he drawled, concentrating on the floor.

"So look at me," she challenged.

He didn't want to. He couldn't remember ever giving her keys and he was annoyed at himself. He didn't even really know her.

"Go away."

"I know you lost your friend, but this is ridiculous." She was pointing around the room and it made him dizzy.

46

"So leave," he managed, before sinking farther into the Lotus.

"I'll leave when you shower, change your clothes and dump those fucking bottles."

Her intervention was not welcome.

"Just go," he pleaded.

"I can't."

"Get out of here," he moaned.

She wasn't budging. He used all the strength he could muster to be as threatening as he possibly could be.

"Get out of my house! I don't want you. I have nothing to say to you. I don't even like you."

He picked up a bottle and swallowed the dregs.

"You're just upset," she said calmly as she stood up to regain some power. "You're just drunk."

He looked up at her glassily, sneering at this stranger, who on reflection was not even that attractive. If she didn't want to leave he'd make her want to.

"I am drunk and you're a whore." He lit another cigarette, satisfied she would be soon gone.

"You asshole," she observed. "You're the whore. You're the one can't make a relationship work, so don't put your shit on me."

He didn't care enough to answer.

Tears were spilling from her eyes. "I wanted this to work but it takes two." She was moving to the door.

"Haven't you forgotten something?" he said, closing his eyes, relieved.

She turned and looked around, confused.

"My keys."

She threw them on the glass table, knocking a can full

of sodden butts onto the floor. He didn't look at her again. She left, slamming the door. He opened his eyes and the tears that had refused to come for so long ran freely.

Acceptance

Anne and Richard suffered like the rest of us. They felt disbelief, anger, depression and guilt but they also had each other and in one another they retained the security and hope that the rest of us had lost. When Richard felt overwhelmed, Anne was right by his side. When Anne found it unbearable, Richard was holding her tight. They missed their friend but thanked God they had one another.

One week after their inheritance party they sat together on their couch, holding on to one another and watching John make his groomsman speech at their wedding. He was tugging at his tie and grinning while his hands involuntarily shuffled telegrams.

"I'm not going to keep you long . . ." A pause. He grinned. "Unlike Anne's ma."

The assembled guests laughed on cue. The cameraman panned to Anne's mother laughing and feigning embarrassment while mouthing, "Oh stop!"

The action over, the cameraman returned to the speaker.

"I'm just going to read a few greetings from people who didn't care enough to come."

Again the guests laughed. Anne in her wedding dress was smiling widely. Richard was wiping his eyes, grinning at his new wife.

Four years later Anne was watching her dead friend on-screen and crying in the arms of her husband. They held each other, watching John as he lined up to kiss the bride, laughing and making smacking noises with his lips. Waving them off, hugging them and spinning them around, intoxicated by their joy. They cried but they laughed too. They couldn't help it; he was funny when he wanted to be. They told stories of when he was smart and when he was stupid. They talked about his bad habits and his favorite sayings. They recalled the good times and some of the bad. They remembered him well and in doing so they achieved acceptance.

Chapter 6

The Bear, the Rabbit . . .

I woke up on Friday morning. John was dead a month. I hugged his pillow, which still smelled of him because I'd made sure to spray it with his aftershave when I'd eventually washed it. It was still early and I didn't have to be in school for a few hours so I tried to sleep, but my body refused to cooperate. I was wide awake for the first time since the accident. I kept closing my eyes, but they burned to open. Frustrated, I sat up and really wanted to cry, but my eyes remained dry. After several attempts I gave up and crawled out of bed. I sat in the bath on my own, playing with the taps with my toes, but that got boring pretty quickly. I lay there remembering John's arms around me. I remembered our first kiss on the wall outside my house, his look of sheer delight the day I produced a packet of condoms in the schoolyard, our time in America, our home, our dreams, his face, his smile, his eyes, his heart and still no tears.

What the . . . ?

I felt sick. I wanted to cry for him because crying was all that I had left and now it would appear that even that had been taken away. It wasn't fair.

"Fuck this!" I screamed to the shower curtain. *"Fuck the lot of it!"* I roared. *"Fuck you, God!"* I yelled to the ceiling.

Not content with God out of it, I attacked the rest of His family.

"Jesus, Mary and Joseph, you bastards!"

Then I moved on to Allah and Buddha just in case and in the end Judas even got a mention.

"Why?" I begged. "Why did you take him, God, you greedy bastard? Why couldn't you let him live?"

Not surprisingly, I didn't get an answer, but as I got out of the bath I slipped and for a fleeting second I thought it might be retribution, so I gave the ceiling the fingers and mumbled, "You'll have to do better than that, fuck face!"

After that I made my way around the house, being careful to check that all electrical appliances were safe before using them.

★ ★ ★

It was the last class of the day and my students had been on their best behavior since my return. When I entered the classroom, instead of chaos, I was met with silence. The smart-asses weren't being smart, the chatterers were silent and the swots were slow to raise their hands to share their knowledge. I was subdued and fragile. My pain was naked and it had a rippling effect on all who witnessed it, including my students, and I felt bad for them. Grief filled every room that I entered like a fog that only lifted when I left. It was the last class of the day, I was teaching history to First Years and we were concentrating on the Reformation. I asked Jackie Connor to read a paragraph on the Lutheran church and switched off. I was staring out the window at two pigeons' heads butting one another on the school roof when I heard Rory McGuire calling me.

"Miss? Miss? Are you okay?"

I emerged from the haze and smiled at him. "I'm fine, Rory. Why do you ask?"

He looked around at his classmates, whose eyes were cast to the floor. He cleared his throat. "Well, Miss, Jackie finished the paragraph five minutes ago."

I felt tears spring to my eyes and I looked toward the ceiling and God.

Oh fucking great, this morning I begged you to let me cry and nothing. Now in front of twenty-five teenagers, you fucking . . .

I didn't finish the thought. Instead I tried to pull myself together. "Does anyone have any questions?" I asked cheerfully.

The class remained silent.

"Right. Good. Okay."

I looked on my desk for the book, but I couldn't see it. I must have appeared panicked because Jane Griffin in the front row handed me hers.

"Here, Miss, we're in the middle of the page."

I smiled at her, embarrassed. "Thank you, Jane."

I looked at the book but reading was difficult. I kept telling myself *only ten minutes to the bell*, but then my heart started racing and my palms began to sweat. I wondered if I was having a panic attack.

52

Pull yourself together, I told myself again. I tried to concentrate, but finally I gave up and asked David Morris to read the next paragraph and while he did, I prayed that it would take us to the bell. When it eventually rang the entire class exhaled and they almost ran from the room. I sat at my desk with my eyes closed and my head in my hands, taking refuge in the darkness. I hadn't noticed that Declan Morgan had remained sitting at his desk. I heard someone say "Miss" and I looked up.

"Declan, I'm sorry, I didn't realize you were still here. What can I do for you?" I enquired without meeting his eyes.

Declan was looking straight at me. "I just wanted to say that I was sorry about your fella. It was a terrible thing that happened to him."

His kindness threw me. I was touched and I desperately wanted to cry again. "Thank you," I managed.

He got up to leave and then he stopped. "Miss?"

"Yes, Declan?"

"Can I tell you a joke?"

I smiled despite myself.

He dropped his schoolbag on the ground and walked up to me. "There was a bear and a rabbit taking a shit in the woods. The bear turned to the rabbit and said: 'Hey, Rabbit, does shit stick to your fur?' The rabbit said, 'No,' so the bear wiped his arse with the rabbit." He smiled as though to ask, "Do you get it?"

I should have admonished him for his bad language but instead I laughed, and when he saw me laughing, he laughed.

"That's a great joke," I said.

"I know," he grinned and he reminded me of John as a teenager. He turned to leave.

"Declan!" I called involuntarily.

He stopped.

"You live down the road from me, don't you?" I enquired.

"I do."

"Would you like a lift home?" I asked.

He smiled. "Only if you let me drive."

I laughed while advising that there was no way in hell. He waited for me while I collected my things and for a few minutes everything was normal. Declan opened the door for me.

"Thanks," I said gratefully and we both knew that I meant it.

★ ★ ★

That night Clodagh arrived with another stew from her mother.

"How long is she going to keep making me stews?" I asked her.

"Not long. Another six months or so," she answered, smiling.

I put it in the freezer on top of the stew and lasagne she had made me the week before.

Clo sat at the counter and continued, "She just wants to help, Em."

I nodded and I wished I could feel normal again. I turned to her, smiling. "One of my students told me a joke today—it was very funny."

She looked surprised. "Tell me."

"Well," I began and paused, realizing that I couldn't remember it. "It was about a bear shitting on a rabbit or something. It was really funny," I said lamely.

"A bear shits on a rabbit? It sounds hilarious," she smiled. "Jesus, Em, we really need to get you out."

We laughed and it was the first time we had enjoyed a second together since the accident. The fog was dissipating and I thanked Declan in my head once more. Later we sat in the living room with coffee and I asked her how Seán was. I hadn't seen him much since the funeral. He had called around a few times, but I pretended I was out and hid behind the curtains, watching him walk down the road. I couldn't face him and now it seemed like he couldn't face me.

"He's fine," she said, but she was a brutal liar.

"What's wrong?" I asked.

"Nothing," she replied.

It made me angry. "I wish you'd talk to me!"

"What's that supposed to mean?" she answered, hurt.

"Stop freezing me out. John's dead, not me. Why can't you just talk to me like you used to." Tears burned my eyes for the fourth time that day, which was considerably less than the day before.

She looked at me, her eyes glassy. "I really miss him, Em!" She was crying. "I feel sick all the time and I don't know what to say." She continued, like a torrent: "I should have some insight or wisdom because of my dad, or maybe it's because of his death that I know there is nothing I can do to make this any better. I wish I could say the magic words. I wish I knew them. I should, but I don't."

I was so relieved. I sat on the couch beside her. I told

her that everything was going to be all right and we hugged.

Suddenly we were having our first real post-John conversation. She told me about a wealthy client of hers who kept sending her flowers. She talked about Seán, how he had become withdrawn, and of her fears that he was smoking way too much hash. He had promised her that he'd stop, but she wasn't sure whether he was just saying it to get her off his back.

She told me that two weeks previously Anne had missed her period and did a pregnancy test in Bewley's café, but it turned out negative. I couldn't believe that Anne hadn't told me.

"Well," she said, "with everything you're going through . . ." she trailed off and thought for a second, then continued unabated, "Which is something we'll all stop doing."

We both smiled. She got comfortable in her chair.

"Em, in the spirit of openness, there is just one more thing."

"What?" I smiled.

"Please stop wearing John's deodorant. It smells like shit on you and it's weird."

"Point taken," I agreed, sad but relieved. "To tell you the truth, it gives me a rash."

We sat in silence, listening to the stereo, and after a while I asked her if she still thought about her father. She thought for a minute before she answered.

"Every now and then," she said, before going on to tell me that, although he had been gone a long time and she hadn't really known him, once in a while she'd see someone walking down the street or she'd find a picture of him or see a rerun of a show that her mom said he'd liked, and when she did it made her smile. It wasn't much to hold on to but it seemed to be enough. She told me that her mom said the pain goes. I recalled my vague memory of her crying in her bunny slippers and the doctor taking her screaming mother upstairs all those years ago. I still couldn't imagine the pain in my chest ever subsiding, and somewhere deep down I didn't want it to. She was right, she didn't have the magic words, but what she did say helped a lot.

Chapter 7

The Bodyguard and the Graveyard

John was dead six weeks. I had promised Clo that I would visit Seán, but I had been putting it off. I was thinking about him as I drove home from school. Declan was sitting beside me in the car, searching through my tapes and slagging off my taste. I was attempting to stand up for myself, but failed miserably when he pulled out Meatloaf and held it up.

"You're not serious? Meatloaf? He's cack."

I couldn't deny it but of course I tried.

"He's great. It's a great album, full of songs that . . ." I had nowhere to go and it was obvious. I gave in. "Okay, fine, he's cack," and tried to explain that it was a phase.

"Really?" he said, still holding up the tape. "What phase was that? The vomit phase?"

I laughed but stopped suddenly when he pulled out the soundtrack to *The Bodyguard*.

He shook his head from side to side and I nodded,

embarrassed. Nothing was said as we both knew there was no defense. I dropped him to his door. He got out of the car.

"Hey, Miss, tomorrow I'm going to introduce you to some real music."

He legged it up the path and I made a mental note to buy aspirin.

★ ★ ★

I was sitting at home alone. Clo was on a date with Mark, the client who kept sending her flowers. Anne and Richard were at some fund-raiser and I was bored. I picked up my keys from the coffee table and played with them for a few minutes before grabbing my coat and heading for the door. As I approached, the doorbell rang. I opened it instantly. Seán was standing there.

"Hi," he said and then he noticed I was holding my coat. "You're going out. I'm sorry, I should have phoned."

I was really happy to see him. I smiled and told him that I was on my way to see him. He brightened and came in. I made coffee and he sat at the counter. He was uncomfortable and apologized for his distance. I told him it was okay, that I understood.

"I did phone a few times but when—"

"I know," I interrupted and put his coffee down in front of him, trying not to spill it, but my hand was shaking slightly. I sat opposite him and continued. "I just needed some time. It was selfish—"

"No, that's not true!"

But I was determined to make things right. "You lost him too . . ."

I wanted to continue and apologize, but he took my hand and squeezed it.

"I was afraid I'd lost both of you," he said.

"Me too," I stammered.

Neither of us mentioned the mistaken kiss. It was too complicated, too embarrassing, too sad and too pathetic. Neither of us spoke about our guilt, but it was impossible to ignore it as it was painted into every facial expression.

If I hadn't gone back inside for the lighter. If I hadn't leaned down to kiss him. If he hadn't told me I was beautiful. If I hadn't dawdled, too embarrassed to move. Our lips met and John had died.

Sitting together was strange, unfamiliar. All that had gone before was dead and buried with John. We had to find a new way to communicate. I was no longer Seán's best friend's girlfriend. I was just me and of course we had a bond, the kind that is built up over time. We'd shared so much throughout college and now our adult lives, but I'm not sure either of us knew if it was enough to hold on to. We would have to start again with one another, a new playing field. Our comfy and safe flirtation was now behind us, our link now missing.

I made tea and we sat in silence.

"I was drunk," he said after a long time.

Oh God, he's talking about it.

"We all were," I said after a time.

"I shouldn't have kept you," he mumbled.

"I can't talk about it."

"I'm sorry," he said.

"It's not your fault. It's mine."

He was welling up. I couldn't stand it. I couldn't bear to see him broken. I wanted to hug him but couldn't.

What would John think?

"I heard a good joke the other day," I said hopefully.

He wiped his tears and looked at me strangely. "Yeah?" he said.

"Yeah," I agreed, hoping I'd get it right.

"Go on then," he encouraged.

"A young girl is lying in her bed in the Rotunda hospital. The old nun comes up to her and asks her for the name of her newborn baby's father. The girl says she doesn't know his name. The nun is puzzled and asks her why not and the girl says, 'Listen, sister, if you ate a can of beans would you know which one made you fart?'"

Seán laughed. I smiled. It was funnier when Declan told it.

"Who told you that?" he asked.

"A kid from my class—you'd like him. He reminds me of . . ." I didn't finish.

He smiled.

He looked tired. Black circles ringed his brown eyes, making them unusually dull. His skin looked dry and sore, hidden under three days of stubble. He'd lost weight, so much so that his clothes looked big on him. He scratched at his new growth absentmindedly.

"Do you want to go and visit him?" he asked.

"I can't," I said. "Not yet."

Over our fourth cup of coffee the void was closing. We managed to find our neutral ground. We spoke about a movie coming out and the actor who had been caught with his dick in a prostitute's mouth. Somehow this led to a conversation about a nasty case of crabs he'd picked up a few years ago.

"I thought my dick would fall off," he confessed.

Somehow Seán with an itchy dick amused me. "Did you tell John?"

"Yeah."

"He never said anything."

"I made him swear," he said.

"So where'd you get them?" I asked, delighted by the diversion.

"Candyapple."

"Brian!" I exhaled.

"Yeah, Brian," he laughed.

He stayed until after nine. We watched an episode of *The Bill* together. It was nice watching TV with someone. When he was at the door I asked him to take care of himself and stop drowning his sorrows in drink and drugs, and to eat. He maintained that he was already on the road to recovery. I wasn't so sure. We hugged and it wasn't weird. We agreed to look out for one another because we were friends.

I had lied. I was ready to see John. In fact, I had planned to go to the graveyard the very next evening and I needed to be alone. I had bought a little rosebush to plant. John wasn't a particular fan of roses but it looked pretty in the shop. It was Doreen who gave me the idea. She maintained that sometimes it helped to have something to do. I thought it was a good idea and even if I hadn't, she had me in the car and on the way to the garden nursery before I could back out.

"When in doubt dig a hole," she said, while Elton John sang about a rocket man on the radio. "I saw Seán on Grafton Street the other day. He looks terrible."

"He's fine."

"Oh, I don't know—he was drinking a lot during the funeral. You'd want to watch him."

I was concerned, but didn't mention that Clo had the same fears.

"I'm sure he's fine, Dor. We all have our ways of coping."

"Getting locked isn't coping, darlin'."

"He said he was taking care of himself."

"I hope so," she said, patting my knee.

"Me too," I mumbled.

★ ★ ★

It was raining again. I was walking around in circles trying to find John's grave. I found myself walking across strangers' resting places in an attempt to shorten the journey. The reality of what I was doing only dawned on me when I tripped on a wreath on the grave of a woman named Mary Moore. I jumped off.

"Sorry, Mary, I didn't think."

I walked on, using the moss-filled pathway that surely would be my own end. *I'm going to slip and break my sodding neck.* I bitched at myself for wearing high heels. As if John would notice.

Eventually, after checking nearly every gravestone in Section D, I found him. It was weird. Suddenly I was standing alone in front of a sodden pile of soil covering a box and in that box lay John, his fair hair still spiked with gel the way he liked it. His eyes closed, his beautiful face relaxed, his mouth a thin line. I didn't know what to do. It was like a job interview where the interviewer refuses to speak. I stood in the rain for a long time. I could feel my trousers sticking to my legs. The pointed toes of my leather high-heeled boots were curling.

Damn, I love these boots. I shouldn't think about boots. I'm here with John. Concentrate.

Doreen had been right: the tree was a fantastic idea. The rain had softened the ground. I took the little garden shovel from my bag and began to dig a hole and while I dug I found chatting easier. I no longer pretended that he was still here. I chatted as one would to a dead person. I was over the denial. I was mostly over the anger and I had bargained enough in the hospital to last a lifetime.

"Doreen's worried about Seán. So is Clo. I think Anne is too—she mentioned him twice yesterday on the phone. He's been drinking a lot, smoking too. I told Dor he'd be fine, but I'm not sure." I was having difficulty, having hit rock. "Clo's fine. She's met someone—his name is Mark. He works in a garage. Apparently he's very attractive. I haven't seen him yet. He sounds nice. I hope it works out."

I stopped talking for a moment to concentrate on levering the rock out of its comfy spot. "Got ya!" I was talking to the rock. I fit the rosebush into the hole I'd just created. It fitted perfectly. Now all I had to do was cover it over and, bingo, a lovely rosebush.

"Anne thought she was pregnant. She wasn't. She says she's glad. I think she's upset though." I felt a pang of guilt. I hadn't been ready but that's all over now.

The tree was suddenly lopsided.

"Crap!" I tried to straighten it, catching my finger on a thorn. "Ow! Stupid bloody tree!" I began removing some of the soil while pushing at the tree gently. "Noel's quiet these days. He's kind of distant. I think he feels guilty, God turning out to be a total bastard and all." I could hear John laughing in my head. "He's different since you left, but then I suppose we all are."

The tree began to right itself. I held it while packing the soil around it to ensure it held.

"I'm fine. That doesn't mean I don't miss you. I miss you all the time. Wasn't there a song called 'Without You I'm Nothing'? Maybe it was a book, or a film. I can't remember. Anyway, without you I'm nothing. I'm fine though. But I've no idea where I'm going or what I'm doing. Jesus, I'm not even sure if I know who I am. It doesn't matter though. I'm fine."

The earth felt solid around the rosebush. I stood up to survey my work.

"It looks good. I bet it'll be lovely in the summer. I'm thinking about putting fencing around your grave. You wouldn't believe the amount of people who walk on the graves around here."

I left soon after. I hadn't cried. I hadn't even moaned—well, not really. I had been strong. It was a good thing to do. I was a survivor, just like my dad had told me I'd be. I walked to the car with my shovel in hand.

I'm terrified.

Chapter 8

Mama

For three months my mother and Anne were vying for the world record in how many times a day they could phone me. Eventually after I threatened to cut my phone line, they stopped. It was time to pick up the pieces and move on, but the problem was there was still the issue of the driver.

A simple blood test had revealed the driver to be sober, unlike his victim. An inquest revealed that the driver had been going at a reasonable speed but when John, drunk and stoned, had stepped out in front of him, he was unable to brake because the brakes on the car he had had serviced that day were faulty. A further investigation was leading to a possible conviction for the mechanic who had supposedly serviced the car. I didn't know who these people were and I didn't want to. I wasn't like those people you read about, desperate for justice. How could the imprisonment of some unknown mechanic make up for a life? I didn't feel the need for redemption through someone else's misery. It was easier to convince myself that it was just a random, terrible accident.

My mother was confounded. She felt that I couldn't move on until the person responsible had paid for their crime. I felt I couldn't move on unless I let go of recriminations or maybe I felt John and I were as responsible as the mechanic, the driver. We all had our part to play.

The driver did not feel like I did. The driver did not want to leave well enough alone. He needed to communicate. He needed John's parents and me, the girl who he had watched cry over the dying man, to know that he was so very sorry. He had spoken to John's mother at the inquest. He managed to shake John's father's hand, but I had not gone and he desperately needed closure.

I picked up the letter from the mat inside my front door. It had probably been there a week before I bothered to lean down to retrieve it and the various bills and bloody pamphlets off the floor. I opened the bills and glanced at them momentarily to ensure I wasn't being ripped off. The bank would automatically release the money so no need to worry about any late payments. I was briefly grateful that the bills came out of my account as changing all the utilities into my name would have been a nightmare. I instantly binned the pamphlets. I opened the cream envelope without thought. I unfolded the matching writing paper without consideration. I read the return address on the top right-hand side of the page without recognition. I had read two lines before my heart jumped and my pulse raced, causing the hand holding the letter to become unsteady.

"Oh God."

"Dear Emma, My name is Jason O'Connor and I was the driver who was behind the wheel the night your boyfriend, John Redmond, was killed."

I folded the page back and sat on the sofa, placing my hand between my knocking knees.

Go away.

I called Clo. She was harassed in work but told me to stay where I was and she'd get to me as soon as possible. I waited. Every now and then I played with the paper in my hand, tempted to open it, but as I did fear took hold and I closed my hand over it, crumpling it like my John would have crumpled upon impact. I wasn't brave enough. This letter was bringing me back to that night with such clarity I could taste the wine on my breath. I could feel the cold air, the hard ground and John's bloodied hair in my hands.

I was still sitting in the same spot when Clo let herself in three hours later. She must have seen the terrible effect this unsolicited letter had on me because she didn't speak. She opened the claw that used to be my hand and took the letter. Then she gently opened it and smoothed it on her leg.

"Do you want to read it?" she asked.

"No," came my firm reply.

"Do you want me to read it?" she asked.

"I don't know," I answered honestly.

"I'll make tea."

I nodded, following her into the kitchen like a ghost on roller skates. We sat at the counter, letting our tea go cold.

"Maybe I should read it to myself first," she offered.

"No."

I didn't want her to have to keep it from me if it was too upsetting. Her own life was hard enough.

"Read it," I said, although I still wasn't sure I'd be able for what came next.

"Okay," she exhaled. *"Dear Emma, My name is Jason O'Connor and I was the driver who was behind the wheel the night your boyfriend, John Redmond, was killed. I have written to you many times. All of these attempts have ended up at the bottom of a bin. What can I say? What can I say to make your life better? I have nothing to offer except my deepest sympathy and my deepest regret. I know how hard it must be for you to hear from me but I can't move on. I can't live my life without telling you how sorry I am. If I could do anything different I would. I've gone through that night so many times, over and over again. If I had left home a little later, if I hadn't stopped for petrol, if I hadn't gone out at all.*

"I was married last year, and my wife Denise gave birth to a little girl last May. Money was tight. I knew the car needed a service and I chose the cheapest place. I'm so sorry. If only I had spent the extra money. I see you in my dreams most nights. Your face, your horror, is imbedded in my mind and I don't know if I'll ever get over the fear. It chokes me. I'm so sorry. My wife wonders if I'll ever be the same, but then how could I be? I drove my car and a stranger died. I'm so sorry. I wish I could turn back time, but I can't. If I could take his place I swear I would.

"I'm so sorry. Jason."

Clodagh was crying. I sat still, absentmindedly stirring my cold tea. It occurred to me that I hadn't thought about the driver, not even once. I hadn't thought about what this terrible accident had done to him and his family. So much pain. Clodagh was hugging me and I tightened my arms around her.

"It will be okay," I heard myself say.

I kept the letter under my pillow for three nights. I read it until the paper was positively grubby. I couldn't just ignore the man. It was so much easier to ignore him when he was just the driver. Now he was a person in great pain who had as much control or lack of it as I had.

It took me hours to pick the card. In the end I went for the plainest one I could find and inside I wrote two words: *"Thank you."*

I posted it before I lost confidence and then I walked away from the post office to meet my brother for lunch.

I didn't tell Noel about Jason. He was not himself. His eyes were circled, his brow furrowed. I tried to find out what was going on, but he fobbed me off with his standard-issue work excuse. I knew that there was more going on, but having faced one demon that day I wasn't looking for another one. He picked at his food like a tubby gymnast hoping to lose a few pounds by merely playing with food as opposed to actually eating it.

"Are you sick?" I'd asked early on.

"No. I'm fine. Just tired," he'd replied.

"Okay." I smiled. If something were wrong he would have told me.

"How's Seán?" he asked.

"Good," I lied.

The truth was, he wasn't doing so well. He had become withdrawn, working too hard, and although his days of impersonating Shane McGowan were behind him, he was still relying on the crutch that is alcohol a little too much for my liking.

"No, he's not," Noel said while attempting to loosen his collar.

"What do you mean?"

"He came to see me last week. I think he needs counseling."

"You think everyone needs counseling."

My brother was like Oprah: he believed in communication. I don't know why—he certainly didn't learn that behavioral pattern at home. Noel went on to tell me that Seán had visited him at home. Father Rafferty had let him in and he had waited there, watching Sky News and debating whether the world was nearing its end for an hour and a half, before Noel had made his entrance. They had retreated upstairs and Seán had admitted that he was depressed or at least he thought he was. He put this down to the fact that he couldn't seem to enjoy anything: work, eating, sleeping, sex. I noticed that although Seán was comfortable mentioning sex, he hadn't mentioned that he was drinking to excess. Noel told me about their little visit because he felt that I was the only one who could help.

I wondered. I was useless. He disagreed.

"He really cares about you. You need to talk to him."

I thought I already had.

★ ★ ★

I met Seán in the park, my idea—no alcohol. He looked better than he had in months although the light that once brightened his brown eyes was still nowhere to be found. We sat on a bench dedicated to an old man who had paid for the installation of the pond. I didn't beat around the bush because, although it was summer, it was way too cold.

"I want you to go and talk to someone."

"What?" He was laughing as though nothing was wrong.

I wasn't in the mood for messing. "You need to talk to someone. Better again, you need to stop drowning your sorrows."

"No, I'm not!"

I was in no mood. "Listen, Seán, you can say what you want, but we're all worried. Clo, Anne, Richard—and you know Richard, he doesn't notice anything—and Noel."

"You spoke to Noel." His tone was cool.

Shit, I shouldn't have included Noel.

"No!" I said with mock horror, then added as innocently as I could, "Have you been speaking to him?"

"I'm fine," he said.

"Piss off!"

He looked at me with curiosity. "Piss off?" he repeated, intrigued.

"Yeah. Piss off!" I said emphatically.

He laughed.

I didn't find the situation so amusing. "Oh, that's funny. Yeah, it's all funny. You're falling apart and it's a real laugh."

He stopped laughing and moved to a defensive stance. "What the hell do you want from me?" he asked, but as soon as he made the query, it was obvious that he did not want my response. He was, however, going to hear it.

"I want you to take your head out of your arse and I want you to face up to the fact that John is dead and there is nothing that you or I or anyone else can do about it. And you drinking your face off for the rest of your days and giving up, well, that's fine. But know this, your friend John, he would give anything to be here sitting on this bench looking at those stupid ducks swimming in circles and he wouldn't piss whatever life he had left down the toilet like you are doing." It was a mouthful and Seán was startled but I wasn't finished. "Now, you can get help or you can piss off because the rest of us need you. We need you to be well and happy and strong like the old Seán because we need him back." I was crying again. I didn't even notice because crying in public was no longer alien.

We sat in silence for a long time. He played with his scarf, an old college one that he dug out every winter.

"I'm not an alcoholic," he said.

"Prove it," I challenged.

Silence. Then, "Okay. I'll see someone."

I took his hand in mine and it was icy. We walked out through the arched gateway and onto the busy street, still holding hands. By the time we hugged and parted at the end of the street his hand was warm.

I walked home and lay on my bed with Leonard, the lost kitten who nobody was looking for, now my growing companion. I fell asleep to the sound of his purring, hoping against hope that, if I could never have John back, at least the old Seán would return.

Seán did go to see someone. I can't tell you what they talked about because that would remain forever between them. He stopped drinking for a while just to ensure that he could and, when he went back to it, it was only socially. He began to find the acceptance that the rest of us had managed despite ourselves and it wasn't long before he returned to brighten us like he used to.

Anne had other problems. She had tasted death and now she craved for life. She admitted she'd been upset that day in Bewleys', when she had taken the pregnancy test. Her reaction to the white window was vastly different from mine. While I had cheered, she had mourned. While I had celebrated what I never had, she had grieved. Another blow so soon. Richard was blissfully unaware of the cause of his wife's distress. He put it down to her missing her friend like he did and it would never have occurred to him to ask.

Anne and I had met in English class. We found ourselves sitting together on the second week and after that it was just habit. We were alike, as both of us weren't particularly sure what we wanted from life, both of us falling into an arts degree, hoping that at some point along the line we'd find our path. When she met Richard he became her direction, like John was mine. It was nice to have someone around that wasn't career- or goal-oriented. As much as I loved Clo we never shared that ambition that burned so brightly in her. Anne was a homemaker. You could see that the first time you laid eyes on her. She was a Benetton-jumper-and-silk-scarf–wearing, Rose-of-Tralee homemaker. Richard was in economics, but he came across as the literary-tweed-jacket, leather-patch-and-jeans, professor type. They fitted, like a well-bound book. Their only problem being that now, after six years, they found themselves on different pages.

Meanwhile, Clo found herself in a relationship with

her admiring client Mark. He wasn't married; she had wasted no time in confirming that fact. He didn't appear weird like the guy she once dated whose all-consuming hobby was the collection of butterflies; nor was he a stalker, again an improvement on the men she had managed to attach herself to. It was comfortable and he was very sweet to her through all the grieving stuff. After four months it was possible that this one was a keeper. She didn't boast about it; she was sensitive to the fact that I had lost my love and certainly wasn't about to shove her new one in my face. Still, she was happy and her happiness had the pleasant effect of rubbing off on me.

We had no secrets. We had built sand castles together. We'd shared adolescence together, from mud pies to blow jobs to losing our virginity to death. Nothing was sacred from one another. How could we change the habit of a lifetime?

"So what's he like in bed?"

"Unbelievable."

"Fuck off!"

"I swear, I came the first night. The first night, Emma! Do you know how long it was before I managed an orgasm with Des?"

"Six weeks."

"Six weeks and I'm not saying he was bad. I mean, Jesus, Butterfly Man was bad."

We were drinking wine on her bed, half watching a video about a string-vest-clad Sylvester Stallone climbing rocks in the snow.

"He does this thing with his finger. My God, it's unbelievable."

I laughed. John used to do a thing with his finger. God, I missed him.

"You know, I haven't slept with someone that good since Seán," she continued.

My head jerked involuntarily and it hit hard against her wooden bedpost. My face flushed red while I steadied my wineglass.

"Are you okay?" she asked.

"I'm fine," I spluttered, embarrassed and attempting to hide the fact that the one time my two wanton friends had sexually collided bothered me. I had no idea why my two single friends having sex had upset me, negating the possibility of meaningful conversation. It was definitely better to avoid the subject.

"Are you sure? Your face has gone red."

I flushed more. This was a problem I'd had since I was a kid: any kind of embarrassment was further compounded by a blood rush to the head.

"I just hit my head," I said, knowing she knew the blush better than I did, as she had been on the receiving end of it too many times.

"You hate it when I talk about Seán," she said after a while.

She was right. I tried to explain my embarrassment away. "It's just . . . it's Seán, you know?"

She didn't know.

"When it's another guy," I went on, "one I'm not friends with, well, then the graphic images are entertaining but with Seán—I can see him. It's embarrassing." I was lying— that wasn't it, but I didn't know what was and what I'd said made sense.

"But John was my friend and you still filled me in on the gory details. I don't get embarrassed."

Shit, she was right.

"Yeah, I know, but when we met we were all kids. God, if I didn't tell you about him I couldn't tell you about anything."

She was smiling at my inexperience.

"Anyway, I'm a prude. Deep down."

She laughed. "You are such a prude!"

"All right, no need to bang on about it." I was smiling but, deep down, as well as being a prude I was a little disconcerted.

What is my problem?

Chapter 9

The Priest, the Stranger and the Unwanted Child

We hadn't gone out together as a gang since that night. Anne decided it was time. She decided bowling was an easy option. I wasn't so sure. I hated bowling. Anything that involved a ball and throwing caused me anxiety, although at least whilst bowling nobody would be actually throwing a ball at me, so I conceded. Clo was delighted, she being adept at pretty much any sport she tried. Also she felt it was a great way to introduce the rest of us to Mark.

"It's perfect," she announced. "Three and three, we can have a match. Girls against guys."

Mark would take John's place, filling the gap that he had left. My heart sank into the pit of my stomach, making me want to vomit. It must have been reflected in my twisted facial expression.

"I'm sorry," she offered, realizing what she had said.

"Don't be silly," I replied while fighting the urge to

throw up. Life goes on and she was right: without Mark the teams would be uneven. She was so excited at the prospect of actually going out with someone long enough to introduce him to her friends, who the hell was I to ruin it for her?

"I'm really happy for you, Clo," I said.

"I know you are," she smiled.

"I don't mean to be a miserable cow."

"I know you don't."

"I bloody hate bowling."

"I know you do." She was laughing.

"I'm really crap."

"Yes, you are."

"Remember the time John threw a basketball to me in fifth year?"

"It hit you in the face, knocking you out."

"I ended up with a big fat lip for five days."

"And your nose hasn't been the same since."

"Jesus!" I immediately felt the shape of my nose.

She was still laughing. "Joke, Emma."

I laughed, embarrassed that I had been so easily fooled. I had wondered often if grief had made me a little thick. This notion had now been confirmed.

★ ★ ★

Clo and I entered the bowling alley together; Anne and Richard were already practicing in lane two. Seán was buying his dinner, which amounted to a hot dog and a bag of crisps. Clo spent her time clockwatching, wondering where Mark was. It was only five minutes after the stated meeting time, but she was used to being let down and the concern on her face made me pity her. Ten minutes later a man entered and she instantly jumped to her feet, smiling and waving as though she hadn't a care in the world. Mark. He was attractive in a kind of upper-class Sampson-haired, thick-neck kind of way. If he'd have bulked up he could have been a gladiator. He waved and pointed toward the café, indicating that he was getting a drink. She waved him on, happy to now be able to concentrate on the match ahead.

Anne was busy attempting to brush up on her bowling skills but unfortunately for her she was as rubbish as I was. Clo suddenly realized that by playing with the women she was on a losing team and Clo hated to lose.

"I was thinking, why don't we mix up the teams?" she asked innocently.

"No way," Seán said while wiping mustard from his chin.

"Why not?" she whined.

" 'Cause Em and Anne are rubbish," Richard noted before bowling a perfect strike.

"It's supposed to be fun," Clo said with audible disgust, but the lads weren't buying it.

"Then you won't mind playing with the girls."

"Crap," she muttered under her breath.

Mark arrived back with minerals for everybody. We all took turns to shake his hand and welcome him into our little world. He seemed nice.

★ ★ ★

The game was over and the lads had beaten us hands down. Clo was attempting to take it all in good spirits, especially as she had managed to have the best game. Mark had been the weakest link in the men's team. He seemed embarrassed by his failure in the eyes of strangers, but his humiliation was eased early on when I had managed to drop the ball on my foot twice. I bloody hate bowling.

We went to the nearest pub. The others were celebrating a great game while Anne and I celebrated the fact that the great game was over. It was one of those huge super pubs, with three floors, and yet it was packed on a Thursday night. We pushed our way past college students drinking shots while a rubbish rock band played in the background. We headed to the second floor where Enya sang about an "Orinoco Flow," whatever the hell that was. There were seats and a girl to serve drinks.

"Standing around screaming at one another over a shit rock band while gulping down shots versus Enya and a seat, that's the difference between your early and late twenties," noted Seán while making himself comfortable in an armchair.

"Yeah, we're getting on," Richard added before waving at the waitress.

The women stayed quiet, not wishing to discuss the aging process.

Clo needed the loo and I followed, afraid I'd get lost if I attempted the journey myself. It wasn't until we were coming back that I recognized my brother sitting in a corner with a woman. I waved and walked over while noticing he was downing his drink and making a "let's finish up" gesture to his company. Clo was behind me when I reached the table.

"Hey, stranger," I said smiling, happy to have bumped into my brother in a super bar of all places.

"Fancy meeting you here," he said a little too exuberantly.

"We were bowling," I said, waiting for an introduction to the woman, who was keeping her eyes fixed to the floor.

"You bowling?" he laughed.

"Yeah," I said.

"Hi, I'm Clo." Clo held out her hand to the stranger we were now both wondering about.

"Hello. It's nice to meet you," the pretty stranger said, briefly looking up. Obviously we were interrupting something.

"We were just about to leave," said Noel.

He stood and the stranger followed suit.

"Seán and Richard are over there," I said, pointing into the middle distance. "Why don't you join us for a drink?"

"I can't. I have work to do," he said without meeting my eyes.

"Right."

The stranger had her coat on.

"Well, I'll see you at the parents' on Sunday," I said.

"Yeah. Okay. See you on Sunday."

The stranger said bye and they walked quickly out of the premises, leaving Clo and me standing watching them leave.

"What was all that about?" Clo asked suspiciously.

"Probably a parishioner who needed advice," I guessed.

"Does Noel meet a lot of parishioners in the pub?"

"It's as good a place as any," I said, totally convinced.

"Okay," she said, totally unconvinced.

I laughed. "He's a priest, Clo."

"He's a man, Em."

"You have a sick mind."

"I suppose I do."

"Yeah, well, you don't know Noel. He didn't have any girlfriends before becoming a priest—he's definitely not going to go there now." I was laughing at the absurdity of it.

She smiled. "She did look stressed-out."

"Yeah," I agreed. "She's probably going through a separation or has cancer or something."

"Grim," she said, nodding. "I don't know how he handles it."

"I know," I agreed but I hadn't a clue.

★ ★ ★

Seán was dedicating himself to becoming the new face of the male magazine world. He wrote funny, engaging articles about topics he couldn't care less about and it paid his bills. His somewhat limited spare time was devoted to writing about things that did matter to him, which nobody got to see. I worked hard with my classes and every now and then I even went out, but truthfully life seemed a little empty. My friends and I stayed close, clinging to each other more than ever, our loss making us more careful with our friendship.

It was late on a Friday evening five months after John died. I was lying on the couch, watching TV. The doorbell rang; it was Clodagh. I knew immediately something was wrong because, normally perfectly turned out, she arrived at my place looking like she had been dragged through a hedge. She greeted me with the words "fucking asshole" and her mascara was halfway down her face. I presumed she had had a fight with Mark, but I was only partly right. She hobbled into the kitchen and it was only then I noticed one of her heels was broken. She asked for a coffee and plonked herself down on the counter stool, flipping off her shoes one foot at a time while holding her head in her hands.

"Did you have a fight with Mark?"

"You could say that."

"Well, I'm sure it's not the end of the world."

I would like to note in my defense that before John's death I would never have uttered such a platitude, but once you hear enough of them it's hard not to. Anyway, her response was in the form of a dirty look.

"Sorry. That was a stupid thing to say. Tell me what's going on?"

She was looking at the carpet, which could have been cleaner. "Mark and I have broken up."

I couldn't believe it—they had seemed to be getting on so well. "Why?" I asked.

"We had an argument."

She paused. It was like pulling teeth.

"And?" I encouraged.

"We had an argument over me being pregnant."

She looked up from my dirty carpet and I nearly fell off the chair.

"You're pregnant?" I managed to blurt out.

"Surprise," she said in a sarcastic tone. There were tears in her eyes.

I didn't know how to react to the news, so I concentrated

on attacking her ex-boyfriend. "That bastard, what did he say?"

She sighed. "He basically said that if I was, it had nothing to do with him."

I was choking on outrage. She just looked tired.

"Why do I always go for such total pricks?" she enquired.

I was asking myself the same question. "I don't know, Clo," was all I could muster.

"Fuck him, Emma! Okay? Fuck him! He's no longer my problem. This," she pointed to her stomach, "however, is."

I hugged her, remembering the day I'd dreaded the blue line, remembering that hours later John was dead and I was alone. It really could be worse. I knew that now. I didn't say anything. I'd never told anyone about the day my boyfriend died. It was too painful. Somewhere in the back of my mind I realized that if I had been pregnant I would be full term by now. I'd still have a little part of him. But this wasn't about me.

"I'm going to have an abortion," she said.

"Because of Mark?" I had to ask.

"No," she answered categorically. "I've known about this for over a week. I've being doing a lot of thinking and if that prick had let me finish before launching into his I'm-not-ready-for-commitment speech, I would have told him the same thing."

It's funny: a year ago if Clo had known that she was pregnant a whole week before telling me I would have been pissed off, but now I understood.

"You're sure?" I had to ask.

She smiled weakly. "Obviously, I'll have to go to London. Will you come?"

Of course I was going. "I've wanted to go to London for shopping for ages." I looked at her, waiting for a response.

"I knew you'd be there for me," she said, relieved.

We moved into the sitting room and talked about stupid things and after a while we were giggling and laughing. Our joint desperation reunited us; our trepidation for our futures, our quest for answers and our fears reduced us to the children we once were. We were forced to confront our pain and together we laughed in the face of it.

Clo had her mouth full of apple pie when she started to laugh loudly.

"What's so funny?" I asked.

"Mark," she laughed.

I was starting to giggle again. "What about him?"

She looked up at me, still laughing. "When I told him and he was being an asshole about it, I got really angry and said—" She laughed again and covered her mouth. "Oh no! It's too bad."

She had my undivided attention. "What? What did you say?" I enquired urgently.

"Well," she began, "he asked what I was planning to do about my little problem."

I wanted to find him and punch him in the face.

She continued. "I said: 'What do you want me to do? Squat down and scream "get out"?'"

We roared with laughter and we continued laughing until she cried. She cried for a long time that night, but she knew she was doing the right thing and I knew no matter what happened I'd be there for her. She stayed over and we planned our trip to London. That night became a turning point. It was the first time that I managed to forget about myself for a whole evening— well, almost a whole evening.

Chapter 10

A Trip, a Miss and Confession

I woke up to the phone ringing by my bed. I fumbled for the receiver, dropped it and while retrieving it noticed the clock read 6:30 a.m. I sank back into my pillow with the phone to my ear.

"Hello," I said into the duvet.

It was Anne. "Hi, just giving you a wake-up call."

She was in the car heading toward Kerry and I could hear Richard fiddling with the radio stations.

"It's six thirty in the bloody morning," I mumbled.

She, of course, was already aware of the time. "You still haven't packed and the last time you and Clo took a trip together you missed the flight out and back."

I couldn't argue. She was right, but having said that, our flight wasn't until three that afternoon and I still had a half day of school before me.

"I'm up," I said wearily.

She disagreed. "You're not up until you're standing—now, get moving!"

I sat up. "I'm up."

She didn't believe me. "Stand up and move around," she ordered.

I gave the phone the fingers.

"Are you up?"

I put my feet on the floor. "Right, I'm up. Jesus, Anne, ever consider joining the army?"

She noted how amusing I was before shouting an order at Richard to "pick a bloody station."

"That's better," she told both of us. "Well, Richard and I are going to pick the pair of you up on Sunday evening. Clo gave me the flight details. Try and make it, Em. I really hate sitting around airports."

Clo and I had obviously noted the irony that Anne so desperately craved the baby that Clo didn't want. We discussed not telling her, as we felt it would be insensitive. However, after much debate, we both agreed not telling her would be the greater evil. She had taken it well. Anne was a trooper.

"Okay," I agreed.

"Tell her we all love her and everything's going to be okay."

"I will," I agreed again.

"Okay, we'll see you on Sunday. By the way, Richard says hi."

"I heard him. I'll see you on Sunday." I replaced the receiver and got back under the covers while telling myself it would only be for a few minutes. I woke up an hour later.

"Jesus!" I shouted. "Jesus Christ!"

I jumped out of bed and ran to the shower. Half an hour later, I was throwing anything I could find into a bag while eating a slice of toast. I managed to get marmalade on my favorite top.

Crap, I thought, flinging it into the wash basket.

Five minutes later I was sitting in my car. I kept thinking I'd forgotten something. It was beginning to bother me. I looked at the house. The cat had enough food to last a week, the door was locked and the oven had never been turned on. I had my travel bag, tickets and keys. What was missing? I started to back out of the driveway.

"Oh for God's sake!"

I pulled back into the driveway, got out of the car, opened the door and ran up the stairs and into my spare bedroom.

"Seán, Seán, get up!"

He mumbled and turned over.

"Get up! I'm dead late."

"Just a few more minutes," he pleaded.

He was a nightmare in the mornings, nearly as bad as me. I needed to do something to get him out. I went into the bathroom and filled a glass with water, walked back to the bedroom and poured it on his head. He jumped up.

"Christ!" he yelled.

I wasn't in the mood. "Let's go, come on, I'm dead late and it's your fault."

He got out of bed. "How do you make that out?" he enquired, smirking.

I ignored him. He had arrived on my doorstep at half two in the morning, after attempting unsuccessfully to get a taxi home after a night on the piss, and I was in no mood for conversation.

"I'll be downstairs. You have five minutes or I'll lock you into the house for the weekend."

Knowing I was serious, he quickened his step. I left him to it. He arrived downstairs an impressive two minutes later.

"Let's go," I said, walking to the door.

"What, no toast?" he asked, grinning.

His charm, or lack thereof, was annoying me. I grabbed two slices of bread and handed them to him.

"There you go, take them home and toast them."

"Lovely," he noted, looking at the scrunched-up bread in his hand.

Two minutes later I was back in the car with Seán beside me, pulling out of the driveway for the second time.

Doreen was on her doorstep.

"Howya, Emma! All right, Seán! Stayed the night again, I see."

She was smiling. We had become even closer since John had died. She was so kindhearted and after sharing way too many Friday nights watching *The Late Late Show* together, she really wanted to see me get laid and it was nice, but her timing was bad.

"Hey, Doreen! I couldn't get a taxi last night!" Seán shouted out the window.

"That's what they all say," she laughed.

"Well, the next time he'll have to walk!" I shouted, still pulling out.

"That's right, love. Give him a hard time. They're all a bunch of bas . . . oh, hello, Father."

I turned to see Noel heading in our direction. I

stopped. "Oh for Christ's sake!" I rolled the window down fully. "Noel, I'm dead late for school."

He smiled. "I can see that. I'm just going to grab the spare key. I left my jacket in your place the other night." He banged the top of the car. "Go on. Have a good time."

I hadn't told him why I was heading away for the weekend. I hated lying to him, but having said that I wasn't going to mention the abortion because that would be stupid. "I'll call you when we get home." I waved, smiled and took off before he could say anything.

I looked in the mirror to see Doreen nabbing him, presumably for a cup of tea, a speciality of hers.

Seán looked at me.

"What?" I asked.

"How come *I* don't know where the spare key is?" he asked.

"Because you'll use it," I answered.

"Lovely," he repeated. He was quiet for a minute. "Hey, Em, tell Clo that I'll be thinking of her."

I smiled. "Tell her yourself."

★ ★ ★

I made it into class five minutes after the bell rang. My students were enjoying their freedom. I apologized for my tardiness while they applauded me. It was English so I grabbed my copy of *Romeo and Juliet*. As it was a play, instead of having the class read it, I would always ask them to perform it. Each day I'd pick the players required for the particular scene we were going through. I felt it would enable the students to remember the play, key parts, etc. The class felt it was my sick nature and of course a small percentage of it was.

"Hands up for Romeo?"

Nobody raised a hand. I surveyed the room.

"Okay, Peter, we haven't heard from you in a while. Jessica, you're Juliet. Who wants to be the Nurse?"

Nobody answered.

"Right, Linda, you're the Nurse."

"Ah Miss, I was the Nurse last week!" she groaned.

"So I'll expect an Oscar-winning performance."

The class laughed. Isn't it funny that the most banal of statements can appear funny in a classroom, church or a wedding speech?

Anyway, Peter began to read. A few seconds later James jumped in his seat and the class started to titter.

"Peter, just a second. James, why are you jumping?" I asked.

James was rubbing his ass. "Declan keeps stabbing me with his compass, Miss."

I sighed long and loud and looked toward Declan. "Declan, why are you stabbing James?"

"Miss, he's a bleedin' liar."

"Language, Declan," I admonished.

"Jesus, Miss, I only said bleedin'!"

The class laughed.

"I'm warning you, Declan. Why are you stabbing James?"

He sighed a sigh very much like my own. The class laughed again. "It was more of a poke, Miss. He won't let me look into his book."

I asked him where his own book was.

"I forgot it."

This was the third time in a row.

"Where are you going to be after class, Declan?"

A groan. "Talking to you, Miss."

"That's right," I agreed. "Peter, take it from the top."

I heard Peter mumble, "Jesus," but let it go. Life's too short.

After class Declan approached me.

"Where's the book? And please don't tell me you forgot it because I didn't get much sleep last night and I'm liable to do something serious."

He nodded. "Okay, but don't go mental."

He waited for me to agree, but eventually realized I had no intention of making any promises, so he continued. "I sold it to Mary Murphy for a tenner," he admitted, smiling.

"You sold your copy of *Romeo and Juliet,*" I repeated.

"Yeah," he grinned, "for a tenner."

"And what do you propose using for the rest of the year?" I enquired, genuinely interested.

"I can pick one up, secondhand, for a fiver in town tomorrow. That's called a profit, Miss. I learned that in Commerce."

He was grinning again. I was battling not to.

"Declan."

"Yes, Miss."

"Close the door on your way out."

He beamed. "I knew you'd understand."

I smiled. I couldn't help it. "Oh, I won't be able to give you a lift this afternoon. I'm taking a half day."

"No problem. Have a nice weekend."

I watched him leave and I was glad I knew him. Teachers should not have a favorite student and, if asked, I would never have admitted that he was mine.

I was clearing my desk when Eileen, the science teacher, came to the door.

"Emma, there's a call for you in the staff room."

I didn't take much notice. "Okay, cheers, I'll be right there."

She stayed. I looked up.

"It sounds urgent."

I got flustered. Urgent meant something bad. Someone could be dead. My heart started to beat faster, my ears ringing.

I ran to the staff room and picked up the phone.

"Hello," I said urgently.

"Hello, this is Nurse O'Shea. I'm calling from Holles Street Hospital."

"Yes," I managed, praying I'd be able to hear her over my beating heart.

"Your friend Clodagh Morris has asked me to call you. I'm afraid she's had a miscarriage."

No one was dead and I thanked God in my head.

"I'll be right there," I told her and hung up.

I sat down as Eileen came in.

"Is everything okay?" she asked.

I smiled an exhausted smile. "My friend just had a miscarriage."

She sat down beside me. "Oh, that's awful. The poor girl, was she trying long?"

I looked at her. "Trying to have a miscarriage?"

She looked at me oddly. "No, trying for a baby."

I was embarrassed. "Sorry, I misunderstood you. Can someone take over my classes? I really should go."

"Of course," she smiled.

I got up to leave.

"I suppose this means you'll have to put off your shopping trip," she said.

"Yeah," I nodded.

"Oh well, another time," she smiled and waved me off.

"I hope not."

* * *

I met Seán in the hospital car park. We walked in slowly, neither of us sure what to say. Clo was sitting in Outpatients. She looked drawn. A pregnant woman was tending to the crying toddler sitting next to her. Seán and I sat on either side of Clo. She smiled at me but her eyes were puffy.

"I was always a cheapskate," she said.

I grinned. I didn't know what else to do. Seán took her hand and told her that it wasn't meant to be.

She laughed bitterly. "I wish I knew that before we shelled out on the plane fare."

She had cramps. I told her that I'd call a nurse, but she said it wasn't bad enough for painkillers.

"You're both being so nice to me. I feel like a cheat. I was going to get rid of it. It was my choice and now it's gone and everyone is being too nice." She started to cry and the toddler joined her.

"When you come out you can stay with me for a while, just until you get back to yourself." I wasn't inviting her: I was telling her.

She told me no and that she'd be fine. She just wanted to go home. I understood, but I was disappointed because I really wanted to mind her, just like my parents had wanted to mind me all those months ago. Seán told her that Anne and Richard were on their way.

She was annoyed. "Oh for God's sake, they must have been halfway to Kerry! There's no need for all this."

Seán laughed. "I think Anne is using it as an excuse to come home and I know I used it as an excuse to get out of a particularly boring lunch meeting."

"Besides, they can go to Kerry anytime. The house isn't going anywhere," I offered.

"I don't want people making a fuss. I feel rubbish enough."

Her lip was trembling and I wanted to cry for her, but being fully aware that it wouldn't be the greatest help in the world, I bit down on mine. Seán decided to change the subject.

"I still can't believe they're thinking about moving there."

"I know," I agreed.

"Kerry. Weird."

"Whatever floats your boat," Clo noted.

We agreed.

"I've never been to Kerry," I mused.

"Me neither," said Seán.

"Maybe it's nice there," Clo said wistfully.

"Yeah," I agreed and then we sat there, silent, until the nurse approached to let Clo know she could go home. We walked her to her car, hugged her good-bye and waved her off.

As we walked to my car, Seán remarked that I looked sad. I *was* sad. I admitted that when I'd got the call I had panicked, thinking that someone was dead, and that I was so relieved when I found out what it was. It was only when I walked out of the hospital that I realized someone had died and, whether the baby that Clo was carrying was wanted or not, whether she miscarried or had an abortion, something that was alive inside of her last night was dead today and that was sad. He put his arm around me and told me we'd all be fine and I knew we would, but for that moment I wasn't thinking about us.

★ ★ ★

That evening I went to Confession because Confession was still the best place to chat to Noel. There wasn't a queue. There never was. Usually, it was just the same two old ladies. I waited for them to confess their sins and tried to imagine what two "auld ones" could get up to that was so bad that each week they'd have to seek absolution and spend so much time doing it. When the last one came out I entered the box. It was cold and the pew was hard on the knees. I briefly wondered if it was fair to have it be so hard, considering the majority of those who knelt on it were over sixty. Noel slid back the little sliding door that revealed the grille that separated saint from sinner.

"Hey," I said.

"Hey, Em, we've got to stop meeting like this," he grinned.

"Well, if you'd ever pick up your phone I wouldn't have to kneel to chat to you."

"I thought you were going away for the weekend?"

"Change of plan," I said. "Clo had a miscarriage today."

His eye twitched. It always twitched when he was surprised or not sure what to say.

"It's okay," I said. "She wasn't ready to have a baby."

"Maybe God was listening," he said.

I laughed bitterly like Clo had done before me. "I doubt it. He never listened to me." I knew I was opening a debate that I normally steered away from with Noel, because I never wanted to hear what he had to say about God and I didn't like to fight with him, but today I wanted to hear what he had to say, just so I could tell him to shove it and maybe make myself feel a little better.

"Can I ask you a question?" I asked.

"Go on," he said tentatively, sensing that I was looking for a fight.

"Okay. How do you know He exists?"

"Who? God?" he asked, playing for time.

"No, Santa," I replied sarcastically. "Of course God."

"I just do," was his reply.

"Not good enough," I challenged.

"Okay, it says so in the Bible."

I couldn't believe it. "That's it? 'It says so in the Bible'?" *That's why he gave up his entire life?* "Okay, let me ask you this. What if it was discovered that the Bible was just another made-up novel written thousands of years ago by some guy who smoked a lot of pot? Would you believe in God then?"

He laughed. "Someone would have to smoke a lot of pot to come up with that story."

"Be serious," I begged.

"Okay, Em, I will," he told me. "The Bible is just the guide. God is a feeling I have inside. He's part of my soul."

He smiled and I wondered if he was smoking pot.

Obviously sensing my dissatisfaction, he continued, "Okay, you don't believe in that. But what about all the people who have experienced miracles? What about the people who have seen Our Lady?"

That's easy, I thought to myself. "A hell of a lot more people claim to have been abducted by aliens and they're called lunatics."

I was pleased with my argument but he laughed.

"I'm serious, Noel. Do you ever worry that you're wasting your life on someone who doesn't even exist?"

He stopped smiling and became pensive. I wished he would just pick a fight, but he wouldn't.

"My job is to help people. How can that be a waste of my life? God's in all of us, Em."

Was he trying to convince himself or me? I thought about it for a minute.

"You're such a sap, Noel."

"Indeed," he agreed.

"I better go."

He waved while I attempted to stand on broken knees.

I sat in the empty church for a while, looking around me. Religious statues lined the walls, the Virgin and Child being the most prominent. I looked toward the marble altar surrounded by golden gates. The stained glass window depicted Jesus, bloody and dying, his mother at his torn feet, looking desperately toward heaven, and I took a moment to appreciate its macabre beauty.

A long time after that, Noel reminded me of that day and admitted that while I was enjoying the view he was inside his little box crying.

Chapter 11

Ron the Ride

Seán was staying over in the spare room a lot, especially since Christmas.

Anne noticed.

"So what's going on?" she asked casually over coffee in a packed coffee shop.

"Nothing," I replied.

She didn't accept "nothing," believing Seán's visits were more to do with me than with transport difficulties. I didn't want to talk about it.

"How long has it been, Em?"

I was confused. "How long has what been?" I asked, pissed off. I really just wanted to have a cup of coffee.

"How long has it been since you've had sex?" She whispered the "sex" bit.

I thought to myself, *I'll pretend not to hear her*, but I knew she'd scream the word if she had to.

"Does it matter?" I asked.

"Yes," she replied.

I sighed at her the way I sighed at my students. She was aware but didn't care, as she felt the matter had to be addressed. It was just over ten months since John had gone, so therefore it seemed to me that it was obvious I hadn't slept with someone in over ten months.

"Since John, of course," I answered, irritated that I had to state it. "Ten months."

"Ten months, Em!"

"So?"

"Em," she said seriously, "you turned twenty-seven years old in October."

"You promised you would ignore my birthday," I moaned, trying to change the subject. I had spent my birthday pretty much the same way I had spent Christmas, under my duvet. I began to wish I was still there.

"And I did ignore it," she said, shaking her head from side to side.

"That includes not mentioning it and besides, you sent flowers," I argued.

"You're changing the subject."

"So, what are you saying?" came my weary reply.

"So, he's not coming back." She sounded a little sad, as though saying it made John's disappearance a little more real.

"I know," I agreed.

"Maybe you should try to get out there." She was smiling at me, like that would make her advice easier to take.

"Get out there! You think just because it's a new year I should forget him?" I said in disbelief.

"No, of course not—nobody is forgetting what you

and John had. But—I know this sounds harsh—he's gone and he's not coming back and you are twenty-seven and alone and we all—"

"Who are 'we'?" I asked, annoyed.

She didn't answer quickly enough.

"You were talking about this behind my back!" I said.

Her smile faded. I almost heard her think, *Oh shit!*

"Who's 'we,' Anne?"

She thought for a minute before answering. "Richard, Clo and Seán," she blurted out.

My mouth fell open. "Oh my God! You had a fucking conference."

She was fumbling for words now. "That is not the case and you know it. We're just worried."

It was obvious to me that these people had fuck all to worry about if the big topic of conversation was my getting laid. I was hurt.

"My sex life is private, and it's not for you to discuss!" I was whisper-shouting.

"Look, it wasn't planned. It's just that Richard knows this solicitor—he's really nice and he's been single for over a year and . . ."

I stopped listening. I couldn't believe it. I couldn't believe that she thought it was okay to be having this conversation with me, here in this stupid packed coffee shop.

"So, you see, that's how the conversation started and Clo and I really feel it's time to move on."

I had missed the middle bit. Shit, they were talking about me behind my back and that was enough. I couldn't believe that Clo and Anne were discussing my sex life with Seán and Richard. It was humiliating.

"Well, actually Seán was pretty quiet," she admitted. "He does spend a lot of time in your place. Is there something we should know?"

"Nothing's going on between Seán and me. He was John's best friend," I said, disgusted at her lack of consideration.

"Okay," she brightened. "So you can meet Ron."

I looked at her and repeated, "Ron?"

"Yeah, Em, the solicitor."

I wanted to tell her to piss off, but after she talked for a long time, I found myself agreeing to meet a guy called Ron. It appears I was lonelier than I thought.

★ ★ ★

A week later I'm in my bedroom getting dressed to go out on a date at eight with Ron. My first date since I was sixteen. I had bought a dress, but decided I didn't like it. Clo and Anne were there, as helpers and spectators. They were drinking vodka and arguing whether red or black was a better choice of color. I was a nervous wreck, like a bad flyer facing a long-haul flight.

"What if I hate the sight of him?"

"You won't," said Anne.

"How do you know?"

"He's a ride," she responded.

"He's a ride?" asked Clo.

"Yeah," said Anne.

"So why have you never set him up with me?" Clo challenged. We laughed and she smiled at herself. "Anyway, just as well, I'm off men," she reminded us.

We knew and wondered how long it would last.

105

It was nearly time for him to call. Clo and Anne were giddy on vodka and I was two minutes from a serious case of the runs.

"Where's Richard?" Clo asked Anne.

"Oh, he's out with Seán," she responded.

I hadn't mentioned my date to Seán. I wasn't quite sure how he'd take it, being John's best friend. It made me nervous.

"Does Seán know I'm going on this date?" I asked, trying to appear casual.

"Yeah, I'm sure Richard mentioned it," Anne replied while fixing my hair like I was a two-year-old.

"Is that a problem?" asked the ever-vigilant Clo.

"No," I responded, lying. "It's fine."

The doorbell rang and I wanted to vomit.

"Answer the door," Anne prompted.

"Right," I agreed. "You'll stay in the kitchen. I will leave with Ron." I could barely make myself say the name Ron. "And then you will go home and not be here when I get back."

They both agreed to those terms so I opened the door and greeted my blind date.

"Hi, I'm Emma," I said.

He smiled. "Ron Lynch. Sorry I'm late."

It was one minute past eight.

"You're not late," I pointed out while grabbing my coat.

I needed to get him out fast before Clo lost her resolve and attempted to check him out, like my mother had done with John all those years ago. "Let's go."

"Okay," he smiled.

We left and I walked down the path to his sports car thinking, *Jesus, Ron is a ride.*

The curtains twitched as we took off and I knew that Clo was giving Anne a hard time for not introducing Ron to her. We sat in silence, occasionally turning our heads to smile at one another. He asked me if I wanted to listen to some music.

"Great," I said overenthusiastically.

"Any requests?" he asked and I thought it a bit stupid seeing as we were in a car.

How much choice could he have? But I remained polite. "What have you got?"

"What would you like?"

I really didn't care. "Bruce Springsteen," I said.

"Which album?" he enquired.

Now he was just showing off.

"Well, which one do you have?" I said, smiling.

"All of them," he replied.

I gave up. "*Born in the USA*," I demanded.

He used a remote control and a few seconds later Bruce Springsteen was in the car singing "I'm on Fire." It was truly impressive, in kind of a "wanker" way. He smiled at me and I smiled back, trying to get comfortable in his bucket seats. We made it to the restaurant before I got to hear the title track and I made a mental note to go out and buy the album. It reminded me of making out in John's bedroom, which we had often managed even though his mom had made us leave the bedroom door open.

"Are you ready?" he asked.

"Excuse me?" I was miles away.

"We're here." He pointed to the restaurant.

"Right. Great."

How many times was I going to say "great," I wondered, while trying to get out of his car and still retain my dignity. That having failed, we entered the restaurant. Obviously it was pretentious: silk walls, lots of lamps, linen tablecloths, silver service, candles, a pianist in the corner, snotty waiters, "the works," as Clo would put it. I really hated eating in places where the staff made you feel like they were doing you a favor by letting you in.

After conferring we ordered from a set menu. The waiter, lanky and smug-looking, scribbled while sighing heavily to signify his distaste at having to serve a heathen who dared to ask for mayonnaise.

"This is great," I said smiling, my face starting to hurt.

"You hate it," he pointed out.

Alarmed, I said, "No," while examining my skirt for lint.

He asked me if I wanted to go somewhere else, but the starters were on the way and for the first time I began to relax, a little.

I looked at him across the table. He was blond, tall—square jaw, broad shoulders and kind of pretty. Not really my taste but a ride, and certainly a lot of women in the place seemed to appreciate him. I kept catching their eyes as they surveyed him and they would turn away and face their uninteresting dates.

I heard myself sighing.

"Okay, you really hate it here," he noted and he was right.

I kept saying it was fine until eventually, after a second glass of wine, when he asked again I relented.

"It's a bit stuffy," I pointed out, embarrassed.

"I know," he agreed. "I was trying to impress you."

I smiled and it was genuine. "So I take it the sports car is not yours either then?"

He laughed. "No, the car is mine. You don't like it?"

"It's okay. I prefer Volvos. They're very safe."

He agreed that indeed they were safe.

I felt like a schoolteacher so I apologized. He laughed and we agreed that blind dates were difficult.

But it turned out that Richard had told him all about me while I knew absolutely nothing about him.

"I'm really sorry about your boyfriend."

I nearly choked. "Thanks," I managed and he was embarrassed and it was visible that he was sorry he mentioned it.

I told him that it had nearly been a year and that I was fine. He told me that he had been at Anne and Richard's inheritance party and had noticed me entering with John. He had asked Richard who I was, but Richard had explained that I was taken.

"I don't remember seeing you."

"Well, you spent the whole night in the kitchen," he recalled.

"Yeah, I remember," I said, smiling weakly, hoping we could change the subject fast.

"I am really sorry," he said again.

"So this isn't really a blind date then," I stated more than asked. "I mean, for me, yes, but not for you."

His face reddened. "Yeah. I liked what I saw."

Fucking hell, I thought and blushed. Mortified, I excused myself to go to the bathroom. I returned and shortly after he asked for the bill.

"We don't have to do this if you don't want to," he said.

"No," I agreed.

"But we could go to a late-night jazz bar that I know," he suggested, brightening.

"Let's go."

★ ★ ★

We headed to the bar and I ordered a round of shots on me while being careful to explain I wasn't an alcoholic. He laughed and told me he'd take what he could get.

"That's comforting," I said and he told me I was a funny girl and for a minute I felt like Barbra Streisand.

He told me about his childhood. It turns out he was born in Germany, but his parents returned home to Ireland when he was two. I was nervous and a little drunk, so I made a joke about the Aryan race, immediately regretting it, but he laughed and I joined in, relieved. We both agreed that first dates are a nightmare and I told him I hadn't been on one since I was sixteen.

"Jesus!" he said.

"Yeah," I agreed and drank another shot.

He told me that before he became a solicitor he was a guitar player in a band in college. I told him John always wanted to be Jimi Hendrix.

"He played guitar?" he asked, interested.

I laughed and said, "No." I asked him if he still played and he said no but that he did sing in the shower.

"Me too," I admitted.

"Oh yeah? What do you sing?" he asked.

"James Taylor," I admitted, my tongue loosened by alcohol.

He laughed. "James Taylor!" he repeated.

"There's nothing wrong with James Taylor," I argued. "So what do you sing?"

"Aerosmith," he replied.

I laughed for a really long time. "Aerosmith! You've a bloody nerve, laughing at me!"

He argued that Aerosmith were the kings of rock and roll.

I pointed out that Elvis held that particular crown.

"Yeah, but he's dead." As soon as he said it his face fell. "Oh my God, I'm so sorry, I didn't mean . . ."

"Hey, it's fine—I mean it hit me hard when I was a kid, but hey, there's always Graceland."

We laughed and I realized that despite myself I was having a good time. We were drunk. He left the car in town and we got a taxi back to my place. He asked the taxi man to wait, so that he could walk me to the door. It was raining hard so I suggested he stay dry, but he wasn't having any of it. He walked me the three meters to the door.

"I had a really good time," he said.

"Me too."

"Can I see you again?" he asked.

"I'd really like that," I replied, my stomach somersaulting.

He leaned in and kissed me and I responded before pulling away, aware the taxi man was watching us.

"I'll call you," he told me.

"Okay."

I waved him off.

The taxi man drove away and, once they were out of sight, I took a minute to process the incident. I had kissed a blond man called Ron, on the doorstep of John's home. I looked up into the rainy night.

I still love you, John. A kiss doesn't change that. Say hi to Elvis.

I walked into the house with rain on my face. As suspected, Anne and Clo were still there, passed out on uncomfortable chairs in the living room. I climbed the stairs to my bedroom, smiling. I'd kissed a guy called Ron.

★ ★ ★

Seán hadn't called in three days. After school I headed into town and dropped into his office. He was in a meeting so I said I'd wait. I sat in the waiting area reading magazines until he emerged, frazzled. I stood up, but he didn't notice me. I called out. He appeared surprised.

"I haven't heard from you—I thought we could get a drink or something."

He looked like he was about to make an excuse but conceded. "Okay, give me a minute."

It was awkward. We got to the bar and ordered a drink before either of us spoke. He was first.

"So how did your date go?"

"Good," I answered.

"Clo said you kissed him." His smile wasn't reaching his eyes.

"Clo talks too much." I laughed and tried to change the subject. "What are you working on?"

112

"An article on smear tests."

I was sorry I asked. "Right," I said, remembering I'd missed an appointment with my women's health clinic.

"So do you like him?" he pressed.

"He's nice."

I took a slug from my drink.

"Nice," he repeated.

This was getting annoying. He was pissed I had gone on a date and it was really obvious, despite his pathetic attempt to conceal it.

"Have you something to say, Seán?" I asked, irritated.

"No," he responded.

"So why the attitude?" I asked angrily. "Do you think I should join a fucking convent?"

"No," he repeated, "of course not."

"So, then, what is it? I had a date with a guy and we kissed. Big deal. It's been nearly a year since John . . ."

I couldn't bring myself to say "died," not when I'd been talking about kissing another guy in the same breath.

Seán apologized and said he was being stupid and that he was happy for me. I told him he didn't have to be happy for me yet and reminded him it was only a kiss. He laughed and it was genuine. He told me he was going out with an accountant that night. My turn to pretend, but I was much better at concealing my true feelings, so I smiled and told him I hoped it went well. We hugged before I left and I found it hard to let go. He held me so tightly that in his arms I felt safe, like I had with John, and I knew that this was because he was my friend.

I walked out into the street. The sky was gray, but

light managed to stream through the clouds like a silver highway leading to another world beyond our own.

It didn't mean anything, John. It was just a kiss.

Secretly I was glad that Seán was upset by the kiss and I spent the journey home convincing myself that I was glad because it meant that he was thinking of John.

* * *

Two weeks and three dates after I'd met Ron, he invited me to his apartment. He would cook the meal and I'd bring the wine. This invite meant one thing. Sex. He wanted to have sex. I wasn't sure if I wanted the same thing. I'm not going to lie to you. I was hornier than a schoolboy on a hot day. It had been so long, but then there was John to consider. What about him? I picked out four outfits and laid them on the bed. I showered for a long time. I sat on the loo, my feet in a basin while I shaved my legs.

Just in case.

I returned to my bedroom to find that my choice of outfits had gone from four to three. Leonard was nestling comfortably on my black velvet dress.

"Bollocks!"

Dressed in green silk, I looked in the mirror. John used to say that green brought out my eyes and even Seán had admired this dress. Not that it mattered what he thought, but he was a guy and he had good taste. My black hair rested on my shoulders. I wished that I'd gone to the hairdresser but it was too late. I put on my makeup slowly and carefully. It had to be right.

Just in case.

I fixed my Wonderbra, shoving my chest upwards and outwards. I kissed Leonard, who struggled to get away. He jumped from the bed and legged it in case a hug followed. It would appear he wasn't in the mood. I picked up my velvet dress, now covered in cat hair, and shoved it in the wash bag. The green dress was definitely a better fit.

Oh God, what am I doing?

I was shaking in the taxi. The taxi man wasn't a talker and I was glad. He turned up the heat without a word. I prayed I wouldn't start to sweat. He pulled up at the fancy apartment block in Donnybrook.

"That will be eight quid, love."

I fumbled for my money and handed him a tenner. "Keep the change," I muttered while collecting up my bag and attempting to open the door at the same time. I awkwardly exited. He waved as he pulled out of the driveway. Momentarily I thought about calling him back, but I didn't. Instead I watched him leave, the automatic gates closing behind him. I exhaled like an Olympic runner before a race. This was it. I felt like I was entering the lion's den.

I buzzed his apartment.

"Push the door. I'm on the third floor." His voice was light and happy.

I leaned on the door and it opened easily. I watched myself enter in the large mirror hanging at the end of the corridor. The lift opened in front of me and I entered cautiously. I pressed on the button marked "3" and stood facing the closing doors.

Last chance to leave.

Outside his door I felt foolish. He was waiting for my

knock. I was waiting for a sign from John. Nothing was happening. I bit my tongue and raised my hand. The door opened before I managed to make contact. He was wearing an apron with a picture of a duck in a chef's hat on it. He was smiling.

"Hi," he grinned, "you look incredible."

The fear went away. The door swung open and I walked into a gentle kiss. He took my coat and directed me into his sitting room. High ceilings, white walls, dark wooden floors and funky vibrant art lined the walls. An expensive chocolate-brown velvet couch sat in the center of the room facing a thick dark wood fireplace. The TV and sound system covered the entire corner of the room. Other than that, the room was empty. It was stunning. The apartment was huge. It even had a separate dining room. It was smaller than the sitting room, but just as impressive. We ate a meal that tasted like it had been prepared by a top chef as opposed to a solicitor. I was slightly embarrassed that I'd let him see where I lived. He must have thought I was a knacker.

"So what do you think?" he asked, grinning.

"It's stunning. It's like a museum. A bloody nice museum."

He laughed.

I was slightly perturbed, not having made a joke.

"I meant the food," he said, aware of my confusion.

"Okay, I'm an asshole," I admitted.

"I'm really glad you like the place." He smiled and it made him look beautiful.

I laughed unself-consciously.

After the meal we moved to the sitting room and sat

together on the soft couch, drinking the wine that I was glad I had spent a fortune on.

He told me about his past, where he'd gone to school and the reason he chose the legal profession. It was clear that he, like my friend Richard, came from money. He was more of a playboy though: that was very clear. Still, tonight he wanted to play with me and after the second bottle of wine I was ready to play with him. We were talking about Madonna. Don't ask me why. The conversation came to a natural end and we both felt a kiss in the air. We simultaneously put our glasses on the floor. We both turned to one another. He put his hand on my neck and I could feel his warmth. He pulled me toward him and I leaned in. We kissed soft and long. His hand moved down my back and when it rested at the base of my spine I felt ready to explode. We stripped in the sitting room. The couch felt good against my skin. His body felt a hell of a lot better.

Jesus, I'm doing it. I'm really doing it!

We moved to the bedroom—again fantastic; candles lit the room and it had a view to die for, but never mind about that. He laid me on the bed, which was soft and inviting. It was obvious he had a housekeeper and I made a mental note to shop for new sheets. He was on top of me and then inside of me and we were moving together. I stopped thinking. He was sweet, attentive, passionate, sexy and we had a really good time together. We didn't know one another three weeks ago and now we had shared this night of music, candles, wine, roses and great sex.

Afterwards he slept and I sat on his cold marble

bathroom floor and cried for the boy who had waited nearly two years for sex with me. The romance I had enjoyed earlier left when I came. The magic revealed itself to be nothing but a parlor trick. I felt so desperately sad, it hit me like a truck. I couldn't go back in there so I left in the middle of the night, feeling like an adulterer.

Ron called the next morning and I let the machine pick up. He hoped I was okay. He had a really great time and he wanted to see me that night. All I wanted was the ground to swallow me. I rang Clo and told her that I wasn't sure that I wanted to see him again. She told me it was perfectly natural to be unsure and scared, but that I deserved to give this guy a go. I didn't want to hear that. I wanted her to tell me to dump him. So after I hung up, I called Anne. She told me pretty much the same thing as Clo had and then went on to describe how fantastic Ron was and what a great match we were. I certainly didn't want to hear that so I called Seán. He said he'd come over and I said there was no need. He came over anyway and brought a bottle of wine. I told him I had spent the night with Ron.

"Go on," he said through gritted teeth, obviously hoping I wouldn't do the female thing and tell him anything too personal.

I tiptoed into the conversation, aware of his fear. I told him I really liked Ron, he was a lovely guy and we got on very well and that he was great. He appeared to be more comfortable with the line of conversation than I had originally anticipated. This was encouraging.

"Go on."

I told him that I didn't want to see him again.

"Why?" he asked, without hinting emotion or judgment.

The others had not asked that and I was unprepared. I thought about it.

"I just don't have the heart."

He smiled. "Well then, wait until you do."

Suddenly I didn't feel so pathetic. Just because I didn't want something with Ron didn't mean I wouldn't want something with someone else. I had slept with someone. That was a start and, who knows, the next time I slept with a guy I might even stay the whole night. I had choices; I was a nineties woman. A weight had been lifted. That night I called Ron and told him I thought it was a bit too soon for me to be seeing someone. He was nice about it, but the call was short.

Anne was devastated. I think she had my future entirely planned and this meant she had to go back to the drawing board. Clo asked me if it would be okay if she had a go at him, before laughing her ass off—the way she always did when she found herself funny. And so I was single after three brief weeks. I felt like a sixteen-year-old again and it made me smile.

Chapter 12

One Year and Counting

And then it was March again. I woke on the morning of John's anniversary having not really slept. Nine o'clock, my mother called. I knew it was her so I let the machine pick up. I stirred my coffee as the machine beeped.

"Emma, it's your mother. Pick up the phone. I know you're up. Emma!" Silence. "Your father told me you weren't planning on attending John's memorial Mass. What are his parents going to think? I know you're in pain, love, but you're an adult and you can't . . . look, everyone will be expecting you. Buck up, darling. I'll call you in an hour." She hung up.

I knew she was right, but I had convinced myself that I was sick. My head ached. I didn't want to go, but she was right: I was an adult. I didn't feel like one. I told you before that grief is selfish by its very nature. At funerals we cry for ourselves, for our pain, our loss, our suffering and it doesn't go away after a week or a month or even a year. The problem is that after a certain amount of time it's unacceptable to be selfish and therefore unacceptable to grieve. I missed being allowed this luxury but again, she was right. I had responsibilities. I went to the toilet and vomited. I threw my guts up and swore I'd never drink a bottle of vodka on my own again. I showered and was dressing when Seán called. He let himself in, having interrogated Noel on the whereabouts of my spare key. I came down the stairs and he was pouring himself some coffee.

"Rough night?" he asked.

It appeared that I looked like shit.

"You could say that," I replied and sat, waiting for him to serve me.

"I told you I wasn't going to the service," I said a few minutes later, annoyed that no one appeared to have taken any notice of my decision.

"Yes, you did," he agreed while I watched Leonard chase his tail—wondering how it still held so much interest after all this time. "I knew you'd change your mind," he said, wiping the counter where he'd spilled some milk.

I scoffed. "Just because I'm dressed doesn't mean I've changed my mind."

He smiled and looked at my puffy face, which I was attempting to hide with my hands. "Yes, it does. Besides, your mother made me come. The woman actually threatened violence if I showed up without you. Tough old bird, your ma."

I smiled. He was right: she was a tough old bird, and besides, I knew they were right. I had to go. This was not a choice that I could make. John's parents had understood my decision not to attend the inquest but this was different.

"I take it that I should put on some makeup then."

He nodded. "It wouldn't go astray."

I headed up to my bedroom and sat at my vanity table. I picked up a photo of John and me. We were laughing. He had his arm around me and he was whispering something into my ear. I wished I could remember what it was. Of course I was always going to the memorial; I had just been acting like a dick. How could I not go? How could I not remember him on this day? I put on my makeup and kissed the photo.

I can't believe it's been a year.

I came downstairs and Seán was waiting with my coat. He applauded.

"Let's go," I said and he was right behind me.

★ ★ ★

Noel celebrated the Mass. Afterwards we all congregated in John's parents' house. Music played; people drank and remembered him. We laughed and enjoyed one another. My mother sang a song and John's father accompanied her on his out-of-tune piano. John's mother and I talked for a really long time. She told me about the things he used to do and say as a toddler and I told her how John and I were together. Seán and Richard sang "Willy McBride" and Clo told jokes, while Anne and Noel debated on the divorce bill.

I lay in bed that night contemplating the day I'd been dreading. It had been lovely because for the first time in a year everyone who lost John remembered him together, with warmth and humor and it was fitting and right.

★ ★ ★

I was lost in a vast garden surrounded by exotic flowers set in soft green sand. I regarded my surreal surroundings, paying particular attention to a burning bush glowing in the distance. Unsure of where I was or what I was doing, I headed toward the purple sun dangling above a spidery tree because for some reason it appeared familiar. As I walked, leaves appeared to spring from the knotted branches of the tree. I wasn't afraid; it was too warm to be scared. Suddenly I was climbing a hill, my eyes still firmly fixed upon the purple sun that now appeared to spin before me. The hill leveled out under my feet and as I approached the now flowering tree, a gentle breeze brought it to life. Blue poppies danced between the thick foliage that continued to crawl along the cherry-pink branches. The purple sun hopped as though it was a ball being bounced by an unseen but mighty hand. Suddenly it was flying toward me. I didn't duck. Instead I caught it and threw it back.

John caught it and smiled. "And I thought you had a fear of flying balls."

He was grinning and, as he walked toward me, he threw the sun over his shoulder. It bounced once before returning to where it had previously hung.

We were standing together gazing at one another under the bright purple light and it all felt perfectly normal.

"Where have you been?" I asked, as though he'd just returned from a night out.

"Around," he said smiling.

"I've missed you."

"I know. Can you believe it's been a year?" He was grinning the way he used to when we were kids and he thought he knew it all.

"It's a nice day," I said for no good reason.

He looked around and nodded in agreement. "Yeah, it is."

"I still love you," I said casually.

He laughed and his eyes seemed to light up. "You always will."

I laughed. He had always been bloody arrogant. "I had sex with someone else," I admitted, a little ashamed.

"How was it?" he asked, unperturbed.

We were walking together, but I kept stopping just to gaze into his familiarity.

"Okay. Mostly it was crap."

He nodded, accepting that we didn't have to talk about it. We were so close but we didn't touch.

"I thought I wouldn't see you again," I said.

"I'm always here."

I looked around. "Where?"

"Wherever you want me to be."

"Bullshit, you're dead."

"You know what I mean."

And he took off, leaving me to lag behind. I called out. He didn't answer. Determined, I caught up with him and noticed the foreign foliage disappearing around us. The green sand led us to a blue poppy tree. He sat and motioned for me to join him. We looked out of the purple vista, which was becoming a background to a virtual game of Pac-Man, like the one we used to play for hours on end.

"I'm sorry," I said.

John stopped and looked at me seriously. "It wasn't your fault," he said, but then of course that's what he would say.

"If . . ." I whispered sheepishly.

He was laughing again and seeing his wide smile and big eyes reminded me of how we used to be.

"If 'if' was a donkey we'd all have a ride." He laughed at himself and I could feel him take my hand.

I was surprised that I could feel his form, his strength and his pulse. I squeezed hard and he returned the squeeze.

"Where to now?" I laughed.

"Click your heels," he said. He smiled and my heart began to break.

"I'm dreaming," I said, catching the single tear that fell and splashed into my open hand.

John looked around and grinned. "You always did have a big imagination."

"But it feels so real. It's you. I know it's you."

I nudged him and he fell against the tree.

"I have a confession," I said after a time.

"You're falling in love with someone else," he said, smiling.

"What?" I screamed, devastated. My confession had to do with his mother and our lack of contact. "I am not!" I shouted. "Who the hell do you think you are to tell me what I'm feeling?"

"Only you could have an argument with a dead man." He laughed.

"Only you could be dead and yet so bloody annoying," I responded and then suddenly it was funny so we both laughed, but I was still sad that he thought I could love someone else. He must have known that I wasn't ready for him to know that, so he distracted me by holding my hand and whispering memories and then we sat together, silent and comfortable, for the longest time. I felt the time pass and in my heart I knew it was time to leave.

"I should go," I sighed.

"I'll catch you down the road," he said, getting up.

He extended his hand and I held on as he pulled me up. I pulled him in tight and we hugged like old friends or family would at an airport. I could feel his heartbeat and his breath on my shoulder.

"You will," I whispered without tears or fear or sadness or regret.

I pulled away and gave a final wave and then he was gone.

Me in love with someone else! As if! What an asshole! And besides, it's still all my fault no matter what he says.

Chapter 13

Sex, Lies and Videotape

A little over one month after John's anniversary it occurred to me while I was putting out washing that Noel was the only one of us who appeared to have been fundamentally changed since John's passing. I wasn't sure how he had changed, but then I never claimed to be sensitive. I didn't know that the woman I had met all those months ago was the reason for this change; I really was so wrapped up in my own world. While I lurched from one day to the next, so did my brother. His new world was as exciting and pleasurable as it was terrifying and guilt-riddled.

After that night, they had met again and it was during this meeting that they both admitted their feelings for one another. They also both realized that a relationship was out of the question. They agreed that they were adults and, although they both admitted to their loneliness, they decided that friendship was their only recourse.

This worked well for a few months, the only problem being the more they knew about one another, the more they confided in one another, and the more they saw each other, the more difficult it became to deny the heat that they generated in one another. Noel had never felt this before. As a teenager he was too shy to bother with girls. As a young adult he was so desperate to become a priest that he had no time for women, but now he was just like the rest of us, working for a living and going home to nothing. He had the confidence that comes with being a man and the time to think about nothing else.

Early on he had visited the bishop to seek guidance from a man who could share his agony and counsel him. It didn't work out as he had hoped. The bishop had been kind but firm. He gave little of himself away, nor did he empathize.

"You made a vow," was his argument. "Like marriage, in good times and in bad. You are a priest."

Noel agreed. He knew what he was but he desperately needed to hear something else, although he wasn't sure what.

"What can I do? How can I get back to being the priest that I was?" he asked, praying the old man had an answer.

"Don't see her anymore."

That was it. That was the great solution to Noel's desperation. Noel thought about it. "I can't. I love her."

He left the bishop's home, realizing for the first time that he was in love and when he called to her house later that night it wasn't to say good-bye.

They had been sleeping together for six months. He

had never felt so many highs and lows in his sheltered world before love. He prayed endlessly and listened for God's word, but no words came. He had a life now, one outside God and the Church, and it was real. This woman was real. She would wrap her arms around him and keep him safe in this unsafe world. She would kiss him tenderly when he wept and she would give him the kind of pleasure that he had never known. He was happier than he ever had been in his life and it was tearing him apart.

How could I not see it?

★ ★ ★

Richard was desperate to move to his new country home in Kerry. Anne really didn't want to go. She was a city girl at heart. As usual, Richard would get his own way. The plan was give and take. Unfortunately for Anne, our friend Richard wasn't used to giving so much as taking. Clo, Seán and I went to their home to help them pack for their move to Kerry. Seán brought beer, but there was little time to drink it. The movers were on their way and very little was boxed up. Anne was turning into her mother, shouting orders at her husband while cleaning every available surface, terrified to be remembered by strangers as "dirty." Clo made her a cup of tea. We got to work, boxing, marking, asking stupid questions like, "Where does this go?" to which Anne or Richard would shout, "In a bloody box!"

I walked around their empty house and it was weird. We couldn't actually believe they were going ahead with it. When everything was boxed away, Anne made lunch and we ate silently in their empty kitchen. It felt like a funeral.

"I can't believe you're really going," I said for the fifth time.

"Neither can I," Richard responded excitedly.

Anne remained silent. She had been quiet all day and everyone, bar her husband, was acutely aware that she didn't want to move to Kerry. We finished lunch. The movers still hadn't arrived.

"Bastards," noted an agitated Anne.

We sat in silence waiting for the movers. Richard was off in his own little world, dreaming about golfing and catching fish. Anne appeared to be frozen like a deer caught in headlights. Clo and I were wallowing in self-pity brought on by our friends' departure.

Seán eventually got pissed off. "Hello, can someone please talk?"

Nobody was listening to him.

"Hello?" he repeated. "Right, that's it! I'm having a beer."

He got up and went to pick up his bag of warm beers while mumbling that he couldn't believe they had sent off the important things like chairs and the bloody fridge first. He started to drink. Clo came out of her coma.

"Hey, what about the rest of us?" she asked, disgusted.

"Oh, *now* someone speaks!"

She smiled. "You'd be surprised what I'd do for booze."

He thought about it for a second. "No, I probably wouldn't."

She grinned. "Oh yeah, you're probably right."

I hated when they flirted, especially when it included a mention of their little fling. I asked for a beer to change the subject. Anne and Richard decided to join us rather than beat us. So there we were, drinking beers in an empty house while waiting for the movers to come and take our friends' possessions and, with them, our friends. Clo perked up after her second beer.

"I met someone during the week," she said.

This sparked considerable interest because since her miscarriage she had decided all men had pricks and therefore were pricks. This meant that they should be avoided at all costs.

"Who?" I asked.

She told us he was a graphic designer who had worked on her last ad campaign. They had gone to lunch together a few times and really got on. She hadn't slept with him, but she was definitely interested. She said he made her laugh and he was kind. She especially liked the way that he always offered her food from his plate. He was cute in a "Mulder" sort of way. He had great teeth and they both loved the same films. We all agreed that he sounded great, but guessed that he was lying about liking the same films because Clo's taste in entertainment was up her arse.

I reminded her that she had declared herself a lesbian the week before. She nodded, noting that it had seemed like a good idea. However, when she really gave it some thought, she realized that men may be pricks but women were bitches and, besides, Page Three just didn't do it for her.

Clo's new love interest was called Tom Ellis. She was going to meet him for a drink later and she was quite excited about it. For a minute I envied her, but then I remembered most dates involved hour-long conversations

131

based on star signs and I was glad to be heading home to Leonard.

The movers arrived and we all helped them haul Anne and Richard's worldly possessions into the van and then they were ready to go. Everyone was out in the garden. Anne had gone inside to take one last look around. Richard was busy discussing the directions with the movers. After a while I followed her. I found her in the kitchen.

"Hey," I announced myself.

"Hey, yourself," she smiled. She looked like she was about to cry.

"It's going to be great in Kerry. The house is fantastic; it's by the sea, for God's sake. And the place looks great, and if you want you'll find a job there, no problem. You're only sixty miles from Cork and that's got everything that Dublin's got—" I was on a roll but she cut me short.

"It doesn't have my friends," she said quietly.

I knew how she felt. "It's not like we can't talk on the phone and Richard still has business in Dublin. You can come up and down as much as you like and we'll visit you. It'll be great," I said, trying to comfort myself as much as comfort her.

She brightened. "I know, I know and you're right. Kerry is beautiful and the house is beautiful and the people seem great, and it's a really quaint little village and Richard loves it. It's a great place to bring up kids and I know we're lucky, but I just hope that we're doing the right thing."

I hoped they were too. I wanted to say, don't go. I'd

even volunteer to unpack all the boxes. But I just put my arm around her. "It's going to be great," I repeated.

She smiled. "Promise me, just because I live somewhere else, you won't forget about me. Okay?"

I laughed. "Christ, Anne, you spend more time on the phone than an AA sponsor. I couldn't forget you if I wanted to."

We laughed and Richard came in to call us. He took one look around.

"Good-bye, kip!" he cheered.

Anne mumbled "men" under her breath and we locked the door behind us. We all hugged at their car. Richard reminded us to visit them at Christmas. We all agreed. Seán and Richard made plans to head to the UK for a soccer match the following month. Anne and I cried. Clo was busy taking photographs, which happened to be her new hobby. They drove off and Seán, Clo and I stood at their gate waving.

"And then there were three," Clo whispered and I felt like crying again.

Seán rubbed his hands together. "Who's coming for a pint?"

Clo refused, based on her need to go home, shower and beautify herself for the lovely Tom Ellis. I agreed. Leonard could wait; he'd gone through three tins of cat food for breakfast. It couldn't be healthy.

We sat in Seán's local and discussed Clo's impending date, which led to us discussing our own sad and depressing single status. I hadn't attempted to date since Ron and Seán's last encounter turned out to be some sort of a stalker. We sat with our pints, resigned.

"So do you ever hear from Carrie?" I asked. Carrie was the name we'd christened his stalker, her real name being Janet.

"No, thank Christ. I heard she's seeing Pete, in accounts," he said.

I couldn't believe it. Carrie was a looney. "So I presume Pete does know she's a lunatic?"

"Well, if he's spending time with her he must," he replied and smiled at himself, satisfied with his smartness.

"Don't be smart, it's very unappealing," I said and continued, disgusted. "I can't believe you haven't set him straight."

"You'd do the same thing," he pointed out.

I was outraged. "Of course I wouldn't."

"Yeah, you would. If you had some nutcase banging down your door every five minutes and he found himself a distraction, there's no way you'd jeopardize that."

I shook my head. "There's something wrong with you."

"You'd do the same thing."

I changed the subject because he knew that I knew that he was right. After another few pints I began to talk about the future. I was worried because, the way I saw it, Clo had been out with a lot of guys, all of them total assholes. I had found one guy, the perfect guy, at sixteen. He was The One and now he was gone. By sheer statistics I was bound to end up going through years of dating complete dicks before ever, if ever, meeting the right guy again. And what if I didn't ever meet the right guy? What if I just got so pissed off sharing my lonely little world with Leonard and his eating problem and I decided to marry some dick, just to have someone? I was feeling a little panicky.

Seán laughed. "That's not going to happen."

"It could," I argued.

"No way," he stated.

"Why? Why no way?" I enquired.

"Because," he smiled.

"Because what?" I pushed.

"Because you'd never settle for that."

I smiled.

It was a nice thing to say until he followed it up with, "You're too high maintenance."

But I chose to ignore that.

We fell silent again. It struck me, despite all our chat, that Seán seemed preoccupied. He was staring at his drink and fiddling with his left ear.

"You seem a little off form," I said.

"Do I?"

"Yeah," I nodded.

"Based on?" he asked, intrigued.

"You know the way I pick invisible lint when I'm nervous?" I asked and he nodded to confirm that he did. "Well, you pull on your left ear."

He grinned and took his hand away from his ear. "You want to know what's wrong?" he teased.

"Yeah."

"Why?"

"Partly to help and partly to feel I'm not the only one with concerns."

He laughed. "It's delicate."

"Delicate? Delicate how?"

"Well, you know I work in an office with ten women and twenty guys."

I nodded. I did know.

"Okay, so you sleep with some of those women and it's cool, but then you sleep with some more and, well, women talk."

The conversation had taken an interesting turn and the gossip in me was screaming, *Get to the point!*

"It turns out that a few of them compared notes and there's something written about me on the ladies' toilet wall."

"What?" I asked, silently wondering if I really wanted to know.

He cleared his throat. "Seán Brogan gives good head."

I nearly choked on my drink.

"Now when they're together they whistle when I pass. I feel violated," he continued, having resumed pulling on his left ear.

I really didn't know what to say. Part of me wanted to laugh and the other part wanted to pick invisible lint from my trousers so I folded my arms.

"Wow. That's terrible," I managed, hoping I wasn't about to blush. I felt sorry for him. He should have had a guy to talk to. I was useless.

"It's a bloody nightmare. Carrie's in on it and that bitch has pictures!"

"Sweet Jesus!" I said, now feeling hugely uncomfortable.

"What would you do?" he asked, seriously.

"I'd just keep my head down," I said and suddenly he was laughing and I realized what I'd said and quietly died.

Keep my head down. I cannot believe I just said that.

Then I found myself laughing too.

After a few pints, Seán decided never to sleep with

136

someone he worked with again and we both drank to his very wise choice.

I got home around ten; Seán was meeting some girl that he didn't work with. The TV was on and I could hear the kettle boiling in the kitchen. As I lived alone, this was troublesome.

"Noel?" I called out, raising my umbrella while making a mental note to go for the bollocks. "Noel? Is that you?"

I had my back to the stairs and was aiming my umbrella at the half-open sitting room door.

"Hey!" I heard behind me and swung around, making stabbing motions with my umbrella.

"It's me—Noel! Don't kill me, please!" he said, smiling, while holding his hands up.

"Jesus Christ, Noel, you scared the shit out of me!" I said, visibly shaken.

"Sorry, I didn't mean to frighten you. I was in the loo and please don't use the Lord's name in vain." He always had a bloody cheek.

"It's my house! I'll say whatever I want." I dropped the umbrella onto my foot as I spoke. "Jesus Christ, my foot!" He went to speak but I was too quick. "Shut up! It's my house!"

He told me I'd survive and then I followed him into the kitchen. He made coffee and told me he had been worried that I'd feel extra lonely now that Anne and Richard had moved to Kerry. He did have a bloody cheek, but he was also bloody kind. I swore I was fine and after my few drinks with Seán I was telling the truth. I told him about the graffiti on the ladies' toilet wall and we had a laugh at Seán's expense.

Then out of the blue Noel noted thoughtfully, "I suppose that's one of the reasons priests should remain celibate. 'Father Noel gives good head' just doesn't sound right."

I laughed. "I don't know—apparently there are a lot of priests that do!" I laughed again loudly at my joke.

He looked uncomfortable.

I apologized, suddenly realizing the comment wasn't in good taste. (Excuse the pun.) "Sorry, Noel, sick joke."

"It's okay." He smiled, but the mood had changed.

I asked him what was wrong.

"Nothing," he replied.

"Come on," I goaded. "It's obvious there's something up, even to me, and I'm renowned for being self-absorbed."

He smiled. "That's true."

I encouraged him to talk and he did. He told me that he had been lonely for so long. He had spent so many years defending his celibacy that he refused to question why it was necessary, until now. He had met someone. She was a social worker, in her early thirties and separated from her husband; they had hit it off. He said that she was beautiful and funny. She was intelligent and told him where to go when he was boring her and nobody did that except for his family. He said that she made him feel like a man. I sat in silence and listened to him, telling me about the color of her hair, and I watched him smile as he remembered it. He spoke of her warmth and her wide smile.

He told me that one look from her made him question all that he was and all that he wanted. From his description I knew he was talking about the woman I'd seen him with in the pub all those months ago. I was dumbfounded. I was usually quite good at giving unsolicited advice, but I was speechless, busy trying to get used to the idea of my brother being a sexual being. But it was more than that. All these years I had believed that his beliefs were enough to keep Noel warm at night, enough to keep him company on winter evenings, enough to make up for living a life alone, but I was wrong. Nobody is built to be alone, especially those who dedicate their lives to caring for others.

I wanted to tell him to give it all up and run off to Jamaica with her, but I recognized that I didn't have a clue what he was going through and that in most situations there is no easy answer.

"Jesus!" I said, before quickly apologizing. It was the least I could do under the circumstances.

We were silent for a while.

Then I ventured to ask, "Have you kissed her?"

"We've been together, Em," he responded, without being able to face me.

"Oh," I said, suddenly realizing why my brother looked so desperate. *So what?* I wanted to scream, but knowing it wouldn't be helpful I swallowed the words. "Are you in love?"

"Yes," he mumbled

"What do you want to do?" I asked gently, afraid my question would break him.

"I just wish that I could be a priest without having to sacrifice everything. It's not fair. I spend my life marrying couples and christening babies and I'm never ever going to have any of that and when I look at her I want it. I want to wake up next to her in the morning. I want to have the kids run into our bedroom at six o'clock on a

Saturday morning. I want to go to parent-teacher nights and apologize for my kids not being able to shut up in class, but the problem is I need to be a priest. I can't imagine my life doing something else. I know it's what I'm here to do." He sank his head in his hands and he cried like a baby. "I'm just so lonely, Emma."

I held him close and I told him that everything would be fine, hoping that it would be. He apologized, embarrassed to be sharing his problems as the unpracticed often do. We sat in silence for a while.

"Life's a bitch," I said.

"Indeed," he agreed.

We laughed.

"It's got to get better than this," I said.

"Yeah," he sighed.

"It will. You just have to work through it. Right?"

"Right," he answered sadly.

He said he should go, but I wanted him to stay. He didn't argue.

Later, I was lying in bed processing his revelation. He passed, returning from the toilet.

"Night, Noel!" I called out.

"Night, Mary Ellen!" he called back.

I smiled at him.

Christ, I can't wait to tell Clo.

Chapter 14

Three's Company

It wasn't long after our little conversation that Noel split up with his one true love. She needed him to make a choice; she could no longer watch him tear himself apart.

"No more guilt," she had demanded.

Noel knew that it would not be possible. He couldn't give up being a priest and, in admitting that, he was forced to let go of any hope that he had allowed himself over the past year. It was over. She cried desperately, as did he. She begged him to stay with her and he pleaded with her to understand. The hurt was immense. She was clinging on to all they had and he was desperately trying to let go. He left her crying, sitting on her doorstep in a nightdress and slippers. He walked down the street blinded by tears, his heart breaking and the sound of her desperation in his ears.

Oh God, what have I done?

Noel didn't see her after that. She had picked herself

up from her step and walked inside, closing the door on him and their aborted future. He went back to the house he shared with Rafferty, who was blissfully unaware of his predicament.

He found it difficult to be alone in his room. He needed people around him. Someone that made him feel normal. Someone who wouldn't judge and who would understand that he needed time to heal. He started spending more time in my place and I was glad of the company. We fell into a routine. Noel would stay three or four nights out of seven. He wasn't a great cook, but much better than me. I'd come home to find a shepherd's pie in the oven and Noel cleaning the kitchen.

He liked to keep busy and I liked that he liked to keep busy because cleaning was definitely not my scene. Of course I did it, but it depressed me. I wasn't meant for cleaning. I was a messer. We'd watch movies together and sometimes he'd take out John's video games and I'd watch him play them as intensely as John had once done. He was sad and sometimes he looked like he'd been crying, but then other times he was almost like the old Noel. Almost.

★ ★ ★

Seán split up with the latest girlfriend but, worse, he was suffering from writer's block. He had been working on a novel for over six months and initially it had been going well, but he had reached an impasse and his computer terminal was taunting him. He evacuated the house at any given opportunity. Once he realized that Noel was spending time with me he joined the gang. The house was starting to get a little packed. Now four out of seven nights I'd come home to Seán and Noel drinking tea and fighting over the remote.

"Noel, I am not watching reruns of *Starsky and Hutch*!" I roared over the blaring theme tune.

"Ah, come on!" they both pleaded.

"Oh, sweet Mother," I sighed.

There were twin beds in the spare room so every now and then they both would stay over. I could hear them chat and laugh through the wall and it felt like camp. They'd talk into the small hours. I'd wake up cranky and queue for the shower. When I got to the fridge the milk would be gone and my toast would mysteriously vanish when I turned my back. We were relying on each other too much and we were doing it in my house. It wasn't healthy. I knew things had to change.

One particular evening, when Noel and Seán were having a few beers in front of Ireland versus Latvia, Clo called with her new boyfriend, Tom. Noel and Seán were more than happy to share their beers; I just wanted a quiet night in, but was obviously outvoted. Tom was delighted, drinking beer and watching soccer, and he was clearly enchanted with the two people responsible for his newfound joy. The lads quickly bonded while discussing the importance of good defense and their own idea on team strategies, each believing that they knew better than the Irish coach.

Clo and I escaped to the kitchen.

"I didn't realize it would be a full house," she said.

It was never anything but and for some insane reason I actually missed being alone so I exploded. "It's a nightmare! They're here all the time. It's not like they don't have any homes to go to! Jesus, I just want to be able to curl up and read a bloody book or not have to watch *WrestleMania*."

"So tell them to go home," she said.

She was right. Enough was enough. Still, I didn't want to frighten them away completely. I would miss them. It's not like they weren't a good laugh sometimes and deep down I did have a soft spot for *Starsky and Hutch*. I just didn't want to have to queue for the bathroom four times a week.

"I'll tell them," I said.

I asked her how Tom was.

"Lovely," she smirked.

They'd been seeing one another for a month and had not slept together.

"Tomorrow's the night," she grinned.

"About time," I noted.

"You can't talk," she pointed out.

She was right. I shut up.

"I'm thinking of wearing my black V-neck dress. What do you think?" she asked.

"You've made him wait to get his leg over for more than a month—I think you could wear dog vomit and he'd jump your bones."

"Good point," she said and smiled. "I'm going to cook for him, some soft music, candles . . . I even bought silk sheets."

She had style, I'll give her that.

"Nice," I said.

"Yeah," she agreed.

We both daydreamed about warm bodies for a few minutes.

"What about you?" she asked.

"Nobody," I said.

Seán walked in, took three beers out of the fridge and made a joke about Noel's taste in men. I laughed and watched him walk out.

"Are you sure?" she asked.

"What?" I enquired.

"Are you sure there's no one?"

"There's no one," I told her firmly, but I was lying to both of us. She didn't push and I didn't want her to.

"Hey," she said after a while, "would you like my vibrator?"

I looked at her, waiting for her to burst into laughter. She didn't.

"It's really great, compact, you can fit it in your handbag and I won't need it after tomorrow night." She was smiling.

Jesus!

It was a lovely thought, but I told her that she should keep it for a rainy day, while attempting to hide my discomfort.

"Emma, you're such a prude," she smiled.

"Indeed," I agreed.

Clo and I moved into the sitting room. Tom and the lads were getting on like old friends. I later discovered that initially Tom was slightly perturbed at the notion of hanging out with a priest. I suppose he was worried about conversation. Most people find it hard to talk about anything other than the weather to a priest for fear that they may incriminate themselves in the eyes of God. However, he took his cue from Seán, who wasn't ever afraid to share his feelings, God or no God.

Clo was beaming. Tom put his hand on her leg as he talked with the others and she made jokes that made everyone laugh. It was nice to see it and it made me wish I had someone to touch my leg. I looked over at Seán and he was smiling at me. We looked at each other for only a moment before reengaging in conversation, but it felt close. Close and a little weird due to my stomach doing a little flip like it had the first time John had introduced me to him in the college bar.

When Clo and Tom had gone, Noel and Seán sat me down.

"We know we're in the way," Noel said.

I blushed red-hot while attempting to mumble the words "no" and "don't be silly."

"I heard you in the kitchen," Seán said, smiling.

I'd been caught. At least they seemed to be taking it well.

"I'm sorry," I mumbled, still embarrassed.

"Don't be," Seán said. "We didn't mean to turn your home into a frat house."

Noel smiled at the idea that he of all people would be responsible for turning my home into a frat house.

"It's not that," I admitted.

"What then?" asked Noel, not because he was insulted—it was just his usual concern.

"I'm afraid that we're all relying on one another too much. I mean, how long can this go on? If I get too used to having you around, well, then, what will I do when you leave?"

And there it was. I'd admitted it, my real concern. I was afraid that if I let my part-time lodgers get under my skin, then it would be too hard to let them go and they weren't mine to keep. It was simple really. They both smiled.

"We not going anywhere," said Noel.

"Just home," said Seán.

They stayed that night and the next morning they left together and I waved them off. I closed the door. Alone again, but it wasn't so bad.

★ ★ ★

The next night Clo slept with Tom. She rang me the following morning. He was still there, asleep. She was wired. They'd had a great time. It hadn't worked out exactly as she had planned. She had forgotten to buy a lighter or matches to light the candles. She'd attempted to light them from the gas oven but only succeeded in covering her hob with wax. The wine tasted like cheese and her meal was an utter failure. Tom arrived to his very stressed girlfriend's home having picked up a pizza, a reliable bottle of vino and a video. They munched on pizza, sipped on wine and laughed their way through *Screwballs*.

"*Screwballs?*" I didn't believe her.

"I know, it's mad. It's his favorite film too."

I was dumbfounded. He really did share in Clo's shit movie taste. "Wow!"

"I know," she said. "The sex was great," she went on, "but I don't want to go on about it because if I do I might jinx it. It's all about breaking patterns, Em. I'm making changes."

"Good for you," I admitted, not really sure what she meant.

147

"Yeah," I could hear her smiling down the phone line, "I'm going to marry him," she said with great confidence.

I agreed it was a distinct possibility that he was The One now that the *Screwballs* thing had come to light.

Chapter 15

Soccer, Betazoids and the Exit

Seán had somehow found the inspiration he required to return to his book. He concentrated on finishing his first novel, something he had talked about doing since the first day we met. He'd work on his articles, then push them aside and get lost in his book for hours and hours at a time. He didn't read time anymore, nor did he care, which was especially frustrating if he had agreed to meet you for lunch.

Noel started taking on extra work. He had some club or social or group to attend almost every night.

I didn't really have anything to get lost into, no escape. I just taught the kids, came home, marked some copies every now and again and that was it. I was bored and now that Noel was so busy I was forced into the confession box just to see him again.

"Hey." I smiled when Noel pulled back the little sliding shutter.

He sighed. "So you're back."

"Well, you haven't been around so much. I just wanted to catch up with you."

"You know where I live," he stated, smiling, because we both knew there was no way that I was ever going to get myself caught talking about famine with Father Rafferty.

"But you're never there," I argued, avoiding the subject of his aging housemate.

He was beaten and surrendered accordingly. "So how about we take this outside?" he said, before adding, "My ass is numb."

Apparently there were all kinds of ways to suffer for one's God and a numb ass was definitely one of them.

We went to a coffee shop. It was late in the evening and the coffee shop was full of students. I looked around and smiled at them, the memories of my own college days seeming distant. Noel noticed my contemplation.

"The passage of time is a funny thing. Sometimes I wish that I could hold on to just one moment, stop time, just for a while," he said.

I smiled. "I know exactly which moment I'd like to hold on to."

He sighed, looking suddenly sad. "Me too," he said.

"Are you all right?" I asked.

"Fine." He smiled again. "Actually I'm glad you came to see me—it saves me a trip."

"Oh yeah?" I said, intrigued.

"I was thinking of going away for a while," he told me.

I panicked. "Where?" I asked, praying he would say Bray rather than Bali.

"I'm thinking of taking a sabbatical to travel, see a bit

of the world God created. I bang on about it enough—
it's time I experienced it."

Now I was really panicking. I couldn't lose him too.
"You want to travel or you want to run away?" I asked,
devastated that he was leaving me.

"Ouch!" he said good-naturedly. "And the answer is I
don't know. But I have to work things out. I can't keep
carrying on the way I am, my heart not in it. I need to
find what I've lost."

I wanted to tell him he was talking rubbish and not to
go, that he could work out his problems here, that I
would help him, but I knew I couldn't help and that he
needed to get away and find the peace he was looking for.

"What if you don't find what you've lost?" was my
only question.

"Then I move on," he said.

He was doing the right thing. I knew it but it was
killing me. "I think you're brave. I'll really miss you." I
was smiling, but tears were rolling down my face.

He wiped them away and held my face in his hands.
"I love you, Emma," he said.

"I love you too, Noel," I responded.

We hugged and over his shoulder I saw the students
sniggering and whispering about the priest and his
girlfriend. If only they understood his position, maybe his
pain wouldn't be such a joke.

★ ★ ★

Clo decided we weren't spending enough time together
as a group. She organized a night out.

"Dinner, a movie, a few drinks," she said.

"A movie," I repeated. "Don't you mean a film?" I enquired sarcastically.

"Em, get with the times. Everyone calls films movies these days. Jesus, you're such a granny!"

I laughed. "I'm twenty-seven," I pointed out.

"That's the problem," she counseled. "So, are you in?"

I enquired as to who was going.

"You, me, Tom, his friend Mick and Seán."

I wasn't convinced. "Seán said he'd go?"

"Yes," she replied firmly.

"Okay, so this is not you and Tom trying to set me up with his friend?"

She shook her head. "Oh, Em, always so suspicious! Nobody's trying to set you up. It's just a night out."

I phoned Seán. He confirmed he would be there so I agreed to go.

We had arranged to meet in a pizza place at half six, just in time for the early bird menu, as Mick kept reminding us. Seán was late. I was beginning to think he wasn't coming and this caused great personal concern as Clo and Tom were still at the fawning phase and Mick was boring the arse off me.

"You know what the greatest thing about *Generation* is?" he asked.

I hadn't a clue what he was talking about.

"No," I replied.

"Cultural diversity," he stated and slapped his hand on the table as he spoke to emphasize the importance of it.

"Really?" I smiled while trying to grab Clo's attention. This was difficult. Tom was whispering into her neck—

she was miles away. I was stuck. I looked toward the door. It wasn't opening.

"You see, the *Star Trek* crew had a Vulcan but that's it. The rest were human. *Generation* has a Klingon, a Betazoid, an Android and Colm Meaney, which is so cool. After *The Commitments*, he's really got out there and made something of himself. I mean, where are the other fuckers?"

"Good question," I said while sneaking another look at my watch and planning to punch Seán's face in. Half an hour and fourteen *Star Trek: The Next Generation* plotlines later he arrived.

"Sorry, I'm really sorry, I got caught up," he announced as he pushed in beside me, much to Mick's annoyance.

"This is Mick." I smiled at him.

They shook hands.

"Mick was just telling me all about *Star Trek: The Next Generation*," I said, smiling.

Before Seán got a chance to comment, Mick asked him if he liked *Star Trek*.

"No, I think it's a load of bollocks," he said, smiling.

Mick was thankfully quiet after that.

We went to see a *Silence of the Lambs* rerun at the IFC. I sat between Seán and Mick. Mick started to whisper in my ear—he was a talker. I hated talkers. I mean, what's the bloody point in going to see a movie if you're going to talk the whole way through it? It was driving me insane so I kicked Seán. Mick started whispering again, telling me some bullshit fact about serial killers.

Seán leaned across me. "What? You'll have to speak up. I can't hear you."

Mick sat back uncomfortably. "Nothing."

"Shit, sorry, I thought you were saying something."

Seán smiled at me while I tried to hide my grin. Mick didn't whisper after that.

We went for a drink, insisting it would be a quick one. Mick was tired so he went home. I sighed with relief. Once in the pub, after the movie postmortem was completed, Clodagh and Tom announced they were moving in together. I couldn't believe it, it had been so quick, but I was happy for them.

"Why not? We could all be dead tomorrow."

Seán and I congratulated them and stayed on to celebrate their good news. They left together and we shared a taxi home.

"It's a bit quick," he thought aloud.

"When you know, you know," I replied.

He looked out the window. "How do you know, Emma?"

"You just do," I responded.

"When?"

I was confused. "What do you mean?"

"When do you know?"

"You just do."

He remained quiet for the rest of our journey. I looked out at the passing lights and daydreamed about being Clarice Starling and kicking Hannibal Lecter's ass while Seán sat silently looking ahead. Obviously, I hadn't a clue what I was talking about.

★ ★ ★

A month later my parents held a going-away party for Noel. They had a banner in the sitting room that read

"Bon Voyage, Noel." There were vol-au-vents, sausages and sandwiches everywhere, making it difficult to find a place to sit. Seán, Clo and Tom came. Anne and Richard were meant to but he got the flu and Anne was playing nursemaid. I looked around the room at my parents' and Noel's friends, the banner and the food. It reminded me of the inheritance party and I thought of John for maybe the first time that month. The guilt made me feel a little weary. I needed air. I went into the garden.

Seán followed.

"Missing him already?" he enquired.

"Noel? No, he'll be back," I responded, not turning to face him.

He walked over to me. "I'm nearly finished with the book."

I asked him for the fifth time that week if I could read it.

"Not for a while. You'll be the first though," he assured me.

I wasn't content with this and begged on the basis that he was nearly finished. I was dying to see what kept him locked away for hours on end. He thought about it for a minute.

"You won't like it. It centers around a soccer team . . ."

Oh Christ, I'm going to have to read a soccer book!

I must have drifted off for a few moments because although his mouth was moving I wasn't really registering the words.

I can't believe I haven't thought about John for so long.

"You didn't hear a word I've just said," he challenged.

"Soccer?" I said. "A soccer team in a small country village," I continued hopefully.

He smiled. "Don't worry—you don't need to be David Beckham to enjoy the story."

"Right, great, I can't wait."

Who the hell is David Brickham?

★ ★ ★

Everyone left and there we were, a family standing in front of one another, wondering who would cry first. Noel's flight left at ten. It was seven and the hours were counting down way too fast for my poor mother. She made herself busy cleaning plates while I swept. Dad and Noel went into his study. They were there awhile. Mom was trying not to cry.

"He'll be okay," I tried to reassure us both.

"He's heading into the frigging jungle," she said, a tear escaping her brimming eyes.

"Cuba is hardly the jungle."

"Bloody Communists."

"Mom!" I called out, distressed at her inability to embrace a PC attitude.

"It's uncivilized."

"Jesus! You don't know anything about Cuba," I said, disgusted.

"And you do," she noted sarcastically.

She was right. I hadn't a clue but I wasn't about to let her racism stand. "It's got some nice beaches," I mumbled, trying to remember something from *The Travel Show.*

"Great. He can die on a nice beach."

"Now you're just being silly."

"Am I?" she asked shrilly.

"He'll be fine," I said, sorry I'd opened my mouth.

"That's all we can hope for. He's only ever been to Spain on a family holiday and even then he had the runs the entire week. Why couldn't he just stay in Europe like everyone else?"

I exhaled and shook my head, much like I did when my class disappointed me.

"You know I'm right," she said. She sat down at the kitchen table. "Why couldn't he be like a normal man and get some young one pregnant and have to marry her like Mary Matthews's son. He has three kids now and he works in the bank."

She was crying so the word "bank" came out as "baaa . . . ank."

"He has to do what he feels is right," I said, not believing it because, like my mother, I wanted him to be like Mary Matthews's son too.

"Do you think he'll ever come back to us?"

"Of course he will."

I put away the brush and sat beside her, putting my arm around her shoulder.

"I just wish life wasn't so hard," she said in the small voice she had left.

"Me too, Mom," I said, hugging her. "We all do."

★ ★ ★

The airport was a nightmare. Mom cried openly. I was trying to hold it together, but it was too hard. My brother was leaving me. Who would listen to my shit now? Who would have the answers, even if I didn't like them? I missed him already and he was standing in front of me, trying desperately to grin. I knew he was excited, but I could also feel his fear. I wanted to wrap him up and take him home. I couldn't imagine how hard it was for my mother.

Dad was stoic. He shook hands with his son and patted his shoulder. "I'm proud of you, son."

Noel smiled at Dad and hugged him tight. "Proud of you too, Dad."

Dad nodded the way men do.

Noel took Mom in his arms. I hadn't noticed how strong he looked until he enveloped her.

"I love you, Mom. I'll make it home for Christmas."

"You promise?" she cried out while fixing the collar of his jacket. Old habits die hard.

"I promise."

We watched him walk through the glass doors that would lead him to Cuba and away from us. He waved one last time. Dad smiled at him and then he was gone. I turned to see my father dissolve in front of my eyes. Tears fell down his face and he made a noise I'd never heard before. He put his hands to his face and the tears streamed through. My mother put her arms around him and they stood there hugging one another.

"We'll see him at Christmas," she said.

My dad nodded like a small boy. I stood by, heartsick. We all walked to the car and we drove out of the airport in silence.

I got home to find Leonard eating a plastic bag. I wrestled it out of his mouth. He minced out of the room, disgusted that I'd interrupted his idea of a perfectly reasonable snack. The lights were off. I left them off and turned the TV on. I remembered the way that Noel had called over when Anne and Richard went to Kerry. He wanted to ensure I'd be okay. Now he was gone and there was no one to call around.

Another one bites the dust.

He loved Queen. I smiled.

My brother could have been a really great homo.

Chapter 16

The Pox

Anne rang. Richard and she were trying for a baby. There was only one problem: they'd been trying to get pregnant for months and nothing was happening.

"Do you think I should get tested?" she asked.

I remembered Noreen the biology teacher in my school had been trying two years before she had her little girl.

"No, it's way too soon. It just takes time," I said confidently.

"I don't know—we've been doing everything possible."

I argued that results came with time. Besides, I felt that if there was any testing to be done it should be on both of them.

"What? You think that there's something wrong with Richard?" she asked defensively.

"No, I didn't say that. I don't think there's anything

wrong with either of you, but if you are going to get tests what's the point in testing only one of you?" I answered, panicking. I wasn't in the humor for an argument.

She thought for a minute. "Do you think it has anything to do with me being on the pill?"

I was confused. "What? You're still on the pill?" I asked, amazed.

"Emma, don't be such a spaz," she laughed. "I mean, the fact that I was on it for so many years."

I thought for a minute. "Well, does it say anything about that on the box?"

"No," she admitted. "Maybe we'll try a bit longer."

"Good idea," I agreed.

The rest of the conversation centered on the fact that she had to drive thirty miles to find a decent shopping center. I was tired and my head was aching. I hadn't slept very well that night and I felt hot.

"I have to go," I said. I just wasn't able to talk.

"Okay, but don't forget I'm in Dublin tomorrow, so I'll see you for dinner."

I agreed I wouldn't forget and hung up the phone. I took two painkillers and dragged myself up the stairs to bed.

I woke up a few hours later and felt a whole lot worse. I stood up to drag myself to the mirror and noticed large red spots appearing all over my torso.

"Sweet Jesus!" I roared.

I moved closer to the mirror and took off my robe to examine myself more thoroughly. This revealed nasty red spots appearing before my eyes.

"Fucking great!" I sighed. "I've got the pox."

I remembered that my parents were away on a short break to Edinburgh and I wanted to cry. The doctor arrived an hour later and confirmed I had picked up a nasty case of chickenpox. One week's solitary confinement and all the calamine lotion I could lay my hands on were prescribed. He left and I stared in the mirror, waiting for spots to appear on my face and praying that they wouldn't. I phoned Clo and she laughed.

"It's not funny," I whined. "If I scratch I could be scarred."

"So don't scratch," she advised, still laughing.

"That's all very well for you to say," I said. "My skin's crawling. I feel like Indiana Jones in *The Temple of Doom*."

She was silent for a second. "I don't get that."

"What?"

"*The Temple of Doom* thing," she said.

"You know, the spiders," I said.

She didn't know.

"You know, when all the spiders were dropping onto Indiana Jones and his girlfriend."

"I think that was in the first film," she said.

"Well, what was the first one called?" I asked.

"I can't remember," she responded after a moment's thought.

I thought about it for a minute. "Me neither," I conceded.

Clo hadn't ever had chickenpox so she couldn't visit. Anne was trying to get pregnant, so I was the last person on earth she wanted to have dinner with. Richard wasn't a candidate on the same grounds. My parents and Noel were away so I was alone and I really,

really wanted to scratch. I sat watching daytime TV, which made me depressed and bored. Boredom encouraged scratching. I made something to eat, but it stuck in my throat. After nearly choking, I lay down on the couch and complained to myself about having to work with teenagers. One of them had carried the pox germ into my class. *Bastards.*

★ ★ ★

I woke up to the sound of the doorbell. I panicked as any infected person would.

I stood behind the closed door and shouted, "Who's there?"

"It's Seán," came the reply. "Let me in!"

"I can't," I whined. "I've got chickenpox."

He laughed. "Clo told me. Let me in."

"I can't," I whined again. "It's very contagious."

"I've already had it!" he called back.

"But it could give you shingles," I moaned.

"Emma, open the fucking door please!"

I opened the door. The light hurt my eyes. He stepped in. I looked up at him.

"Fine, but don't blame me if you get shingles. Your brain swells and you die."

He laughed, enjoying my flair for the dramatic. "Where did you hear that?"

I pointed to the brochures the doctor had left me. He picked them up and read. He smiled. "I think you're a little hysterical."

"Really," I said snottily. "Well, if you had the pox you'd be hysterical too."

He laughed and I realized that despite his condescension I was really glad he came.

"I brought videos, ice cream and extra calamine lotion."

My hero.

We settled into a movie. He made me wear mittens, so eating the ice cream was a challenge, but I made the effort, as it was the first food that didn't induce dry retching. A lot of it ended up on my face, which I cleaned on my mittens.

"Very sexy," Seán laughed.

"Ha, ha," was my only retort. I wasn't able for much more; my illness had made wit a real challenge.

"No, really, you're sitting there in flannel pajamas covered in red angry little spots, wearing mittens with ice cream all over your face. I am seriously turned on."

He was grinning, delighted with his little joke.

"Arsehole!" I was too sick to compete with his witty wonders. "Fuck off!"

"Good comeback—do you mind if I take notes?" he replied annoyingly.

I threw a pillow at him. "I'm sick. I have chickenpox. I could die," I whined, seeking pity.

He burst out laughing. "You could die!" he repeated for his own pleasure.

It sounded a little hysterical when he said it. I tried to redeem myself. "It says it in the pamphlet," I informed him plaintively. "Adults can get shingles, which in rare cases can end up with the aforementioned brain swelling and subsequent death,"

He was still laughing. "You have chickenpox. You're

going to feel crappy and itchy for a few days and then you're going to be fine."

"Fine," I agreed, "it's possible I may not die, but I am very fragile so piss off with the teasing."

"I wasn't teasing," he laughed. "You look stunning."

I tried to keep a straight face, but when I noticed the large brown ice cream stain on my pajamas I gave in and laughed. I was a bloody state and he was hilarious, the king of comedy, and I'm sure as attractive with the pox as without it. Secretly I hoped he'd get it so that we could test the theory. He put calamine lotion on my back and made me cups of tea. We watched the film together and when I needed to go to the loo he helped me remove my mittens. At ten he tucked me up in bed, ensuring my medications were lined up on my locker.

"Why are you still single?" I wondered aloud as he fluffed my pillow. "You'd make such a good boyfriend." I snuggled up.

For the first time since I'd known him he blushed. I was instantly aware of the awkwardness, which hung thickly in the air like a fart in a lift full of strangers. I pretended that I was sleepy, not really sure what had caused the sudden change in atmosphere. He backed out of the room.

"Good night," he said.

I closed my eyes, but I could feel him looking at me for a few seconds before he closed the door.

What's up with him?

He stayed over and made me breakfast. I walked into the kitchen while he was preparing a tray. He was disappointed by my sudden appearance.

"I was going to bring you breakfast in bed," he said.

I smiled. "I'm feeling a bit better."

I thanked him for coming over. He told me to sit down and handed me tea and toast. I sat while he toasted more bread.

"John's dead one year, four months and two days," I said out of nowhere.

He turned to face me.

"Really," he said.

"Yeah. I used to know offhand, but lately I have to try to work it out," I admitted.

He remained silent.

"Do you think he can see us?" I asked.

"What?" he replied.

I asked again. He said he didn't think so.

"Why? Don't you think it's a possibility that he can see us?" I challenged.

"No. Em, I don't want to think about that. I want to believe that he's somewhere better than this."

He sounded sad and I wondered why. Maybe it was a stupid question. I was just tired. I didn't want to upset him.

"I'm sorry. You're right. He probably is somewhere better. Why would he stick around?" I said, attempting to be cheery.

He turned back to his toast. "Someday you'll let go of him, Emma. I hope it's sooner rather than later," he said, straightening in his chair.

I played with my toast. "Me too," I said to the back of his head.

He left soon after that. His mood had changed and I was glad he was going as I was feeling sad and stupid. Of course he didn't want to hear about John first thing in the morning. It was depressing. He missed his friend. That's why he was acting oddly. He was moving on—that's why he wanted me to move on. It all made sense.

Except it doesn't.

★ ★ ★

Ten days later and feeling a good deal better I decided to visit the grave. I hadn't been in a long time. Time to check up on my tree and catch up. It was a crisp dry day in late spring. The trees were full and the air still. I was careful not to stand on anyone, instead sticking to the path that led me to the little tree I'd planted months before. It was blooming. Three red roses and two buds perfectly poised over the new headstone upon which his name was written.

In loving memory of
John Redmond
1972–1998
Sleeping with angels

It was nice. His mother must have picked it.
I wish he were sleeping with me.
I sat down on the dry ground.
"Hey, stranger."
Nothing.
"Sorry I haven't been around in a while."
Nothing.
"I miss you though."
Nothing.
"Seán has been minding me. I had chickenpox. They're

nearly gone. He's been very good to me. I couldn't have asked for a better friend. Do you have friends?"

Stupid question.

I looked up at the sky.

"I wish I could hear you just once, just to know you're okay. The dreams are gone now. You used to come every night. I haven't seen you for months. I wonder, will I see you again?"

I stared at his headstone for an answer. None came and then it dawned on me. I couldn't remember the sound of his voice.

Oh my God!

Tears started to pour out of my eyes, fat and loud like a leaking tap. I racked my brain but it was silent.

Oh my God!

I ran from the graveside, no longer worrying if I was jogging on someone's beloved. I got to the car and I was out of breath.

I can't remember. I can't remember!

I drove away as fast as I could. I was so ashamed.

How could I forget so soon? What is wrong with me?

I got home faster than I should have. Then I pulled apart my sitting room, my kitchen and my bedroom until I found the answering machine tape at the back of my locker where I'd put it months before. I tore the current tape out of the machine and put it in as quickly as my fingers would allow. I pressed play.

"Hi, you've reached six four zero five two six one. John and Emma are somewhere exotic so leave a message and if we like you we'll call you back."

And there he was. Relief washed over me. I still had

the tape: even if I couldn't keep him in my head, I could keep him on tape. I thanked God for answering machines. I told myself everything was going to be okay, but it wasn't. How could it be? I was a mess.

Jesus, why can't I get it together?

Chapter 17

Unlucky for Some

The summer had passed uneventfully and it was October, Friday the thirteenth, and my birthday to be exact. I woke up to my mother's rendition of "Happy Birthday," followed by "For She's a Jolly Good Fellow." I happily listened to her attempt. Although I was twenty-eight I was in good form. Why not? My friends and I were going to Paris for the weekend. I'd never been and I couldn't wait. My bags were packed from the night before. I was alert and excited.

Leonard was a dead weight on my legs. I tried to move him, but Leonard was not cooperating. I gave up and lifted him to the side. He sighed like an old man disturbed by his grandchild. He flipped over with his paws in the air, waiting for his morning tummy rub. Once I'd removed his dead weight the feeling in my legs returned. In the shower I sang about love. I was going to Paris after all, I might as well get into the spirit. I was dressed and ready to go when Clo and Tom came to pick me up. We were

meeting Anne and Richard at the airport and Seán was
already in Paris. He had to interview a French rapper for
an article he was doing on the global phenomenon that is
hip-hop. It wasn't his area, but his colleague had come
down with a nasty case of pneumonia and he was forced
to step into the breach. He was asked to follow this rapper
for one week, kind of a week-in-the-life-of type thing.
Once the rest of us discovered he would be staying in his
own apartment, it wasn't long before we had arranged to
use his free accommodation and my birthday as the
perfect excuse to get away.

We flew into a tiny airport surrounded by a lot of
fields. Not exactly how I'd pictured Paris. We were herded
onto a bus, which took another hour and a half to get
into the city, but I didn't care. Tom and Clo were sitting
down the back, locked in their own little world of
romance and laughter. Anne and Richard sat opposite
me. He was reading out passages of a guide to Paris while
she took notes of particular points of interest. I watched
the road pass beneath us, listening to my Walkman and
looking forward to seeing Seán. I had missed him all week.
I hadn't noticed how much I relied on him. Now that Clo
had found her soul mate she didn't have as much time for
her ordinary mates. Not that she wasn't around—it was
just that now she had someone to consider. Anne and
Richard lived in Kerry. The last time I'd heard from Noel
he was in South America picking fruit. Seán was single
like me, so it made sense that we spent more time
together. It had been a long week without him and I
couldn't wait to catch up.

He was waiting at the bus stop—conveniently placed

outside an Irish pub. Anne and Richard were the first to greet him. He was smiling and talking animatedly as I descended the steps. I was really looking forward to a hug, but when I reached the ground I realized the reason for his excitement. He was introducing the blonde beauty beside him to our friends. She was a tanned, tiny-waisted, knitted-top and perky-tits Frenchwoman, kissing Richard on both cheeks while he grinned and his wife stood back smiling pleasantly.

Seán was busy so I went to collect my bag from under the bus with a heavy heart. I wasn't in the mood to hang around with the French despite my location. Clo emerged from the bus and descended the steps, admiring the view of this Paris backstreet, wearing pink cashmere, sunglasses and lip gloss. She could have been a movie star alighting from a private jet. Despite the month, the skies were blue but sunglasses were definitely not required. Tom was behind her carrying her handbag, makeup bag and her carry-on luggage, which she had refused to put under the bus. I suddenly realized I was surrounded by couples.

Ah crap!

We didn't bother with the Irish pub; Seán had too many places that he wanted to show us. Françoise, or Frankie as he liked to call her, was the rapper's sister and she'd taken a shine to our friend the first day he met her. They had been inseparable for a week. This was mainly because he was ghosting her brother and she was her brother's PA. She hung over him like a cheap suit while we ate lunch outside a pretty little café in Montmartre. Everyone was talking excitedly about what he or she wanted to do and where he or she wanted to go. Their conversation faded into the background while I took time to adjust to our new addition, the lovely Frankie, who seemed to warm to everyone but me.

It was only when we were paying the waiter that I took time to look around. It was beautiful. Old cobbled streets, artists painting, American students and young couples on the footpaths all around. Little cake shops displaying fancy cakes and fresh bread, the smell of which wafted through the streets. The mopeds, the bikes, the attractive Frenchmen who whistled at the girls who walked by confident and nonchalant, well used to being admired. The Sacré Cœur stood majestically in the background. I could see its spire from where I was sitting.

It didn't feel like a city: it felt like a cosmopolitan glamorous village that belonged to another time and place. I was in love.

★ ★ ★

We were following Seán and his French loaf back to the apartment. Clo was busy taking photographs of pretty much everything that moved or stood still, birds munching on bread crumbs, cute shopfronts, a bike, a couple kissing, a waiter serving coffee to an old man wearing a silk scarf. She looked like an American tourist. She just kept clicking, afraid she'd miss something. Tom was ably assisting by pointing out anything she could have missed.

"That car is cool."

"Got it."

"The old woman."

"Got her."

"Oh wow, look at that carousel!"

"Get on it."

He complied, smiling and waving.

"Pretend you don't know I'm here—just sit on the horse and look wistful."

He sat and attempted wistful.

"Got it."

Anne and Richard laughed at them while holding hands and whispering about making a baby in the city of love. Frankie walked ahead with Seán, her hand inside his back jeans pocket, signaling to all that his ass was taken. I just looked around, taking it all in. I felt like I was as close to heaven as is possible. The blue sky seemed to come from the ground beneath me. It was all around. If there were villages in the sky they would all look like Montmartre.

We reached the apartment and took an old, ornate and ludicrously small lift to the top floor. The wooden floors smelled of polish, the windows were tall and encased in pretty white wood. The kitchen was small with a little oven and a large fridge. The sitting room was surrounded by glass looking over the busy street below. A large painting of a young girl cycling through a tree-lined street hung on the wall. She looked happy, but then why shouldn't she be—she got to live in Paris. There were three bedrooms, all immediately taken by the couples. I got the pullout in the sitting room.

"Are you sure this is okay?" Seán asked.

"It's fine," I nodded. "I'd rather this than walk in on a couple first thing in the morning."

He nodded. It was a good point. It was obvious that

everyone was intent on having as much French sex as possible. He pointed to the stereo.

"There's a stereo."

"I've got earplugs."

He nodded again, grinning. He turned to join the others, who were rammed into the kitchen, attempting to work out the coffee machine. He got to the door and he turned as though he was going to say something, but words appeared to fail him.

"What?" I asked hopefully, although I wasn't sure what I was hoping to hear.

"What do you think of Frankie?" he asked.

"She seems nice," I lied. She was arrogant and stuck out her tits whenever she wanted to make a point.

"Yeah, well, it's not like I'll be seeing her after Sunday," he said, searching my face for an expression.

I wasn't sure what kind of expression he was looking for so I just smiled.

"A girl in every port," I laughed.

"Yeah," he agreed, but he obviously didn't find it as funny as I pretended it to be.

★ ★ ★

We ate in a quaint little restaurant of Frankie's choosing.

"It's for the French," she said mysteriously.

It was an odd thing to say, as we were in fucking France so who else would it be for?

She must have copped my expression. "Not the stupid tourists. Good food, good price, no ripoff," she noted before sipping on her cheap wine.

Great, we're stupid tourists.

Clo smiled before taking a picture of the flower-framed window. The waiter took our orders. I was looking forward to the rack of lamb, having earlier chosen something that turned out to be wolf meat.

"*Comment voulez-vous votre viande, Madame?*"

"Excuse me?"

"Your meat, how would you like it cooked?" Frankie intoned while shaking her head knowingly at the waiter. *Bitch*.

"Well done." I didn't look at either of them, instead concentrating on the menu.

"*Bien cuit,*" she translated.

He nodded at her and walked away.

"It's so authentic," Anne said.

I could see Frankie give her the same look I have given Americans who say "everything is cute and small."

Clo and Tom were holding hands under the linen tablecloth. I was a gooseberry at my own birthday dinner. Seán must have noticed my pathetic demeanor. He raised his glass and the others followed suit.

"Here's to the birthday girl—may she always stay beautiful!"

I blushed. The others laughed and smiled. Frankie looked me up and down, making it quite obvious she had no idea what he was talking about. You could almost hear her thoughts: *You have to be beautiful to stay beautiful.*

I didn't give a toss. It was a nice thing to say, so screw her. The waiter arrived with our meals. Mine was last, of course. Everyone made a big deal about waiting until eventually it was obvious their food was getting cold. When my meat eventually arrived it was barely cooked. The waiter almost dropped the plate in front of me and walked off before I could register the blood flowing into my potato gratin. I cut into it, revealing pink flesh.

Oh my God, it's alive!

Richard was the first to notice my horror. "I thought you said well done?"

Anne peered at my dinner plate. "It certainly took long enough."

"Jesus," was all I could manage.

Frankie leaned in to see what all the fuss was about. "What's wrong? It's fine—eat!"

I really didn't like her. "I asked for well done," I said snottily.

"It's not blue. It's cooked. Look, brown." She was pointing at the outside of the meat.

I was pissed off so I held up what looked like road-kill on my fork. "Look, it's pink and bloody," I said sarcastically.

Seán, realizing this could get nasty, called the waiter back. He appeared over me, looking down.

"Yes," he said.

The bastard could speak English.

"I asked for well done," I said, attempting to match his arrogance.

"Yes," he said and he walked away.

Everyone stopped eating.

"What a prick!" Clodagh intoned while Tom nodded his head in agreement.

"Sorry, Em, they are a bit funny about their meat," said Seán.

Frankie smiled as though she had secured some sort of

victory. I pushed the plate away and poured a large glass of wine.

Happy birthday to me.

★ ★ ★

The nightclub was on a street just off the Champs-Élysées. Music blared, people danced, big comfy booths lined the walls around the dance floor. They were full of young men watching the half-naked girls gyrating with one another. Unlike in Ireland, there was no queue at the bar. At least something was going my way. I ordered a double vodka and Coke and sat at the edge of the booth that Frankie had managed to secure.

"VIP will open soon," she said.

"Are we going into the VIP?" Clo asked excited.

"Of course," she said snottily, as though Clodagh was a little slow. "My brother is a famous French rapper—where do you think we would drink? A barn?" She was pointing into Clodagh's face. Her finger was inches away from Clodagh's right eye.

"Why not? It would appear that you were brought up in one!" Clo said, stepping back from her long finger.

Frankie scowled. "You bore me!"

I wanted to punch her but I was a little afraid of her—she looked like she could be vicious with those long nails of hers. Clo obviously felt the same, as she waited until Frankie's back was turned before giving her the fingers.

Within an hour we were in the far more salubrious VIP room. Frankie marched us in like she owned the place. Anne, Clo and I hung back, not too concerned about whether or not we got in. Our need to bitch was way too strong.

"What a bitch!" Anne said.

"She doesn't like us," Clo smirked.

"Yeah, well, she can piss off," I concluded.

"There's our girl," Clo laughed.

The bouncer was looking at us quizzically.

"We're with Françoise," Anne told them.

"Who?" the bald bouncer with the pecks asked.

Exactly, I thought, pleased with myself.

Tom came back to the door. "They're with us," he smiled at Baldy.

"Go ahead," he said and unhitched the red rope between us ordinary folk and French celebrity.

The room was dark and only lit by candlelight. Each booth was circular with high backs so as to give those with high profiles the illusion of privacy. We found a booth with Frankie's brother's name on it. His posse was already ensconced. Introductions followed. I just nodded mutely while Seán shook hands with his new friends.

"Where's Pierre?" he asked.

"Bar," one of them answered.

I sat beside Seán just to piss Frankie off.

"What do you think?" he asked.

"Great if you like banging your glass off your teeth."

"I love the dark," he grinned.

I smiled. It wasn't so bad. Clodagh and Tom were slow dancing to a fast track. Anne and Richard were in a deep conversation. Then Frankie shoved her tongue down Seán's throat in a bid to get his attention. Some French guy tried to make conversation, but with the loud music and the fact that his English was about as good as my French, we gave up after mere seconds. Frankie looked up from her tongue job.

"Pierre!" she waved.

Pierre, a tall brunet with golden highlights, gleaming smile and a body carved out of precious stone smiled at his sister. He said good-bye to a waif-like model that I recognized from *Vogue* and she retreated into her own dark corner. He approached and smiled at one and all.

"Do you mind if I sit?" he asked and I shoved over.

"I'm Pierre."

"Emma."

"Ah, Seán's friend," he smiled.

"Yeah," I nodded.

"You like Paris." It wasn't a question.

"Beautiful."

"You're dark Irish, not ginger!" He laughed at his own joke.

"You're observant," I said, attempting to be snotty, but it wasn't as easy to be snotty to Pierre as it was to his sister.

He smiled. "Fire," he said.

"Excuse me?"

"Fire in your belly, no? You dark Irish."

I just smiled. I hadn't a clue what he was trying to get at. We sat for a while sipping at our drinks. He spoke to the others about his musical career and his chart success, tour dates, press responsibilities. I'd never heard of him.

Boring.

I smoked. The great thing about Paris is that smoking is not only tolerated, but also condoned, and although I was normally a light smoker, the circumstances ensured that I would make use of this reprieve. I lit another smoke. He took it out of my hand and dragged on it long and hard.

"Thank you," he said, grinning.

I just lit another cigarette. This Frenchman was way too smooth for his own good. Still, he was pretty. I liked looking at him, especially when I realized that Seán was staring. After all, he wasn't the only one who could score.

"Would you like to dance with me?"

"Maybe later," I answered smugly.

Bet you're not used to hearing that, are you?

He was intrigued. I could tell he was used to women falling all over him.

"Come with me?" he said and stood up.

I found my hand in his and suddenly I was on my feet and crossing the dance floor. He was commanding, I'd give him that. I could feel Seán and Frankie's eyes on our backs and when I looked around to wave neither of them looked too happy.

He took me outside to a private balcony that overlooked a little courtyard full of trees, flowers and little fountains lit up by blue lights. We sat on the bench and he put a fresh cigarette in my mouth and lit it. I inhaled and smiled at him, hoping he didn't notice that I was feeling a little light-headed. He touched my hair.

"I like dark."

"The blue lights are nice."

"I meant you."

"I know."

"You're single, no?"

"Yes."

"Seán told me about his friend, your boyfriend. I'm sorry."

I had been feeling pretty smug. Smug and dizzy, but this really threw me. "Oh," I stammered.

"I didn't mean to cause pain."

"You didn't," I smiled convincingly.

"Good. Life is for living."

"I never realized I was in the presence of genius." I said it before I'd managed to think about it, but luckily enough he found my jibe entertaining.

He threw his head back and laughed. "I like you Irish. I like Seán. He's fun."

"Yeah."

"Not so much for me as my sister."

He was laughing again and I laughed too—his giggle was infectious. We sat in silence for a time and it was comfortable. I could feel his thigh resting against mine. The night sky was lit up with stars and it was like they had been hung there especially for us. I hadn't looked up into a dark sky in so long. I felt like I was in a Van Gogh painting. Things were beginning to look up. I had a moment of realization. I was sitting on a VIP balcony with a French god. It was true that I'd never heard of him, but millions had. He was a celebrity.

What the hell was he doing hanging out with me?

"How many girls are wishing they were me right now?" I asked out of nowhere.

He smiled, enjoying my honest questioning. "A lot," he grinned, flashing a sexy little crooked tooth.

"So why are you wasting your time with me?" I said. "You *are* wasting your time, you know," I added, putting him straight. I wasn't about to have sex with some French celebrity.

He wasn't perturbed. "I never waste time," he said brightly.

I laughed. He was sexy. I could see Clodagh through the glass door. It was obvious that she was the scout sent to report back to the others. She grinned and gave me the thumbs-up. He caught her and mimicked her gesture. She jumped back and pretended she was talking to someone who gave her a dirty look before moving on. We laughed together as she made a hasty retreat.

"Your friend, does she think I'm wasting time?"

"My friend doesn't think."

I didn't mean it, of course, but I was really enjoying our banter. A slow French song I didn't recognize played inside.

"We will dance now, yes?"

He was standing over me with his hand outstretched. I gave him my hand and he pulled me from the chair. I was standing in front of him, waiting for him to make the next move, but he was happy to let me stand against his chest for a moment before he took me in his arms. Suddenly we were dancing. He smelled good. He put his hands through my hair and cupped my face, ensuring that I had nowhere to look but his face. It was a pretty face and he knew it. The trick was not to get lost in his eyes. I focused on his mouth. That was a mistake. Suddenly his pouting French lips looked like a chilled Coke bar in the desert.

Oh my God!

"I'm not planning on sleeping with you." I said it more for my own sake than his.

"Why not?" he asked.

Good question. I hadn't thought about that.

"You don't like me?"

"If I didn't like you I wouldn't be dancing," I said, glad my series of blushes was hidden beneath the dark sky.

He laughed. "I like you. You are different."

"Everybody's different—sometimes they just act the same."

He smiled and nodded his head. "You are smart."

I was beginning to get bored with his observations. "You like to point things out, don't you, big man?"

He laughed again.

I liked it when he laughed.

"Let's go." He was raising the stakes.

"Go where?" I was marking time.

"Let me take you to my home."

I snorted.

"Attractive," he grinned.

"Cheers," I smiled, remaining cool, although deep down I wished I hadn't made a noise through my nose.

"Come," he said and I found myself succumbing and following his lead.

He grabbed his jacket and my bag. I was impressed that he could so easily determine which bag was mine, seeing as there were at least four under the table. Seán and Frankie were staring at us. Anne and Richard were dancing. Clo approached from the rear.

"Are you leaving?" she asked, obviously excited by the prospect.

"Yes," Pierre answered before winking at her.

Seán sat back in his seat.

"See you, Seán," Pierre smiled warmly at his new friend.

"Yeah, see you."

Seán couldn't seem to manage a smile. Frankie was horrified. I grinned at her and she pouted while staring back, ready to take a slice out of me. Pierre and I walked out together. I pretended not to notice the girls in the club staring and pointing and even ignored those who attempted to touch and grab at him as he passed.

What's that all about?

We were escorted out by nightclub security. A car and its sleepy driver were waiting outside.

"Rue Boissière"

"Oui, Monsieur Dulac, tout droit."

We settled into the backseat. He put his arm around me.

"Don't worry. I won't bite. Unless you ask."

"I won't ask."

He grinned. "Maybe. Maybe not."

"You're sure of yourself."

"And you are not."

Damn. Game, set and match to Mr. Dulac. I grinned. The driver sped through Paris at an alarming rate, so much so that at one point I felt like screaming, "Slow down, you lunatic!" I was getting edgy, but to Pierre it was just another night. I made myself relax. When the car stopped I sighed with relief.

"Let's go." He took my hand and helped me out of the car.

We were in his apartment block before I got time to catch my breath. He was used to making fast exits. The lobby was like that of a 1920s hotel. Brass was the predominant feature. It had dark red walls and bright modern art lined them. We got into the brass lift—again it was a tight fit.

What is it with the French and tiny lifts?

I looked at the floor, signaling that I had no ambition to make out in a confined space. He continued to grin like the cat that got the cream or, in Leonard's case, the entire contents of an ice-cream van. Once inside his apartment, I began to wonder what I was playing at. It was getting a little intense. I had no idea where I was or what I was planning on doing. He took me to the sofa and sat me down. It was a chaise longue, red and dangerous-looking. He put on some music. I didn't recognize it. It was French jazz. He poured drinks from a bar that filled the corner of the room. He handed me vodka with a splash of Coke. I could have done with more Coke, but I wasn't complaining.

He moved in toward me, and my heart was racing. We were about to kiss and then the strangest thing happened. We talked. I mean, really talked. He asked me about John and I told him. I told him things, some of which even Clo wasn't party to. He told me about the girl who had broken his heart by leaving for America. She had never returned. A few years after they split she had died in a fire. He didn't compare our pain and it wasn't a competition.

We laughed a lot. We had the same outlook, same sense of humor, same ideals. There were differences too. He was a hip-hop god while I was a teacher. He loved to sleep around while I wasn't that way inclined. He was arrogant and I was self-conscious. But we had fun. He told me sexy stories and I pretended to be a little bit more shocked than I was, purely because he enjoyed my horror too much to let him down. We drank into the early hours and fell asleep together on top of his covers. I woke a couple of hours later and he was awake and staring at me.

"Hello," he said, smiling.

"Hey," I mumbled, attempting to cover my mouth.

I could smell mint on his breath. He'd obviously brushed his teeth while I slept.

"Where's the loo?"

He pointed. I entered the en suite and coated my finger with toothpaste. I cleaned out my mouth as best I could, splashed my face and reentered. He was waiting, knowing that I had been preparing myself for something other than merely going home. He was under the covers. I walked over and he held the sheet up to allow me in. I obliged and then we were kissing, French kissing.

What followed? Well, all I can say is if he could sing as well as he could shag, he deserved his god-like status. Better again, when it was over I didn't cry.

A few hours later he kissed me good-bye before giving his driver orders to take me back to Seán's apartment.

"Will I see you again?" he asked.

"No," I grinned.

He nodded. "Sad." He smiled.

"Thanks," I said and I meant it. I really had needed to get laid.

"You're welcome." He patted the roof of the car and the driver took off.

I didn't look back. I knew he wasn't watching.

★ ★ ★

Clo and Tom were still in bed. Anne and Richard had left hours earlier to make the most of the day. I was in the kitchen fumbling for the coffee beans. I felt someone enter behind me. It was Seán, in pajama bottoms, nothing else. I grinned at him, but he was too angry to respond in kind.

"Where the hell were you?" He was pointing and his finger shook ever so slightly.

"Excuse me?" I said defensively.

"What the hell is this? I've been up half the night worrying about you!"

His finger fell to his side, but his face retained all of its anger.

"You know where I was. Stop being an asshole!" I was matching his tone. "You're not my father."

"No, Emma, I know who you were with and judging by what I've seen this week, that could've meant anywhere or doing anything. How was I to know that he hadn't got bored after an hour? You don't know him."

Every ounce of joy I had felt as I drove away from my romantic evening was taken away. The fleeting freedom from guilt was gone. He was making it dirty and wrong. He was saying I was one in a long line of women, I was nothing and that I should feel bad.

I'm not going to cry.

Tears stung my eyes but I refused to let them fall. Anger was filling my throat, my voice battling to get past it. "You are a hypocritical bastard! It's all right for you to fuck everything that moves, but it's not okay for me to have one night. Your French tart sucks on your ear all through dinner and that's fine. After all, you're a stud—but me, well, I'm just a sad old slapper. Don't waste your time worrying about me, Seán. I don't fucking need you!"

He blanched. I'd never actually seen anyone do that before. His whole face lost its color instantly like I'd turned off the switch.

"I didn't mean it like that. I didn't mean that you . . . I'm sorry. I was just worried." His overreaction didn't make sense.

Liar. He had ruined everything. "What did you mean then?" I yelled.

"We're friends," he mumbled.

"Oh, so are all my other friends going to come in here and scream at me?"

"No." He was shaking his head, looking for an answer.

"So what is it then, Seán?" My voice had grown weary. It was getting harder to hold off the tears.

"I . . ." He stopped and looked around for nothing in particular.

I waited.

"I . . ." He stopped again.

What the hell is wrong with him?

"I'm sorry," he said and he walked out, leaving me standing alone with a half-open bag of coffee beans and I was crying.

Damn it.

I was still crying and hunched over my espresso when Clo emerged from her room. I had my back to her when she entered. She was clapping. I felt her arms around my shoulders.

"You are such a dark horse. Pierre Dulac! I mean, I know we've never heard of him, but who the hell are we? By God, when you do it, you do it in style!" Her voice was full of excitement.

189

I looked up at her and her smile dissipated.

"What happened? Did he hurt you?"

My tearstained face belied the truth about my romantic evening.

"No," I sighed. "Last night was perfect and so was this morning—that is, until I got here."

She put her hands on her hips, something she often did when confused. "I'm not with you."

"Seán," I mumbled.

"Seán?" she probed.

"Seán seems to think I did something wrong last night."

"He what? What do you mean?" She pulled up a stool and sat beside me, her cheek resting on her arm resting on the counter.

I looked down at her and shrugged my shoulders, signaling my bewilderment.

"He was roaring at me." I was crying again. I couldn't believe how crappy I was feeling. It was so unfair.

"Don't mind him. He's being a dick. You have a shower and change your clothes. We'll get out of here, do a bit of sightseeing and then we can have lunch and you can tell me all about last night."

She was smiling again. I felt a little better. I had an amazing night and I could either let Seán take that away or not. I chose not.

Seán was locked away in his room with Frankie when we left. We didn't leave a note. Tom went to meet Anne and Richard, honoring our preexisting commitment to meet them for a trip down the Seine. Clodagh had explained that we needed some time alone and he was happy to oblige. We picked up a Métro map and we were off. First stop, Hotel de Ville for a coffee. We were sitting in the bar downstairs, drinking coffee and smoking cigarettes even though it was only ten in the morning and I usually don't smoke until after one, but when in Rome . . .

Clodagh had ordered croissants, which I was devouring, having suddenly realized that I was starving. She was smiling patiently, waiting for me to tell her about celebrity sex, but not wanting to push it. Suddenly she brightened like a little bulb had come on inside her head.

"I know! Let's play a game. I'll tell you something personal if you tell me."

I laughed—she was so obvious. "Okay. You first."

She nodded her head, preparing herself. "Okay. Tom is divorced."

My face fell. I'd expected her to say something stupid just to get me talking. "I thought he wasn't married?"

"He isn't, he's divorced."

"Oh my God! When did he tell you? Was he married long?"

"Emma, this isn't about me. It's your turn," she sighed, signaling that discussion was not part of the game.

"Okay. I didn't have sex with Pierre last night."

"What?" she almost roared.

An old man looked over and grunted.

"What?" she whispered. "You didn't have sex? Oh my God, Emma, I'm so fucking disappointed. Why not?"

Her face was a picture and I was beginning to forget Seán.

"Clo, this is not about me. It's your turn," I smiled.

Two can play at this game.

191

"Fine." She straightened up in her chair. "Tom has two kids. Mia is nine and Liam is four."

I think I may have blanched. "Two kids?"

She nodded.

"Have you met them?"

"Your turn."

I was beginning to tire of this game. "Fine, I had sex with Pierre this morning."

She burst out laughing. "Yes. Oh yes! Thank you, God!"

We were both laughing.

"What was it like?" She was jumping slightly in her chair. It was time to end this charade and find out what was really going on with Tom, because shag or no shag, that's what we really needed to talk about.

"You tell me about Tom and his kids and what it all means and I'll tell you about my morning with Pierre Dulac."

So she told me.

Tom was seventeen when his girlfriend got pregnant. They had Mia. He got a job in a computer factory. He was married and had a mortgage at twenty-one. He worked hard during the day and did computer courses by night. She got a job in a flower shop. They had Liam. Tom opened his business. He became successful quickly, but he was never home. His wife met someone at the flower shop. She had an affair. He left. It was messy for a while, but amicable in the end. They both realized that they had been going through the motions. They had just married too young. She did well in the divorce. She'd since remarried and he saw his kids on weekends. He told

Clodagh about his past on their first date. She had met his children and, although it was clear she wasn't Mary Poppins, they were getting on all right. She was happy and it didn't matter.

"Are you sure?"

"Initially it was a worry, especially with my luck. That's why I didn't say anything. I needed to work it out for myself."

She was worried I'd be offended that she hadn't told me, but deep down she knew it didn't matter.

"You're in love."

"Yeah, I am," she agreed smiling. "First time for everything," she added, laughing.

Wow, Clo was in love. There was light at the end of the tunnel.

I'd like to be able to say that we spent the rest of the day in museums, galleries and old Parisian churches but I can't. We shopped, buying in Old Navy, Gap, Naf Naf, the list went on. We bought dresses, shoes and bags. Clodagh bought a watch. We ate lunch outdoors, watching our fellow shoppers go by. We looked in Prada, Gucci and Chanel just for a few minutes, then out the door before one of the beady-eyed salespeople spotted us, blew a whistle and kicked us out. In the late afternoon we walked along the winding little backstreets, absorbing the atmosphere.

It was after eight when we got back. Anne, Richard and Tom were playing poker in the sitting room. Frankie and Seán were out. Anne made tea and we filled her in on our day. She talked about the *Mona Lisa*. It had been a letdown and her feet were killing her. She loved the galleries and had bought a painting that would be shipped to Kerry. Tom was in great spirits, having thoroughly enjoyed his sightseeing. He and Richard bonded over a mini-case of seasickness on the *bateau-mouche*, but they had recovered enough to enjoy four pints in the afternoon.

We were all starving so Anne left a note telling Seán which restaurant we would be in. Over dinner Tom showed us pictures of his kids. Everyone was happy and in good spirits. I aimed for the vegetarian option and got fed. It was a good night, but Seán was missing. It reminded me of our fight and all the ugly things we'd said. I felt tired. The others wanted to go for a drink, but I made my excuses. They blamed my weariness on having had a good ride and they were partly right.

Clo and Tom walked me around the corner to the apartment. They waited until I was inside before they walked away arm in arm. I sat on the sofa and lit up. Seán entered from his bedroom quietly and sat down next to me. I handed him a cigarette. He took it gratefully. We sat in silence.

"You were right. I'm an asshole."

"You're not an asshole. You're just an insensitive tosser," I smiled. It was impossible to stay annoyed with him.

"I would never intentionally say anything to hurt you."

"I know."

"I'm sorry."

"I know."

He looked so lost I couldn't help but put my arms around him and we hugged.

"Where's Frankie?" I asked mid-hug.

His arms stiffened. "Gone."

I remembered that Pierre and his posse were heading

off to Canada that afternoon. She was part of the posse so it made sense.

"Oh well," I sighed, "at least we have each other."

He kissed the top of my head and we lay in one another's arms exhausted and fell asleep.

Chapter 18

The Sound of Music,
Plastic Tits and Bruce Willis

It was coming up to Christmas and I was dreading it. I had
to look forward to at least three Christmas parties, which I
was being forced to attend, battling to get Christmas presents,
crowds, wrapping, extending my Visa credit, "Jingle Bells,"
queuing in the post office for four hours, marking
Christmas tests and Wham's bloody "Last Christmas" on
the radio every five minutes, culminating with Christmas
Day spent with my parents fighting over the remote. At
least Noel was coming home. The rest of it was almost
worth it. I was wrapping presents when the phone rang.

"Hello?"

"Emma, *crackle, crackle* . . ."

"Hello?" *Crackle, crackle* . . .

I shook the phone, something I always did when I had
a bad line. It never helped, but it felt like I was doing
something.

"Emma, *crackle, crackle*. It's me, Noel."

"Noel, is that you?" *Crackle, buzz, crackle.*

"The line is really *crackle, crackle, crackle . . .*"

"Noel, oh my God! Where are you calling from? It's so good to hear your voice!" *Buzz.* "Damn this line."

"Goa *buzzzzzzzzzzzzzzzzzzzz.*"

"Are you okay?" *Crackle, crackle, crackle.* "When are you coming home?"

"Em, I'm not. *Crackle, crackle, crackle . . .* Tell *crackle, crackle* that *crackle, crackle.* Sorry. I'd *crackle* to but I'll call on *crackle* day."

"What?" *Buzzzzzzzzzzzzzzzzz.* "You're not coming home?" My heart sank.

"I *crackle* time *crackle* love you *crackle* I'm *crackle.*"

"You're what?"

"Fine!"

"I love you too!" I shouted.

The line went dead.

"Fuck!"

How was I going to break this to the parents?

Oh Noel, please come home!

I was upset, then pissed off, then really pissed off. He had called me with the bad news so that I was the one who had to break it to our parents. He was doing God knows what in Goa and I was left on the receiving end of their wrath.

That's like something I'd do.

I decided to get it out of the way as soon as possible. I fixed myself a hot port and dialed home.

Bloody Christmas.

★ ★ ★

There was one bright side to the season. Clo, Tom, Seán and I were heading down to Kerry to spend New Year's Eve with Anne and Richard and I was really looking forward to that. I missed them and I couldn't wait to see their place and to get out of Dublin. I was excited so I planned to grin and bear the rest of it. That was the plan—the reality was somewhat different.

Tom ran his own graphic design company, which meant that he threw a company Christmas party. Clodagh attempted to entice us to attend.

"It'll be great," she said.

I didn't want to go and complained loudly. She told me to shut up. It had been over a month since Paris and as soon as we returned to Dublin the old unsocial me had taken up residence once more. She was fed up of it.

Seán didn't complain—he was in a party mood. He'd met some New Yorker who was working with the magazine for two months. She was an executive type, blonde hair, tall and big tits. Basically, most women's worst nightmare. Despite his vow to never date a co-worker again, he appeared smitten and needed an excuse to ask her out. Tom's Christmas party was perfect.

I was busy getting ready. The doorbell rang. I ran down the stairs, cursing the pizza man. It was Seán. He was early.

"You're early," I said while trying to towel-dry my hair.

"Yeah," he agreed. "I had a late meeting in town."

"How'd it go?" I asked while running up the stairs, not waiting for his answer.

He made himself at home. The pizza man arrived and he paid him. I arrived downstairs fifteen minutes and half the pizza later. He looked up from the near-empty box. "I was hungry," he said.

I sat down and started to eat the remains. "So how did it go?" I asked again, this time actually awaiting the answer.

"Good." But he didn't appear happy.

"What's wrong?" I asked.

"Nothing," he answered.

This was annoying. I knew that he had something to tell me. I could always tell when he was holding back.

"Well?" I said.

"Well," he repeated.

Christ, it's like talking to my mother. I gave him a dirty look.

"Okay," he surrendered, "my boss called me in to his office and asked me if I would like a promotion."

I was delighted. "Oh my God! That's amazing. Congratulations. What's the job?"

He wasn't smiling. "Editor," he said unhappily.

"Wow," I said cautiously. "Amazing."

"Yeah," he said. "The thing is, it's editor of a new sister magazine. I'd be based in London."

I stopped smiling. "London," I repeated.

"Yeah," he said while looking at my clean floor.

"London, England?" It just came out.

"No, London, Spain." He almost laughed.

"Wow." Then I repeated the word "London" because I was having difficulty allowing it to sink in. I felt a lump in my throat. *Oh my God, I'm going to cry.* To give myself something to do I picked up the pizza box and put it in the bin, then turned away to make coffee. He was silent. "That's great," I repeated.

"You think so?" His voice was small.

"What's the money like?" I asked, delaying a response. *What was I supposed to say? Don't go?*

"It's good money," he repeated dully.

Seán loved Dublin. Unlike most of us, he never complained about the dirt or the late bus. He lived in Joyce's Dublin. He acknowledged the beauty of this ancient city, the old, the new, the tradition, its people and of course the old-fashioned *craic*. He actually got excited when he stood at the taxi rank on Dame Street. He'd spin around, observing the glory of the Central Bank and Trinity College, the two concrete works of art that closeted him.

"This is where Stoker first thought of the idea for Dracula," he told me once.

I remembered laughing at him one cold night as he pointed out the Central Bank lit up in all its glory. "You can see how these buildings inspired him, can't you?" he had said, seeing something that I would never see.

He would miss Dublin and I would miss him. I didn't want to turn around because my eyes were filling up.

"It's a good opportunity," he said for both our benefits.

I stuck my head in the fridge, feigning difficulty in reaching the milk.

Don't cry. Be a friend. This isn't about you.

I turned with milk in my hand. "It's great news. You should be really proud. I'm really happy for you." I smiled, hoping to convince.

He looked down. "Great," he repeated.

I tried to brighten. "So when are you leaving?" I asked, afraid of his answer.

"The end of January."

"That soon?" I managed.

"That soon," he agreed.

My heart sank as I smiled widely. "That's great," I repeated once too often.

He wanted to leave, so he called a taxi while I pretended to look for some lipstick. I sat on my bed and I wanted to bawl. My head felt heavy so I held it in my hands.

"Fuck," I said to the wall. *What can I do? I can't tell him to stay. That's selfish. I can't tell him that losing him would be unbearable, because I'm not his girlfriend. We're just friends.*

I missed him already and I felt sick, but we had a party to go to. I put on more lipstick. The taxi came and we left.

We arrived after nine. The party was in full swing. Clo was drunk.

"I drank too much wine at dinner," she confided. "And I didn't eat enough dinner at dinner. The chicken was foul." She laughed at her devastatingly witty comment. She could see that I wasn't amused. "Jesus! Who shoved a fork up your—"

I interrupted, "Seán's leaving."

"He's just got here," she pointed out.

"He's moving to London at the end of January."

She sobered up momentarily. "You are joking."

"Do I look like I'm joking?"

"Did you ask him to stay?" she asked.

I was taken aback. "Of course not. It's none of my business." I was annoyed by her question and wondered whether she was keeping up with our conversation or having her own one in her head. "What the fuck would I ask him to stay for?"

She put her hands in the air. "No reason, Emma. No reason at all. I'm going to the bar." She left.

What the fuck was that?

★ ★ ★

Tom was talking to a female member of his staff. He was smiling and making small talk and I had no interest. Clo had disappeared and I briefly wondered if she had already retired to the cloakroom for forty winks. I looked around and sipped at my vodka. Seán was standing at the bar, talking with his blonde coworker.

Bitch.

He caught me watching them. I smiled at him, embarrassed, and then scanned the room, pretending that I was looking for Clo. I finished my drink. Tom noticed and another one magically appeared. Clo returned from whence she had gone.

"Where did you go?" I asked.

"I needed to pee. How long has Tom been talking to her?"

"Not long."

"Bitch!" she whispered.

"What have I done now?" I asked, pissed off that I had bothered to come out.

"Not you. Her!" She pointed out the woman Tom was talking to.

I asked what the problem was and she told me that Tom used to go out with her.

Who cares? Seán's moving to London.

"So?" I said unhelpfully.

"So. She's a bitch," she replied.

Tom came back to the table with his hands up. "I was only talking to her."

Clo pretended she didn't know what he was talking about.

Tom smiled. "It's a Christmas party and I was with her a long time before I knew you. She's a nice girl who's engaged to an insurance broker," he said sweetly.

She smiled, delighted. "I'm sure she's lovely. Still, she'll always be a bitch to me," she said honestly.

"And why is that?" he asked.

"She had her tongue in your mouth."

He nodded his head and it seemed to put her case to rest. He grinned. Then he put his tongue in her mouth. She giggled and they started necking. Clo had an amazing ability to be able to neck and yet still clear at least four more drinks. I was still on my second. Watching Seán and the blonde flirt was choking me. I was staring. He had his back to me so it seemed pretty safe, that is until the blonde bitch noticed and pointed it out. He turned to meet his audience and I smiled widely, got up and walked up to them, mortified.

"Hi," I said. I shook her hand. "I'm Emma. I've been waiting for an introduction, but you know what Seán is like." I was grinning, but it was stupid grinning.

"Julia," she replied shortly and we shook hands.

I asked them if they wanted a drink. They said no. "Cool," I said.

Cool—what, am I fourteen? Then I told myself I was an idiot.

I needed to go to the loo.

Clo grabbed me en route. "Are you going to the loo?"

"Yeah."

"Thank God. My back teeth are floating," she admitted, hanging on to my sleeve. Halfway across the floor she buckled, so I carried her the rest of the way. I held her up while waiting in the endless queue. She asked me what I thought of Seán's blonde. I said I didn't know.

"I think she's great," she said.

I let her go and she fell to the floor.

"Unfair!" She wagged her finger while getting up.

"Sorry," I muttered and resumed holding her. "How would you know anyway?"

She squared up and I could tell she was seeing four of me.

"You haven't spoken to her once."

She disagreed. Apparently Julia had made it to the party an hour before Seán and me.

"American women are so independent, aren't they?" she noted.

"Are you taking the piss?" I asked, annoyed.

She laughed. "You just won't see it." She threw her head back, hitting it on the wall. "Ow!" She was rubbing her head. "Oh God! I'm so drunk. Why didn't I eat the chicken?"

We were next in line so I shoved us both into the cubicle and sat her on the loo.

"I didn't mean it earlier. She's a shit, really," she said while peeing loudly.

I smiled. She was funny when she was drunk.

"I'd still like to know where she bought her tits," I said a little wistfully.

Clo started laughing and fell to one side. I righted her.

"That was money well spent," she pointed out.

I laughed for the first time that night.

"Hey, Em?"

"What?" I replied.

"Do you think people will mind me peeing in the sink?"

"You're not peeing in a sink."

"Oh good." She nodded her head and I passed her the toilet tissue.

I bought her a pint of still water on the way back. She sat drinking it and giving me the thumbs-up every now and again. Eventually she recovered long enough for Tom to drag her to the dance floor, where they swayed to "Lady in Red."

I nursed my vodka and Coke. I must have looked like a loser because a drunken fat guy in a red suit approached and asked me if I wanted to kiss Santa. I politely declined his invitation.

"Come on. How could you resist this?" he asked while thrusting his crotch forward. "Want to dance?" he insisted.

I said no again and tried to turn my back on him, but the table full of drinks made it difficult.

"Come on. You look so sad sitting there."

He was pissing me off now.

"I don't feel sad," I said through clenched teeth, but he wasn't going away.

"Come on! It's Christmas. Loosen up, for fuck's sake!"

That was it. I'd had enough. "Look, mate, no doesn't mean okay, it doesn't mean maybe and it sure as shit doesn't mean ask me again. I'd rather look like the biggest loser in the world than dance with you and feel nauseous. So do us both a favor and fuck off!"

He absorbed my little speech. "Dyke," he said before walking away.

I composed myself and looked around for Seán. He was in a corner kissing the blonde bitch. I felt sick. I looked around for Clo, who was now headbanging to Europe's "The Final Countdown."

I picked up my coat and walked over to her. "Clo, I'm going home."

She looked at me blurrily. "Home?" she repeated, sounding disturbingly like ET.

"Yeah," I agreed. "The place where I live. It's getting late."

She became alert. "Did you call a taxi?" She grabbed my hand.

"I'll get one on the street," I said, trying to break away.

"Hold it," she called out. "You'll never get a taxi on the street."

She was right but I needed to get out of the place.

"I'll wait in line. I need the air. I'll be fine," I replied.

She hugged me. "I am drunk and you are an asshole sometimes, but I do love you," she said, smiling.

"Cheers!" I said, backing out.

Tom waved mid-head bang. I didn't say good-bye to Seán.

The queue at the taxi rank was endless. It was cold and I just wanted to get home. It was only a twenty-minute walk so I thought, *What the hell?* and headed up the street. George's Street was busy, full of people trying to hail taxis and cursing them when they whizzed past. I walked quickly and as I walked the streets got darker, the people disappeared. Suddenly I was on my own.

The story of my life.

I quickened my pace and was passing an alleyway when I heard a scream. I turned. I heard another muffled scream and then a thud. I stopped and held my breath, straining to hear.

"Shut up, you fucking bitch!" a male voice roared.

I heard a girl cry.

"Please," she was begging.

I heard a wallop and then her cries. I didn't think. I just took my hands out of my pockets and walked into the lane. He was lying on top of her. Her shirt was torn. Her face was bruised and her arms were pinned down. He was bearing down. She was staring at me wide-eyed, begging me with her tears. He tried to open her fly and she cried out. He put his hand to her throat while I watched. It was as though I was featuring in a stranger's nightmare. I walked toward them. I couldn't help it. It seemed like I was being dragged. He didn't seem to hear me approach. He was too busy pulling at her pants and grunting. I hated him with everything inside me. I desperately wanted to hurt him. He pulled at his zip with his free hand and cursed under his breath. I scanned the alley, my eyes coming to rest on an old brush handle. I walked three steps and picked it up. He heard me and looked around. I ran at him and started to hit him, hard and blindly. He fell off her. I kept hitting him over and over again. He raised his hands to protect himself. I kept slamming the brush handle down on top of him. She tried to drag herself away and lay on the ground by the wall, holding her ribs and moaning.

"Get up!" I screamed at her. *"Get up now!"*

I was still hitting him.

She was petrified, but she started to get up slowly and painfully. He rolled away and jumped up. I kept showering him with blows, but he was focused now and he was swatting them away. Our eyes locked. He was unsteady. I wasn't afraid—in fact I was exhilarated at the prospect of knocking him down.

"Come on, you piece of shit!"

I was Bruce Willis in a dress.

"You're going to be sorry!" he warned venomously.

He was wrong. I wasn't one bit sorry. I smacked him on the side of his head with the brush handle. He fell against the wall. I smacked him again. He stumbled. Then I did the most unbelievably stupid thing I've ever done. I dropped the brush handle and ran at him. I grabbed him by the balls and squeezed them as hard as I could. He was down and I made the most of it. I punched him in the face not once, not twice, but three times. He was groaning and he wasn't going to be getting up for a while. The girl was holding on to the wall crying. I grabbed her hand and we ran out of the alley and up the street. I saw a man and his girlfriend walk toward us holding hands, and I screamed. I screamed my head off.

"Help! Help! Help!" I shouted over and over again.

The girl collapsed, hysterical.

"Help us!" I cried.

They did. The police were called. We were taken to the hospital. She was badly beaten up. Her lip was bleeding, her ribs broken, her face bruised. My fist really hurt and my head ached. I was in shock, but aside from that I was fine. I sat in the exam room, numb and disorientated, while a student doctor dressed my swollen fist.

What is going on?

The doctor left and a policeman entered with a notebook.

"Hi, remember me? Jerry?" he said.

"Hi, Jerry," I replied automatically.

He smiled at me. "Well, Emma, your friend is doing really well. She's going to be fine."

"I don't know her," I mumbled. "Did you find him?"

"No, love," he said, "he was gone."

I briefly wondered how he had managed to walk with his bollocks in his mouth, but didn't share my concerns.

"That girl has a lot to thank you for," he said. "But for the record, it's never a good idea to tackle a maniac on your own. You should have called for help."

He was right. I didn't argue. I couldn't believe what I'd done. A bump was appearing on my head—I couldn't understand it.

"He never touched me," I said.

"You probably gave yourself a bash with the brush handle," he smiled.

"I didn't tell you about the brush handle," I said suspiciously.

"Yeah, you did, in the hallway five minutes ago."

I couldn't remember.

"You're in shock."

"Oh," I said, wishing I was home in bed.

"Do you want me to call a doctor?" he asked.

I must have looked terrible. "Where is she?" I asked.

"She's in X-ray. Her mother is with her."

"Good," I replied.

"Do you remember anything about him?" he asked, probably not for the first time. I couldn't. I could only remember her. I didn't know if he was tall or small, old or young, blond or brunet, black or white. I couldn't recall one single thing about him. I was embarrassed and frustrated by my inability to help.

"It's all right," he soothed. "It's been a long night. Who can they call to pick you up?"

"Seán." His was the only name that came to my head.

* * *

Seán arrived just after five in the morning. Jerry brought him behind the curtain. It was obvious from the start that he hadn't been told what had happened. He looked at my bandaged hand and my swollen forehead.

"Oh my God! What happened?"

"I'm fine," I said, deeply relieved to see him. "I'm sorry I got them to call you. I couldn't think of anyone else." I was embarrassed. Jerry was still standing there. Seán noticed this fact.

"Did they tell you what happened?" I asked.

He was having trouble keeping up.

"No," he said, eyeing Jerry. "I was just told to come and get you. Were you attacked?" He looked like he was scared to hear the answer.

"No," I smiled. "I did all the attacking."

His face fell. He turned to Jerry. "Oh my God! Is she under arrest?"

Jerry smiled. I tried to interrupt but Seán was stern. "Emma, I'll handle this." He turned to Jerry. "I'm really sorry, she's never done anything like this before, and the past year has been very stressful."

Jerry started to laugh. "Your friend isn't under arrest. In fact, some would say she's a hero, or is it heroine?" He winked at me.

I smiled, grateful that he held my stupidity in such high regard.

Seán interrupted. "Excuse me, could somebody please tell me what's going on?"

Jerry decided to give us a moment.

"I beat up a rapist," I said. He looked like he didn't understand what I was saying so I continued, "I was walking past an alley, heard screaming—he was trying to rape this girl so I grabbed a brush handle—"

"Brush? Handle?"

"Yes, and I beat him with it. Then I grabbed him by the balls and punched him in the face until he fell on the ground and we escaped."

It sounded surreal even as I was saying it. My head was hurting and my fist stinging and for some reason tears were streaming from my eyes.

"Jesus Christ, Emma," he said almost under his breath, "you could have been killed."

He sat down on the spare chair and reminded me how insane it all was.

"I couldn't leave her," I cried.

"I know," he said, but his tone was weary.

I started to sob. He took me in his arms and held me really tight while I cried in his arms for what seemed like a really long time.

★ ★ ★

The doctor checked my head and pronounced me okay to leave. I wanted to see the girl, so Seán took me to the second floor, where she was sleeping in a private room. I looked through the glass at her mother, who was sitting quietly, watching her. The woman was shaking and looked broken. I remembered what that felt like. The girl lay in a drug-induced sleep. We didn't belong there so we left. Outside we sat on the steps of the emergency room, waiting for a taxi and sharing a cigarette.

"Whatever happened to Ireland being the land of saints and scholars?" Seán asked.

"They fucked off and built America," I responded.

The taxi pulled up.

"Let's go home."

He pulled me up. In the taxi I asked where Julia had gone. He told me she wasn't his type and we left it at that.

Chapter 19

The End of the Line

I woke up the next morning in my own bed and sighed with relief.

It's all just been a terrible nightmare.

Then I felt my face. *Holy shit!*

I jumped out of bed and stumbled to the mirror. I sat down and stared at my poor swollen eye, which was turning at least some of the colors of the rainbow. It hurt to cry, but I did it anyway. It wasn't because I was sad—instead it registered as pure fear. In the cold light of day and in the privacy of my own bedroom I found that I was really scared. I wasn't Buffy the Vampire Slayer. I didn't do any kind of karate. I hadn't even attended a self-defense class. In fact, the one and only time I hit someone I was five and to be truthful, it was more of a hair-pulling incident than actual slaps. I pondered this. I certainly couldn't have ever been compared with any kind of daredevil. Even at the carnival I was the one sitting on the bench minding the coats, while everyone else lined up for the roller coaster. I couldn't bring myself to go on a Ferris wheel. I even had a fear of flying balls, for God's sake. Who the hell did I think I was last night? I could have been killed or, worse, that fucker could have got his dirty paws on me. So what the hell dragged me down that lane? I felt a little nauseous and suddenly it dawned on me.

"John?"

I looked around the room suspiciously.

"John? Are you here?"

I'm losing my mind.

I got back into bed and stayed there for the rest of the day.

★ ★ ★

As anticipated, Christmas Day passed off uneventfully. I didn't mention my tangling with a rapist to my parents, fearing coronary attacks. Instead I told them that I had fallen while drunk. My mother ranted for twenty minutes, my father laughed and Noel rang, managing to bail me out of trouble even from a distance. It was good to hear his voice. I missed him and wished he were home. He was happy, having a ball, and I was happy for him. Our parents were so delighted to hear his voice that they didn't dwell on his broken promise. We didn't have long to talk. Dad had taken up most of the call talking about the weather.

"Call me when you get home," Noel said and gave me a number before hanging up.

I couldn't wait. The day was long. I was bloated. My

mother insisted that we watch *The Sound of Music* and it was never-ending.

I got home after eight. I pulled out the number and called Noel.

"What's wrong?" he said.

"Nothing," I said defensively.

I couldn't believe he could sense trouble from a million miles away. And the truth was that I was bothered. My encounter with scum had left a bad taste in my mouth.

"Tell me," he said.

So I told him my sad and sordid tale.

He didn't interrupt until I finished. "You're a modern-day Good Samaritan," he said.

I laughed. "If Good Samaritans kick people's heads in, then yeah, that's me."

"Well, I did use the term 'modern,' " he noted.

I smiled. "You're not angry?"

"You did what you had to and it worked out. I'm proud of you."

I wasn't about to tell him my theory about John. I wanted him to stay proud as opposed to him fearing for my sanity.

"What about you?" I asked.

"I'm great. Not kicking heads in, but living and it's really great."

I laughed, genuinely happy. "I miss you," I said, not being able to help myself.

He told me he missed me too and I wanted to reach out and touch him.

"When are you coming home?" I whined.

"I don't know," he replied.

"Are you still a priest?" I asked.

Silence.

"I don't know," he said.

"Okay. I love you," I said.

"I love you too."

"How's Seán?" he asked.

Suddenly I felt sad. "He's leaving for London. He's going to be an editor of some magazine over there."

Silence.

"Maybe he needs something to stay for," he said.

"That's not up to me," I replied.

"Maybe." Then he added, "John's been gone awhile."

I knew this but didn't know why he had suddenly said that.

"I know," I said.

"Happy Christmas, Emma!"

"Happy Christmas, Noel," I replied.

I put down the phone and opened a bottle of wine.

"Happy Christmas, John," I said and took the bottle to bed.

When I lay down, I was drunk. Unable to sleep, I lay there in the stillness and I wondered if John could see me. Was it possible? Was heaven a place from where he could look down whenever he wanted? Could he still touch me? It frightened me to think that he was somewhere, knowing that sometimes I forgot to think about him for a whole day or week or month, knowing that the pain in my heart had dissipated. And although I still missed and loved him, I had to look at his picture to really see him. What if he knew that I couldn't remember the sound of his laugh? What if he knew about . . . ?

I would rather he just slept. Noel would have said it was God's way, His plan, and that life goes on. I felt like a traitor. Maybe he didn't want me to get on with my life, maybe he wanted me to love him until death reunited us, and maybe he did send me down that lane. Did he? Did he want me to help that girl or was he sending me a sign. Noel said once that I thought of death as a punishment, but he saw it as a gift. Noel thought everything was a gift. If someone punched him in the face he would have thanked him. I asked him once if he really believed that he had all the answers. He told me he didn't. He just believed. That was the problem: I didn't know if I wanted to. I fell into a drunken sleep, only to wake to my doorbell.

Doreen bustled past me. She had a boxed fruitcake in her hand.

"Thanks," I said when she put it down on the counter.

"Let me look at your face," she ordered.

She took her time examining my swollen eye. "How's your hand?" she asked.

"Good."

I flexed it to show her how well I was doing. I made tea. Doreen preferred tea—coffee made her edgy.

"Seán called me," she said. "I'd no idea I was living next door to Walker Texas Ranger. He's worried that you've lost your fucking mind."

I wondered why he'd called Doreen.

"He called you?" I asked.

"Of course he did. Everyone knows how great I am in a crisis. I worked on the Samaritans Help Line for a year, you know. I've heard it all."

I laughed. "There's nothing to hear."

She smiled. "There's always something to hear, love," she corrected me knowingly.

I told her I had no intention of chasing any more rapists down alleyways.

"That's not what I'm worried about." She waved her hand in the air dismissively. "It's time to move on," she said out of nowhere, but I instantly knew to whom and what she was referring.

"There's nothing to be concerned about, Dor, really. I have moved on," I said, looking at the counter.

She reached out and held my face in her hand and looked into my eyes.

I couldn't escape her.

"Where's the girl I used to know? Where's the girl with the smile that could melt the hardest of hearts? I know you're in there somewhere, behind all that pain and guilt."

I wanted to cry. She held my face. Something cracked inside and I gave voice to the feeling I'd run from all these months.

"It's my fault! If I hadn't gone back inside!" Tears burned in my eyes.

She looked at me hard. "Listen to me, young lady, there's no such thing as 'if.' You can't change what happened. It was never up to you."

I shook my head. "He didn't want me to go back inside."

"It doesn't matter."

"He told me to leave it—he just wanted to go home."

"It doesn't matter."

"He'd be here today."

"No! He wouldn't."

I pulled away. "Why?" I cried, matching her tone.

"Because, Emma, it was meant to be," she said calmly.

I shrank back and we stayed silent for a while. She took my hand and rubbed it, allowing me to absorb the facts. I did but she didn't know the full story.

"Dor, I don't feel him in my heart anymore. It hasn't been even two years and I can't feel him. He deserves better. I hate this." I was crying.

She softened. "Let me ask you this. If it was you who died, wouldn't you want him to carry on, to be happy?"

Of course I would, she knew that. I nodded.

"Why?" she asked.

"Because I loved him!"

"And he loved you," she said.

I sobbed and nodded and she smiled.

"It's time to let him go, love. Holding on just hurts both of you," she said gently.

"Dor?"

"Yes."

"Do you think he can see us?"

"Probably, every now and again. It must be very frustrating for him."

"What do you mean?"

"Well, he has moved on."

I nodded and deep down I knew it was time for me to do just that.

★ ★ ★

We were on our way to Kerry. Tom drove, Clo was in the front and Seán and I were in the back. I was happy to leave Dublin, happier to be sitting beside Seán. Being close to him made me feel safe.

It was a long drive. After five hours of sitting, we pulled into a long, winding driveway lined with trees. We couldn't help but be impressed. The house loomed large; the porch light gleamed in the distance. Tom honked the horn. Anne and Richard stood waiting for us. My arse hurt. So did Clo's—she keep lifting her arse off the seat, rubbing it and saying, "Christ!" a lot.

Seán jumped out of the car first. He and Richard hugged. Clo and Anne danced around together wildly. I stood back smiling. Tom stood back with me, observing.

"Richard, Anne, you remember Tom," I said.

I realized instantly it was a stupid thing to say. They had spent an entire weekend in Paris with him after all. Anne made a big deal about my eye as we made our way into the house. She asked if I was okay.

"Just glad to be out of the car," I replied.

Richard grabbed my hand. "Hey, Rambo!"

I smiled.

Anne couldn't wait to be filled in.

"But I told you everything on the phone," I said, despairing.

She stopped filling the kettle while I looked around her kitchen, which was the size of my entire house.

"Emma, a story is only a real story when it's told face to face," she said.

"Since when?" Clo enquired.

"I want to hear everything," Anne ordered, ignoring her.

"She punched him in the face." Clo talked as though she was there and smiled. "And she kicked him in the nuts."

"It was more of a squeeze," I corrected.

"Who'd have guessed you were so vicious?" said Anne and they both nodded at me approvingly.

Seán watched us in silence; he was definitely not as impressed as the others. I was glad of it, as I had no intention of ever repeating the performance. Richard appeared from the sitting room.

"How's the poor girl?" he asked.

"Fine," I said.

Although I wasn't sure that was the case. I had only spoken to her mother once briefly on the phone. She thanked me and said that she was taking her daughter away on a holiday, which didn't necessarily convey that the girl was fine, but I was hoping for the best.

Tom and Seán found Richard's PlayStation, so we didn't see the lads for most of the night. Anne, Clo and I sat in the kitchen drinking wine and looking out onto a beautiful stone patio, which looked onto a river. It was pretty breathtaking. Clo and I were in heaven.

"This is some place," Clo commented.

Anne smiled. "Yeah," she agreed before changing the subject.

We knew she wasn't totally convinced about living in Kerry, but looking around it was difficult to sympathize. Clo put on a CD. Anne asked how Leonard was.

"Yesterday I caught him trying to swallow his toy mouse," I replied.

Clo laughed and told Anne that the week before he

had managed to get into my fridge and mangle everything in it.

"That's so weird," Anne said.

"Tell me about it. He managed to suck down three lamb chops and half a bottle of white wine!"

Anne thought I should take him to a vet. Clo disagreed and defended his healthy appetite.

Anne was disgusted. "There's nothing healthy about a cat sucking down three lamb chops with a bottle of wine."

"Half a bottle," I corrected.

She gave me a dirty look before asking if he was fat. He was nearly two years and he shared the same dimensions as a medium-sized dog.

"He's big-boned," I said.

Clo backed me up. "It's just his breed," she offered.

Anne gave us both another one of her patented dirty looks. "Emma, bring that poor cat to the vet," she said in a tone reminiscent of Doreen.

I nodded my head in defeat and had to admit my cat had a problem. I briefly wondered if I was a bad mother.

All of a sudden Anne was giggly and explained that she wasn't used to drinking as she and Richard had been following a strict diet, which included no alcohol consumption, for the past two months.

"Why?" Clo asked, shocked.

"To increase our chances of having a baby," Anne whispered, even though the lads were in a sitting room about four miles away, in what Clo described as the west wing.

Clo thought about it for a minute. I smiled because I knew what she was thinking. "Funny, I thought most women got pregnant after a decent meal and a few Bacardi Breezers. Or is that just me?"

I choked on my wine. Anne was silent for a minute before noting, "That's a good fucking point."

We laughed for twenty minutes. Seán arrived in, victorious. He had beaten Richard at Time Crisis.

"Really? How boring," Clo noted before grabbing his arse.

He told her she hadn't a clue while getting a few beers from the fridge. Anne was still laughing.

"What's so funny?" he asked.

"Booze," came her reply.

Clo and I laughed stupidly.

"Right so," he said and left.

We were halfway through a second bottle of wine and Anne was slumping.

"It's shoo good to have you," she slurred.

Clo and I smiled. This was the first time we'd been together in months and she was right, it did feel really good.

Richard showed us to our rooms while Anne was having difficulty finding her own. We all said good night. Five minutes later there was a knock on my door. It was Richard.

"We didn't really get a chance to talk," he said.

I hated when people said this to me. There was a tone that wasn't difficult to recognize. The tone that told you a lecture was on the way.

"I know what you're thinking and I haven't come to give you a lecture."

Yeah, right.

"I just wanted to make sure you were all right," he said, smiling. The smile didn't fool me.

"I'm fine," I said.

"Good," he said. Then came the dreaded, "But I was thinking . . ."

Right on cue.

"It wasn't the safest thing in the world, you know, attacking a rapist. Some would say it was a bit mad."

He was looking at the floor. I followed his eyes. The floor was marble.

Nice.

"I don't have any plans to do it again."

He smiled. "Good."

He proceeded to tell me how upset Seán had been.

"Really," was my jaded reply.

"Yeah," he responded.

His smile faded. "He really cares about you."

My face reddened. "I know," I replied.

"Do you care about him?" he asked accusingly.

"Of course." I was taking umbrage.

"He said he's going to London," he continued unabated.

"It's a good opportunity," I said, sitting down, still hoping he'd leave.

"And that's what you told him?" he asked.

"Yes."

We were both getting pissed off.

"If you have any feelings for him, and we all know you do, I suggest you pull your head out of your ass and tell him."

I couldn't believe it. *Cheeky bastard!* "Kerry is making you mean."

"I call them like I see them and we all know I don't see much," he said, smiling. He headed toward the door while I sat there dumbfounded at his sheer nerve. He turned. "Hey, can we keep this little conversation between ourselves? If Anne knew I spoke to you, she'd kill me. Good night." He winked at me. "I do love you, Em, but sometimes you're blinder than I am."

Not really—your wife hates her new life.

He was gone.

I lay down but I couldn't sleep. I kept thinking about him saying that everyone knew I had feelings for Seán. Clo had never said anything. She made jokes, but then she made jokes about everything. Anne hadn't mentioned it either. Maybe Seán knew. I blushed. I was twenty-eight, in a dark room on my own and I was blushing.

"Jesus, I really need to talk to Clo."

Clo and Tom were asleep. It was just gone one in the morning. I knocked on the door and let myself in. Tom moaned.

"Tom," I whispered.

He turned in the bed, still sleeping.

I walked closer. "Tom," I repeated.

He was still in the land of nod.

"Damn," I whispered. *I can't believe they are asleep already.* I moved closer again and shook him.

"Tom!" I called into his ear.

He shot up in the bed.

"I'm up, I'm up," he said, looking around, realizing it was pitch dark. He focused blearily on my crappy dressing gown.

"Christ, Em, what time is it?" he asked, rubbing his eyes.

"I'm really, really, really sorry but this is an emergency. Could we swap beds?"

"What?" He sounded surprised at what appeared to me to be a perfectly reasonable request.

"I really need to talk to Clo," I begged.

He looked over at Clo, passed out and dribbling.

"She's asleep," he noted.

"I know just how to wake her. Really, this is an emergency. My room is two doors down on the left."

"Okay," he agreed, beginning to sense the urgency of my situation.

I smiled and waited for him to exit the bed.

He sat looking at me.

"What?" I asked, getting irritated.

"I need to put something on," he said, embarrassed.

"Oh, right, sorry," I agreed and turned my back to him.

He got out and struggled to put on his shorts and a T-shirt. He left and I sat into the bed.

"Hmmm, warm." The marble floors looked great, but they were bloody cold. "Clo," I whispered.

She moaned.

"Clo." I shook her.

"Ten more minutes," she mumbled.

I shook her harder. "It's Em, I really need to talk to you," I said, still shaking her.

She didn't jump or even open her eyes.

"What the . . . ?" she mumbled.

I turned on the light. She opened her eyes slowly.

"This better be good," she warned.

"I'm in love with Seán," I said.

226

It was funny because I hadn't intended on opening the conversation that way.

She sat up and faced me. "Well, it's about time," she noted, half smiling.

I was panicked. "What the hell am I going to do?" I asked.

"Tell him," she said.

"Easy for you to say," I said, trying to get comfortable.

"Easy for you to do," she replied. "He's in love with you and you're in love with him. Simple." She reached for her cigarettes.

"Do you really think so?" I asked.

She lit her cigarette and took a drag. "I know for a fact. He told me last year."

I couldn't believe it. "Why didn't you tell me?" I almost screamed.

She looked at me knowingly. "Because we both know you would have freaked out and kicked me."

I thought about her answer and in light of recent events I really couldn't argue. She was right. I would have freaked out. I wasn't ready.

"But you're ready now," she said, reading my mind.

I felt butterflies in my stomach. I'd forgotten how that felt. It was nice, but also a little troubling.

"Jesus," I said.

"Jesus," she agreed.

We sat in silence and she finished her cigarette.

"Where's Tom?" she enquired after about five minutes.

"I sent him into my room."

She laughed.

"So how do I tell him?" I asked.

"Just jump him."

Wise counsel, but not the kind I was looking for. It must have been written on my face because she continued pretty quickly, "It's not rocket science, Em, you just have to say it."

We sat in silence again.

"You don't think it's unfair to John?" I asked, needing to hear her say the word "no."

"Don't be a prick," she replied.

"Close enough."

And that put an end to that line of questioning.

"Okay," I agreed, "I'll tell him." I smiled at her resolutely.

"Good," she said, putting out her cigarette. "Now turn off the light and get some sleep."

I obeyed and lay down.

I'm in love with Seán, I thought as I drifted into a peaceful sleep.

★ ★ ★

We all met at breakfast. Clo had politely warned Tom not to open his mouth about the previous night's sleeping arrangements and he dutifully complied. We sat together at the breakfast table.

Anne was hungover, mumbling, "No eggs."

Clo and Tom were playing footsie and grinning stupidly at one another. Richard was eating toast and writing an itinerary for the day's events. I don't know what Seán was doing as I couldn't look at him, fearing I would blush and vomit simultaneously. I remember thinking that this could become a real problem before Richard interrupted my thoughts.

"I've a big day planned. We're going to take a hike up the mountain. Then I'm going to show you some local woods. We've booked a fishing boat for the afternoon and then, if you're feeling up to it, I was thinking about taking in a game of golf for an hour before dinner. I'm thinking of eating around eight. How does that sound?"

Clo laughed and told him it sounded like hell. Anne threatened to kill him, but Seán thought it sounded great and I briefly wondered what I saw in him. I recovered to add my concerns.

"If we do all that and eat a big meal at eight, we'll be asleep by ten and it's New Year's bloody Eve."

Anne and Clo agreed. I thought Tom was getting up to give me a standing ovation, but he was just heading to the fridge for some milk. When his thirst was finally quenched he agreed with Richard and Seán. It was the girls against the boys and I didn't like the odds. Anne's will to fight was diminished and Clo could be bought by a promise from Tom. It was obvious that yet again Richard would have his way.

Richard briefly wondered why he didn't have a hangover and I prayed that at some point it would kick in. It didn't and, as we piled into his Range Rover, I cursed God again. Seán was sitting up front. Clodagh, Tom, Anne and I were sitting in the back. I caught Seán smiling at me through the rearview mirror. Something made me wave and suddenly I felt awkward. I noticed myself fixing my hair twice within the space of five minutes and started to panic. Anne was wedged in beside me. She leaned over and I jumped, terrified she was about to vomit.

"What's wrong with you?" she asked.

I relaxed. "I thought you were going to throw up."

"I'm fine," she assured me, gray-faced and smelling of wine.

I remained unconvinced. "Do you want the window seat?"

She leaned in again. "No. So what's up?" she whispered.

"Nothing," I replied.

"You're lying," she whispered a little louder.

"I don't know what you're talking about," I whispered back, trying not to sound panicked and worried that Tom would hear her.

"There's something going on. You're quiet, you've been fixing your hair since you got into the Jeep and Clo told me about last night." She smiled and leaned back in the seat, some color returning to her cheeks.

"I was going to tell you," I whispered, embarrassed and mentally punching Clo in the face.

"It's about time," she laughed.

I blushed, realized I was blushing and blushed some more. Realizing that I was now blushing more, I blushed even more. It was a slippery slope so I hid my face in my lap. Clo leaned over Tom, fearing that I was sick. "Emma, are you sick?"

Richard stopped the car. Seán climbed over the seat.

"Are you okay?" he asked, concerned and so sweet.

Still the color of beetroot, I decided to answer from my lap. "I'm fine," I said.

"Can you lift your head up?" he asked.

Fuck off, my brain silently begged.

He wasn't going anywhere, so I raised my reddened face to meet his.

Clo burst out laughing.

"Richard, please drive on," I said with all the authority I could muster.

Seán returned to the front seat, slightly confused.

Clo mouthed the word "sorry" but it was obvious she wasn't because she was still laughing. Richard drove on. Anne was too sick to laugh, but I could sense that she would hold her stupid grin all the way up the bloody mountain. I closed my eyes and leaned against the window. My eyelids were protecting me from my audience and my inner voice repeated, "Be cool, be cool." After a while I began to wonder who I was trying to fool. Seán knew I wasn't cool and he didn't seem to mind. Then again, now that I realized I loved him, the least I could do was try not to make a fool out of myself at every possible turn. But it's not like I could change. The problem was that he knew me too well. It was all very confusing. Later, when Richard stopped the car so Anne could throw up, I found myself looking out the window, smiling at the beauty and forgetting my stupid little world for a while.

We started our mountain hike around eleven. We were still walking at three. Richard, Seán and Tom walked ahead, talking about football, motor racing and oohhing and ahhhing at flora and fauna. Clo, Anne and I lagged behind. Initially we were really enjoying ourselves. Anne felt much better. The scenery was beautiful, it was dry and although it was cold the skies were blue. That was great for about an hour. Three hours later it was wearing thin. We were lost and the lads were too busy being retarded to notice. We managed to keep ourselves busy by discussing the object of my newly discovered desires. The conversation ran the usual course. I was nervous and unsure. They were excited and felt it was a dead cert. I talked rubbish and they told me how fantastic I was. I talked some more rubbish and Clo complimented my hair. Then I remembered *Friends* and I froze. I stopped and looked at Clo and Anne. They looked back.

"What?" Clo asked, more to get me moving as opposed to talking.

"*Friends,*" I said.

They looked blankly at me.

"Ross and Rachel," I said, believing it enough for them to catch on.

It wasn't.

"And?" said Clo.

I couldn't believe it. *Friends* was her favorite TV program. It was perfectly obvious what I was getting at.

"Ross is secretly in love with Rachel for ages, but he doesn't say anything—he's just her friend. He's always there for her. He's her rock. She's just come out of a big relationship. She's all over the place while he waits in the wings. And when eventually she realizes that she's in love with him, he's seeing a Chinese chick. Last week she ended up on her face in the airport."

I finished my homage to the American sitcom long enough to take a badly needed breath.

Clo smiled. "Emma, it's fine. Seán isn't with a Chinese chick—he's over there trying to look up a deer's arse."

I remained uncomforted. "It's an analogy," I said.

Anne smiled.

"What?" I asked.

"Nothing," she replied.

I wasn't budging.

"It was just a funny episode," she grinned.

Clo linked my arm and started walking with me. She reminded me that my life wasn't an episode of *Friends* and also pretty accurately predicted that the Chinese one wouldn't last long. Ross and Rachel were bound to get together. I wasn't sure, as consummated love wasn't always a ratings winner. I knew this didn't make for a good argument so I just shut up and walked.

We eventually found a pub and everyone was starving. It was three thirty and Richard's whole itinerary was messed up. The girls cheered. The lads had to concede. Playtime was over. We all ate way too much and whiled away a very pleasant three hours drinking Irish coffee and melting by the fire. We didn't make it back to Anne and Richard's until after eight. We all had hot showers, changed our clothes and only started cooking the dinner at nine. We drank wine, although Anne stuck to weak beer. Everyone was helping out, setting the table, sorting out some music, stirring sauces and filling glasses, while bumping into one another. It was a definite case of too many cooks. I got my jacket and decided to go for a cigarette.

I sat on the bench outside, looking out into the darkness with only my cigarette to light the way. I heard footsteps behind me and my heart skipped because I knew it was Seán.

"I thought you'd given up," he said.

I smiled while he sat. "I did," I answered, exhaling. "You're watching me fall off the wagon."

He smiled. "Mind if I join you?" he enquired and I wanted desperately to kiss him.

I handed him a cigarette instead. We smoked silently, although I was having a full-scale conversation in my head.

Seán, how's your cig? Oh good. Listen, by the way, I love you and I'd like to shag here and now.

We sat in silence.

Then he asked me what I was smiling at.

"Nothing."

We returned to silence. I started to feel the pressure. I needed to say something, anything to start a conversation. The tension was thick in the air. I couldn't think of anything, which was ridiculous—we'd been friends for years. I kept wondering why he wasn't talking and wishing that he'd speak, but he just smoked. It was getting weird so I decided just to open my mouth and say the first thing that came to mind and to hell with the consequences, so I did.

"Happy New Year, Seán."

He looked at me. "It's only half nine."

I smiled. "I know," I said and took a drag out of my cigarette, wishing I could smoke quicker.

This was too hard. I was a coward. I didn't have the courage of my convictions. I was weak and I was scared. It was funny, I had no real idea that I was in love with Seán until last night and now suddenly the prospect of losing him was sickening. Seán had told Clo that he was in love with me, but he was drunk and it was over a year ago. Maybe he's moved on—that's why he's going to London. London was Seán's Chinese girl! I'd blown it, left it too late. He was going to London and I had missed the boat. Saying something now would be stupid. It would just make things difficult and it could definitely ruin our friendship. It hadn't even been two years since John died. By the time we finished our never-ending cigarettes I had decided things were best left as they were. We walked down the path to the house and he put his arm around my shoulder.

"You look sad," he said.

I smiled at him and hugged him close. "I'm not sad. I'm happy to be here," I answered. I felt his warmth and I wanted to tell him after all.

★ ★ ★

We ate dinner and drank wine. Anne even managed a glass or two. We moved into the sitting room. It was raining outside. Richard had lit a fire. The TV was muted and the stereo sang. Seán sat beside me and I felt like the whole room was waiting for something to happen. He didn't notice. He was busy scribbling in his notebook. Anne asked what he was doing. He told us he had an article to write for the following Tuesday and he was taking some notes. Clo chastised him for being a nerdy swot. She couldn't believe it was thirty minutes to midnight on New Year's Eve and he was working. He defended himself by noting his articles were always a great conversation piece, while conveniently ignoring the fact that the conversations invariably ended up in arguments.

This time, he needed to define the modern woman.

Clo laughed. "Easy. A great date, a shit housewife."

We laughed and agreed she was right.

He grinned and took it down. He looked up at me. "What about you, Em? If pearls, high heels and a duster defined women in the fifties, what describes women in the nineties?"

It was a good question. I was unsure of my answer. He looked up from his notepad.

"Well?" he said.

"Do you want the glossy magazine answer?" I knew he always wanted the glossy magazine answer.

He grinned and nodded.

"Okay," I began. "*Cosmopolitan* leads us to believe that the modern woman works hard, pays her own bills, carries her own condoms, isn't adverse to a one-night stand. She can cook, fix a flat tire, do the splits, give birth in a pool without the benefit of painkillers, retain the figure of a well-endowed sixteen-year-old well into her sixties, is an uninhibited lover, a football fan, has a large music collection and enjoys lewd jokes."

The others were laughing while Seán was scribbling wildly and I wondered why he didn't just read *Cosmopolitan*. He looked up after a minute.

"What do *you* say?" he asked.

"She's free," I answered without thinking.

Clo broke into "Working on the Chain Gang." The others joined in, but Seán just smiled and nodded his head while I sat thinking about what I'd just said.

I'm free.

He asked Anne, if she could pick to live the life of any female TV character, who it would be.

She thought for a minute, sloshing her beer and grinning widely. "Lois Lane."

He asked why, although it seemed pretty obvious to the rest of us.

"Superman," she nodded, grinning. She didn't need to say any more.

Clo nodded her head in agreement, before noting that she'd like to be Pamela Anderson in *Baywatch* and Tom supported her choice enthusiastically. I said Dana Scully. However, when Clo pointed out that she was overworked, had a gross job, no boyfriend and was always in a crisis, I briefly wondered about my mental health and quickly switched to Jasmine Bleeth, Pammie's friend in *Baywatch*. Clo gave me the thumbs-up.

Richard turned up the TV. It was five to twelve. I was sitting next to Seán.

Christ.

I briefly considered lighting a cigarette, but I didn't want Anne to know I was still smoking. Suddenly everyone was smiling at each other and yelling out the countdown. My bladder throbbed and I feared I would pee. All roared a collective "Happy New Year!" Anne and Richard kissed and held one another. Clo and Tom were sinking into the chair together. Seán and I smiled at one another.

"Happy New Year, Em," he said and my heart stopped, making it difficult to respond.

He smiled and pulled me into him and I swear it kick-started my heart. I was buzzing like a teenager, but then he kissed my cheek and pulled away.

"Happy New Year," I mumbled and we stood there awkwardly, waiting for the others to pry themselves apart. After that we listened to eighties music and got drunk.

Clo and Anne followed me to bed. They were troubled that I had not taken advantage of the New Year's kiss with Seán as discussed and agreed upon earlier that day. I apologized for being pathetic. Anne was sympathetic, but Clo was having none of it, telling me to take my head out of my arse, which now was becoming a common theme. I whined that there was nothing I could do about it.

Clo grinned knowingly. "Of course there is, you can go to his room."

Anne nodded her head in agreement. It was after three, but my protestation was falling on deaf ears. Clo reminded me unnecessarily that we were driving back to Dublin the next day and time was running out. She and Anne walked to the bedroom door.

"It's now or never," Anne said.

"Amen," Clo bowed her head.

Noel had mentioned he was thinking about going to New Guinea during our Christmas Day phone call. I briefly wondered whether or not he had made it there but had forgotten him by the time they had closed the door behind them. Alone in a dark room, I was faced with a decision that could potentially lead to the worst humiliation of my life. I could just go to his room and tell him or go to bed and let him go.

Suddenly I realized I had no choice. I had to tell him or I'd go insane. The only thing I had to do was work up the courage so I moisturized, washed my teeth, put on lip balm and stood leaning against my door for a really long time. It was the threat of neck cramp that moved me in the end.

I got to his door and I was in a state, but I knew there was no turning back so I knocked really loudly.

"Who's there?" he said.

He sounded awake. I hadn't counted on him being terribly alert.

"It's Emma," I managed.

The door appeared to open instantly. He said, "Hi," and I said, "Hi." I told him I needed to talk. He let me in. The curtains were open and a half-moon peered through the glass. I adjusted my eyes to notice the curtains were floor length. The window was a patio door, which led to a private patio, which overlooked the water. It was really beautiful. I walked over and opened the patio door. He smiled.

"It's a great room."

I couldn't believe it; I didn't even have an en suite. He followed me out onto the patio. I was staring at the love seat positioned beside the potted plants.

"I don't have a patio," I moaned.

He smiled. "Did I show you my en suite?" he said, almost laughing.

Then he showed me into his private bathroom behind what appeared to be a wardrobe to the unsuspecting tourist. It was plush, the bath was round and it smelled like Coco Chanel. I couldn't fucking believe it. Here was Seán staying in the Ritz while I was down the hall in the bloody Holiday Inn. While I was contemplating Anne being a dirty bitch, Seán was waiting for me to give him a reason for my visit. So when I finally recovered from the indignity of being given a dodgy room, I followed him back into his idyllic one. He sat on the bed and I sat beside him. The injustice forgotten, I was forced to deal with the issue at hand. My heartbeat increased; my muscles tensed. He asked if everything was all right, while looking at me weirdly. I assured him I was fine, but my insane, hysterical grinning probably left him with some doubts. As the seconds passed he began to look scared for my sanity. This was not the strong start that I'd hoped for, but I persevered. This was the moment I was going to tell him I loved him. I exhaled and let it out.

"I don't want you to leave," I said.

Damn, I meant to say I love you.

I hadn't stuck to the plan and this was new territory. His mood changed and he looked at me intensely.

"Why?" He sounded a little hoarse.

I momentarily prayed he wasn't coming down with a cold and then I answered him as honestly as I could manage.

"Because I'd really miss you."

Damn, damn, why can't I just say it?

I wanted to look away, but his gaze held mine. His eyes were moist and wide and sad. His mouth was soft and inches from mine. He was wearing nothing more than a tracksuit bottom and although his eyes riveted me I could feel the closeness of his chest. Jesus, I was weak for him.

"Why, Emma?" he asked.

I love you.

"Why would you miss me?" he challenged.

"Because . . ." My voice left me.

"Because what?" he asked urgently.

"Because I love you," I said a little too shrilly. Yet still, at last I'd said it. I think I exhaled.

"You love me?" he repeated skeptically.

I nodded in agreement because it was true.

He smiled. "You? Love me?"

"Yes," I agreed.

"Not just as a friend?" he queried.

"No, not just as a friend," I confirmed.

He leaned in closer. "How long?"

I answered honestly. "A long time."

He smiled. "I love you too," he said grinning.

And then we were kissing and oh and my God, the boy could kiss. And then we were touching and it didn't feel weird—instead it felt good, really good, too good to explain. I don't remember a single thought that entered my head. I just remember the most intense sense of bliss. We managed to get naked with surprising speed and dexterity. It was as though we already knew each other intimately. No head-banging, no awkward fumbling, no misplaced hands. It was as though we fitted somehow.

He was lying on top of me naked when he asked, "Are you sure?"

I looked up at him. "Yeah," I agreed, laughing.

I pulled him to me and he was laughing and then we were kissing again and he was inside me and oh my God, the boy could . . .

Afterwards we lay in the round bath in Seán's impossibly cool, Coco Chanel-smelling bathroom, naked and warm.

"What are you thinking?" he asked when he caught me smiling.

"What took me so long?" I said.

He laughed. "You're slow."

It made me smile because he was right. I was slow but then nobody's perfect. We talked all night, lying in one another's arms, about the past and about the future. He told me he wasn't going to London and I was so happy that I cried.

The next morning we got breakfast in bed. Richard,

Anne and Tom had kindly got up early especially to bring us eggs. We hugged onto the sheet, having only slept twenty-five minutes, startled and feeling pretty naked while they grinned wildly and said things like, "Good on you!" and, "We figured you'd have worked up an appetite!"

It felt like at any moment one of them would whip out a camera and yell, "Cheese!" And then they were gone and we were looking at each other freaked out and then we were laughing and I felt sixteen.

Chapter 20

Chucky, a Homecoming and the Cow

It was a crisp, cold day in January, gray except for a laser-like light beam that penetrated the earth through a clearing in the clouds. The ground was dry and hardened by the cold that crept through even the thickest of clothing. My hands were blue under my bunched-up sleeves. I walked past the gates and meandered through the line of graves that led the way to John. My nose hurt and I could feel the skin around my lips chapping. I quickened my step and vowed to say what I had to and leave. I reached my destination minutes later, but found that on this ungodly cold morning I was not alone. John's mother, Patricia, was cleaning the headstone. I momentarily thought about hiding, but her eyes met mine and I was caught.

"Emma!" She smiled warmly, despite the freeze.

"Patricia!" I called out a little too cheerily.

She approached with her arms outstretched and I walked

into her embrace. "I haven't seen you in such a long time."

I apologized profusely, face reddening.

She sensed my guilt and immediately put me at ease with her wide smile. "It's so good to see you."

"You too, Patricia." I meant it, despite my embarrassment.

I picked up a sponge and together we cleaned. She talked about her neighbor who had won a trip around the world and I talked about school. When the headstone was gleaming she asked me if I wanted to join her for a coffee. I hadn't managed to speak to John, but I was having such a lovely time with her and coffee meant warmth.

The skies opened as we made our way back to our cars. We were both soaking as we entered the coffee shop. A nice old dear took our coats and hung them on a stand by the door. We sat near the open fire that roared in the corner and we slowly began to melt. A waitress took our orders and we sat looking at one another like old friends who had been apart longer than they would have wished.

"You look happy," she said.

The guilt returned.

"Are you happy, Emma?" she asked kindly.

"Yes," I admitted.

"Good girl," she nodded.

I didn't want to tell her about Seán because that would be unfair. It would have hurt too much, my being happy with John's best friend while he slept underground. It turns out I didn't have to.

"And Seán?" she asked.

"He's fine," I said, blushing.

"Your mother told me about you two and I'm happy. I'm so glad, Emma. We were all worried that you wouldn't find someone."

Oh my God. I should have said something.

I couldn't look at her.

She laughed. "You're so sweet."

"I'm sorry, Patricia." I felt like crying but I was wet enough.

"There is no need to be sorry," she said.

"I still love him," I said apologetically and a little pathetically.

"I know, me too, but he's gone and we're here."

She was so wise. Suddenly I missed her. "Seán's great," I grinned.

She laughed. "I'm sure he is—he's had enough practice."

We both laughed and clinked our coffee mugs. It was so good to see her. Later we hugged by the cars and promised to keep in touch. I realized on the drive home that I didn't have to tell John. He knew and was happy for me.

★ ★ ★

The weeks after Christmas flew. Seán moved in with me in early February. Everyone was delighted for us except Leonard, who was suffering intensely on a new diet. Lack of food compounded by a new housemate ensured a violent reaction. Initially he showed his displeasure by peeing on Seán's side of the bed, so we ensured the bedroom door was always locked and this worked well for a while until one night Seán, finding it difficult to

breathe, awoke in the middle of the night to find Leonard
asleep on his face. I woke in time to see Leonard hit the
opposite wall, do a kind of flip thing and land on his
chubby little legs. Seán explained the situation while
Leonard sat at the end of the bed with his neck craned,
staring at him venomously. It was only then that I noticed
the door was closed. I looked at Seán, who appeared
locked in Leonard's eyes.

"You left Leonard downstairs when we were going to
bed, right?"

He nodded in agreement.

I pointed to the door.

"How did he get in here then?" I asked.

Seán went pale. "Jesus, he's like Chucky," he whispered.

We sat looking at the cat for a really long time,
attempting to work out how he had gained access to
Seán's face. Eventually the cat gave in and meowed at the
door. I let him out and attempted to make light of it.
Seán slept sitting up that night and we never did work it
out.

The next morning I mentioned it to Doreen, who had
dropped in to escape her husband, who had recently
joined the Green Party. Apparently he was separating her
rubbish and trying to talk her into getting a system
installed to recycle their waste. She sat at the kitchen table
while I made coffee.

"I mean, for Christ's sake, Emma, when I married him,
I never agreed to bathing in my own recycled urine."

I agreed it was more that any vow could withstand.
Leonard passed us and I watched him head into the sitting
room. I ran over and closed the door and sought advice

from my older and wiser friend. I explained the troublesome events of the previous night.

"How did he get into the room?" she asked.

I told her I didn't know.

"Weird," she said.

I was hoping for more. She got up, opened the door a crack and looked out at Leonard, who was sitting by the window watching a bird hop across the lawn. Sensing her presence, he turned to stare at her. She stood for a minute, analyzing him before closing the door.

"He's starving," she said.

I didn't understand what this had to do with my cat being a psycho.

She sat down. "He's got that supermodel haunted look," she laughed.

I still wasn't getting it.

"When did you put him on a diet?" she asked.

"Just after Christmas," I answered.

"And when did Seán start staying over?" she asked.

"Just after Christmas," I answered.

"Well then," she said, "there you go. He equates starving with Seán. He probably thinks that if he kills Seán he'll get fed."

I wondered. "You could be right."

"I'm over sixty, love. I'm always right."

And I believed her until she asked me if I'd ever considered putting Leonard into therapy. I complained I was already paying a fortune for a dietician. She nodded sagely and reminded me that I could always have him put down. I think he heard her because when she was leaving he made a run for her legs. Dor didn't move—she just

looked down at his chubby little face and threatened to
break it. He backed off.

"A firm hand is all it takes," she said and left.

I looked at Leonard. "Cop on!" I shouted and bravely
turned my back on him and walked into the kitchen.

Later I informed Seán of what I now believed to be
Leonard's issue. He agreed the theory had merit. We
decided that he should be seen to give Leonard his meager
meals. He did and the cat pissed on his food. We gave him
nothing else all night, locked our bedroom door and Seán
resumed sleeping while sitting up. This lasted three days.
On the third day the cat ate his lo-cal steamed chicken
and after that there were no more murder attempts.

The weeks and months passed and, while Leonard lost
weight, Seán and I got used to being a couple. Initially I
had been concerned about him moving into the house I
once shared with his best friend. We discussed getting a
new place together, but then rents were getting more
expensive. I loved where I lived and so did he. We did
buy a new bed, but when I couldn't bring myself to
throw out the old one he suggested that we move it into
the spare room and throw out the spare bed instead. He
wasn't jealous or threatened or even annoyed at my
position. Instead he understood my reasons and I loved
him more for it.

★ ★ ★

Noel had been gone over a year. Seán and I were at my
parents' for Sunday dinner. My father's veins were at him,
my mother had a headache and I had my period. Seán put
on a brave face while surrounded by misery.

"So how's work?" he asked my dad.

"Painful," my father responded dully.

He asked my mother how her bridge lessons were going.

"I'm rubbish," she said.

He started to age before my eyes. I felt sorry for him.

"Seán's been promoted," I said brightly. They bucked up and were pleased for him. "He's going to be editor of a new magazine being launched in May."

My mother was thrilled because the title "editor" impressed her. However, she couldn't help but note that men's magazines are full of rubbish.

"I mean, what the hell do men know about anything?" she asked.

I laughed her off while Seán and my dad smirked at one another like they had a clue.

The phone rang and it was Noel. My mother nearly stood on my father in her attempt to get to the phone. Instantly their mood improved. My mother was beaming and punctuating every sentence with the word "son," while my dad insisted on shouting into the phone even though it was a good connection. When I eventually got to talk to him he told me that he was in Africa. I imagined him with a tan, stubble and hippie hair, snorting coke and playing poker with shady characters, until he mentioned that Sister Augustino and Mother Bernadette had dropped him into the village to make the call. I told him about Seán and me. Of course he already knew about us and called me slow. It had been four months since we'd spoken and I missed him dreadfully. I called him a cheeky bastard to my mother's utter disgust.

"Emma, for God's sake!" she almost cried.

I could nearly hear Noel smile. I asked him when he was coming home and he said sometime that year and then I said good-bye because Seán kept digging me to give him the phone. When he got it he wasn't doing much talking—instead he nodded a lot, then he took the phone out into the hall.

On the way home I asked him what he and Noel were talking about, but he just smiled and said nothing. I found this very annoying and reminded him of my freakish strength, but he still wouldn't budge. As soon as we got home he distracted me with sex and I soon forgot what was bugging me.

Two Sundays later, Seán couldn't make it to dinner at my parents so I trudged over alone. My parents and I sat at the dinner table and were discussing Leonard's dietary progress when the doorbell rang. My mother got up to answer it. Dad and I were discussing the fat content in tuna when we heard my mother scream. My heart sank and my stomach turned. My father jumped up, but I was ahead of him. We ran into the hall expecting terror; instead we found my mother wrapped around Noel and Seán grinning beside them. My father enveloped his son and my mother. It was like a scene from *The Waltons*.

"Hey, Em," Noel said, grinning over my father's shoulder. "Did you miss me?"

My parents parted and I grabbed him and held on tight. My dad stood back, watching his children with tears in his eyes. Noel escaped me and he went back to Dad. They hugged tight and my dad cried. My mother gave Seán three desserts as a reward for bringing her son home, so he ate while Noel told us of his travels, showed us photographs of exotic places and handed out trinkets from around the globe. He was relaxed and when he laughed his eyes sparkled. Eventually my parents, worn-out by excitement, went to bed, leaving Seán, Noel and me alone together, three old friends catching up on one another's lives.

Noel was thrilled that Seán and I had finally found each other. (His words not mine.) I called him a sap. Noel called me a hard-ass and Seán agreed. I couldn't help but remember John and how he and Noel had such a good friendship. The thought, although fleeting, made me smile. Seán glimpsed my smile and squeezed my hand, returning me to the present.

It turned out that Seán had confided his feelings for me to Noel a long time ago.

"You weren't the only one who came to Confession, Em," Noel told me.

Seán laughed, remembering getting carried away during one of their confessional chats and lighting up a cigarette. Noel had smelled smoke and thought the church was on fire.

We talked most of the night about African culture, Asian technology and about what amazing creatures elephants were. It was Noel's first night home so neither of us brought up the future. We didn't want to push him into revealing his plans.

★ ★ ★

Clo arrived over to my place the following Saturday. I was lost in laundry. She was beaming.

"What?" I asked.

251

"Tom asked me to marry him," she replied.

I dropped my washing basket.

She laughed and did a little happy dance. "I said yes."

I tripped over the washing basket, but managed to hug her without further injury. It turns out they had been sitting at home watching *This Life* and during an argument as to whether Miles was sexy or a pain in the arse, Tom asked her to be his wife. Just like that. They were going to buy the ring that afternoon. We sat together in the kitchen.

"It's funny the way things work out, isn't it?" she asked.

"I suppose," I said and I knew what she meant.

"For so long I thought the next wedding would be you and John."

I smiled at her. "Me too," I said.

"Do you think he would have liked Tom?"

I nodded my head. "Definitely."

She smiled. "Yeah. Tom would have liked him too."

She asked me if I still missed him. I told her I did.

"But you wouldn't change your life now?" she asked.

I told her I didn't have the power to change anything and that for the first time I understood why and I wouldn't want to change it—after all, if I did control life and death I'd probably fuck it up.

"This world is a chessboard and we are mere pawns," I declared with an air of pomposity.

She looked at me blankly.

"We just have to try to enjoy the game," I attempted to explain.

"Shut up," she said, putting me back in my place.

I laughed. "Okay, but you know what I mean."

"Nobody knows what you mean when you go off on

one," she smiled. Then, after a while, she said, "It's good to see you happy."

"You too," I smiled.

Everything was going to be all right, at least for a while, and I could live with that. Seán was my future, I was in love and maybe there was a part of me that was in love with him from the first time I met him. I definitely thought he was a ride. I smiled as I remembered. She asked me what I was smiling at so I told her. She agreed he was a ride.

"Life's funny," she said sadly.

"Yeah," I agreed, but nothing was going to upset me on the day that my best friend announced she was getting married.

"Tom's a ride too," she noted.

"Oh God, I know," I agreed.

Doreen arrived in with a packet of biscuits. She plonked herself at the kitchen table.

"You're not going to believe what he's playing at now," she said and we both knew she was talking about her husband.

Clo laughed and put on the kettle.

Dor proceeded to tell us he was on a protest march against the felling and selling of trees. Clo noted that maybe he had a point. She'd read somewhere that trees were important. Doreen told us they were Christmas trees.

Clo loved Christmas trees. She thought about it for a minute. "Oh, who cares? Dor, I'm getting married!"

Doreen put her cup of fresh tea down. "You love him?" she asked.

"More than shoes."

"Does he love you?"

"More than football."

Doreen finished her interrogation by asking whether he had any interest in the Green Party.

"Not that I know of."

"Good. All the best of luck to you, love."

I wondered what Doreen was like when she was in her late twenties. I wondered would Clo and I be sitting together in our sixties complaining about our husbands' latest schemes or our kids being ungrateful bastards, handing out advice to youngsters living next door and making an assortment of cakes over which any problem could be discussed.

Clo and Doreen left together, Clo to meet her fiancé to pick out a ring, and Doreen to get her husband out of a tree. I returned to laundry and was just about to start ironing when Noel arrived.

"You got a haircut," I wailed. I had really liked his shaggy-hair look.

He just smiled. "I'm meeting with the Bishop tomorrow."

"You could have worn a hat," I advised, but he just smiled.

"Not for this," he said, grinning.

He looked older but happier. The lines that had appeared around his eyes over the past year served only to highlight the light that twinkled from within.

"What are you going to say?" I asked with my fingers crossed.

"I'm a priest, Emma," he said in a tone that suggested a happy resignation.

I don't mind admitting that my heart felt heavy in my chest. I concealed my disappointment by cleaning the counter. I hadn't expected it. I thought that his adventures around the globe would have confirmed he didn't belong to the Church, but then again, Noel wasn't me.

"But what about never having a family, love or sex? What about watching other people live their lives but only ever nearly sharing in every experience? What about being alone?" I asked, becoming surprisingly upset by his revelation.

He took my hand. "I've experienced a lot of things over the past year. Some of them were great, exciting. Everything was new and a challenge, but I've seen things, Em, things that people should never have to see, let alone experience."

He told me about his trip to the Sudan and in particular a tiny four-year-old boy who was dying of malnutrition. His body was tortured, bones grated on the thin skin that covered them, muscles twisted, belly bloated. He was blind, the gift of the health that he had been born with stolen. This little creature was alone. His mother had died a month previously and my brother found him lying and dying on a dirty camp bed calling for her. When Noel held his hand, tears rolled down his gaunt face. He clung on, desperately afraid to be abandoned once more. He was four years old and he knew he was dying. My brother sang to him. He caressed him and when he went into renal failure, he lay with him in his arms praying out loud and kissing his wet cheek. This little man would never have the life that we took for granted. He would

255

never know the sweetness that life brings. He would only ever experience loss and pain. *Why?*

His story hurt deep inside. It made me remember how good we have it. Even when we lose we often win. What about him? When would he win? Noel had sat with him for two days. He performed the last rites and then the child had died in his arms and Noel swore he was smiling. It seems my brother's presence was all it took. His nickname was Bassa and he wanted to be a doctor when he grew up. Noel stopped talking, tears streaming down his face. I was speechless and I could feel my cheeks burn.

"He's my family, Em."

I sat there choking on sorrow for the boy I never knew and for my brother, who'd watched him die.

"You're going back."

My heavy heart was beginning to crack.

"I'm going back," he nodded.

"You could be an aid worker."

"I'm a priest."

We both cried, but then we both knew he was doing the right thing and, although my heart hurt and my ears buzzed, I felt so proud to know him. I held him in my arms.

"I love you."

"I love you too, Em."

That was the end of that conversation.

★ ★ ★

A week later I was in town shopping with Clo. We were looking for an outfit for her engagement party.

"Does my arse look big in this?" Clo asked for the fourteenth time.

"You're a size six. How could your arse look big in anything?" I replied for the fourteenth time.

My feet were killing me and I wasn't in the mood for shopping. Eventually she picked out a black dress, which looked remarkably similar to the eight black dresses she already had in her wardrobe. I mentioned this, but my comments weren't appreciated.

"Emma, you haven't a clue," she said while marching to the counter.

I was too hungry to argue. Shoes were bought and we were ready to get some food. I was practically crawling and Clo was ratty. We had just ordered when her mobile rang. It was Tom's work number. She answered but it wasn't Tom. I watched her smile fade and the color drain from her face. Tom had collapsed and had been taken to James's Hospital by ambulance. We left the restaurant without a word. We got to the car with very few words.

"He'll be fine," I said, terrified I was wrong.

"I know," she said, her words hollow.

Neither of us believed it. She drove insanely and I didn't complain. We ran into the hospital, almost landing on the information desk. Clo's father had died of a heart attack and standing at that information desk I knew that she was silently convincing herself that Tom was now doing the same thing. Her body shook, she was wringing her hands and when she attempted to speak to the nurse her voice had left her. I held her tight, terrified, waiting for the pain. She cleared her throat and enquired about her fiancé. The woman smiled at her and checked her computer. Clo closed her eyes, but mine were fixed on the woman and her computer. She looked up at us still smiling.

"He's in surgery, dear," she said happily.

Surgery was good. Surgery meant he wasn't dead. Her father hadn't made it to surgery. John hadn't made it to surgery. This was good news and we both felt it. Clo sighed. Tom wasn't dead and then we both registered that there was still time for that. People die in surgery, and what terrible thing could be wrong with him? Clo went white again and I think I joined her.

"Is it his heart?" she asked, already crying in anticipation of this stranger's answer. Her tears were burning her eyes and she was holding my hand so tight, fractures were possible. The woman looked at her screen again.

"No," she smiled. "Suspected appendix, dear."

The word "appendix" sank in. We both looked at one another.

"Suspected appendix?" Clo asked, color returning.

"Yes, dear. He shouldn't be too long," the woman confirmed, her smile fixed.

"Suspected appendix," I repeated to ensure we weren't sharing in a happy hallucination.

"Appendix," Clo confirmed smiling and then we were laughing a little hysterically and we kept laughing. Clo was leaning on me with her knees close together, looking like she needed a pee, and I was wiping tears from my face and trying not to snort.

The woman's smile faded. Obviously, she thought that we were lunatics. This made the situation funnier. I needed to pee. Clo had a pain in her face and, fearing that we

were very close to being escorted out of the hospital, Clo regained some composure.

"I'm sorry," she said to the woman, "but would you mind telling us where the ladies' is?"

Then we burst out laughing again and she suggested rather coldly that we should consider leaving the premises until we'd composed ourselves.

So there we were sitting in Clo's car outside the hospital. When we eventually calmed down Clo turned to me.

"Do you think he'll be out of surgery yet?" she asked.

I looked at my watch. "I think it's only a twenty-minute operation."

She got serious. "Jesus, Em, what am I going to do?"

"What do you mean?" I asked.

"He'll be back in his room soon and we're barred."

"No, we're not. The woman merely asked us to compose ourselves."

"We looked like assholes in there. Appendix is serious. I didn't mean to laugh—I was just so relieved it wasn't his heart."

"And I was glad he wasn't run over by anything," I admitted.

"Do you think he'll be okay?" she asked suddenly, paling a little.

"Were you okay when you had your appendix out?" I asked.

"Yeah," she admitted.

"Was I?" I asked.

"Well, you moaned a lot as I recall, but then you were always a bloody moan as a teenager," she grinned.

"Well then, they caught it in time, they're operating. He'll be fine."

"His brother Rupert is in there," she said before noticing I was picking lint from my trousers. "Stop it!"

"Sorry," I said, knotting my hands in my lap. "You wanna go in?"

"Not yet. I can't stand Rupert," she admitted.

"Oh yeah?" I asked, interested. She hadn't mentioned him before.

"Bloody know-it-all," she mumbled.

Once I'd ascertained Tom's exact co-ordinates from the frosty woman at the desk, and having at least an hour to wait before Tom got out of recovery, we headed to the canteen, ordered unwanted bacon and cabbage and waited for Seán.

We waited for over half an hour. Our dishes were long cleared away. Our coffee was cold. We had that uncomfortable feeling that sitting at an empty table when there are fifty people with trays looking for a seat brings. Eventually a blue haired, bandy-legged, arthritic old lady stood over us roaring to her friend in the queue.

"I can't go on, Delores, my knees have given up!"

We took the hint and stood outside, drinking stale take-away coffee amongst a group of smokers, one of whom was nice enough to offer us a cigarette each.

"No, thanks, we're off cigarettes," Clo admitted a little sadly.

Fifteen minutes and two smokes later Seán arrived. Tom had at last been moved to the third floor.

His brother Rupert was sitting by his bedside. "Where the hell were you?"

I instantly didn't like him.

Tom was attached to a drip, dribbling and in a drug-induced haze, but he smiled when he saw Clo.

She leaned over and kissed him while pointedly ignoring his brother. "I'm really sorry—you were already in surgery by the time we got here."

He smiled and nodded.

The brother looked at her disbelievingly. "You work only ten minutes from the hospital."

He had a kickable face.

She just smiled and responded calmly. "Well, we're here now."

"Better late than never," he mumbled.

"Why don't you shut up?" Clo suggested while still smiling. Tom giggled, although it wasn't apparent whether he found Clo funny or whether he was seeing pink elephants pole dancing.

His brother remained unimpressed. "He could have died, you know."

Clodagh smirked. "He's fine."

"Appendix is potentially life-threatening and no laughing matter," Rupert snarled.

Clo's smile faded. "Oh shove it up your arse, Rupert," she said and Tom laughed.

He was with us after all.

Chapter 21

A Hen, a Whisper and Silver Linings

The wedding was less than three months away and I was meeting with Anne and Clo to go shopping for wedding lingerie. Anne had insisted on flying to Dublin for the event, afraid that her distance would mean missing out on the smallest of things. She was desperately lonely and everyone bar her husband knew it. Post-Christmas had been particularly difficult for her, but knowing this did not make seeing her any less shocking. She had put on over three stone and it looked like someone had taken a bicycle pump and used it to blow her up. I couldn't believe it. Clo was silent, a rarity in itself. We both composed ourselves and greeted her a little too enthusiastically, if truth were known.

She sat and grabbed the menu. "I'm starving," she said and I prayed Clo would remain silent.

She did and unfortunately so did I, for a long two minutes.

"I think I'll have the steak and chips, chicken wings on the side and can I see the dessert menu now?" Anne went on as if everything was normal.

I regained my speech. "The steak is great," I said.

"What?" Clo queried absentmindedly while still focused on her growing friend.

I repeated that the steak was great.

"Right," she said, staring.

This wasn't going well.

Anne looked away and called a waiter. Clo and I looked at one another. She had mentioned nothing about weight gain on her numerous calls to us both and it was a shock.

Later we were in Brown Thomas looking at underwear. Anne wandered over to the shoes and Clo took the opportunity to discuss her size with me.

"Christ, Anne's got big," she said, followed by, "Did you see what she managed to eat?"

She had ended up sucking down steak and chips, chicken wings, a slice of double fudge cake, a muffin and two Snack bars. I agreed this wasn't like her but argued against bringing it up.

Clo was adamant. "There is obviously a big problem—excuse the pun. As her friends, it's our job to find out what the hell is going on, sort it and put her on a diet so that she can fit into the bloody bridesmaid dress!"

"I knew we bought those dresses too early," I said, shaking my head.

"You are joking. We've all been pretty much the same size for the last five years!" Her hands were in the air and she was beginning to sweat.

It was a good argument and I agreed our friend's
sudden weight gain was puzzling and ill-timed, but added
that if she wanted our help she'd ask for it and so far Anne
was acting like there wasn't a problem. We could always
return the dresses—and maybe she was happy with her
new size and it was only other people's small-mindedness
that would be the cause of her unhappiness.

Clo looked at me and said, "I love you, Em, but
sometimes you talk out of your arse."

I informed her that it was a fact as I'd seen it on *Oprah*.
She laughed and made some smart comment about Oprah.

"Excuse me, Clo," I began snottily, "Oprah Winfrey
has done more for women, fat people, skinny people and
minorities in America and the world than most politicians,
presidents and royals since the beginning of time.
Furthermore, I believe that when she makes a point it's
based on medical and documented fact as opposed to
relying on the old adage that agreeing with anything
outside your realm of experience means talking through
your arse."

Clo looked at me and smiled. "Em, you're right and
maybe Oprah's right, but something's going on and I'm
going to find out what."

At least I got her to agree to wait until we were back
at her place and I remember promising myself that I'd get
pissed.

We got back and it was late. My feet were swollen, Clo
had a headache and Anne was hungry, again. I opened a
bottle of wine and handed Clo a glass, which she used to
wash down a couple of headache tablets.

And Anne gave out to her for abusing her body.

Oh Christ, here we go.

Clo swallowed and smiled. "Speaking of which," she began, "Em and I were just talking."

I couldn't believe she'd included me in her crusade. I was losing color while Anne listened to her intently.

"You've really packed on the pounds."

Now Anne was starting to lose color. Clo must have noticed, but carried on regardless.

"In a really short space of time. It's just not right."

Anne was silent. I was mortified.

Clo continued. "It's not like you're Oprah or anything. You've never fluctuated more than half a stone in your life."

I was appalled that she had the audacity to bring Oprah into this and in such a negative light.

Anne looked at me with hurt in her eyes, so I decided to speak before Clo's version of kindness killed her. I really didn't know what to say. This whole thing had got out of hand. It felt like an intervention and who the fuck were we to intervene? What did we know? The girl had put on some weight. So what? I wondered what Oprah would say.

So I asked her if she was unhappy and she answered by bursting into tears. Clo and I sat beside her on the couch. Clo handed her some wine and tissues. Her eyes were puffy and sore.

"I hate Kerry!" she wailed. "And now apparently I'm a fat pig!"

"Okay, you are fat but you will never be a pig," Clo said gently, as though she had just said something helpful.

Anne stared at her incredulously. I pretty much

265

mirrored Anne. Years of working in PR had obviously addled Clo's brain because she didn't seem to notice our bemusement.

"And besides, even with the extra pounds you're still more attractive than some skinny people I know!" Clo added triumphantly.

Anne looked at me and I looked at Anne and Clo sat looking at us both, grinning like she'd just waved a magic wand. We sat for a few seconds before Anne burst out laughing.

"You really are the shallowest person I know but I still love you," she said, nudging Clo, and Clo smiled at her, acknowledging her shallowness and glad to be accepted.

"Everything's going to be fine," I piped up.

Anne wondered how.

"You're going to sit Richard down and tell him that you're homesick and then you'll come home," I said, like it was a problem easily solved.

Living in Kerry was Richard's dream. He loved residing in a small and beautiful place surrounded by mountains and lakes. He loved the views, the slow pace of life, the people, the quaint bars, the good food and the silence. Kerry gave Richard peace, but Anne was a city girl. She found beauty in architecture, noisy restaurants, city lights, the theater, museums, Brown Thomas and the Shelbourne. She loved the noise, the people, the queues and even the traffic.

"Do you know there isn't one traffic light in the entire town?" she almost cried. "How the hell am I supposed to live like that?"

We nodded in agreement. It seemed insane. She

further argued that her husband would never agree to leave Kerry, adding that she was ready to hang herself.

"Why not compromise?" I asked. "Why not live in Dublin during the winter and Kerry in the summer?"

Anne thought about it. "But the summer is only three months of the year."

"Exactly," Clo grinned.

Anne smiled and added how lovely Kerry was in the summer. "I wouldn't mind Christmas there either. It's really nice at Christmas," she said, brightening as she spoke.

"Well, there you go then," I said, as though it was decided.

"More wine?" Clo offered, as if to seal the deal.

Anne's smile turned to concern. She wasn't as convinced as us, but then again, a problem is always simply resolved when it's not your own.

So we drank. We drank to our health, to Clo's wedding and to Anne's diet and then we drank some more because for most people in their twenties being heavy is a crime while drinking yourself to death is perfectly acceptable. People are insane.

Seán picked me up just after eleven. Anne was passed out on the couch with a blanket over her and an empty glass in her hand. Clo tried to take it, but Anne wasn't letting go.

Clo and I said our good-byes and Seán escorted me to the car. When we got home, he made me a coffee and ran a bath. I lay in it for the longest time just thinking. Seán brought in a refill. He sat on the floor by the bath the way John used to do. He offered to wash my back the way John used to do. He took care of me the way John used to do and I realized that I was happy, truly content. I was twenty-eight and living in rented accommodation. I was a teacher on a bullshit wage. I had a car that broke down once a month and a cat that made Roseanne Barr appear stable. But as Seán towel dried my hair I was at peace.

Later in bed we turned into one another and I told him of Anne's unhappiness and subsequent weight gain.

"I'd move to the moon for you," he said.

I laughed. "I take it that's the moon or nowhere?" I said.

"Obviously," he replied, grinning.

He kissed me and it still felt like the first time. We had run out of condoms, but we made love anyway and afterwards I lay in the dark smiling.

★ ★ ★

Anne returned to Kerry the next day. She was hungover, but determined. Richard picked her up from the airport. He turned up with flowers and she told him they needed to talk. What ensued was a blazing row during which the flowers were severely damaged. Anne wanted to go back to Dublin. Richard wanted to stay in Kerry. She argued homesickness. He argued his distaste for Dublin. He argued she hadn't made an effort to fit into the Kerry lifestyle. He had made a lot of friends, but she refused to socialize. He further argued that after a year they had made a new life for themselves there. He pointed out the obvious: they had a home, they were trying for children and she had agreed to move to the country. She disputed that it was more difficult for her to make friends, but when challenged she couldn't give a reason why. She pointed

out that they still had an apartment in Dublin and plenty of money to buy a house. It was also apparent to her that so far they had been unsuccessful at getting pregnant and besides, there were perfectly good schools in Dublin anyway. They screamed and roared. He, disappointed because she was giving up so quickly, she, disappointed because her husband was either completely blind to her pain or didn't care. Richard was used to getting his way and Anne was used to giving it to him but she couldn't do that anymore.

At four in the morning, she packed her clothes and drove to Dublin. Richard woke on the couch to find his wife gone and a note with the word "Choose" written on it.

★ ★ ★

It was two weeks since Anne had walked out on Richard. In that time she had dropped an entire dress size, which Clo unhelpfully described as a silver lining. I was worried. She had gone from overeating to not being able to hold down soup. She set up home in their Dublin apartment, which was a penthouse and nicer than my bloody house, but it didn't stop me from wondering if Anne felt like she was slumming it. Each day she waited for Richard to call, but he didn't and she was devastated. She'd ring me sobbing so loudly her pain was impossible to ignore.

"I left and he doesn't care!" she'd wail.

I tried to be positive, but the evidence was weighing in favor of her statement.

"He's a selfish bastard!" she'd roar.

I sympathized while being careful not to agree, afraid

269

that if and when they got back together she'd hold it against me. Women can be funny like that.

"Where is he, Emma?" she'd cry plaintively.

Good question.

"Why can't he just meet me halfway?"

Better question.

"Does he even love me?"

Scary question.

I wanted her to stay with Seán and me, but she didn't want to leave the apartment just in case he called. She sounded really depressed and it frightened me.

One night I tried to call her. She didn't pick up. She hadn't left the apartment in two weeks and she had been very down during the day. She could have been out, but deep down something told me she wasn't. I called again. No answer. I was getting very nervous. Something was wrong. I could feel it—that terrible dread was creeping into my bones. I got into the car, but of course it wouldn't start and Seán was out so I called a cab, but nothing was available for over an hour. That was too long. There was no direct bus so I went to Doreen.

Doreen had been a nurse. I told her to bring her medical bag. We reached Anne within half an hour after my first unanswered call. There was no answer at the main door so we entered the building with a pizza deliveryman. He didn't notice us follow him in and, if he did, thankfully he didn't care. We took the lift to the top floor and I rang the bell. Nothing.

"Emma, this is ridiculous—she's probably with her parents," Doreen said, leaning on the wall.

I rang the bell again and pressed my ear against the door.

"Doreen, listen," I said urgently, sure that I had heard something or someone.

Doreen pressed her ear against the door and then looked at me. "The TV?" she questioned while repositioning her ear.

Now we were both listening intently. A man passed us and stopped.

"Can I help you?" he said.

"No, thanks," I said nonchalantly, attempting to appear normal.

"I'm the caretaker, so if there's a problem?"

"Yes, actually, we'd like to get in. Do you have a key?" Doreen asked with authority like she owned the place.

The man smiled at her audacity. "Yes, I do have a key, but I can't just give it out, you understand."

I had returned to pressing my ear against the door. "Shush," I said hurriedly. "I can hear something. It's her. I can hear her."

I could hear the word "help" being called out faintly. Doreen went back to listening. The man approached and looked for space so that he too could listen.

Doreen was becoming impatient. "Listen, there's a young woman in there and we think that she may need help. So you run along and get the key and if we're wrong we'll apologize and bid you good night, but, if we're right, you'll be a hero."

The caretaker contemplated this for a moment. "Give me a minute," he said and left.

By the time he returned we were both full sure that we could hear her calling out and I was screaming that everything would be fine to a wooden door. He let us in and followed. The sitting room was empty and the TV was on. The kitchen was clear and so was the bedroom. I made my way down the hall and to the bathroom with Doreen and the stranger following tentatively behind.

I tried the door. It was locked.

"Anne!" I called out.

"Em!" a small voice called out from behind the door.

"Anne, let me in!"

"I can't!" she cried.

"Why not?" I asked, looking at the two others behind.

"I've pulled my back out! I can't move."

I pushed at the door.

"Stop!" she cried out. "I'm naked!"

"Jesus," mumbled the caretaker. I guess he was expecting a quiet night and a naked, injured woman certainly wasn't on his "to do" list.

"Calm down, love. We have the caretaker. He'll take care of the door," Doreen said while gesturing to the caretaker.

"Doreen?" Anne whined.

"Yes, it's me, love. Everything will be fine."

"I'm naked," Anne reminded us.

"It will be fine. I'll cover his—what's your name?" She looked at the caretaker.

"Jim."

"I'll cover Jim's eyes when he removes the door."

Jim looked nervous. I could hear Anne mumbling something about God. Jim disappeared to find his tools. Doreen and I kept Anne talking. It appears that she hadn't eaten all day and the likelihood was that she had fainted in the shower. One minute she was standing under hot water, the next she woke up on the floor unable to move. I tried to calm her, but she wasn't having any of it and I could understand: an accident is bad enough; a naked accident was like pouring salt into the wound.

Doreen remained upbeat. "Sure it isn't something you can tell your grandkids?" She was smiling at me, sure that her words would bring comfort, but I knew better and when Anne started to cry so did she.

Jim returned and began unscrewing the hinges.

"Why don't you just kick it down," I asked.

"You want me to kick down a solid mahogany door?" His voice was laced with the smallest hint of sarcasm.

"Well, yeah," I replied.

Anne screamed that he was not to kick down the door. She did not need a door landing on top of her or indeed a handyman on top of a door landing on her. Doreen reminded her to be calm. With only one hinge to go I insisted on taking over. He complied a little too willingly and I wondered if he was gay. With the last hinge removed, I alerted my naked friend that I was about to enter.

"Wait!" she screamed.

We all stood motionless.

"Jim?" she called out.

"Yeah?" he said hesitantly.

"You can go now. Thanks for your help," she said from the floor.

"Right then," he smiled and almost ran out the door.

Doreen sighed. "Men. Bloody useless."

I pulled the door over and saw poor Anne arse up and facedown.

"You could park a bike," Doreen laughed.

She was right. I had expected Anne to be lying flat, not bent over and on her knees. It was a bloody awkward position and I wondered how she'd managed it.

"Yes, thank you, Doreen," Anne noted, not amused.

I covered her with a bath towel and then followed Doreen's instructions and we lifted her to her feet. She was still bent forward and Doreen worried that it was a slipped disc.

We called an ambulance when it became perfectly apparent that Anne was going nowhere in a sitting position. I dressed Anne while Doreen gave the operator directions. While we waited, Doreen interrogated Anne as to the cause of her accident.

"Okay, so you were dizzy. You hadn't eaten. When did you eat last?"

"Yesterday—maybe the day before." Anne looked like she was going to be sick but maybe that was because she was bent forward.

"You must be starving," said Doreen. "Why don't I make a sandwich for the ambulance?"

Anne's sideways glance said it all, but Doreen carefully wiped the hair from Anne's face and spoke gently to her. "I know you're stressed and I know you're having a bad time but, love, you have to eat—otherwise you end up naked on the floor."

Anne mumbled something about a yogurt in the fridge. I spoon-fed her and we waited. Over an hour later the ambulance men arrived.

Doreen was agitated and didn't mind letting it show. "It's a bloody disgrace," she kept mumbling as the ambulance men lifted Anne into the ambulance. "Is this what we pay our taxes for?" she asked the young man who was busy trying to inject a muscle relaxant into Anne's back.

He tried to ignore her, but she repeated the query until he was forced to answer her. "Sorry, missus," he said.

This seemed to suffice. I thanked her and told her I'd let her know how we got on in the morning.

"No problem, love. See you in the morning for a coffee."

And then we were on our way to the hospital. The injection meant that Anne could lie flat, but it was obvious she was still in pain.

In the hospital at last and behind a curtain I stood, holding Anne's hand. She was crying and my heart was bleeding for her. I thought about calling Richard, but then I was afraid that it would only make things worse. When the doctor arrived I was given a respite so I called Seán and he commiserated and told me to leave Richard to him. When I returned Anne was drowsy.

"I've given her something to help her sleep," the doctor said kindly.

"Thanks," I said automatically, realizing suddenly that I could do with some sleep. "Is she going to be okay?" I asked as he was leaving.

"Fine, although it looks like she's torn a muscle. It's sore but a week's rest should do the trick."

"A week," I repeated just to be sure.

"Maybe two." He winked and left.

"Easy for you to say, mate."

I left Anne asleep in a private room. It was after two a.m. when I got home. I fell into bed and Seán cuddled me close to him.

"Did you talk to Richard?" I asked.

"He was out. I left a message."

"Jesus!"

"Don't worry, he'll be here," he said confidently.

"Are you sure?"

"Absolutely."

"She's starving herself," I said guiltily.

"She'll be okay."

"Do you think it's 'cause Clo and I called her fat?"

"It probably didn't help." He sighed. "But her real problem is in her marriage."

"Still, I'm going to kill Clo."

And then I was asleep.

★ ★ ★

The next morning Doreen kept her word and in so doing woke me at the crack of dawn. We drank coffee together and she appeared happy with the doctor's diagnosis.

"A torn muscle is much better than a slipped disc," she noted before digging into a slice of toast.

"I suppose so," I said, not really knowing much about either ailment. "I just hope that everything will be okay between Anne and Richard."

"It'll be fine," she said. "Nothing like an accident to remind people what life's about."

I thought about her statement for a moment and then agreed.

"And what about you?" she asked from nowhere.

I wasn't sure what she was getting at.

"Well, Miss Psychic. If you hadn't insisted that there

was a problem and that we hightail it over there, she'd probably still be lying on the floor arse up."

I hadn't thought about that. "Jesus," I said.

"Jesus indeed," she agreed.

"What's that all about?" I asked.

"Who knows?" she said and then she smiled to herself knowingly.

"John?" I asked conspiratorially.

"Maybe," she smiled the same smile.

"Jesus," I said.

She nodded.

"I wish he'd fuck off," I said wistfully, not sure that I was particularly happy with my ex and his penchant for sending me on missions of mercy.

Doreen laughed. "Yeah. I know what you mean."

She left and as I drove to school I wondered if John really had sent me another message from the grave or was I just super-sensitive since his passing. Either way, before his death I was never known for my intuitiveness. I also thought about the fact that I seemed to be spending a large portion of the last two years in and out of the bloody hospital. By the time I reached the school car park, I was convinced that John had looked down on us. He had seen trouble and he had helped us and it didn't freak me out. I apologized to him for my earlier comment. I didn't want him to fuck off. It made me happy to think that maybe he was still around looking after us and as I parked the car I realized that I no longer feared life and death blurring into one. I knew he was continuing, that he was being taken care of, that he was at peace and that I'd see him again in another world, at another time. Seán would be there and Clo, Anne and Richard and we would be fine and for the first time in a long time I thought about God and His plan and I believed. Noel would have slapped his thigh.

After school I headed to the hospital. Anne looked a good deal better and although she found it difficult to sit up at least she was horizontal, which was an improvement on the night before. She was pitiful, weak and terribly afraid, and my heart broke for her.

Clodagh arrived, breathless, as she had run out of a meeting to make the strict visiting hours. Richard hadn't appeared yet, which was worrying. Anne was apologizing to Clo, worried that in her present condition she wouldn't be able to be a bridesmaid. Clo wasn't worried. She had full faith that Anne would recover and if she didn't Tom had a cousin that would fit into the dress.

Seán had been speaking to Richard daily since the breakup and it emerged that he, like Anne, felt like the victim and was similarly depressed and mute. Seán tried to talk him into making the first move but it was no good. He was stubborn and so used to her caving in that he felt it was only a matter of time. Seán had tried and failed to reach him. He had no idea how badly his wife was suffering and it seemed that he didn't care. As far as Richard was concerned, Anne had walked out on him so why should he care? Sean had tried to explain that relationships were give and take and that maybe he should consider giving in just this once. Richard called him an asshole and hung up. Sean cursed and blamed me for insisting he interfere.

In the end, where Seán failed, Clo had triumphed. She had a bellyful of it and so two days into Anne's injury she managed to locate him through his PA. He was in Paris tending to an apartment that he was letting. It appears he was having problems with the non-paying tenants and he had decided to evict them personally. She called his hotel room from my place and told him how it was, as only she could.

"Richard, it's Clo, don't you dare hang up. Richard? Right, it's like this. You and Anne have been together since first year in college. She's your wife now. You're apart and miserable and we, your friends, are really worried about both of you. So here's the wake-up call. You're a spoilt bastard and you've had your own way since forever, but you're married now and that means compromise. Anne is in hospital, having fainted from starving herself—now I'll admit I may share the responsibility there but the fact is that now she's done her back in. She's desperately unhappy, in agony and you are supposed to love her. So get off your arse, get home and do something about it. Oh and by the way, from now on check your bloody messages."

She fell silent and I wished I could hear what he was saying. After a few seconds she handed the phone to me.

"He wants to talk to you."

I said hello and he asked me if Anne was all right.

"She's really hurt herself and it could have been a lot worse," I said and I believed I wasn't exaggerating.

I told him that Anne had done everything she could to try to make him happy and it was about time he returned the favor. I reminded him of the good advice he had given me and I hoped he would accept mine.

Clo grabbed the phone and added, "Don't be a dick all your life."

She hung up.

"Clodagh!" I screeched. It had seemed to go well until she called him a dick.

"I'm sick of him," she noted.

"But for Christ's sake! Calling him a dick is hardly the best foot forward."

"We've tried everything else and besides, a fact is a fact."

"Lovely," I noted.

She grinned. "You worry too much. You're so like your ma."

I threw a cushion at her. "I am not," I said, disgusted.

I have to point out that I'm not sure why this analogy upset me, as aside from loving her, I am also very fond of my mother, but it did.

"You," I said.

"You," she countered.

"You," I furthered.

This line of argument continued until Seán arrived laden with shopping and a large brown envelope. Leonard immediately jumped down from the window and followed Seán into the kitchen, desperate to be fed. Seán obliged before returning to the sitting room, lighting a cigar.

Clo and I looked at him.

"What are you doing?" I asked.

"Celebrating," he noted.

"Oh yeah?" Clo asked.

"Yeah," he agreed.

"Celebrating what?" I ventured.

"My book. It's being published."

Our jaws fell.

"No!" Clo said.

I was on my feet. "Oh my God!"

I was so excited I thought about puking. This was something I thought about a lot lately. My stomach was on edge. Still I was extremely happy, delirious almost. Seán was jumping up and down in the one spot. I was clinging on, enjoying the ride.

"That's incredible," Clo said, genuinely pleased.

"It could be on the bookshelves as soon as Christmas," he noted proudly while holding me tight.

"I could do the PR!" Clodagh almost screamed. "I'd love to do a book launch!"

I laughed. She was such a media whore. He was dancing and inhaling his cigar and he was forgetting that it was a cigar as opposed to a cigarette that was to be his downfall. Five minutes later he felt sick.

Clodagh left soon after. At the door I wondered aloud if we had done the right thing in calling Richard. She told me that we had and begged me not to waste the night worrying when there was so much to celebrate. She was right.

★ ★ ★

Our phone call had worked. Within five hours Richard was by Anne's bedside holding up the piece of paper that she'd written "Choose" on. The word "Choose" had a line through it and underneath was written "You." It was a real movie moment, but instead of falling into his arms (let's face it, she wasn't in a position to) she stood (lay) firm. They had to make changes in their marriage and they would either fix it or walk away. They talked for hours and for the first time Richard listened to his wife. She articulated all that bothered her and it turned out that there was a long list to get through. He agreed that he had been a dick and actually apologized. He hadn't meant to be such a dick and he admitted her fall had frightened him. He had thought that if he held firm she would come back, but for the first time in his life Richard realized that the world didn't revolve around him. They talked into the early hours and eventually it was agreed that they would try to live in Dublin for the majority of the year. Richard was giving in to his wife's wishes and, despite the discomfort, she was elated. Equality at last.

Chapter 22

Blue

I woke up at seven a.m. The alarm hadn't gone off and it was unlike me to wake before it. I felt restless and looked over at a peaceful Seán. I thought about waking him to discuss Anne's impending hen night, but decided against it, as my feeling was that he wouldn't be too pleased. I got up. He found me in the bath half an hour later. He offered to make breakfast, but I really didn't feel like it. He offered to give me a back rub, as my body seemed to ache. I stood up and felt dizzy. He noted that I was pale while handing me a towel. He helped me from the bath and was concerned, but the bath water had been hot so I promised it was no big deal. I tried to force-feed myself a piece of toast, but the sight of it made me queasy.

Please, God, not the flu, I silently prayed as I got into the car. This night was to be Clo's hen and there was no question that I wouldn't be there. I headed to school, praying that if it was the flu the kids had it too. They didn't.

Damn, I thought as I prepared myself to educate thirty rowdy students.

★ ★ ★

Declan came up to me after the lesson.

"You all right?" he asked.

"I'm fine," I smiled, feeling a little better.

"You sick?" he asked.

"No," I smiled.

"Hmmm," he said under his breath.

"What's 'hmmm' supposed to mean?" I attempted a smile.

"You're green." He pointed at my face.

"Are you thinking about going into medicine, Declan?"

"No," he answered flatly. "I'm going to manage pop groups, work them like dogs, make millions and retire at thirty-five." He smiled and leaned forward. "Did you ever hear Jackie Lynch in third year sing?" he asked.

I said that I hadn't.

"Nice little voice on her and not a bad looker. A bit of makeup, the right clothes, she could be a little ride." He grinned and added it was a pity I wasn't ten years younger.

I let it pass because he always entertained me and, to be truthful, at my saddest and before Seán, I swear there were days when I thought it was a damn shame he wasn't ten years older. I watched him leave and wondered how long it would be before I was reading about him in magazines. I felt much better by lunch. I ate, which was to be a big mistake. I lost said lunch rapidly, but by the afternoon I felt better again. It was now obvious that I was coming down with some sort of stomach bug and prayed it wouldn't fully kick in until the next day.

★ ★ ★

Seán was home before me, waiting by the door. He was smiling and holding a bunch of balloons in one hand and a box of my favorite chocolates in the other and he had a rose between his teeth. I laughed.

"Well?" I queried suspiciously.

He had to spit the rose out to speak. "They're giving me a two-book deal with an option for four," he said, beaming.

I screamed. "Oh my God, you're such a ride!"

"I know!" he agreed, shouting.

I jumped him. He dropped the balloons and the chocolates, much to a slim-lined and deprived Leonard's joy, and, while we tore each other's clothes off, Leonard tried to gnaw through packaging. We celebrated with champagne in bed from five to eight and then I had no option but to leave for Clo's hen. He understood and besides, we had the whole weekend to celebrate. The good news was that I was feeling great, full of love and champagne and ready to party. Clo hadn't trusted us with the arrangements for the hen, saying we'd make an arse of it. Instead she took full charge, advising that any hen arriving with a plastic or mechanical mickey would be asked to leave. No wigs, no ball and chain, no crowns, no T-shirts, no phallic foods. This was a night about women together, clubbing, getting pissed and going out with a bang. There were ten of us, all dressed in little black numbers with big hair, lots of makeup and high heels. We

entered the first pub, sat in a line at the bar and drank a
row of shots and then another. The third was on the
house.

We took a table and drank cocktails, talking about Posh
Spice, diamonds, health spas, the tax system, Caribbean
holidays and men, Clinton, phone sex, *Big Brother,* Kid
Rock, Palestine, Nostradamus, babies, weddings, Clo and
the future. She was glowing, intoxicated and having a blast.
We headed to a club and danced for hours while Anne
stood painfully and yet waving from the side of the dance
floor, then on to the next club to play pool, sit on couches,
smoke cigars, drink some more, fall off the couches, then
drink some more, hoping that nobody noticed.

At four the management called us some taxis.

Anne had improved greatly, still a little stiff, but she
was loosening with alcohol. Clo helped her into the taxi,
afraid that her hen may have been too much for her
injured friend, but Anne was adamant that it was a night
for celebration and she was not about to miss a second of
it. Richard was away so she invited us back to her place
for another toast. Anne filled our glasses and we held
them high. She remained standing, as sitting was still a bit
of a challenge.

"We wish for you everything good and more!" she
smiled and we clinked glasses.

Clo wanted to make a toast. "To the many men I
turned down tonight and to the many men I'll be turning
down for the rest of my life! Good luck to one and all!"

We laughed and Anne raised her glass.

"One and all!" we repeated.

I didn't make a toast—I was too busy drinking. Anne

made herself comfortable on the floor, drinking from a straw so she didn't have to move her head. We sat up until six talking about the past, our teenage years, college and our summer in the States, the people we met along the way, the people we lost along the way. Clo reminded me of my dream wedding, John standing on the altar, George Michael singing at the reception. I laughed. Now when I daydreamed it was of Seán and George Michael didn't really figure. It's funny how the world works, how we win and lose, how we can never really know what's ahead though we never stop planning. How we survive and move on. There's a sadness that comes with survival, but also more joy to be had. We agreed Clo had earned hers. She deserved the best because to us she was the best, the brightest, the funniest and the truest, and Tom was a good man and although we three, sitting there, had long ago realized that life isn't all roses and behind every silver lining lies a big dirty cloud, we also knew that we would always find comfort in one another and after all, isn't that what being a hen is all about?

★ ★ ★

The next day I suffered. I suffered like I've never suffered before. Truly the pain in my head was tantamount to a bomb going off deep inside my temple. At one point I considered that I might be having an aneurysm. I even thought about going back to the hospital. Why not? At this stage they all knew my name. I lay in bed with a cold cloth carefully placed over my eyes and moaning to ensure that I hadn't lost the power of speech. I felt sick but then again, that was to be expected. I had drunk my own body weight. An unusual side effect of this particular hangover was painful breasts. They also felt a little bigger than usual and were extremely tender to the touch. I opened my top and there were little brown rings circling my nipples.

Interesting.

Seán was in the office playing catch-up, which is something he often did on a Sunday. I was alone except for Leonard, who was engaging in a staring match with Old Mrs. Jennings's cat across the road. It was after two when I eventually made it out of bed. I puked and instantly my stomach felt better. However, my head was still reverberating when Doreen called to share in the events of the previous night. She made tea while I was only too happy to detail the kind of hangover I was experiencing. She didn't seem too concerned.

"Yeah, well, it serves you right."

"Thanks a lot, Doreen."

"Yeah, well, what age are you? Really, Emma, sometimes I wonder about your generation."

I began to wonder why I bothered. I made a face and she laughed. "It's not funny. I was supposed to mark essays today. I can't see straight. I want to puke." Then for some reason I added, "And the odd thing is, my breasts are tender."

"Tender how?" she asked.

"Just tender, sore," I said dismissively.

"How sore?"

"Oh for Christ's sake, sore!"

"What else?" she asked.

I wondered about whether I should mention the brown rings and then I wondered, if I didn't, would it be something I should have mentioned and I couldn't once I'd slipped into a coma.

"Brown rings around my nipples."

This statement was met with a silence that was unusual for Doreen. "Brown rings," she repeated in a voice that suggested concern.

"It's a bit weird, isn't it?" I queried briefly, considering whether or not it was the effect of too many sun beds in my early twenties.

"How have you been feeling lately?" she asked.

"Fine," I said and then I thought about it. "Actually not really fine. Last week I could have sworn I had a touch of food poisoning and then yesterday I felt like I was about to come down with the flu. I was kind of dizzy."

"You are dizzy," she sighed.

"Excuse me?" I responded with great indignity.

"Emma, it's obvious."

But nothing was obvious to me.

"When was your last period?"

I began to twig where this conversation was heading and I would have laughed only laughter caused pain. "About two months ago," I said, smiling.

"Two months ago!" she nearly shouted.

"I know what you're thinking but it's no big deal. I'm as irregular as a Dublin bus." It was true. As a teenager I'd be lucky if I got six periods a year. I'd pretty much regulated in my twenties, but then John died and I'd been all over the place ever since.

"Emma, despite your irregularity, would you not consider taking a test?" she asked, not particularly comforted by my menstrual history.

"No."

"Well, I think you should."

This was not what I needed to hear today of all days. "Really, Dor, it's fine."

"I'm sure it is, but that doesn't mean you're not pregnant, love. Brown circles are a real giveaway."

Bollocks.

She had to go to her son's football match and she left warning me to get a test. I stayed on the couch, attempting to block out the conversation we'd just had. By four I couldn't take it anymore. I got into the car, drove to the nearest chemist and bought headache tablets and a pregnancy test.

Here we go again.

I got home to find that Seán had still not returned from the office. I went to the bathroom, opened the box, struggled with the foil wrapping and peed on the stick.

Three minutes.

Initially my mind was blank and this I guessed was due to the fact that I had killed millions of brain cells the evening before.

Two minutes.

Holy crap, that minute passed really quickly.

I thought about Seán and I smiled because even though I'd been sick as a pig when he left that morning, he had managed to make me laugh and I couldn't even remember how.

One minute. Jesus, time is flying.

I wondered how he'd feel if I was pregnant but it was a fleeting thought and surprisingly, I couldn't manage to muster concern.

Odd.

I looked at my watch. Three minutes had passed. I didn't hang around. I turned the stick over to reveal the thickest bluest line I ever saw. I sat mesmerized by this line for a long time.

I'm pregnant.

I let this new information sink in. The word "wow" would best describe how I felt. I wasn't worried, but I should have been freaking out. Let's be honest, it's pretty obvious that I have a tendency to freak out, but on this momentous occasion I was completely relaxed. I felt in control and happy and then I remembered I had drunk a ridiculous amount the previous evening. I was slightly perturbed, but that lasted a mere minute. I had known a girl in college who was six months gone before she realized that she was with child and she drank like a fish for all of those six months. The little one emerged intact and was declared healthy. One night wasn't going to do much damage and I'd ensure that there wouldn't be a repeat performance.

I'm pregnant.

I phoned Doreen and she was around almost before I'd managed to replace the receiver.

"I told you," she said, hugging me. "Are you all right?" She pulled back and pushed the hair out of my face so that I couldn't hide.

"Aside from a bloody headache, I'm fine," I admitted.

"Oh, this is so exciting!"

Suddenly I was smiling because she was right. It was exciting.

"I love babies. Their smell, their little feet, the way

they feel when they lie sleeping on your chest. Oh, I miss my babies," she lamented.

I was now grinning so hard that my face started to hurt. I was having a baby and I was looking forward to it. We hugged and she nearly suffocated me. She made me something to eat even though I insisted I wasn't hungry. She wouldn't hear of it—apparently I was now eating for two. I did ask her about what I would say to Seán. When it actually dawned on me that I hadn't told him I confessed I felt guilty that she was the first to know.

"Rings around your nipples!" she said. "I knew before you did, you bloody eejit!"

Good point. She was laughing.

I'm such an idiot.

★ ★ ★

It was after seven when Seán eventually made it home. I was lying on the couch watching *Blind Date,* screaming for Number Two. He plonked down beside me, glad that I had recovered sufficiently to care who the slapper in the tiger print chose for her date in an amusement park in Scarborough. I felt a little nervous, but not as nervous as I should have. He grabbed the remote and switched the channel.

"Did you eat?" I asked without thought.

"I grabbed something on the way home."

I concentrated on the TV. Madonna was singing about sex.

He got up. "Do you want a beer?"

"No," I smiled.

He left for the kitchen and I wondered when I was

going to tell him. It's hard to explain, but all the feelings that I would have expected to feel, like shock and fear, just weren't there. I did care about his reaction, but something deep down inside couldn't let me worry about it. It was definitely not in line with my usual behavior and this alone should have caused alarm, but I was locked inside a weird place, a blissful place.

He arrived back with a beer and sat down, putting my legs across his lap. He winked at me and I smiled.

"I did a test today."

"Oh yeah?" he said while staring at the TV.

A young blonde presenter was talking animatedly about the top-ten hits.

"Yeah," I said while silently admiring her boots.

"What kind of test?" he asked, probably admiring her tits.

"A pregnancy test."

He choked on his beer; foam was escaping from his mouth and rapidly making its way to his chin. His head flicked in my direction.

"I've been feeling kind of crap lately."

"I know, and . . . ?" he responded. He didn't appear alarmed or even that shocked, just inquisitive, like possibly it could be a good thing.

"Doreen said I should take the test."

He didn't flinch. "And?" He really wasn't one for beating around the bush.

"And she was right."

"She was right?" he questioned and I could see excitement build in his eyes.

"I'm pregnant," I said and I couldn't help smiling

because I knew his face, I knew his eyes and I knew that he was happy.

He put down his beer and he turned to face me. "Are you absolutely sure?" he asked and the fear in his voice was the good kind.

"It was blue," I said, my voice filled with sudden emotion. I started to cry but my tears were the happy kind.

He cupped my face in his hands. "Are we going to have a baby?" he asked and I briefly thought about putting it in writing.

"Well, I hope it's not two," I laughed.

"I'm going to be a father," he said and then he was crying and we were hugging. "I'm going to be a dad," he repeated and then we both cried like babies, which was ironic, considering that I had one living in my belly.

A while later we went upstairs and carried out a second test just to be sure it was blue just like the first one and we sat together on the bathroom floor, looking at this blue line and dreaming about all it meant. That night we lay together in one another's arms making plans. We were definitely going to have to get a mortgage and that wouldn't be a problem. We had steady jobs and a few quid put away. We decided not to tell anyone, at least not until I was three months gone and besides, Clo was getting married and neither of us wanted to take from her limelight. Doreen could be trusted as long as we kept her away from everyone. A lot of people lost their first baby but neither of us was willing to think about that. We both wanted this baby. We hadn't realized it, but now it was clear this was the best thing that could ever have happened.

The joy I felt filled my once-weakened heart and made it whole.

Of course we thought about John, how could we not? I told Seán about the test I'd carried out the day that he died and for the first time I admitted to myself and to him how badly I had felt. But this was different. We were older and wiser. We were better prepared and stronger. It didn't mean I didn't love John. It just meant that I wasn't ready then. I did feel bad, but then Seán squeezed me tight and the guilt melted away.

"I love you," I said.

"I love you too, Mammy," he grinned.

"Okay, seriously, don't call me Mammy," I said. "I prefer Mom, Mum, Mam or even Ma."

Oh God, I'm so excited I need to pee.

Chapter 23

Love, Marriage and Baby in a Carriage

It was 9:30 a.m. on the day that Clo was to marry. I was kneeling on the bathroom floor chucking my guts up. I wiped my mouth and cursed Seán and his healthy sperm. I was a bridesmaid, which was distressing because my last fitting had been two weeks previously, leaving the dress a little tight. My Wonderbra, having given up the ghost, remained in my underwear drawer and I briefly wondered if I could get away with big knickers. Unfortunately the fact that my dress was grafted on meant that big or even medium-sized knickers were an option I didn't have. I fixed my hair, slapped on some makeup and waddled into the kitchen where Seán stood, looking fabulous in a suit, making breakfast.

Bastard.

I had kept my word and not told anyone else about the baby and it had been harder than I could ever have imagined, especially since it appeared to all who knew me that I was merely gaining weight. I didn't even look pregnant—instead I looked kind of podgy. Clodagh had returned the bridesmaids' dresses, afraid that Anne would continue to starve herself in a bid to fit into hers. She'd decided on a pattern and hired a dressmaker, who was not oblivious to my ever-changing size, as the dress fittings acted like a kind of cruel monitor. While I was increasing in size Anne was decreasing and poor Clodagh and her hardworking dressmaker were getting quietly distressed. The dress was silk and a further insult to my burgeoning hips. I had briefly toyed with the notion of pulling out, but I quickly returned to my senses and instead resigned myself to the fact that I would have to carry out my duty, thick or thin.

Now I pulled at my new silk skin and worried that breathing would become difficult after a feed. I pretended to smile.

Seán laughed. "You look great."

"Shut up," I moaned. "I look like a pig."

"I always had a thing for bacon." He pretended to smell the air and although it was childish I couldn't help but laugh along. Suddenly I felt hungry and he was so yummy I wanted desperately to strip him, jump him and wrestle him to the ground, which made me wonder if, under the circumstances, I was a tad weird.

★ ★ ★

The wedding service was going beautifully. Clo was stunning in white silk with dark skin, a long veil and a smile that lasted. Tom, originally nauseous, saw her and then relaxed. The vows were done. They went without a hitch. They lit the candle and the church didn't burn down. When the singer was supposed to sing, she did and she did a fine job. Everything was going so well. I was standing on the altar beside the bride. It was hot, my dress was beginning to pinch, my feet hurt and my head was spinning. I really needed to sit down but the priest was a talker.

Just keep it together for five more minutes. Don't faint. Do not faint. Please do not faint.

I was sweating and couldn't work out what the priest was saying, but it must have been good because the crowd clapped. Clo and Tom began walking down the steps of the altar, the rest of the wedding party following. The photographer was snapping photos of the happy couple.

Just walk down the steps, I told myself.

Unfortunately my luck had run out. Just as the photographer shouted the word "cheese!" I crumpled, only to wake up on my back, looking up at the priest, bride, groom and Seán.

"I'm so sorry," I mumbled, attempting to get to my feet. "Church is hot," I mumbled again. Seán was helping me up when the back of the dress split. The crowd remained silent as I was helped out the side door with a jacket wrapped around my waist. Air helped me but not the dress—there was no cure for the dress. Clo and Tom were fussing, but I begged them to go back to their wedding day.

"I'm fine. I swear. I'm so sorry."

Clo just smiled. "You're just a limelight hogger, Em."

I laughed and added sincerely that nothing could steal the limelight from her. She truly was stunning, the day was going great and I was a mere blip that should be ignored. She laughed at my embarrassment and agreed with Seán that it was best if I went straight to the hotel. Once inside our hotel room and with what was left of my dress off, I felt considerably better. I looked in the mirror and everything seemed to be a little bigger than it had been earlier that morning. I wasn't sure if I was just imagining it. Seán was lying on the bed, waiting for me to join him.

"You need to lie down," he kept saying.

"Do I look heavy?" I asked.

"No," he almost snorted. "I told you, you look great."

I sighed.

His smile turned to a frown. "Is that what this was about? Are you on some stupid diet? You know you can't diet while pregnant."

I joined him on the bed. "No. Of course not—if I was on a diet I wouldn't have eaten half a bucket of chicken, a large fries and a side order of onion rings last night, now would I?"

He had to think about it for a moment before he agreed. He had taken off his shirt. The room was warm, his skin was hot and he looked hotter. I suddenly felt a lot better. I kissed him, he smiled and I kissed him again and untied his pants. His smile grew and suddenly I was on my back and my tits didn't feel so sore anymore. He stopped to put on a condom and I wondered why, but then he was a creature of habit and I didn't want to ruin the momentum. We'd moved and were up against the wall when the door opened and Anne and Richard were in the room. We didn't notice until we heard Anne's scream. Richard said a delicate, "Excuse us," and he pushed her out the door. Fortunately for me, Seán acted as coverage which was a good thing. I would have died if Richard had seen my newly acquired wads. We heard the door close, looked at one another and burst out laughing. Seán briefly worried that Anne had seen his arse but when I reminded him that everyone had seen his arse when Ireland beat Italy in the '94 World Cup, he relaxed. We got dressed. He was back into his suit. I got into a black knitted and blissfully stretchy dress.

We met Richard and Anne in the lobby.

"Feeling better then?" Anne asked brightly.

"Yes, thanks," I agreed, blushing.

Richard and Seán grinned at one another and went to the bar. I ordered water. Anne ordered something stiffer.

The bride and groom arrived shortly thereafter. I had missed the photos outside the church, but Clo didn't mind. I apologized about the dress but she couldn't have cared less. She was delirious and had the J-Lo glow. She was just glad that I was feeling better. Anne remained silent, which I remained very grateful for. The photographer beckoned us and we smiled for the camera, swapping places with the in-laws, out-laws, friends and neighbors until eventually our photo duties were completed and it was time to eat. Again I was grateful, as I was hungry enough to eat a Grand National winner. The food came and went. The speeches were hysterical. Tom's brother Rupert actually managed to be warm, even a little funny, and I wondered if I had misjudged him in the hospital—after all, he had been merely concerned about his brother undergoing surgery. Then he told a joke about women having no brains and I realized my gut feeling had been the correct

one. Clo's mother and her stepfather wore proud smiles as they laughed at the stories told about their daughter.

★ ★ ★

After the meal Anne, Clo and I went up to the bridal suite. Clo was putting on makeup. Anne was fixing her dress and I nipped into the loo for a quick puke. I turned on the taps so as to cover the sound but they were those sprinkler ones, a lot of power, very little sound. I threw up and then I threw up again and again and again. I could hear talking outside. I retched loudly and it stopped.

"Em?"

It was Clo.

"Yeah?" I called out as brightly as possible.

"Are you okay?"

I started to say "great" but it started with "gre–" and ended in vomit.

Anne was at the door. "Let us in!" she yelled dramatically.

"It's open," I said with head in loo.

They walked in, both with concerned looks on their faces.

Clo appeared terrified. "Oh my God, did you have the mussels to start?"

"Yeah, they were lovely," I said from the bowl.

"Oh Jesus! It's food poisoning! Half the wedding ate the bloody mussels!" she cried out.

I attempted to argue but my mouth was full. Clo looked like she was about to cry. Anne was quiet. I stopped vomiting.

Oh, the relief!

I was washing my face while adamantly denying the

charge of food poisoning. The two girls were eyeing me carefully.

"Emma, are you on drugs?" Clo asked seriously.

I took time out from the sink to look at her in her face, just to ensure she wasn't joking. "What?" I asked incredulously.

"Well, one minute you're fainting, the next it's wanton sex and now you're throwing up. You remember that one time I took coke? Exactly the same."

"I'm not on coke," I said, embarrassed that Clo was now aware that I had forgone the church photos in favor of a shag against a hotel wall. "I was feeling better," I added lamely.

Clo thought about it for a split second. "Fair enough," she nodded happily. "So it's not coke and it's not food poisoning."

I agreed it wasn't either of those two things.

"So when are you going to tell us you're pregnant, Em?"

I sighed, relieved. "Now," I said weakly, not really sure whether to laugh or cry.

"You're pregnant!" Anne squealed.

"I'm three months," I admitted.

Clo said, "Oh my God!" a lot before asking if I was sure.

"Positive," I replied. "I took a test."

Anne said that sometimes the test can be wrong, but seemed content when I said that I'd taken two, followed by a hospital visit, which had further confirmed my status. Anne asked if Seán knew and I confirmed that he did and that he was as happy as I was. Clo hugged me, but I pushed her away, terrified that some puke would find its way onto her dress. She laughed and Anne hugged me while dismissing my fears. I held her tight, comforted by her positive response.

How many books have Anne and Richard read on pregnancy and how much effort is it taking them to get to a place Sean and I came to by accident?

"I'm so happy for you," she said selflessly and when she pulled back she was smiling genuinely, but it was hard to ignore the tears forming in the corner of each eye.

Clo was jumping up and down. "I'm going to be an auntie!"

Anne and I dared not argue. We finished making ourselves up and headed for the party.

★ ★ ★

Seán and I were on the dance floor, swaying to one of George Michael's slow ones. He was holding me close and I could feel Anne's stare burn through my back. She wanted me to admit I'd spilled the proverbial beans so that she could hug him and drag me into a corner so that we could talk about babies all night. I had begged them to keep their mouths shut. I knew this directive would be exceptionally difficult for Anne. Having said all that, Seán and I had agreed that we would tell our parents first and I had promised to hold my tongue until then. Then again, I had promised Anne that I'd tell him that I'd told them on the way down from the rooms. It was getting a little complicated.

He's going to kill me.

So there we were, dancing at a wedding, ironically to George Michael. Seán smiled at me. I wondered how long his smile would last. I really needed to pee.

303

I'll tell him after I pee.

Anne and Richard were now dancing beside us. She caught my eye and mouthed: "Tell him." I wondered if my bladder would hold. "Spit it out," she mumbled as they circled us. It was a lot of pressure on both bladder and mind. This song was like that New Year's Eve cigarette—never-ending.

"Seán," I said.

He bowed his ear to my mouth.

"I told Anne and Clo about the baby," I whispered nervously.

He cautiously nodded his head.

"I know we said we'd wait but I've got the all clear and—"

"I told Richard and Tom," he sniffed, spinning me around.

I absorbed this information. "You asshole!"

"What?" he asked innocently.

"I was in bits. I thought that I'd broken this big pact."

"Well, you did—it just so happens that so did I."

He was grinning the way he did when he was pleased with himself. And suddenly it was real. I was pregnant, two pairs of shoes for three people. Of course it had been real when I was puking, getting fat and crying for no reason, but now Clo and Anne knew so it was really real. I wasn't crying, but a tear managed to creep down my face and drop to the floor.

"I'm really happy," I told his feet.

He pulled my face up to meet his. "Me too."

Our noses met and at such close proximity his eyes appeared to dance. Of course it could have had something to do with the strobe lighting. I gave Anne the thumbs-up and she and Richard descended, closely followed by the bride and groom. We were all hugging and kissing and patting each other on the back and my once-broken heart felt mended and full.

★ ★ ★

I recognized the garden bursting with exotic flowers emitting from the soft green sand. The burning bush still glowed in the distance and, no longer unsure of where I was or what I was doing, I headed purposefully toward the purple sun dangling above a spidery tree. While climbing the hill I smoothed my skirt and fixed my hair, all the while my eyes fixed firmly upon the purple spinning sun. The hill straightened out as I approached the flowering tree on which the blue poppies danced on cherry-pink branches. Once again, an unseen mighty hand threw the purple sun my way. I bounced it and threw it back.

John caught it and smiled. "You're back," he said while throwing the sun over his shoulder.

We hugged.

"I needed to see you," I said, as though visiting the dead was normal.

"I'm intrigued." He sat down under the tree and I joined him, squinting at the light show in the sky.

"Clo got married today."

"Yeah?"

I nodded.

"The fourteenth of July, 1989, she swore she'd never marry," he said.

"What's your point?" I grinned.

"She owes me twenty quid." He laughed and I gave him a dig.

"She's really happy. Tom, that's her husband. He's a laugh. You would have liked him."

"Good," he said and I noticed he was sitting still and staring like Gandhi.

"I still love you," I reminded him.

"You always will," he reminded me. I wasn't ready to tell him about the baby.

"So did you send me down the lane that night to get my head kicked in?"

"I can't take the credit for that, Xena." He grinned. "But I bet it made good TV."

I gave him another dig. We sat in silence while I absorbed some courage.

"You were right," I said, trying my best to have him face me.

"Oh yeah?" he said, seeming a million miles away.

"Last time, when you said I was falling in love. You were right." The words out, I bowed my head, no longer wishing to see the color of his eyes.

"I'm glad."

"Glad," I repeated, disgusted. "What kind of a word is 'glad'?"

He wasn't following.

" 'Glad' is a Pollyanna word," I said. "It's a fifties, G-rated-movie word, isn't it?"

"You want another word?" he asked, grinning.

"No, you're all right," I admitted, finished with my tiny tirade.

"He loves you as much as I did," he said, nodding to himself.

Wow! I thought. Of course he didn't need me to fill him in. He'd known all along.

"So how much is that then?" I ventured, but he just laughed me off.

"You want to walk?" he asked and a yellow pathway opened up in front of us.

"No," I said. Even asleep and dreaming I was exhausted. I had one more thing to say. "So there's no need to tell you that I'm pregnant then?"

He shook his head. "No need at all."

"So are you glad?" I asked in my best sarcastic voice.

He nodded, laughing. "Very."

Suddenly we were walking away from the tree and upon the yellow path, despite my weary legs.

"*The Wizard of Oz,*" I said, smiling at the yellow bricks beneath me and at the memory of Judy Garland in her beautiful ruby slippers.

John stopped and looked at me seriously. "Do you want ruby slippers?" he asked like a father would of a spoilt child.

"No, it would be too much," I whispered sheepishly.

He was laughing again and seeing his wide smile and big eyes reminded me of how we used to be.

Suddenly there was nothing but a doorway.

"Time for you to go," he said and I panicked a little.

"No," I complained. "I just got here."

But it was too late. I was awake in my own bed. Seán was passed out beside me with Leonard asleep, curled around his head.

Yellow brick road, I thought. *Christ, who knew I was such a bloody sap?*

★ ★ ★

We were to break the news to my parents the next day and, although I was a grown woman in a strong relationship, I have to admit I was a little scared. After all, there was the issue of marriage. Seán was great, mostly because he was now a resident of Cloud Nine and didn't give a toss what other mere earth-dwelling mortals thought of our situation or indeed us. He was going to be a dad and already he had decided that he was going to be the best dad in the world. We were in the car driving toward my parents' house and I was biting my nails.

"Stop biting your nails," he said without taking his eyes from the road.

"I'm not," I denied.

"It's going to be fine. I bet your dad cries." He grinned.

"I hope not," I said, playing with my hands.

"I bet it's a girl," he said, turning the corner onto our road.

I smiled and then I saw our house and I felt sick. He passed me the sick bag.

"Thanks," I managed, gray and attempting to imbue myself with a sense of steely determination. It wasn't working.

He parked the car outside the house.

"Are you ready?" he smiled, seeming bizarrely excited.

"No," I said, getting out.

"Right then."

I rang the doorbell, forgetting I had a key. My mother

answered the door, instantly recognizing I hadn't used my key and worrying about the implications.

"Hi," I said as breezily as the situation would allow.

"Hi, yourself." She eyed us suspiciously.

Seán waved from behind me, grinning like a clown on acid.

"What?" she said, still holding the door.

"Can we come in?" Seán's voice asked from behind me.

She let us in. We followed her to the kitchen.

"Okay," she announced.

"I'm pregnant." I smiled hopefully, not wishing to drag the matter out. She sat down and remained silent.

Oh crap, we're for it!

"Are you okay?" Seán asked her, while automatically reaching for a glass of water.

She lifted her head and she was smiling.

"Well, I would have liked a wedding first but then again, your brother did give himself to God, so I suppose it all balances up."

"So you're okay with this?"

"I'm fine with it," she said, taking me in her arms before crying. My father reacted pretty much the same way, although Seán lost ten quid because he didn't actually cry.

★ ★ ★

Seán's own father was a breeze. He was an easygoing man. I suppose he had to be—his wife had walked out on him when Seán was a kid and he was left to bring up Seán and his younger brother, James. He was proud and he shared a cigar with his firstborn.

"I knew you had it in you, son," he said proudly.

I rang Noel. He was in New York completing some sort of aid-worker induction course. Seán insisted upon being put on speakerphone.

"So when are you two going to tie the knot?" Noel asked after the preliminary congratulating was completed.

I hadn't thought about it.

"Whenever," Seán piped up.

"Whenever?" Noel questioned.

I remained silent, as we had never discussed marriage.

"Okay," Noel said thoughtfully. "But you are going to get married, right?"

"Of course," Seán said breezily.

I smiled.

Oh, okay. Baby, marriage, this is fine. I'm not having difficulty breathing. Groovy.

Noel was excited and already making plans for the service.

"I could be anywhere in the world," he said. "But I'll be back. You just give me a date and I'll be there," he promised.

★ ★ ★

Yeah, it was all great back then, of course—that's before I got really heavy and swollen. Later, Seán and I lay in bed daydreaming about what our child would look like and thinking up exotic and pretty, but rubbish, names. We laughed and he stroked my tummy, which was really beginning to thicken, reminding me of a rotund basketball player in third year who had attempted to bully me once. Clo had drop-kicked her and she steered clear

after that. I smiled while I lay there, wondering if she'd ever lost the puppy fat that I was now gaining.

★ ★ ★

Two months later I was very fat and my clothes were straining under the pressure. Clo and Anne took me shopping for maternity wear. We went from shop to shop to shop and through endless rails of sailor suits and flower-filled frilly dresses that emphasized every lump and growing bump. I was sinking into a depression and, although Anne remained upbeat, Clo was sharing my devastation.

"I'm never getting pregnant," she muttered when I exited the dressing room in a fuchsia-pink top and trousers that were tight up top yet ballooned around the thighs.

"You look fine," Anne said while attempting to give Clo a furtive dirty look.

I was beside myself. "I'm ugly, ugly, ugly," I repeated, returning to the dressing room to strip off the vile concoction. It seemed to take me forever to find the strength to remove the garment. I was so tired all the time. I'd expected pregnancy to be difficult but this kind of exhaustion was beyond my wildest expectations.

"Are you okay?" came Clodagh's query but it was her knocking that woke me.

"I'm fine," I said, struggling to come to terms with how I managed to fall asleep with one arm out of the God-awful fuchsia-pink top and one arm in.

Later in the coffee shop Clodagh was rambling on about the state of maternity fashion and daydreaming about designing some functional yet attractive clothing,

despite not having a clue about it. I looked at Anne and smiled, always conscious that my growing stomach was a constant reminder of her failure to get pregnant.

"Are you okay?"

She nodded. "I'm fine, Em. Actually I have some news of my own."

I braced myself. I hated when people had news as it usually meant change and that usually upset me. Clodagh was all ears.

"Richard and I are going for IVF," she said.

"IVF?" Clodagh repeated, unsure.

"His sperm count is low. It looks like we'll never get pregnant the obvious way, so instead we're going for insemination."

My face fell.

Clodagh leaned in. "Are we talking about a test tube?" she asked conspiratorially.

Anne sighed. "No."

"What then?" Clo asked, fascinated.

"Richard provides a sperm sample and if it's good quality the doctor inserts it through some sort of catheter. It's not sore or anything, maybe a little uncomfortable."

"Wow. How long before you know if it's taken?" I asked.

"The same amount of time as it takes anyone else. I miss a period—I take a test."

"Exciting," Clo said. "Just think, this time next year you both could be mothers."

"Yeah, well, I'm not counting my chickens yet. It might not work."

"Don't be so negative. You've got to be positive to be positive," Clo said, laughing at herself.

"You really are a bloody moron," Anne laughed.

"Seriously, what are your chances?" Clo asked.

"Who knows?" Anne answered with her hands in the air.

Clodagh nudged her. "So is the doctor cute?"

Anne laughed. "Old and fat. Anyway, I just wanted to let you know."

"You know we'll be there for you, right?" I asked.

"I know," she smiled.

"You, Richard, the doctor and the turkey baster."

She smiled and we laughed together. What else could we do?

Chapter 24

In the Name of the Father

It was a Saturday and feeling unusually sprightly, I decided upon going into town to look for baby clothes. I had no intention of buying, as my mother and Doreen had been adamant when advising that buying for a baby not yet born would bring untold bad luck. Although not usually superstitious, I wasn't about to take any chances and they had both agreed that there was no harm in looking. I looked through rails of little dresses, pink and yellow tops, little blue shorts and jumpers with every kind of zoo animal imprint. I looked at runners, shoes, sandals, all tiny and cute, little gloves, little hats, little vests and socks that were so small I had trouble fitting my thumb into them. I'll admit that although I didn't know whether I was having a boy or a girl, I did spend most of my time in the girls' section. This was mainly due to the fact that everything was so pretty and my recent discovery that I had a weakness for all things pretty.

I eventually pried myself away from pink and proceeded toward the blue section when I saw a familiar face going through a rail of boys' trousers. I couldn't quite place the face, wondering if it was the face of a parent I should be avoiding. She didn't notice me as she was too engrossed in measuring the size of trousers against her child, who was struggling to get out of his buggy. I continued viewing little shirts, hoping that the woman would give me as wide a berth as I was giving her.

She was at the counter paying for her shopping when the little boy turned his head and faced me. I inhaled audibly and the woman next to me, noticing my condition and possibly my pallid color, politely asked if I was okay. I quickly said I was, but I was lying.

The child was Noel—he had his eyes, his face, his curly hair—and the woman was the woman I had met in the bar two years previously. It was Laura, Noel's lover. I was rooted to the spot rather like a beached whale waiting to be shifted. She looked up as she was leaving and saw me. Our eyes met and when indifference turned to terror I knew that she had recognized me. She almost ran to the door and before I knew it I was following her and calling her name. She stopped halfway down the shopping center mall. She didn't turn; instead she just stood there waiting for me to catch up. When I did I could see that she wore the same red face that I myself often did. She was rocking the buggy and looking straight ahead as though she were in front of an invisible firing squad. We both knew the game was up, but unfortunately neither one of us knew where to go from there.

Noel's child was restless, wondering why he was being

pushed back and forth rather than traveling to a new and more interesting destination. We stood together side by side for only a few seconds, but they lasted three lifetimes.

Eventually I uttered her name. "Laura."

"Emma."

"I think we should go for coffee," I said.

"Look, Emma, we really don't have anything to say," she mumbled.

"I think we do," I pushed, knowing by the tone of her previous statement that deep down she agreed.

★ ★ ★

Later in the coffee shop her son, my nephew, relaxed in his pram but we adults were like little bombs about to explode with information overload. We ordered coffees and sat.

"What's his name?" I asked, looking at my nephew.

"Noel," she said, sighing and possibly berating herself for being such a sap as to call her son after the man who'd abandoned her.

"He's beautiful," I said, meaning it. Noel was a handsome man and his son was adorable.

"Thank you," she responded, although I doubt the compliment meant much in light of the situation she had found herself in.

"Does Noel know?" I asked.

"No," she said simply.

"Why not?" I had to ask.

"Are you going to tell him?" she asked, not afraid of getting to the point.

"Yes. No. I don't know." My mind was in a daze.

"Why haven't you told him?" I ventured again, hoping for an answer.

Tears filled her eyes and threatened to trickle down her pink-stained face. My heart bled for her. Maybe it was because I was pregnant and hormonal, or that she was a mother and soon I would be one too. Either way, when I saw her cry, any brewing animosity dissipated. I squeezed her hand and it acted like a tear release. The tears poured and I waited until they too dissipated. Noel Junior was too busy eating a carrot stick to notice his mother's anguish. She explained that she had only found out about the pregnancy after Noel had decided to end the relationship. She had often thought about telling him, but decided that he had picked the Church over her, knowing that he loved her and knowing that he felt he had no choice but to follow a path that would never include her or their child. She had felt it cruel to further complicate his life, having borne witness to the many nights of suffering and torment that he had endured during their affair. She was happy to have been given a child as, at the age of thirty-eight, time had been running out. She had always wanted to be a mother and had long ago reasoned that if God had to take away her lover maybe he had compensated her with their child. I wasn't so sure and although it was evident that she loved Noel and felt she was doing the best for all concerned, I couldn't hide from the fact that my brother had a child and, if I knew, how could I keep it from him? And although her argument was a convincing one, despite any pain it would bring, didn't he have a right to know?

We walked toward the car park together. She asked me

about myself and seemed delighted that I was with Seán and having his baby. Apparently Noel had talked about our unrequited love. At the car she begged me to talk to her before I talked to Noel. She gave me her number and although my discovery of her secret was down to a chance encounter, she seemed to feel responsible for my impossible position. It was easy to see why Noel had fallen for her. She was calm, kind, sweet and friendly even when terrified and with her world turned upside down, and although we had only met briefly once before we hugged when parting.

Poor cow.

* * *

Seán was in the spare room, which had long ago become his study. I charged up the stairs as quickly as my fluid-filled legs would allow. I plonked down on the chair in front of his desk. He looked up grinning and wondering how much money I had mentally spent.

"Noel is a father."

He stood up as though he'd just realized he'd sat on something sharp.

"Excuse me?" he uttered, looking down at me plonked in the chair.

"I bumped into Laura and her one-year-old, Noel Junior, in town."

He sat down. "Noel Junior," he repeated and I nodded in agreement.

I told him all about it while he sat dully looking into the middle distance and scratching his head intermittently.

"This is big," he kept saying until I told him to stop.

I asked him what I should do; keeping in mind that Laura was right, in that telling Noel he had a son would be tantamount to putting a gun to his head. He argued that not telling him would be denying him the chance to know his only son. He was right, but then again so was she. My brain was fried. I wanted to talk to my mother, but then her brain would have been fried and it would only serve to further complicate the situation. Seán and I debated the pros and cons of disclosing Laura's secret for hours. We were both well aware that we were dealing with shades of gray. I couldn't sleep, unable to shut either my brain or bladder into the off position. I felt ill all night, intermittently dizzy even while lying down and so weak that it became difficult to raise my hand to my face.

★ ★ ★

Sunday dinner was a nightmare. Neither Seán nor I could bring ourselves to make small talk with my parents. My mother put it down to my own exhaustion.

"It's perfectly natural. I couldn't keep my eyes open on Noel."

I nodded.

"And what's your excuse, Seán?"

"Work."

"Ah!" she replied before noting that she too was tired.

My father was too busy watching Dublin lose a hurling match on TV to query our silence, probably because of the desperate situation unfolding on the playing field.

That night when Clodagh rang I didn't tell her, not because I wasn't dying to, but because it was already unfair that Seán and I knew Noel's business before he did, never mind my friends. Seán and I talked around and around in circles. One minute he made a point in favor of Noel being told and in the next moment he made a point in favor of him not being told. I followed suit. Neither of us had a clue what to do. Noel was truly happy for the first time in a very long time. The changes we had witnessed in him were hard to ignore. He had found his place among the priesthood and the people who had needed him most. He had rediscovered his path and his destiny. He was at peace. Who were we to take that from him? Still, how could I not tell him?

It was mid-week and Father Rafferty took Confession at five. I had stayed behind to correct essays that should have been corrected at the weekend. It was just after five. I didn't think about it because to do that would encourage me to question myself and I had been doing quite enough of that to last a lifetime. I waddled into the church, hoping against hope that I would find myself alone. I was in luck. I squeezed into the confession box and knelt down on the unforgiving wooden kneeler. Like my mind, my knees felt like they were stuck between a rock and a hard place. At seven months my stomach had grown larger than I could have believed possible. I arched my back, which was killing me, only to find my stomach jammed against the confession box, which was definitely not made with mothers-to-be in mind, but then that's the Catholic Church all over. I made a silent promise not to debate what I perceived to be the evils of the Church as I had far more pressing business to discuss.

It wasn't long before the little shutter was slid back, revealing Father Rafferty, his eyes closed and his head nodding, hand raised in blessing.

"Father Rafferty," I said.

He stayed silent, head bowed, waiting for me to spout the usual formula.

"Father Rafferty," I repeated slightly more forcefully, but yet with respect. He stopped short, opening his eyes and steadying his head so as to focus.

"Emma?" he queried.

"Yes," I replied, happy to have caught his attention without having to bang on the grille, which would have been my next move.

"What can I do for you?" he asked, realizing that I wasn't there to seek forgiveness.

"I need your advice," I leaned in and whispered although the church was empty.

"What is it, Emma?" he asked, coming closer to the grille.

"It's Noel. He has a child."

Father Rafferty paled. "Laura," he said after a time.

"Yes," I answered, not surprised that Noel had confided in him. Although they were very different and generations apart, the two men had a mutual respect and understanding.

"He doesn't know," he said, immediately understanding why I had come to him.

"He doesn't," I answered. "She found out after they parted. She didn't tell him because she knew he was a priest at heart."

"She's a lovely woman," he said with his eyes on the floor, so that I couldn't read their expression, although his tone suggested sadness. "And now?" he asked, returning my gaze.

"And now I know. I bumped into her with Noel

Junior. He's exactly like Noel—he even has a curly cowlick."

Father Rafferty shook his head sadly, but I could see a hint of a smile.

"I don't know what to do," I said, begging for the answer.

His slight smile faded and he held his head in his hand, squeezing his temples. Battling my own headache, I lurched from one knee to the other, hoping to God he'd come up with something fast.

"You can't keep it from him. To do so would not only be a sin against God, but also against nature." He shook his head in his hands as though his words hurt him.

"Noel will leave the priesthood. He won't risk the Church's reputation," I said, mirroring Father Rafferty's thoughts.

"Yes, he will," he said sadly. "It's a pity—not for him but for us. He's one of the good ones."

I could see his hand tremble slightly, but I couldn't tell from his tone whether it was due to emotion or simply old age.

"I'm sorry," I said.

"I'm sorry too," he replied. He looked at me and attempted a smile, but behind his tired eyes I could see Noel staring back at me. Father Rafferty may have been old and unusually consumed by Doomsday, but he was once young and had faced all of the fears, desires and longing that my brother did. He understood the impact, the implications for Noel better than anyone else. He also understood that Noel was being given a chance to be a real father and I don't know if he regretted or rejoiced in his life choices, but in that moment he looked lost. I wanted to cry; then again, I had wanted to cry earlier when I'd ordered cappuccino and it came without chocolate sprinkles.

"Father," I said out of nowhere.

"Yes."

"Would you like to pray with me?" I couldn't believe what I'd just said. I didn't even know if I would remember a whole prayer.

"Yes," he nodded, brightening.

So I started the "Our Father," hoping against hope that he would join in before I got to the middle bit, which I definitely didn't know.

"Our Father who art in heaven, hallowed be Thy name . . ." *Please join in.*

"Thy kingdom come, Thy will be done . . ."

Please, please, join in.

". . . on earth as it is in heaven."

He's joining in, thank Christ! Okay, now I'll just lower my voice so that I can mumble the middle bit.

"Nan nah nan nah nannahnana, and lead us la la la but deliver us from evil. Amen."

Father Rafferty's head was bowed.

I crossed my fingers, hoping he wouldn't launch into another prayer.

He didn't. He blessed himself and smiled. "Thank you, Emma."

"You're welcome," I said, relieved, still not having a clue why I'd even suggested it, but then I'd been acting really weird and I was beginning to worry it was more than hormonal.

"I should go," I said, attempting to get up.

"I hope that I'll see you again," he said.

"Yeah," I agreed politely while struggling to move.

He pulled back the shutter and I was left alone and still kneeling. It felt like I was wedged in. *Oh for fu–*

"Father Rafferty!" I called out while knocking. The shutter went back, revealing him.

"Emma?"

"I'm stuck," I moaned, mortified.

He chuckled and the next time I saw him he had one foot wedged against the door of the confession box while attempting to haul me out.

★ ★ ★

Seán and I had decided that telling Noel about his son over the phone was not the way to go and, as he was still in the western world completing the aid-worker induction course, we felt it only fair that the news be delivered in person. Of course, when I say "we had decided " I really mean "I had decided." As I was unable to fly and no one else knew about the situation, it left Seán in the undesirable position of messenger.

Much later Seán had confided that it wasn't Noel and his problems or the fact that the plane seemed to be flying a little too low that really bothered him on his way across the Atlantic, although neither helped. Instead he spent most of his alone time worrying about his own life and the new demands upon it.

When he later described to me the anguish he had suffered during that period of our life together, I have to admit I felt a little selfish. I hadn't even noticed he was

stressed. Then again, it's so rare to catch a glimpse of someone else's darkest fears. He told me that after the initial glow that came with the announcement of my pregnancy had subsided and the reality of what fatherhood would mean had dawned on him, he found himself in the unenviable position of being wholly terrified. It was probably not unusual for any man in his position to feel somewhat panicky. After all, parenting is no joke. However, in Seán's case there was more to it.

Seán had spent most of his life avoiding the issue of his abandonment and to date he had found this tactic to be successful. However, now while contemplating and awaiting the arrival of his own offspring, the fear and questions that had been instilled the day his mother walked out on her family rose from deep inside and walls he had spent years building slowly crumbled. As I grew bigger so did his fears. Would he be like her? Would he find rearing a child too difficult? Would he fail as a father as she had failed as a mother? His dad had often said they were alike; he had her eyes and her grin. Would he share her inability to be a decent parent? He hadn't mentioned it to me; instead he attempted to fob off his obvious fears but they refused to remain ignored, with the result that his every attempt only served to intensify them. He had tried to be reasonable, he was his father's son, after all, but the questions that he had never bothered with before were beginning to choke him. Why did she leave? He knew why she left his father. Theirs was a marriage born out of duty as opposed to love. She had become pregnant with Seán and marriage was the only solution available at that time. His dad swore that she had loved her children but, if she had, wouldn't she have taken them with her? His dad had said it was more difficult for a single mother in the seventies but if that was the case, why didn't she make an effort now that he was an adult? He hadn't really cared before. Initially, of course, he was devastated by her disappearance, as any child would be, but he got used to the situation, quickly realizing that her absence coincided with the advent of a happier household. Gone were the long arguments and the screaming rows and after a while he found himself more contented and safer, ensuring her return would be met with anxiety and anger rather than with welcoming open arms. He had been very comfortable with her absence for such a long time but now, on the cusp of fatherhood, he wondered whether his ability to walk away from his mother as she had walked away from him was a sign that he was capable of isolating those closest as she had done.

These fears were compounded by his track record. To date his relationships had been fleeting affairs, exciting but without any kind of depth. He loved me—he knew that. He had loved me a long time before it was decent. Initially he had wondered whether he was just coveting the kind of relationship that his best friend had. Deep down though, he knew that wasn't so. It had been hard and then his friend died and he drowned in his guilt, knowing that with John gone his way was clear and regretting every second of the hope that that recognition brought. He had tried to stay away but that was too hard. Now he had all that he wanted for the first time but he wasn't John: he wasn't the steady one; he shouldn't be the first in the group to be a dad. He was the messy one, the guy who couldn't hold down a relationship.

And he prayed: *Oh please, God, don't let me fuck this up!*

So, on his way to see Noel, all these thoughts and memories tormented him and by the time the meal was served he was a wreck. The airhostess who had served him alcohol kindly enquired how he was. He nodded that all was well, but deep down inside he was fighting the tears that hadn't welled since he was a small boy. He tried to sleep but it wasn't working out. The man beside him was snoring, his head against the window, his arm a little too close to Seán's genitals for comfort. He wobbled up the aisle, regretting the last gin and tonic. He stood in the queue for the toilet, hoping his nervous stomach would keep it together, despite his mind refusing to do so.

And he worried. *What if I can't hack it? What if I run?*

Back in his seat his arse felt sore. He pitied the gentleman who had been queuing behind him. His mind drifted back to the problem in hand. What would he say to Noel? How would he break the news that would surely break his friend? The safety-belt light blinked above his head and the captain announced that they were entering an area of turbulence. He and his fellow passengers bounced in their seats, lurching and bobbing until he felt his meal lodge in his neck. It was around this time that he wondered what the hell had made him agree to involve himself in my brother's life, when it was becoming increasingly obvious to him that he was losing control of his own. If he had disclosed his fears to me I could have told him that he had nothing to worry about, that he was one of the most dependable people I knew and that he was his father's son in every way. I could have told him that we had something his parents never had and that a child would only strengthen us. Then again, being hormonally challenged, I could have just told him to fuck off. Despite this, and maybe it was naïve, I knew deep down that we were going to be a family and we would have a happy ending as much as anyone in this world can. He was either too kind or too scared to offload his woes on me. I wish he had. It hurts to think that he was twisted with fear, alone in the air and on the way to New York and a new set of problems.

He did manage to sleep, but it wasn't for long. Somewhere over the Atlantic Ocean he managed to push his own worries to the back of his mind so that he could focus on the job at hand.

Landing wasn't as smooth as he would have liked, but nevertheless he found that he was grateful to be on solid ground, regardless of the wall of heat that seemed to envelop him as he exited the plane. It was May and New York was unusually hot. He felt faint, but carried on regardless. Having only brought hand luggage he was grateful that he didn't have to stand around a carousel for an hour, waiting for bags like his fellow passengers.

He made his way out to the taxis and handed an address to an old man in a grubby suit. It helped that the taxi driver spoke English and had appeared to live in the city for longer then six months. The man spoke about a traffic jam on Amsterdam and shouted at a biker who had cut across him. The radio was loud and the air-conditioning wasn't working. Maybe it was the heat or trepidation or exhaustion but within minutes he was asleep. The man woke him, laughing at the relaxed Irishman. He pointed toward an impressive-looking four-story building, old by American standards.

Seán handed over the money and pulled himself out of the car and onto the street. He stood watching the taxi pull away before he made his way to the door.

Now obviously I wasn't there but Seán has a way of telling a story so that you almost feel like you were there. So keeping in mind that this is not verbatim, it went something like this.

He went into the empty foyer, rang a bell and waited for a response, fixing himself as though he was picking up a girl for a first date.

A smiling middle-aged woman emerged. "Hot day," she said.

"Yeah. I'm looking for Noel—"

"Father Noel?" she interrupted.

"That's right," he said, smiling for the first time that day. At least he was in the right place.

"He's in the diner on the corner," she said, pointing.

He thanked her and exited into the heat again, removing his jacket and rolling up his sleeves.

He could see Noel through the diner window before he crossed the street. He looked good, wearing casual clothes. His hair was a little longer and he was laughing with the man seated opposite him, unaware of the bomb about to be dropped. Seán wondered if he should leave. It might be better to check into his hotel first, maybe shower and change his clothes. Maybe he should eat first, gain his strength. The closer to the window he got, the hotter it seemed to be. His stomach was annoying him again.

Christ, I hope it's not an ulcer.

He entered quietly but the bell on the door gave him

away. Noel looked up automatically and then looked away before realization crept upon his face and he turned back, focusing on his old friend. He jumped up and Seán braved a smile.

"What the hell?" Noel said, confused and delighted.

Seán just smiled, hoping against hope that Noel wouldn't worry until it was necessary. Noel's eyes narrowed.

Too late.

"What are you doing here?" he asked, hugging a weakened Seán.

"I've come to see you."

"What's wrong?" Noel asked, worried that something had happened to a member of his family.

"Nothing's wrong," Seán lied while smiling at Noel's friend.

The man returned the grin.

"You're here on business?" Noel asked, leading him to the table.

"Yeah," Seán heard himself saying. He sat.

Noel's friend leaned across the table to shake his hand. "I'm Matt. It's good to meet ya."

Seán shook Matt's hand. "You too," he smiled, sick that he had lied, yet relieved that he was facing a reprieve.

"Matt's a doctor—he's worked all over the world."

Seán grinned at him. "Ever think of coming to Ireland? We could certainly do with some more doctors."

Matt laughed. "I think there's probably more need in the Third World." He chuckled happily.

"Check out James's emergency room any night of the week and come back to me on that," Seán said, grabbing the menu.

Noel laughed loudly, glad to be reminded of home even if it was its shit health system. "How's my sister?" he asked and not before time.

"Good," Seán smiled genuinely, possibly for the first time that day. "She's getting big."

"It won't be long now," Noel grinned.

"No," Seán sighed and put the menu back. He wasn't going to be able to eat now.

"Congratulations, man," Matt said.

"Cheers," Seán said, wondering whether or not Matt would be saying that to Noel any time soon.

They talked with Matt for a while. Seán reminisced about the time we had all spent a summer together working in New York. Matt talked about 9/11 and the devastation that had overcome some of the areas that Seán had remembered so fondly. Noel was excited about going to some distant land to make it a better place, anticipating what the future held. God love him.

Then Matt ran off to meet a girl. They didn't hang about long. Noel was excited and wanted to show him some of the sights. Seán insisted he had been there, done that and asked if they could go back to Noel's place. He used heat as the excuse and Noel seemed to buy it hook, line and sinker.

They walked back to his hotel. Noel was busy pointing out attractive buildings and cool cars. Seán was busy working out how to break his news. They reached the hotel and Noel talked briefly to the doorman while Seán basked in the air-conditioned foyer.

"It's raining at home," Seán mumbled in the lift.

"It's always raining at home," Noel laughed. He let

them into the room and Seán parked himself in the chair. Noel fluffed his pillows and sat on the bed. "So what do you need to talk about?" he asked, kicking off his shoes.

"What?" Seán asked surprised.

"You're in New York for twenty-four hours and you want to spend it in my bedroom?" Noel laughed. "I don't think so. What's the problem?"

Seán sighed. Of course Noel knew there was a problem, but he had figured that it was someone else's. Why wouldn't he? It was always someone else's problem, just not this time. Noel was looking at Seán with curiosity. It was time.

"It's Laura."

Noel paled instantly. "What's happened?" he begged, obviously shaken, fearing the worst.

"She has a son," Seán found himself saying.

Noel froze. This was a problem he hadn't counted on having to solve.

"He's yours."

Seán couldn't bring himself to look at Noel. Noel couldn't tear his eyes away from Seán.

"What?" he said, although he desperately didn't want him to repeat his previous statement.

Seán guessed as much. "He was one last month. Emma said he's the head cut off you."

Noel's lip began to tremble and his hands began to shake. He didn't ask if Seán was joking. He knew people didn't fly thousands of miles to take the piss. Instead he got angry, so angry his face reddened and eyes hardened. Then he was up on his feet and moving toward Seán, who instinctively rose to his feet to be met by a punch in

the face. He went down, holding his left eye in disbelief. Noel stood over him.

"What are you doing here?" he roared.

Seán was confused to say the least, as he believed that he had just quite categorically stated the reason for his visit.

"Would you rather I didn't come?" he shouted from the floor.

"This is not your business!" Noel roared while backing away from him.

"You're right," Seán said, getting up and brushing himself off. "This is none of my business. I have enough of my own worries." He'd had enough.

He slammed the door behind him but not before he heard Noel thud to the floor.

Noel told me later that for hours he rocked back and forth silently, tears streaming from his eyes. The anger that had so quickly engulfed him had burned itself out just as quickly and now he was left alone, lost and bitterly regretting his outburst. Seán didn't deserve that, but I suppose that day he was wondering what he himself deserved. Was this a punishment? Was it God's way of kicking him out? He had broken his oath. Who was he to think he could get away with it? And I know that he felt cheated and desperate. It was nightfall before he rose from the ground. He picked up a light jacket and headed out onto the streets. He walked in a straight line, following the street that led him away from his hotel and his new life, unaware of where he was going, but desperate to complete the necessary journey.

My brother was Forrest Gump.

★ ★ ★

Meanwhile Seán sat in the coolness of his hotel bar, full from bar food and sipping on a cool beer. His eye hurt and he could see the waitress checking out his black eye. He was confused by my brother's response but a tiny part of him could almost understand it. Finding out you're a father is a big shock. Then again, if it had been Laura who had broken the news, as it should have been, would she have received the same treatment? He didn't think so. So much for gratitude. Maybe Noel would have preferred not to know in the short term and even Seán and his sore eye could admit that it would have been better coming from someone else. After all, at the end of the day he was just the guy who got Noel's sister up the pole. It was hardly a qualification to be the bearer of such weighty news. But he also thought of Noel as a friend and had hoped that Noel felt the same way.

After an hour of mulling it all over in his head, he came to the conclusion that he was disappointed. Disappointed that Noel had reacted to him the way he did and disappointed that he had reacted to the news of his own child that way. Of course it was a shock and of course it would jeopardize his plan, but this wasn't about Noel.

Seán was halfway through his second beer when he understood the real reason he was disappointed with Noel's angry and bitter reaction. He remembered his reaction to his impending fatherhood. He remembered the sheer joy he had experienced, the overwhelming sense of being complete. And sitting in a hotel bar off Broadway with a black eye and a dodgy stomach, he concluded that he would never be like his mother. And in that moment a weight lifted and, for the first time in weeks, and possibly for the first time ever, he was free.

★ ★ ★

Noel walked through the streets of New York for most of that night. He said he reached Christopher Street sometime around four a.m. and there he knelt on the sidewalk and prayed. I did mention to him that he was lucky he didn't get his head kicked in, or get robbed or even harassed. But then it would appear that the weird and scary tend to stay away from the weird and scary. After an hour or so he got up and began making his way back to the beginning. It was after two when Noel knocked on Seán's hotel room door.

Seán was packing away his things, grateful for a late checkout. He opened the door to my disheveled and contrite brother. He allowed the door to swing open and Noel entered while Seán continued to busy himself with his packing.

"I'm sorry."

Seán turned to him. "I'm sorry I had to be the one to tell you."

"I know." Noel sat on a chair similar to the one in his own hotel room. "How's your eye?" he asked, wincing at the purple swollen face opposite.

"Could be better," Seán said, half smiling.

"I really am sorry," Noel said, putting his head in his hands.

"It's not the end of the world," Seán said with authority. "It might even be a new beginning," he added a tad limply, not wishing to receive a second blow to the face.

"You don't think I'm being punished?" Noel asked, shaking his head.

"Do you?" Seán sat on the edge of the bed.

"Maybe. No. Yes. I don't know," he said, resigned to the fact that this was a problem that could not be solved by a night spent on his knees.

"I'd call it a chance," Seán attempted.

"A chance?"

"You have a son, man," Seán said smiling, even though when he did his entire face hurt.

"So why didn't Laura tell me? Why you?" Noel at last asked the obvious.

"I just got lucky," Seán attempted to joke. Noel didn't appear impressed so he moved on quickly. "You chose the priesthood. She chose to have the baby. She didn't want to burden you."

"But you did?" Noel asked, raising his eyes to meet Seán's.

"Emma found out. She couldn't keep it from you. If she could have come herself, she would have," Seán explained as best he could, glad of the chance he had been previously denied.

"I'm so sorry," my brother repeated.

"Don't worry about it. Actually I got some stuff worked out and besides, it's good to know you're not perfect. It was beginning to be a real burden," he laughed.

Noel smiled, nodding his head. "I'm definitely not that."

"And I've got the face to prove it."

Noel accompanied Seán to the airport. He waited until he was to board. At the gate they hugged good-bye.

Seán took a picture of Noel's son from his pocket and handed it to him. He took it and pocketed it for later. That was something he would view alone. Noel handed Seán a letter for Laura. Seán waved as he went through and when he was out of sight the ghost that used to be my brother turned and walked away.

Chapter 25

Dying to See You

I hand delivered the letter myself. It was the least I could do under the circumstances. Laura was pleasant and offered me tea but during my short visit she didn't open the letter. I explained my brother's shock without mentioning the fact that he had been a bit of a dick. Seán had defended him. However, I was not so tolerant. As far as I was concerned, Seán had dropped three hundred quid on the flight. The least my brother could have done was refrain from punching him in the face. Laura was remarkably calm in light of the nasty situation she faced. She was a hippie at heart and I put it down to that, although I don't really know why. She was really sweet about my pregnancy, giving me some teas to try and little hints about bringing on labor. She had had Noel Junior naturally, insisting that squatting was a far superior position from which to expel a child. I tried to smile through her vivid account of the beauty that is birth, while making a mental note to book my epidural on my next hospital visit. Noel Junior played with a cardboard box in the corner of the kitchen while repeating a sound that sounded remarkably like "tosser" over and over again.

"Just ignore him," she had warned.

"Okay."

I smiled, sipping on tea that tasted like tree bark. "He's very advanced," I noted. Being a year old and being able to say something that approached the word "tosser" was no mean feat, even if it wasn't the most desirable of first words.

She laughed, agreeing, and noting that she herself had walked at eight months. "He must take after you then. Noel was on his arse until he was two."

She laughed. "It's a wonder he wasn't on his knees," she said, grinning.

I really liked her. She had a good sense of humor and an inner calm that I was unfamiliar with. It was easy to see why my brother had fallen for her. Aside from her rubbish-tasting teas and an admission that she was a Neil Diamond fan, she was a real gem.

I wanted to confide that I wasn't feeling so good. The doctor had dismissed my endless moaning at the beginning of my pregnancy and now it was a case of the boy who cried wolf. Laura seemed so understanding, but then again this wasn't about me. I decided against seeking her counsel and left when it became apparent that she was waiting for my departure so that she could bury herself in my brother's response to the news of a son.

★ ★ ★

Clodagh and Anne arrived later that night to sit and watch TV and, having succumbed to a number of dizzy spells, it was all I was pretty much fit for. Seán, Richard, Tom and a few of his friends were at a friendly Ireland match. I had noticed that Seán's general humor had improved greatly since his trip and mentioned it to Clo. She however couldn't give a toss about Seán or his humor. She wanted to know the secret I was keeping.

"I'm not keeping any secrets," I denied, going red.

"Emma," she sighed. "Look in the mirror."

I didn't need to. I looked to Anne for support, but it had been a slow gossip week, so she, instead of addressing my gaze, borrowed my usual habit of pretending to pick lint off the cushion. I weakened. Okay, I admit it didn't take much. I was dying to unload myself. I could have sworn the unspoken information was making me feel fatter.

"Noel's a father."

Clodagh nearly fell off the chair. Anne looked at me like I was insane.

"You are having a laugh," Clo said, more out of habit than actually believing that Noel being a dad would be a source of great humor. "Laura?" she asked, having an extraordinary ability to remember even the smallest details of someone else's private life.

"Who's Laura?" Anne asked, confused and already a little pissed off.

It was at that point that I remembered that I hadn't ever spoken to Anne about Noel and his affair. It seemed only fair that I share his secret with only one as opposed to many, but in the cold light of this new information, that action was being seen as anything but fair. Clodagh, immediately realizing that we had both put our foot in it, became unhelpfully tongue-tied.

"I wasn't supposed to tell anyone so I only told Clo," I said hopefully.

"Oh," Anne said, nodding her head. "Fine." She was still nodding her head. This was never a good sign.

Clo jumped in. "And she mentioned it to me by accident."

"By accident?" Anne said, not believing a word of it. "How does that work? Did Emma start off by talking about her day and the words 'Noel's shagging someone' just fell out of her mouth?"

Clo was stuck.

I jumped in. "Anne, he made me swear not to tell anyone."

"Yeah, you said. So you only told Clo."

"Yeah," I said wearily. I was way too heavily pregnant to deal with this.

"Your best friend Clodagh. Of course, why wouldn't you tell her? But me, well, who am I? I'm just in the background and a supporting role in the Emma and Clo Show." She started to get up.

This outburst had taken both Clodagh and me by surprise and neither of us was prepared to respond. I realized she was leaving.

"Anne, it's not like that!"

Clodagh agreed but Anne wasn't buying it. She grabbed her coat. "You know, I'm sick of being the third wheel." She got to the door before Clo stopped her.

I was still stuck to the sofa, battling to get to my feet.

"What's wrong with you?" Clo held the door and got into her face, the way she always did in a confrontation.

"I'm sick of you!" Anne roared from a place deep down. "I'm sick of both of you and your little private club!"

"Oh, don't be so ridiculous, there is no private club," Clo stated calmly and maybe a little dismissively while still holding the door.

Anne had had enough. She tried to pull the door, but Clo wasn't letting her go anywhere, so she crumpled. She burst into tears and sobbed heartily. All the previous aggravation left Clodagh and she stood there utterly confused by Anne's desolation. I had at last managed to get off the sofa. I hugged Anne, figuring that touch is sometimes better than talk. I led her back to the sofa and ensured that she sat before I followed. Clo followed us. We waited for Anne to tell us what was really going on.

"The IVF won't work. Richard's sperm count is not only low but he has serious motility problems also."

"Can't he do anything to improve it?" I said, shocked.

"And you say that *we* don't tell you anything," Clo uttered before really thinking.

I gave her a dirty look while Anne just sat there.

"Sorry, that was a stupid thing to say," Clo noted apologetically.

"No, you're right. I'm really sorry. I'm just really disappointed and I can't really vent to Richard because he feels bad enough as it is. It's making me a little insane." Her tears had ceased, although the pain etching itself into her face was giving me a cramp.

"I'm so sorry, Anne," I said, crossing my arms in a pathetic attempt to cover my pregnant belly.

"You can't have everything," she said, attempt
smile, which really didn't work out for her.

"Of course you can," Clo said unrealistically.

Anne and I eyed her, awaiting the reveal.

"You're rich. There are plenty of kids out there th
need parents. Fill out a few forms and, you know, pick u
a kid."

She smiled at us. Anne looked at me and I nodded,
silently agreeing that Clo had a tendency to oversimplify.

"What?" she said, eyeing us eyeing each other.

Anne admitted that, although she had said that she
would adopt a child if she couldn't have her own, deep
down inside she had believed that she could and would.
She so desperately wanted to carry her own child, to give
birth to it, to rear it, for it to be her own. I understood
where she was coming from. Even though pregnancy was
far from a bed of roses, I wouldn't have traded my
condition for anything in the world. The first scan, the first
kick, the feeling of another human being nestled close to
my heart. I understood. Clo did too. She had
remembered the empty feeling as a result of her own lost
child. We sat together on the sofa, Anne in the middle
and Clo and I on either side, our arms around her, and
Anne cried until she had no tears left.

★ ★ ★

It had been a month since Seán's trip to New York and
Noel had still not made contact. I was eight and a half
months pregnant and exhausted. My previous checkup
had revealed that I was dangerously anemic and, although
the words "dangerously" and "anemic" had been quite

shocking, a large part of me felt vindicated. The doctor didn't seem overly concerned. He recommended a soluble iron drink that tasted like a rugby player's foot and handed me a list of iron-rich foods. It had been two weeks since my visit and despite a seriously unattractive flatulence problem, I was really a good deal better.

It was eight thirty and I needed to be in school.

"Seán!" I shouted up the stairs.

I could hear him scurry from the bathroom.

"I need to be gone," I reminded him.

My condition made driving impossible, so I was relying on Seán to get me where I needed to go, the knock-on effect being that I was late for everything.

"Get down these stairs before I kill you with my bare hands!" I shouted, much like my mother had done throughout my teenage years.

"Right," he said, coming down the stairs. "No problem, Fatso."

I threatened to kick him. He noted I was too fat to raise my leg and we headed to the car. I was cranky, suffering from sleep deprivation, chronic peeing and pains in places I had previously been unaware of.

"Braxton Hicks," Doreen had said the day before over tea in my place with my mother and me.

My mother agreed. "Definitely Braxton Hicks."

"It's just the body getting ready to give birth," Doreen added.

My mother agreed and went on. "Don't worry, love. You'll probably go over. I went two weeks over on both you and Noel." She winced and turned to Doreen. "I had to be induced both times."

Doreen shook her head sadly. "I had to be induced on my Damian. A bloody nightmare," she said.

My mother shook her head in agreement. "Why do you think I only had the two?"

Doreen nodded and drank her tea.

I wish they'd both fuck off.

They both remained silent for a blissful moment until Doreen remembered something that she wanted to share.

"The epidural didn't work on my last," she said. "All it managed to do was delay the bloody labor. Nineteen hours I spent trying to get that child out. He was ten pounds, eight ounces and you know something? Thirty-five years later he's fifteen stone and lazy to this day."

My mother laughed, although I really couldn't see the humor. "Emma was breech," she informed Dor. "No epidural, twenty-one hours, a forceps delivery. I sat on a rubber ring for a month." She smiled for some reason only known to herself.

"And they say you forget!" Doreen laughed.

I had had enough. "Right, it's time for you people to go home."

They both looked at their half-drunk cups of tea and half-eaten slices of apple tart.

"What's wrong?" my mother asked, genuinely confused.

"I don't want to hear your shitty stories. Okay? I don't want to hear about people shoving their hands up my fanny. I don't want to hear about it splitting in two. I don't want to hear about epidurals that don't work, rubber rings, ten-stone babies and what a nightmare inducing is. I would rather not know."

They smiled at one another knowingly and Doreen was the first to speak.

"Sweetheart, in our day no one ever told us anything. The first time we made love was more like an experiment than actual sex. The second time most of us got pregnant and when we went into that delivery room it was terrifying. Ignorance isn't always bliss."

Neither is knowledge.

My mother of course agreed with Doreen and added how lucky my generation was and I halfheartedly agreed that we were really lucky and, as they finished their tea and tarts, I grieved for my poor fanny.

★ ★ ★

We were in the car and I was unusually quiet.

"Ooohh," I moaned.

"What?" Seán asked, slowing the car.

"It's nothing. Just Braxton Hicks," I said, rubbing my side.

"Braxton what?" he asked.

"It's just the body getting ready to deliver," I advised knowledgeably.

"Right," he said unsure.

"Ahhh!" I called out.

"Jesus! Are you sure you're okay?" he asked fearfully.

His concern should have seemed sweet and yet I was having difficulty fighting the urge to hurt him.

"Emma, are you okay?" He was clicking his fingers in my face for some unknown reason.

"Aside from being a fatty with swollen ankles, fat hands, a pain in my back and a bladder the size of a pea, I'm fine. Couldn't be better."

He laughed. "There's my girl!"

I smiled despite myself. *Sexy bastard.*

★ ★ ★

It was my first class after lunch. The morning had been a blur. The Braxton Hicks pains were coming closer and closer together, also a little more painful each time. I was beginning to think I might have been misinformed.

"Take out *Silas Marner*, page one hundred and fifteen," I announced to general moaning. I needed to sit.

"Okay, last night I asked you all to read chapter seventeen. I need someone to stand up and tell me about it, story content, your thoughts . . ." I was feeling pain, real pain that burned like fire. *"Oohhh!"* was all I could manage.

Declan stood up at the back of the class. "Are you all right, Miss?" he asked.

"Fine, Declan. *Ooohh!*" I doubled over.

I suddenly needed to stand. Declan was on his feet and at the top of the class before I could manage to haul myself up off the chair. He helped me stand.

"I'm fine." I tried to smile but then a wave of pain came upon me, my face twisted up and I swore. "Holy fuck!" I cried out.

The class laughed. Declan told them to shut their faces and then he ordered Mary Murphy to call the principal and an ambulance. I wanted to walk but was finding it difficult. Declan held my weight with each pain and he started to rub the base of my back. I was in agony yet surprisingly still aware enough to be mortified that a student was rubbing the top of my arse, but oddly it was helping. The rest of the class were standing around me; the girls were looking a little green and the boys a little greener. Some students had to sit down.

Then it happened as Declan tried to guide me out of the classroom. My waters broke. I felt a gush, then I heard a gush and finally I looked down and saw the gush fall to the floor like a mini-torrent. Patrick Hogan fainted.

The principal entered flustered and followed by an overexcited Mary Murphy.

"I'm in labor," I confirmed, before succumbing to another wave of shocking pain.

Declan took over. "Sir, her waters just broke. She's having contractions about five minutes apart. I think she's going to go."

I was recovering sufficiently to take his words in.

Oh Jesus Christ, I'm going to go.

"Yes, thank you, Declan," the principal answered quite snottily. "I think I can take it from here," he added dismissively.

Another pain.

"Oh my God!" I cried as the principal tried to help me out.

"You have to rub her back, sir!" Declan called out.

"Yes, right," the principal said and then he banged my back like he was burping a baby.

No way, I was not putting myself in his hands. I stopped and he continued in his attempt to drag me.

"Declan!" I called. Then I turned to the principal and told him to go away. He eyed me uncertainly. "I want Declan. He has a clue. You don't."

It was a bit strong, but then there was a child trying to tunnel its way out of my body, so I felt strongly that it wasn't the time for pussyfooting.

The ambulance arrived and it was Declan who got in with me. I handed the principal my list of people to call and advised him that I was entrusting him with a very important job. And so while Declan helped me with my breathing, my boss set about the task of calling Seán, Anne, Clo, my parents, Seán's parents, Doreen and to be fair to him he even managed to track down Noel and I wasn't even that sure where he was.

In the delivery room the pains were coming sharp and fast. Gas and air wasn't cutting it. I called for an epidural, but I was progressing too quickly. Declan held my hand. I was crying, afraid Seán was going to miss it.

Declan tried to comfort me. "He won't miss it," he said.

"He's late for everything!" I wailed.

Declan ignored me, looked up and smiled. I followed his eyes to see Seán, bedraggled and eager.

"Not everything," he said, gowned up and ready to aid delivery.

I felt like I was unwittingly appearing in a bad sitcom or maybe it was just that I'd inhaled way too much gas and air. Declan said he'd leave it to us, but asked if he could take a quiet look before he left.

"No!" Seán and I both said together.

He smiled. "All the best."

And then he was gone and nobody yelled, "Cut!"

Oh Sweet Jesus, I'm having a baby.

★ ★ ★

An hour later, the midwife pushed on my stomach and the obstetrician yelled, "Push!" He really didn't need to because, as the bloody anesthesiologist still hadn't showed up with my epidural, instinct was ensuring I pushed for dear life.

"I can see the head, Emma!" the doctor called out.

"Oh God!" I called out.

Seán was mesmerized. "Jesus Christ!" he said over and over. "I can see the head. I can see the head, Em!"

He was laughing. I wanted to scream until my head nearly fell off, like they do in the movies, but I found that I had neither the will nor the energy.

"Now, one more big push. Come on, Emma!" I heard from between my legs.

"Oh God!" I roared.

And suddenly there you were, laying on my belly, covered in goo stuck to lots of hair, seven pounds eight— five little fingers and five little toes. You were crying and a kind of purple like the sun in my dreams. Seán was crying and pressing Send on a text announcing your arrival. The doctor was smiling at the midwife who was smiling at you and I can't describe the feeling inside. They took you away to be checked and washed and I ached.

I adore you.

And it felt like the credits should roll: *Happily Ever After.*

Seán followed you out of the room so that the doctor could finish up and I just lay there in shock thinking, *Wow!* over and over but then the oddest thing happened. My legs felt wet and I sensed the gush within seconds, then some spots appeared in front of my eyes. I blinked and they got bigger. My hearing became fuzzy, like I'd just been submerged. My doctor shouted at a nurse. I thought I heard the word "tear." There was a lot of movement and noise and although now in a bubble I could feel the room fill. A nurse behind me adjusted the bed. My head was dropped, my legs rose, my blood flowed and my heart slowed.

What's happening?

After that those around me became more and more distant until eventually everything faded to black. It turned out the placenta had torn, the blood loss was significant and this was further complicated by my anemia—easy for the doctor to diagnose but difficult to control.

Seán was holding you in his arms when a nurse told him. He nearly dropped you right then. She took you and he followed her back to where he'd left me minutes previously. The room looked different: machines had invaded in his absence, and I was now plugged in and tube-ridden. Monitors bee-beeped to the tune of my slowing organs. He was stoic, disbelieving, shaking his head from side to side as though to suggest to the universe that, no way, this was not happening.

My parents arrived, having left the house the second they'd received his "it's a girl" text. They had managed to make the journey in a record-breaking twenty minutes and my father was chasing my mother down the hall. A nurse stopped them and suddenly the balloon my mother was holding rose to the ceiling unfettered as her legs gave way.

It was odd. The room faded away and yet I could see

everything. I could see the nurse wrapping you in your blanket with your dad watching over you, five doors away. I could see him nearly drop you and, if I wasn't already dying, the fright would have killed me. I saw them plug me in and Seán watching, unable to breathe, and I could feel his heart lodged in his throat and hear it beating in his ear. I saw my parents argue over how long to pay for parking in the hospital car park.

And it wasn't just the hospital either. I saw Clo delighted with the news and texting me from her car, telling me she was on her way. Anne crying in her kitchen while Richard comforted her with the words, "Our day will come." I saw Noel in the middle of nowhere with desert all around, stopping to turn and stare into space.

"Emma?" he said before he walked right through me.

And I knew. *Oh no, something bad is happening.*

And then there was nothing.

★ ★ ★

I was lost in a vast garden surrounded by exotic flowers set in soft green sand. I regarded my surreal surroundings and laughed. It had been a while since I'd visited. The good old burning bush blazed as brightly as ever. I headed straight toward the purple sun dangling above a spidery tree basking in its glow. It was warm and I was happy. Then I was climbing the hill and waiting for the purple sun to spin before me. The hill straightened out under my feet and as I approached the flowering tree, a gentle breeze brought it to life. The familiar blue poppies danced between the thick foliage that continued to crawl along the cherry-pink branches. I waited for John.

"Hey, Fatso!" he called out, grinning, bouncing the sun like he was Magic Johnson.

I laughed. Only two people could get away with calling me "Fatso." He looked the same. Only I had changed. He walked toward me and then we were hugging.

"You look beautiful." He always knew what to say.

"Seán says I'm like a fine wine."

"Hmmm, fruity!"

"You're a ghost, stop flirting," I laughed.

"It's never too late." He grinned.

"I've just had a baby," I remembered.

"I know. She's really beautiful."

"Yeah, she really is," I smiled.

"Any names?"

"Lots, but she doesn't look like any of them."

He threw his head back and laughed loudly. "Women! Women crack me up. How can a person look like a name?"

"They just do." I gave him a dirty look, which he ignored.

We were walking again, holding hands. He led the way and I followed like a curious child.

"You've seen her. What do you think about the name?" I asked.

"Deborah."

"Please don't tell me you want me to call my child after the first rock star that made you want to touch yourself."

He grinned. "Ah, Debbie Harry."

"Animal," I sniffed. My crotch hurt and my legs felt sticky. I ignored this in favor of looking around for the yellow pathway to appear.

"What's the female version of John?" I asked.

"Joan."

"Oh. I'm not calling her that."

"I wouldn't," he advised.

"How about Joanne?" I asked.

"Joanne." He mulled it over. "Yeah, I like Joanne."

"Me too."

"What does Seán want to call her?"

I smiled. "He wanted to call her Bindy so he doesn't get a say." We laughed as we made our way to the yellow pathway.

"I must get, The Wizard of Oz for Joanne," I said, grinning.

John stopped and looked at me seriously.

"Do you want ruby slippers?"

"Go on then, seeing as it's a special occasion."

He grinned and they appeared on my feet, dazzling and much redder than I had remembered. I sashayed beside him and he was laughing again, his wide smile and big eyes reminding me of how we used to be.

"Where are we going?" I asked, wondering if there would be a Straw Man involved.

He smiled in response and suddenly and overwhelmingly it occurred to me I shouldn't be here. I stopped.

"Did I die?"

"There's still time," he said.

"Good," I sighed. "Am I going to die?"

"I don't know."

"Oh God, I don't want to die!"

Walls sprang up on either side of us and soon they were alive with images of our past. I found myself focusing on the night we first kissed. John squeezed my hand as we watched our younger selves, all tongue and teeth.

"We really didn't have a clue," he said, smiling.

Not today. I can't die today.

I nodded absentmindedly and we moved along to view a different phase of our lives, stopping to take it in as an art critic would an interesting painting. It was the day we finished the Leaving Cert. We were standing under a tree near the basketball court. We were laughing and I was jumping excitedly. Then we were kissing and making a much better job of it. Fellow students were moving and talking excitedly around us and yet we were alone in one another.

I turned around to see John focused on the wall behind me. I looked back at my wall to watch us kissing under the tree near the basketball court and John returned to my side.

"That one lasts awhile," he grinned and took my hand.

"I can't die," I said calmly.

"You still have time," he repeated.

"Did you have time?" I asked.

"No," he admitted and then he turned me toward the wall.

I watched myself lying in my own blood while the doctor attempted to shock my heart out of flat line. I watched Seán's face aging and felt his heart burning while he sat still with his head hung low like he had the night we lost John. I saw my parents desperate and desolate. I saw Clo clinging to Tom, silent but begging me to come back.

I want to.

I saw you less than an hour old, lying alone, already forgotten.

"I can't leave her," I said and John seemed sad.

And then I heard my brother's voice while on his knees in the middle of some desert:

"Our Father, who art in heaven,
Hallowed be Thy name,
Thy Kingdom come.
Thy will be done, on earth as it is in heaven.
Give us this day our daily bread.
And forgive us our trespasses,
As we forgive those who trespass against us.
And lead us not into temptation,
But deliver us from evil. Amen."

"Noel?" I called out but I couldn't see him.

I could see the doctor charging up the defibrillator paddles.

I turned away and John was gone.

"John?" I called out, panicked.

He appeared in the distance.

"Where are you going?"

He winked and pointed into the distance. "Emerald City!" he laughed.

"But I need you!" I cried out with one eye on the wall. The damn paddles seemed to take an eternity to charge.

"Not anymore," he said.

"I love you!" I called out.

"You always will," he laughed and he was gone.

"Clear!" the doctor shouted and I heard the *beep, beep, beep* and then nothing.

★ ★ ★

When I woke you were nearly twenty-four hours old. I'd missed your first day. I cried for many reasons but mostly because of that. I promised I'd never miss another but then those kinds of promises are impossible to keep. Seán, your dad, found it difficult to let either of us go. He rested you in one arm while holding my hand.

"I couldn't have lost you," he kept saying.

"I wouldn't be lost," I told him.

The truth is I could have died and who knows why I didn't. Maybe it wasn't my time; maybe John had a word with a Wizard or God heard Noel's earnest prayer. Maybe it was just blind luck. Either way I'm still here. Sometimes I think about John and I smile. I'm happy he got to name you and even your dad admits Joanne is a far better name then Bindy.

Chapter 26

In the Now

I can't believe it's been five years since you were born and it's weird to try to think of this world without you. A lot has changed in these past years and more has remained the same. We moved out of our little townhouse a year after your birth. Seán got a promotion and had his second novel published, so we could afford to move by the sea. I've never lived by the sea before and I wouldn't live without it again. There's something about it. I'm not sure what it is. Maybe it's its vastness or depth or the ever-changing colors and the comforting sound of the waves lapping on the beach, ever constant, whether it be on a melancholic cold morning or a busy sunny day. I guess when it comes down to it, the sea is as close as we get to another world here on Earth and I like that.

I still work as a teacher and every now and then I have the pleasure of teaching a student like Declan. Speaking of whom, I hadn't seen him in four years and then out of the blue last week he appeared as a VJ on MTV. I couldn't believe it and at the same time it seemed that he was at last fulfilling his own destiny. It makes me smile to think of the boy with the big heart making his way in the world. It also makes me feel old and at thirty-three that's just not right.

★ ★ ★

Anne and Richard have a place the size of a small country pretty close by. It's nice having Anne so close. She dotes on you and spoils you beyond anything that could be determined as reasonable. Richard discovered rally racing a few years ago, much to Anne's utter disgust, but you know Richard—he will not be deterred. He's attempting to race across some desert in the middle of some kip left of nowhere next summer. Poor Anne. The good news is that after five years on a waiting list they have at last received confirmation that in less than a month they will have the baby that they dreamed of. She's Chinese, she's three months and her name is Ming. There has been pretty intensive debate as to whether or not they should keep her name or change it. Richard has come down heavily on the side of a change due to his fear that his daughter will be known as "Minger" all through school. Anne is afraid that they will be stripping her of her identity. Clo is with Richard; rather lose one's heritage than face the nickname Minger. I tend to agree, but we'll see. Either way, little Ming is going to have to come to terms with a lot in this world but she'll be loved and that's what's important. You should see Richard—he's like a little kid. He's been working on Ming's nursery for over a year and he's made a total arse of it. Anne appears to despair but behind it all she can't hide her smile. You've already made her promise that her baby girl won't affect your relationship. There are no flies on you.

★ ★ ★

Clodagh and Tom went through a hard time a few years ago. His company was keeping him way too busy to be deemed healthy even for a career-orientated woman like Clo. Tom's long hours meant he and his wife would soon become strangers. To add insult to injury the fruits of his labor were not worth the massive effort. His competitors were undercutting him, staff was too costly and the tax man was crucifying him. They were fighting more and having sex less. He was tired all the time; she spent most of her time alone. It was a bad time, so bad Clo had considered leaving. She was devastated, but after many a negotiation she found their position to be in deadlock. He needed to put in the hours to keep the business afloat and she needed the husband he didn't have time to be. On the night she packed her bags he came home in time to stop her. Her drastic action frightened him and he admitted that marriage had made him complacent. They talked the whole night through. Tom wound up the business and within a month a job offer that he could not afford to turn down took them to London. The relocation package alone made sense and Clo had always wanted to taste life in a big city. She moved over without a job but her days as the supportive housewife were always going to be short-lived. Four months after moving she was working for a PR company in London. She's still there and loves it. She says she prefers Dublin for a laugh but London for shoes and shoes win. I miss her. It's not like we don't talk on the phone or e-mail one another most days, but distance is hard. I get to see her more than you'd think though. Thank Christ for the low-cost airline. Anne and I get over there every couple of months and she comes home as much. She's still a career girl at heart and has no intention of having any kids or "danglers," as she would put it.

You don't really know Clo—she's just some strange adult that passes through every now and then, but I hope that someday you will and then you'll love her as much as I do.

★ ★ ★

Doreen died last spring. She suffered a heart attack while sitting upstairs on the 16A bus. She was on her way to a peace march with her husband. She was reviewing the route with a map and a compass while her husband laughed at her industry. She nudged him and he said she smiled like she knew something everyone else didn't. Then she slumped on his shoulder. It was a day before her sixty-fifth birthday. Sixty-five seems young these days but Doreen felt old. She had aged in the past few years. Maybe I noticed because since we moved I didn't get to see her as often or maybe it was just her time to be old. She had lived a good and, in her own opinion, a long life and that was good enough for her. I like to think she knew. I like to think that an angel whispered in her ear and told her to come home. I miss her voice and look forward to hearing it again. Her wake was incredible. Her family had planned a surprise party and despite her death the party went ahead as planned. It was the send-off to end all send-offs. There were memories, music, laughter, dancing and song. We celebrated her life and sent her on her way. It was pure Doreen and exactly what she would have wanted, us living it up and her sitting back and enjoying the view.

★ ★ ★

Noel, well, what can I tell you about your Uncle Noel? He came home within a week of your birth and six months later he did leave the priesthood. The first time he met his son was on a Sunday in a park. Laura brought him there on the pretext of duck feeding. They would bump into one another as though by accident. There was to be no build-up. Noel would just slip into his child's life slowly and carefully. Of course, your grandmother took to her bed when told of Noel's paternity and career change. She emerged after a week of sulking and found, despite what the neighbors would say, Noel's new status was the one she had dreamed of all along. Dad was cool about it but that's just him—your granddad is cool. I asked Noel once what was it like to meet his son for the first time. He remembered the ducks and Laura leaning over a little boy who was giggling and as he got closer the little boy looked around and he saw his face and something inside clicked. He smiled at the memory and I knew what he meant.

Of course it wasn't all roses—having to admit that he'd ate the apple to the bishop and a room full of clergy wasn't a laugh. Leaving behind his life and his vocation was no picnic either. He was lost for a while. He was forced to move home and Mom said it was like dealing with a bloody teenager. He and Laura were rocky for a while but spending days in the park or at the movies or in the garden with his son made up for most of it. They got back on track a few years ago and Noel Junior was soon joined by Gina, who at two years old is your arch-enemy while Jamie, her twin brother, has become your unconditional slave.

Noel went back to college too and now works as a social worker. The money's crap, but then money was never an issue for my brother.

★ ★ ★

Last night Seán was holding my hand and I turned to examine his familiar face. He has aged in the past few years. All his boyishness has left him. Instead I was staring at a rugged handsome man. Little lines are appearing around his eyes and each with a little story to tell. His five o'clock shadow makes him look dangerous but his eyes remain forever the same. Sometimes I lose myself in him, his strength, his calm and his humor.

He smiled at me and pushed my hair out of my face. "The first time I saw you I fell in love with you," he said.

"The first time you saw me you didn't even notice me," I grinned, remembering John trying to catch his attention in the Buttery bar, desperate to introduce his girlfriend to his new best friend. "You were too busy chatting up some blonde medical student." I remembered her clearly.

"That wasn't the first time," he whispered, which shut me up instantly. "It was in the Arts Block a few days before that night."

I turned and faced him, attempted to lean on my elbow, missed and hit myself in the face.

He laughed as I fixed myself. "I was drinking coffee, sitting by the wall opposite the library. I saw you coming up the steps. You were carrying books piled on one another. Your hair was in your face, but I swear the light behind you made your green eyes glow. You were stunning and it was obvious that you didn't have a clue about that. I could tell by the way you held yourself. Beautiful women usually have an air of arrogance, but you didn't have that. Of course two seconds later you tripped and dropped your books all over the place. I wanted to help you, but I couldn't move. You picked them up and got up, slowly mumbling to yourself. You were standing when they fell again. You blushed until you were purple." He was laughing.

I hit him playfully, urging him to go on.

"You gave up after that. You just sat amongst the books and lit up a cigarette. Then you put your Walkman on and sang alone, totally unaware of anyone or anything around you and I was in love."

"Wow! I didn't know that," I admitted, remembering the terrible humiliation that he spoke of, and the embarrassing way I used to forget that just because the general public couldn't hear my Walkman didn't mean they couldn't hear me.

"Such a klutz!" he laughed into my ear.

"I'm not a klutz," I argued.

"Emma, you punched yourself in the face less than two minutes ago."

I didn't argue again. "I hated every girl you ever dated.

I even hated Clo for a second or two," I admitted without guilt.

"I know," he grinned.

"I love you," I said.

"You couldn't help yourself," he smiled and I, remembering John, nodded.

"No, I couldn't."

"Till death do us part!" he noted triumphantly.

"And beyond," I mumbled.

★ ★ ★

You were appearing in your first school play earlier tonight. Five years old and already you think you're Halle Berry. You were so cute as the Virgin Mary. Seán caught it all on camera and no doubt I'm going to have to listen to an endless stream of the latest editing techniques this weekend. You forgot your line, my heart stopped but you just burst into the chorus of Outkast's "Caroline." I'm not sure that the Virgin Mary ever sang about someone's shit not stinking, but you made it work. You took a bow and received a standing ovation. It was the best school play I'd been to and I've been to them all. Maybe you'll be the next Halle Berry after all. You went to bed full of orange juice and biscuits.

I retired to my room to finish this journal. I started it on your second birthday because it was on that day, standing in sunlight surrounded by friends, balloons, toys, treats and you aged two, twirling around until dizzy and puking, that I realized I could have missed it. I could have missed knowing you and being there for you and there is nothing that I or anybody else could have done about it.

It was then that I decided to tell you some things about the past and about what I've learned in this life just in case in the future I'm not around. You could treat this as a kind of reference book. More often than not it will be a reference book on what *not* to do but that's okay. I gave it to Clo to see what she thought because maybe some of it was a little sexy for a mother to tell her daughter. She didn't think it was too sexy but then again Clo thinks I'm about as sexual as a green runner bean or an old lady eating grapes. She told me I should have it published, like anyone is going to be interested. I told her she was insane.

"You're insane," she retorted.

"You," I said.

"You," she replied.

"You," I reiterated.

"You," she reiterated.

We went on like that for quite some time. I only mention it because it merely goes to show that adults can often act like children when they think no one is watching.

Anne had already read it. She'd been reading it on and off for over a year now. Every few months I'd hand over the latest installment and she'd read it over a coffee and a few Digestives, laughing or crying, and then together we'd reminisce about the way we were and are. Although she enjoyed trotting down Memory Lane, it concerned her that maybe I was writing some sort of obituary but that's not what this is about. Maybe I'll live to a grand old age and if I do I'll be there and you won't need these words, but maybe I won't and if so this journal is a little insurance and to that end, I just want to end up by imparting the little wisdom I've gleamed to date.

I'm old enough and I've watched too many sitcoms to know that I don't know everything. I can't live your life for you. I can't even protect you as much as I'd wish to. You have to go out into the world and live your own life. You have to follow your heart and make your own mistakes of which you will make many, because everyone makes mistakes and nobody is perfect. Not even that kid with the golden hair and the beauty-queen eyes that will sit opposite you on the bus when you're feeling like some old dog left out in the rain or that boy who every boy wants to be and every girl wants to be with or even the genius being primed to be the next Bill Gates. They will all know pain and hurt and rejection, but they'll also know love and laughter and joy just like you. My life can only ever be a lesson to me. So this is just a heads-up on the four key things that my life has taught me thus far.

After night comes day.

After death comes life.

Even at your darkest time look around because you are never really alone.

You are loved.

Up-Close and Personal with the Author

Pack Up the Moon starts where other stories finish: with an unhappy ending. How did you get the idea for this book and its special beginning?
Mom died when I was seventeen. I was devastated and, much to my utter disgust, life went on. In my early twenties a close friend committed suicide, a few years later I lost another friend, and my father died that same year. At some point it occurred to me that when someone in your life dies, in their absence your life alters and every ending—no matter how painful—is a new beginning.

Describe grief.
Grief is selfish because it is all about you. It's about you needing and missing that person who has gone. And you don't just lose them. You lose the person you were with them; those jokes and moments and that side of your personality they

brought out. Your body collapses because part of you has gone.

There are sad moments in your novel, but it's also full of vitality and joie de vivre. "Day follows night"—this is one of the last sentences of your novel. Has it always been possible for you to believe in that?
In my life there has been terrible sadness but also immense joy. I consider myself very lucky because even during the worst of times there was always love and laughter, so it's always been easy for me to find a positive. I'm not saying I'm Mary McSunshine, but the smallest thing can make me smile.

How important are your friends to you?
Their importance is immeasurable. I'm lucky enough to have a great mix of male and female friends. Your friends are your peers and your peers are the people that give you a kick in the ass when needed; they are the people you learn from, rely on, and laugh with. They say that friends are the family we choose for ourselves, and I don't mind saying I've chosen well!

The novel in a way is formed by experiences on the border of life of death, once Emma herself is in danger of life. Do you think that such experiences generally decide about a life's path?
I think every human being is on the edge of death. One heartbeat too fast or too slow, one cut or knock can end a life in an instant. At the age of

twenty I was hit by a car and was badly injured. I could have died, but luckily aside from an ability to predict frost and occasionally walking like a dude, I escaped without any lasting damage. I'm not sure if my accident changed the course of my life any more than where I chose to work or live or the people I befriended. I believe that every decision, no matter how minor, sets your course.

Before you started to write your first novel, you already had some other professions. Could you tell us something about it? Has it always been your dream to write a book? I started out acting but it wasn't for me, which was pretty annoying as I'd made a big deal about leaving college to follow my theatrical dream. To save face I then worked for a short time as a stand-up comedian. I had some great times but way preferred writing the comedy to performing it. I'm happier on the periphery rather than center stage. Plus you have to be committed to be a performer. You have to love it and I didn't. It was only through trial and error that I realized my true love was writing, which is weird because it should have been obvious. I wrote all through school, loved writing short stories and comedy, and loved studying comedy. Call me a nerd but I used to watch sitcoms and then go to my room and write down all the gags I could remember. I read everything I could get my hands on, including about twenty years of the *Readers Digest*. My mate Enda said that the reason I thought I should act rather than write is simple. I'm slow.

Would you ever perform again?

Recently I've been commissioned to write a TV series and one of the producers joked that I should play a particular role. That thought nearly brought my lunch up. I don't like using the word "never" so I'll just say I sincerely bloody hope not.

In the story Emma's friend Anne is suffering hard from moving from Dublin to Kerry with her husband. Would you feel like that? Do you prefer to live in a city or in the country?

I did feel like that! My parents split when I was five and mom and I lived in Dublin with my gran. Mom got sick pretty quickly after the separation. She suffered from multiple sclerosis. First she needed a cane, then a walker, then a wheelchair. My gran was old and infirm so we all minded each other. When I was twelve it became apparent that we could no longer live together. My mom and gran were taken to separate hospices and I was taken in by my dad's sister in Kerry. Moving there and leaving Mom was the hardest thing I've ever done. I do love Kerry and Kenmare; the town I grew up in is beautiful. I have some fantastic memories of country living but my heart was always in Dublin.

Would you call yourself a believer?

I am a believer. I believe in joy, in sadness, in this world and the next. I believe we've been here before and we'll be here again and that each

lifetime teaches us lessons that will eventually lead us home. I believe in forgiveness, empathy, understanding, and that hate has no place in religion, politics, or the human heart. Call me a tree hugger but I believe in love!

What do you like most about your homeland?
I like driving in the Dublin Mountains with the car stereo on full blast. In Kenmare I love tucking into a bowl of mussels and a pint while catching up on local gossip. I like listening to the rain hit my window at night. I like that when the sun comes out for even a second the Irish get near naked. I like the music and the fact that every bar and restaurant is full of chat and laughter. I like the people because your countrymen are your extended family and no matter how annoying, they are familiar in an unfamiliar world. Oh, and I especially like that I live in the age of transport which means that I can leave.

You preface your novel with a poem by W. H. Auden, and a dedication to your mother. She must have been an extraordinary woman. Would you like to tell us something about her?
She was extraordinary. It was the mid-1970s in Ireland. She was separated when people didn't separate. She was living with her mother who didn't approve of her leaving her drunken husband. She was losing her balance, she was falling, she was left lying on the floor for hours waiting for a six

year old to come home from school to help her up, and yet when I came home she was smiling. She'd tell me to lie on the floor with her and we'd talk about my day. When her legs would shake uncontrollably she'd tell me to jump aboard. When she needed help to the loo or to bed she'd tell me stories and we'd laugh when she'd get stuck as I'd push her up the stairs. My mom was wheelchair-bound and in a home by age forty-two, and sometimes she cried and sometimes she swore but mostly she smiled a genuine smile because she found joy in the smallest of things, and when she laughed those around couldn't help but laugh with her. My mom died at forty-nine. She had often prayed for a cure and she'd holidayed year in year out in Lourdes searching for a miracle. Her greatest fear was to be left unable to communicate. She watched those around her locked inside themselves and it terrified her. She didn't have to worry. One fine day she ate a lunch (my mother loved her food) and went to bed for a snooze mentioning that she wasn't feeling too well. That afternoon one organ shut down after another quietly and painlessly. The hospital called her sister who arrived in time for Mom to say goodbye, and she died there and then with a smile on her face. It was a good death and well deserved. I like to think that in the end my mom got her miracle.